WONDERLAND

IRINA SHAPIRO

To request permissions, contact the publisher at rights@stormpublishing.co

Ebook ISBN: 978-1-80508-148-7
Paperback ISBN: 978-1-80508-149-4

Previously published in 2015 by Merlin Press LLC.

Cover design: Debbie Clement
Cover images: Shutterstock

Published by Storm Publishing.
For further information, visit:
www.stormpublishing.co

ALSO BY IRINA SHAPIRO

Wonderland Series

The Passage

Wonderland

Sins of Omission

The Queen's Gambit

Comes the Dawn

PROLOGUE

Despite my heartbreaking childhood experiences and years of living with a foster family, I'd always given my trust easily, believing that, inherently, people were good and worthy of my faith in them. Some of them proved to be, while others lost their place in my affections and eventually disappeared from my life, having let me down or betrayed me in some way. As I grew older, I began to comprehend that trust is a precious gift, even more precious than love, since we can still love people we don't fully trust.

Just as Alice—who'd been my favorite character growing up —discovered that there was much malice in Wonderland, I'd learned that in the real world, trust is a valuable commodity, one which should never be bestowed lightly or without much consideration, for misplaced trust can carry a heavy price, and at times even cost us our lives.

As I entered the city of London on that ordinary day in September of 1685, I had no inkling that I was about to tumble down the rabbit hole once more, and this Wonderland I'd found myself in was not a dream I could wake up from, but a vivid nightmare, one that would stay with me for the rest of my days.

ONE

London, England

I shivered with apprehension as the forbidding silhouette of the Tower of London came into view, dwarfing the busy streets beyond the thick outer wall and casting a shadow—physical as well as metaphorical—onto everything beneath. Our progress was slow due to heavy traffic on the narrow street at this time of the morning. It was congested with loaded wagons, closed carriages, and numerous pedestrians all rushing to get somewhere. A briny tang floated off the Thames when the breeze carried between the tightly packed houses, but in more closed spaces, the air reeked of dead fish, rotting produce, waste, and at times something I preferred not to name, since it was just too distasteful to contemplate.

I hastily turned away as I caught a glimpse of something bloated and way too large to be a fish hauled out of the water by several ferrymen, who gathered on the muddy banks of the river, scratching their heads and turning out the pockets of their find. Floaters were not uncommon, nor were they treated with any respect. This one would probably end up in a pauper's grave once anything of value had been taken off them and divided among the group—if there was anything to be had.

Hugo seemed oblivious to all the activity around us, having practically grown up in seventeenth-century London. For me, it was all new. I'd been to several villages and the town of Guilford, but the only London I was familiar with was yet to be built. My last glimpse of the great metropolis had been in August of 2013, just before Hugo and I had left it to travel to Surrey and disappear through the passage in the crypt of the local church that would take us back to 1685, a year fraught with danger, especially for Hugo, who was wanted for attempted murder, abduction, and, most notably, high treason for his role in the failed Monmouth Rebellion.

Most of the perpetrators had been arrested and either executed or transported for their part in the uprising, with Hugo being the last, and the most elusive since I'd whisked him off to the twenty-first century to avoid arrest and execution. Generations of Everlys had wondered what had happened to the ill-fated lord who had just vanished one day in the spring of 1685, but none could have possibly imagined that he didn't die a brutal and anonymous death, but actually escaped to the future, where he faced a death of a different kind—a death of identity and a total lack of any desirable future.

I sighed with frustration as I realized that we'd have been safely in France by now had it not been for the rather unfortunate timing of the news that Max, Lord Everly circa 2013, had discovered the passage to the past and followed us to the seventeenth century, only to promptly get arrested in Hugo's place due to the family resemblance. So, here we were, in London, a place where Hugo's capture would mean certain death.

I tried not to think of the Duke of Monmouth, who had recently been beheaded, his execution so brutal and incompetent that John Ketch would live on in history as the most famous executioner of his day. Monmouth's body and his severed head had been laid in a coffin lined with black velvet and interred under the communion table of St. Peter's Chapel at the Tower, but Hugo wouldn't be buried next to Monmouth should he be apprehended. Instead, his head would wind up on a spike as a warning to others, and I would be left alone, pregnant, and unmarried, but most of all heartbroken.

The thought of losing Hugo caused me such acute pain that I did my best not to dwell on, knowing that there was nothing I could do to deter him from his chosen path. A less honorable man would have happily allowed someone else to take his place and escaped with his life, but Hugo wouldn't hear of allowing Max to be tried in his place.

Hugo and Max had history—a brief, but violent one, but it made no difference to Hugo's resolve. I must admit that for one mad moment I'd tried to convince Hugo to leave Max to his fate, but deep down I knew that, despite the danger, Hugo was right. He wouldn't be the man I fell in love with if he allowed an innocent man to take his place and face the consequences. We'd argued all the way from Portsmouth, going over possible solutions and looking for a way to get to Max, but nothing came to mind save Hugo turning himself in, which he would do over my dead body. After forfeiting our passage to France on the *Mathilde* and traveling several days to London, we still had no plan.

I looked with interest at the narrow streets of Blackfriars, lined with half-timbered houses whose upper floors extended so far over the street as to almost block out the light and appear to be on the verge of tumbling. The diamond-paned windows faced each other; the glass glinting in the morning light as we passed.

Hugo tossed the reins of his horse to a young lad and escorted me into a small, but clean inn. I didn't know if the street even had a name, but it was within walking distance of the Tower, which made me even more anxious. Hugo looked nonchalant as he asked for accommodation and brought our few possessions to the room at the top of the stairs.

Being on the top floor had its advantages, since the open window caught a fresh breeze off the river and dispelled some of the other odors coming from downstairs, and it gave us a view of the street and the dreaded Tower. I couldn't see much beyond the wall, but I thought I could just glimpse a portion of the viewing platform situated just behind it.

The Tower still housed the Royal Menagerie, which consisted of many exotic animals, including lions, which were occasionally exercised in a section of the moat by the western entrance. The menagerie had been used exclusively by the monarchs and their few favorite courtiers since its establishment during the reign of King John in the twelfth century, but Queen Elizabeth had decided to open it up to the public, charging three half-pence, or a cat or a dog to be fed to the lions, which also provided entertainment for the masses. The menagerie had been long closed in my day, but it was strange to know that there were wild animals only a few streets away that devoured live animals for the pleasure of the visitors. I supposed in a time when people went to public executions in droves that was to be expected, but it still made me uneasy.

Hugo set down the bags and came up behind me, putting his arms around me and pulling me against his chest. He didn't say anything, just held me, letting me know in his own quiet way that he knew what I was feeling. He had to be scared, although he'd never admit it, having been raised by a stern father in the seventeenth century where men didn't vocalize their feelings, especially when those feelings had anything to do with fear, and he wasn't fool enough not to understand the risk he was taking.

I wrapped my arms around his, wishing that I could hold him forever and keep him safe. Hugo moved our joined hands downward to let them rest against my stomach, which was just beginning to swell. I was in my second trimester, and Hugo and I had hoped to marry as soon as we got to France, but now we'd have to wait. Hugo couldn't marry me using an alias, but to use his real name and reveal his presence in England would be the equivalent of signing his own death warrant. Being a woman of the twenty-first century, I wasn't terribly bothered about being pregnant and unwed, but I knew that Hugo was deeply distressed by his inability to legalize our union and it gnawed at his conscience, making him feel as if he were somehow letting me down.

"Why don't you lie down for a while and rest?" Hugo suggested as I leaned wearily against him. "You must be bone-tired. I'll be back in an hour. Promise," he added hastily as he felt me stiffen.

"Where are you going?"

"I have to purchase some writing implements. I have letters to write," he explained patiently, not wishing to upset me further.

"To whom?" I asked. No one knew we were in England besides Hugo's sister Jane, and even Jane would think that we were in France by now, safe and sound.

"Neve, please don't worry. I have a tentative plan, and you have my word that I will not do anything to put us in danger."

Famous last words, I thought pessimistically.

"What plan?" I demanded, but Hugo just smiled, turned me around, and walked me toward the bed, where he gently pushed me down, gave me a sound kiss, and headed for the door.

Of course, he could hardly stay cooped up in this room, hiding. We had come back to London for a reason, and he had to put his idea into action if anything was to be done for Max. As far as we knew, Max Everly was still alive and being held at the Tower, the trial date not yet set since the prisoner kept insisting that he had been arrested by mistake and was actually one Maximillian Everly and not Hugo Everly whose name was on the warrant.

We had no idea if anyone believed him, or if he had any chance of release, but it didn't seem likely. Max's captors would see it as a ruse to avoid execution by trying to plead insanity, which would never deter anyone in this century anyway. The Crown had no qualms about putting to death a person who was not mentally capable of standing trial if he were believed to be guilty. If a five-year-old child could be hanged for theft, a man of thirty-five could most definitely be executed for treason, even if he were raving mad.

"All right," I finally relented. "Be careful."

"Always." Hugo put on his hat, pulled it down low, and disappeared through the door, locking it behind him. I knew he'd be doing more than just buying paper and ink. He'd stop into a tavern or two to glean as much information as he could. London was buzzing with the news of Lord Hugo Everly's arrest, and whereas there were those who felt that Monmouth had been a martyr to the Protestant cause, the majority felt that the only good traitor was a dead traitor. No one enjoyed a public execution more than Londoners, and the prospect of having another culprit put to death was something worth speculating about.

Currently, the only thing that stood between Hugo and certain capture was his flimsy disguise, which wouldn't hold out more than another few weeks. We'd colored his hair blond and changed the color of his eyes with lenses, but the hair would quickly grow out and reveal the black roots beneath. The disguise was only meant to last until we'd sailed for France, but who could have anticipated Max's arrest? I still couldn't fathom what had possessed Max to walk into the village of Cranley when he knew full well that Hugo was a wanted man, but I suppose he'd assumed that things had quietened down by September and, in his excitement at being able to time-travel, forgot all about the uncanny resemblance between himself and his ancestor.

I tried to rest, but kept tossing and turning until I gave up altogether and went about unpacking our few belongings and having a quick wash before Hugo came back. Now that the morning sickness had passed, I was always hungry, and the smells emanating from downstairs were becoming more and more appetizing by the minute. It smelled like roast beef, boiled turnips, and freshly baked bread. My mouth watered as I thought of the beef. I'd had an overwhelming craving for meat these past few days. Perhaps I wasn't getting enough iron in my diet and my body was sending me a message.

I opened a little pouch and popped a prenatal vitamin into my mouth. I'd been given a prescription for three months and had about two months' supply left, so I took one every other day, rather than every day, to make them last longer. I wanted to give our baby the best chance at health possible, so I tried avoiding all alcohol, which was nearly impossible given that there wasn't much else to drink, and eating as many nutritious things as could be found; a difficult task when people's diet consisted mostly of bread, meat, and the occasional vegetable, which had been cooked to such an extent that it was barely even recognizable.

Since it was fall, I had been able to get some fresh apples and pears, as well as the occasional handful of berries, which were a good source of vitamins, as well as apple cider. The cider still had some alcohol but was much safer than drinking water that was unfiltered and could carry any number of germs and diseases. I tried to drink milk whenever I could; purposely forgetting that it wasn't pasteurized. The cows in this century were grass-fed, unlike the livestock in my own time, so I hoped that the milk was safe.

I tried to ignore my growling stomach as I looked out the window in the hopes of seeing Hugo. The activity on the viewing platform caught my eye, and I hastily turned away as I heard a mighty growl, followed by a roar of approval from the onlookers as the lion devoured its prey. The people milled around for a few more minutes and then began to disperse, the show clearly over as the lion was maneuvered back into its cage. I wondered what part of the Tower Max was held in and if he could see what I'd just witnessed. I hoped not.

My heart lifted as I saw Hugo weaving between the carts and passersby as he dashed toward the inn, a small parcel beneath his arm.

"An hour as promised, and judging by the look in your eye, you're starving," Hugo guessed as he set down his purchases and smiled at my relief at seeing him unharmed. "I've asked the publican to send up our dinner, so you don't have long to wait. Roast beef," he added unnecessarily since the smell of roasting meat filled every nook and cranny of the inn with its appetizing aroma. But, beneath the wonderful smell of dinner, I smelled something else, something that drew me to the table and Hugo's parcel.

I put aside the quills, pot of ink, stick of black wax for sealing letters, and paper, and focused on a little paper packet which nearly brought me to tears because it smelled of home.

"Is this what I think it is?" I asked as I sniffed experimentally.

"I thought you'd be pleased," Hugo replied, confused by my reaction.

"Oh, I am. I just felt homesick for a moment. Thank you, Hugo. Wherever did you find it?"

I opened the packet and stuck my nose inside, inhaling the wonderful smell of tea leaves. The fragrance reminded me not only of endless cups of tea, drunk for pleasure, thirst, as part of any crisis management, and in various places, but also of my foster mother, whose hobbies included reading tea leaves. I was instantly transported to the front room of the little house in St.

John's Wood, the memory of Linda, as she had me call her, poignantly fresh in my mind. I could see her hunched over the table in absolute concentration as she studied the remnants of my tea, her face displaying a dizzying range of emotions as she oohed and aahed, awed by what she saw. Linda came up with all kinds of fantastic stories about my future, making me laugh with wonder at all the adventures that I would have, then she would pour me more tea and give me that extra slice of cake, which always came with a warm kiss planted on top of my head.

Did you foresee any of this, Linda? I thought with an inward sigh as Hugo gently took the packet from my hands and folded it closed.

"We'll save this for later, shall we?"

"I didn't realize tea was readily available in the seventeenth century. I thought it came to England later on," I mused as I tried to overcome my sudden melancholy.

"It's not a popular drink with the common people, not like ale or wine, but there are several coffee houses in London that offer it. Catherine of Braganza introduced it to the Court after she arrived from Portugal and married Charles II, and it became something of a fad among the nobility. It was deemed as being exotic and new, a taste of China. I tried it once or twice at Court, but never developed a taste for it until you made me drink it by the bucket," Hugo joked as he put the fragrant packet into a drawer.

I was about to ask him to go get a cup of boiling water from the kitchen when a young girl appeared with a loaded tray, balancing it precariously on one hand as she swiftly moved Hugo's parcel off the table and set down the food. She executed a brief curtsy and disappeared without a word, leaving us to our meal.

"So, have you learned anything?" I asked as I tucked into the roast beef with relish.

"Nothing that we don't already know. Max is being held in

the Tower under heavy guard. He's been questioned," Hugo
added carefully.

"Is that a euphemism for tortured?" I stopped chewing and
gazed up at Hugo, needing to know the truth. It hadn't occurred
to me until that moment that Max might have been hurt. I had
simply assumed that he was incarcerated, but now that Hugo
had mentioned it, I realized that Max's denials might have
prompted a more "persuasive" type of questioning and shuddered. I couldn't help remembering the torture devices on
display in the Tower of London's museum, the sheer barbarism
of the objects enough to make one break out in a cold sweat.
People in the future certainly hadn't invented torture; it had
been around for a long time, the methods so uniquely grotesque
that even to the modern person who'd seen it all on television,
the cruelty of contraptions like the rack and the iron maiden
were beyond comprehension.

"Most likely, but I don't know for sure. In any case, he has
nothing to tell them other than what he's already confessed to.
He can hardly tell his torturers the truth. Max said that he's a
distant relative who'd come visiting and stopped off at the inn
before making his presence known at Everly Manor," Hugo said
as he reached for my hand. "I hope he's not seriously injured."

"Perhaps he assumed that by September things had died
down and he was in no danger. He couldn't have known that
there were soldiers stationed in the village with the express
orders of arresting you should you return home. God, Hugo, I
do feel sorry for him despite what he's done in the past. I know I
probably shouldn't, but I do. I can't even begin to imagine being
in his situation. He's got no one to turn to, no one to ask for help.
As far as he knows, he's all alone."

"Yes, it must be bewildering, to say the least. Had I found
myself alone in 2013, I would have been at my wit's end, and
there they don't execute people, or even convict them without a

fair trial. Max must be terrified. Is he a religious person at all?" Hugo suddenly asked.

"Not that I know of. I think Christmas and Easter are the extent of his churchgoing activities. Why do you ask?"

"Dying is easier when you have faith. You convince yourself that there's a greater purpose to your death rather than it being just a random act, which in the great scheme of things means absolutely nothing, and your passing is forgotten as soon as the funeral is over. Max was at the wrong place, at the wrong time."

"To say the least," I agreed. "But what now?"

"Now," Hugo said as he pushed away his clean plate, "I get to work."

"Doing what exactly?" We'd discussed several avenues of inquiry, but nothing definite had been decided.

"Bradford Nash keeps a London house. He's rarely there, but there's an elderly couple who are in residence, acting as caretakers and keeping the place safe from burglars. I will write a letter to Brad and insert letters for my sister and Archie, which I will then have delivered to Brad's house. The servant will send a messenger to Surrey. Until the letters are delivered, there's nothing to do but wait."

Hugo's strong profile was illuminated by a single candle, the quill suspended in his hand as he mentally composed letter after letter. I wasn't sure what he expected in terms of help from Bradford, Jane, or Archie, but I'd known Hugo long enough to realize that he had a keen mind and a strategic way of thinking situations through, which I'd never needed in my own twenty-first century world. If Hugo had some sort of plan, then I had to just trust him. He was still scratching away as I drifted off to sleep, tired out by travel and worry.

TWO

The reply from Bradford came in the form of the man himself, who sent word that he'd wait in Westminster Abbey at noon on Wednesday: a place so central and crowded that no one would pay any mind to two men talking in a back pew. Coming to the inn was too risky, since the association between Hugo and his closest friend was well known to the authorities.

Hugo made a circle around the abbey to make sure that nothing seemed out of place, besides the dozens of people milling around, vendors selling goods outside the church, and a service in progress which no one seemed to be listening to. He'd left Neve at the inn, having bought her a book of sonnets to keep her mind from running away with her. Hugo knew she'd worry the whole time anyway, but there wasn't much choice.

Hugo didn't consider himself to be an indecisive man, but the decision to come back had not been an easy one, despite what Neve thought. Having thrown in his lot with Monmouth for his own religious and political reasons, Hugo had committed to his cause, knowing full well what the consequences would be. He'd named his nephew as his beneficiary and put his affairs in order, should anything happen to him, but what happened to him was Neve, and now he had that much more to lose. Hugo had been truly torn between doing the right thing and just turning his back on Max and sailing for France as planned. He had a baby on the way, a baby who would be born illegitimate if he didn't marry Neve soon. He had a responsibility to his lady and to his unborn child, but how could he allow Max to be condemned?

Max was a selfish, conniving bastard, to say the least, but he was innocent of treason, if not of attempted murder. If condemned, Max would most certainly die, and Hugo couldn't look away, couldn't turn his back on the man. He was putting himself, Neve, and their future child in great danger, but he had to answer to his conscience, and his conscience was a cruel mistress. So, Hugo had made a pact with himself. He'd give it a month and do everything in his power to help Max. After that, he'd see to his family and live with the consequences, whatever they were.

Hugo slipped into the abbey and looked around. It didn't have the aura of solemnity that churches normally had, forcing people to speak in hushed tones and look around as if being watched by God himself. Westminster Abbey was spread out and crowded on a Wednesday afternoon, people coming and going and creating a somewhat chaotic atmosphere, which was just what Hugo needed.

Brad was already there, seated in the center of the back pew, hat in hand, his shaggy blond head unmistakable among the parishioners who'd come for the service and were scattered around the half-empty pews closer to the pulpit.

Hugo walked past him twice, but Brad never even noticed the plainly dressed, blond, blue-eyed man who finally slid in next to him.

"This seat is taken," Brad said not unkindly, wishing to get rid of the man. His look was one of annoyance, since there were plenty of other places to sit.

"It's me, Brad," Hugo chuckled.

Brad just stared, open-mouthed, taking in the light hair, sky-blue eyes, and the homespun of a simple merchant.

Hugo sat silently, giving Brad a few moments to take in his altered appearance.

"H-h-how is this possible?" Brad stammered. He knew the voice, and he knew the man once he looked closer, but he couldn't accept the transformation. "Have you been bewitched?"

"No, Brad, I'm still the same man underneath. This is just a clever disguise."

"How could you change your eye color?" Brad whispered, outraged. "Is that a periwig?" He reached up and pulled a lock of hair.

"The hair is real, and the eyes are the same as always. It's just bits of colored glass." He couldn't say that the lenses were made of soft plastic since Brad wouldn't understand, but he needed an explanation that made sense. Brad was an educated, reasonable man, but even he could be persuaded that Hugo was under some kind of enchantment, and the last thing Hugo needed was any more questions about Neve and her origins or supposed powers.

"You put colored glass in your eyes?" Brad was scandalized, but also impressed. "Does it hurt?"

"Not at all. It's specially made. How are Beth and the baby?" Hugo asked, eager to change the subject.

"Oh, very well. Robert is nearly five months old. He smiles and even has one tooth. It's charming. The nurse brings him once a day for me to play with." Brad beamed with pride.

Hugo just smiled, remembering what Neve had said about fathers in the twenty-first century who took care of their children without the benefit of nurses or servants. He'd seen plenty of dads in Hyde Park, walking around with prams, teaching their children to ride bikes, and pushing them on the swings as they squealed with delight. His own father hadn't taken much interest in him until he got older and could be introduced at Court, but the mere idea of the elder Everly playing with Hugo nearly made him laugh out loud.

"I'm glad to hear it. I wish I could see him. And Jane?"

"Jane is Jane," Brad replied somewhat cryptically. "I delivered your letter in person, and she seemed—what is the right word—perplexed. She said she would reply, but when I offered to take the letter with me, she changed the subject."

"That's odd. Is she in good health?"

"She appears to be," Brad replied, shrugging his shoulders.

"And how's Jemmy?" Hugo asked.

He'd never said goodbye to his eight-year-old page, who was more adopted son than servant. Hugo genuinely missed the boy and hoped that Jane was looking after him. She'd never warmed up to the boy but had promised to take care of him until Hugo was able to return to Everly Manor.

"I haven't seen him, but I'm sure he's well," Brad answered impatiently. "Hugo, what are you doing here? Where have you been? When I heard you'd been arrested I came up to London to see you but was denied entry. They said you'd gone mad and were claiming to be Maximillian Everly. If you are here with me, then who on earth is the man in the Tower?"

"He's a distant relative who bears an uncanny resemblance to me," Hugo explained, sticking to the truth as much as possible. "It seems that he came to Cranley and was arrested in my stead. Brad, I need to get him out."

"And how do you propose to do that? Everyone believes him to be you, so the only way to get him out is to present the real Hugo Everly, which I will not allow you to do," Brad said hotly.

"Neve expressed much the same sentiment. But, Brad, I can't allow him to be tried and executed. You know he has no chance whatsoever of proving his innocence. He'll be lucky if he's sentenced to beheading. It can be so much worse."

"I know, old friend, I know." Brad looked crestfallen for a moment. The penalty for high treason was drawing and quartering, a fate worse than death, which made beheading look like the most humane of sentences. Brad nodded in agreement as he turned to Hugo. "Do you remember Gideon Warburton? Beth and I had him to stay the Christmas before last after his mother passed. He's Beth's cousin by marriage," Brad asked, giving Hugo a searching look.

"Can't say that I do. I was at Court the Christmas before last, so I never had the pleasure of meeting him. Do you think he can help somehow?"

"I'm not certain. Gideon is a man of law, but his experience lies mostly in drawing up wills and marriage contracts. He has, however, a very keen mind and likes a challenge. I can consult with him and see what he might suggest," Brad offered.

"Do you trust him?"

"He's a bit odd, to tell you the truth, but I believe him to be a man of integrity. Can you meet me here tomorrow? I'll consult him tonight and see what he proposes," Brad suggested.

"What will you tell him?" Hugo asked, considering the consequences of bringing another person in on their secret.

"I won't give anything away. I'll just ask a theoretical question and see what he suggests."

"Very well. I'll see you here tomorrow at noon. I hope your man has something to contribute because I'm at a loss," Hugo confessed as he smiled ruefully at his friend. "I must return to Neve. Did Jane tell you she's with child?"

"No, she didn't," Brad replied, gaping at Hugo. "When is it due? Are you married then?"

"It's due in March, and no, we're not married yet, but will be as soon as possible."

"And what of her Protestantism?" Brad asked, still baffled

by Hugo's news. He had never imagined that Hugo would compromise when it came to the religious views of his wife. He routinely pretended to be a Protestant in order to divert attention from his more colorful activities, had many Protestant friends and associates but had never been flexible when it came to marriage.

Hugo's first wife had been from one of the most prominent Catholic families in the country. The marriage had lasted all of two weeks before it was annulled by the bride's father who didn't approve of the match and found a physician to swear to non-consummation, despite the fact that Catherine was already pregnant with Hugo's child. Hugo had still considered himself married long after his skittish bride had married someone else and passed off Hugo's daughter as her husband's. The child had died in infancy, but the whole experience had left Hugo heartbroken and remote, with no desire to ever marry again, despite the need to produce an heir to keep the Everly line going. It had taken the appearance of Neve Ashley for him to finally allow love back into his life and finally accept the annulment, which had set him free to marry again.

Perhaps his love for Neve is stronger than his faith, Brad thought, or, knowing Hugo, he'd simply found an acceptable solution.

"Neve will remain a Protestant, but she has agreed to raise the child in the Catholic Church. I think it's a fair compromise," Hugo added a trifle defensively.

"It is, and I wish you both happiness." Brad patted Hugo on the shoulder. "It is good to see you, old man, even if you hardly resemble yourself. I'd given you up for dead, and believe me, I've mourned you every day. I'm glad to see you have arisen."

"Don't start comparing me to Christ just yet. I might have risen, but I'm far from alive; not until I'm free to reclaim my identity and estate and marry the mother of my child in the sight of God."

Hugo shook Brad's hand and slipped out of the pew and into the golden September afternoon. He trusted Brad with his life but wasn't sure how a man of law could help without being told the truth of the situation. He needed an alternate plan, since time was of the essence. Sooner or later, a trial date would be set, and things would move very quickly once that happened.

THREE

"I'm coming with you," I insisted as Hugo prepared to go meet Brad. "I can't stand being cooped up in this room a moment longer. I need air and exercise," I added, as if I needed a reason to want to escape the tiny room. I could take three steps from the bed to the window and back, or just remain horizontal for the duration of Hugo's absence.

"All right," Hugo conceded. "I can't imagine that anyone would recognize you since the only people who've seen you were Captain Humphries and his men when they came to arrest me. Of course, Lionel Finch knows what you look like as well, but I highly doubt he's in London since the date for the trial hasn't been set yet. I'm sure he'll be the star witness, though. Should have killed him when I had the chance," Hugo grumbled warily.

"You don't mean that, Hugo, I know you don't."

Hugo just shrugged, no longer sure he'd done the right thing when he spared Lionel. Lionel Finch had the power to bury Hugo, and we both knew it. His testimony was paramount to the case, and he would relish the opportunity to see his enemy die. Hugo had caused Lionel Finch bodily harm while trying to protect me and had humiliated him by taking his savagely beaten fourteen-year-old wife. Finch would have no reason to believe that the man on trial wasn't Hugo Everly and would not pass up a chance to get revenge.

I firmly put the thought out of my head and followed Hugo down the street. Despite my misgivings, I was excited to be out and about. London was a beehive of activity; a place I knew well in the twenty-first century but felt like a tourist in now. It was truly amazing to see the magnificent façade of Whitehall Palace in the distance, and hard to believe that in a not-too-distant future it would burn to the ground, with nothing remaining but a few drawings and paintings to remind future generations of this gargantuan palace that housed thousands of people, ranging from the king himself to the lowliest servants toiling in the kitchens and stables.

I gaped at the giant construction site that was to become St. Paul's Cathedral. Nearly two decades after the Great Fire, it was still under construction, and wouldn't be consecrated for over thirty years yet. It was strange to see London without the familiar cupola rising over the rooftops, the landmark that screamed "London" to the modern world nearly as much as the sight of Buckingham Palace or Tower Bridge, or the famed Eiffel Tower as the symbol of Paris. Of course, most of London was not made up of famous buildings, but narrow, muck-strewn streets, flanked by houses that overhung the muddy pavements and blocked out nearly all sunlight in some of the more congested areas.

The population of London had grown so quickly over the past few hundred years that the metropolis had spread way beyond the original city wall, claiming the farmland beyond and transforming it into a warren of narrow streets and thriving local businesses. Commerce was taking place all around us, and I was surprised to see that stalls had been set up amid the construction to sell everything from books to hot pies and herbal remedies for every conceivable illness.

The streets became wider and slightly cleaner as we approached Westminster Abbey. I gazed at the spot where the Houses of Parliament would be, but saw another building, not the world-famous Gothic structure with its clock tower piercing the London sky. There was no bridge and no busy intersection, just a muddy crossroads with the abbey rising majestically on the other side. While by the future St. Paul's, there were throngs of people outside, hawking their wares, shopping, haggling over the price of something they wished to buy, or generally just loitering. Several boys were visible in the crowd, their eyes darting around in search of a suitable victim. Anyone who'd been to London before knew to hold on to their purse for fear of being relieved of it before they knew what had hit them.

I nearly cried with joy when I spotted Brad's leonine head. He was gazing up at a stained-glass window in such apparent concentration as to make it obvious that it was all an act. His hands were folded behind his back, and he seemed enraptured of the subject, although his eyes frequently strayed to the door. He walked away as soon as he saw us enter and took a seat in a wooden pew that was furthest away from people milling in the nave, waiting for us to join him. He seemed unusually nervous, and I hoped he didn't have bad news.

"Neve, you look in fine health," he said quietly as I sat down next to Hugo. "Pregnancy agrees with you." I could see that he had lots of questions, but Hugo forestalled him asking any of them by going directly to the crux of the problem.

"Have you been able to find anything out?"

"I have, actually. According to my learned friend, it seems that the basis of any case is to first establish the identity of the accused. A trial cannot proceed if there's any doubt. Gideon advised me that witnesses need to be brought forward who would testify to the fact that Maximillian Everly is not Hugo

Everly. Of course, the more witnesses there are, the better," Brad explained, clearly satisfied with this idea.

Hugo was less impressed. "But if no one can see the prisoner, how can they possibly know if it's me or not until the actual trial, and even then, given the resemblance, they'd need to actually talk to Max to make sure that we are not one and the same."

"Yes, that's a hindrance, but one which can be overcome. If enough people can be prevailed upon to testify without actually seeing Maximilian, such as myself, your sister, your man-at-arms perhaps, then we stand a chance. We obviously know that the man is an impostor, so we don't need to spend time with him to ascertain this fact. Even if a few people can cast suspicion on the identity of the prisoner, the trial can't go forth. They won't release him, of course, but at least he won't be executed for a crime he didn't commit. In time, Maximillian might be set free, once any doubt has been eradicated."

Hugo stared up at the window, his face set in hard lines as he tried to poke holes in this plan. He didn't seem to come up with too many objections since he turned back to Brad, nodding in agreement. "That seems to be the best chance we have, so we must try it. Of course, a man of law must be hired to put this notion forward, since the Crown will not lift a finger to mount any kind of defense. Max is on his own in there. What do you propose, Brad? Can your man be hired for this case?"

"It's already done. Gideon Warburton will visit Maximillian in the Tower tomorrow. He is instructed to say that his services are being paid for by a benefactor. Gideon will report directly to me and will do his utmost to get any information from the prisoner which might help his case. Is there anyone we can contact who can verify his identity?" Brad asked, suddenly realizing that the coin had two sides. "Does he have a wife, mother, child, or even a mistress? It would greatly help."

"There's no one," Hugo answered, his voice flat. "Maximillian has no family."

"Well, where did he come from? I'd never heard you mention him before." Brad was nothing if not persistent.

"I don't know, Brad. I haven't seen the man in years. We never kept in correspondence. I believe he might have been living abroad."

"So how can you be so sure that there's no one we can call upon? Surely there's someone who knows him. Where was he living before coming to Cranley? Did he take a ship from abroad? If he weren't here during the rebellion, he'd be proven innocent. Perhaps there's a captain, or a member of the crew, who could testify that he had been aboard their vessel," Brad insisted.

"Have your man Gideon ask him. Perhaps he can put forth a few names. In the meantime, please send a message to my sister asking her to come to London," Hugo instructed. His brow was furrowed, and I wondered why that should be, but didn't ask. Perhaps he didn't want Jane to worry, but he'd written to her telling her that we never left for France. Seeing us in London wouldn't be any great shock to her.

I had thought that Jane would come to London at the first opportunity, but there was still no word from her. Perhaps she had to make arrangements for Clarence, although he was old enough to stay alone for a few days in a house full of servants, supervised by his tutor. Clarence would probably relish a few days of freedom, hounded as he was by Jane to focus on his studies. At thirteen, the boy never got to do anything fun, and probably missed his uncle, who took him hunting and fishing despite the protests of his mother.

"I've invited Jane to stay at the house when she comes to London. You know how she hates to stay at inns," Brad said as we prepared to leave. "I will send a message once she arrives."

"Brad, don't tell Jane where we're staying," Hugo said as

Brad turned to leave. "She might decide to come see us, and having my sister visit me would be tantamount to yelling my whereabouts from the city walls. I will arrange a meeting when the time comes."

"Of course," Brad replied with a smile. "I will be as silent as the grave."

FOUR

Max Everly hobbled toward the narrow window of his cell, drawn by the raised voices and general commotion taking place down below. He'd seen the wooden structure being built, but, being a man of the twenty-first century, didn't immediately make a connection between the structure and its purpose. Max watched in horror as a young man was led out of an arched doorway across the green and escorted to the scaffold by two burly guards. An executioner was already on the scaffold; his hands gripping the handle of the ax as he swung it a few times for practice.

There was also an elderly clergyman, his face pale, and his lips twitching nervously as he watched the approach of the condemned. The young man looked terrified, but walked with his head held high, shrugging off the hand of the guard on his arm in a last gesture of defiance. He couldn't have been more than eighteen or nineteen, but his courage in the face of death was extraordinary.

A few people stood by, eager for their entertainment, but it wasn't a great crowd by any means. The condemned was probably someone of no account, his death not worth the bother of a public execution.

Max knew he should step away from the window, but he was rooted to the spot, unable to tear his eyes away from the young man as the clergyman spoke to him quietly, offering absolution. The young man shook his head, his face set in hard lines as the clergyman moved away, noticeably angry. The young man crossed himself with an air of defiance, making the Protestant clergyman wince at this singularly Catholic gesture.

This seemed to be a sign for the execution to begin. The guard moved forward to force the young man to his knees, but he held up his hand and sank to his knees of his own accord, laying his head on the block and staring down at the wood beneath him, his hands gripping the sides of the block.

Max winced as he heard the thwack of the ax and watched the man's head fall onto the wood beneath. Crimson ribbons of blood coated the rough planks, dripping between the cracks and pooling at the feet of the executioner, who was accepting praise for a job well done. He'd chopped off the head with one stroke, something that was apparently quite a feat.

The clergyman departed without a second glance as the crowd began to disperse, a single weeping woman left standing by the scaffold. She sank to her knees, sobbing bitterly, but no one paid her any mind. She was of middle years, and it shook Max to the core to realize that she was probably the young man's mother. She reached out toward the head, but one of the guards kicked her hand away with his boot, ordering her to leave. She didn't; she remained by the scaffold until someone came with a handcart to take the body away and throw a bucket of water onto the planks to wash away the blood. Only then did she finally rise and follow the cart as it was wheeled away, her shoulders shaking with silent sobs. Max hoped that she would be able to claim the body for burial since the young man wouldn't get a Catholic service at the Tower. It was a small thing, but to her, it would mean the world, especially since he probably didn't receive last rites.

Max turned away from the window and was violently sick into the chamber pot. His hands were shaking, and his knees buckled as his brain finally processed what it had just seen. This wasn't some historical drama; this was real life. A young man had just been beheaded before his eyes, his crime likely no more serious than theft or assault. A life had been cut short without any fanfare or pity. One strike of the ax and it was all over; no appeals, no retrials, and no life in prison. This was not the lenient justice system of the future; this was a world where people were routinely executed, partially to inspire fear, and partially to keep the cost of incarceration down. The Crown didn't need the expense of supporting countless prisoners for years.

Max finally forced himself to get up off the floor and lay on his cot, curling into a fetal position. He had been in this cell for over two weeks now, since he'd been foolish enough to saunter into the village without any thought to what might happen. He'd been so excited to finally find the passage that all family history had fled from his mind, leaving him feeling like a kid at Christmas. It had taken him months to decipher Henry's diary and figure out how to open the damn passage. The answer had been in front of him all the time, but Henry had hidden the key in plain sight. A drawing of a six-petaled flower. So simple.

He'd only wanted a little taste of seventeenth-century life, not thinking for even a moment that he could be arrested in lieu of Hugo. The soldiers wouldn't listen to a word he said, beating him savagely until he could no longer speak, much less stand. They'd trussed him up and taken him to London in fetters, like an animal, allowing him only some bread and ale on the journey and refusing to uncuff him even when he was desperate for a piss. One of the soldiers had to help him, laughing at him as he'd grabbed his cock painfully with calloused hands and ordered him to do his business.

Since then, Max had been repeatedly beaten and questioned by several different men. His ribs ached unbearably every time he so much as drew breath, and several teeth had been knocked loose. Max's left eye was swollen shut, and his bottom lip split. At least two fingers were broken, as was probably his nose. He could barely get enough air through the swollen nostrils, which made breathing even more difficult. He'd told them the same story over and over, but they didn't believe him. And why should they?

Max could feel the cold, stone wall behind his back. It was as hard and unyielding as his captors. Tears of fear and frustration slid down his stubbled cheeks as his body shook with the shock of what he'd just seen. He might not be next, but his turn would come sooner or later. There was nothing he could do to convince his guards that he wasn't Hugo Everly, and there wasn't a single person he could appeal to for help. Who would believe him? Who would care? Hugo had been branded a traitor and executing him served a double purpose. He'd be punished for his crime, and his death would serve as a deterrent to others who considered plotting against the Crown.

Max let out a mirthless bark of a laugh. He'd wanted to run for Parliament only a month ago, had been planning his campaign and seeking backers. Politics was a dirty business in his own time, but nothing compared to the ruthless, bloody quagmire it was now. In the twenty-first century, a person might risk disgrace, financial ruin, and possibly a tabloid scandal, but this was much deadlier. Backing the wrong horse meant certain death, and Hugo had backed the wrong horse.

Why couldn't he have just stayed neutral and accepted a Catholic monarch? Was he such a religious zealot? Hugo hadn't struck Max as being particularly religious or unreasonable. Of course, he hadn't known him for more than a few hours, but the impression he got was of a man very much in control of himself and his surroundings, despite the fact that he was completely out of his element in the twenty-first century. What had possessed him to throw in his lot with the bastard son of Charles II? Did it mean that much to him to have a Protestant on the throne, or were there other reasons which would remain unknown?

And where was Hugo now? Was he still in the future with Neve, or had he returned to his own time? Unlikely, since Max was now incarcerated in his place. Hugo had avoided arrest by escaping to the future, and Max had stupidly stepped into his place by going to the past. It'd be funny if it weren't so bloody unbelievable. Perhaps Hugo knew Max was missing and was trying to pass himself off as Lord Everly in the future. If Max could be mistaken for Hugo, surely Hugo could be mistaken for Max. Of course, his mother would never fall for the hoax, not for a second.

Max couldn't even bring himself to think about his poor mother. He'd disappeared without a trace, just as Neve had several months before, leaving his mother to jump to her own conclusions. Would she have alerted the police, or would she have finally believed that the passage was real and that he'd gone off into the past? Naomi Everly was way too old and too frail to come after her only son in pursuit, so she would be forced to just sit and wait, hoping that Max was safe and would come back to her. Would she still be there waiting if he ever managed to return, or would the strain of not knowing what happened to him kill her?

He'd had many arguments with his mother, occasionally thought her to be cold and domineering, but he would give absolutely anything to see her one last time, to tell her that he loved and respected her, and to have her lay her gnarled hand on his head in a sign of benediction as she had when he'd told her he'd be seeking a seat in Parliament. She'd been proud of him then, believing Max to finally be living up to his potential, rather than shirking his responsibilities as Lord Everly. What would she think of him now, caged and beaten, but most of all terrified?

Max forced himself to breathe as deeply as he could to stop the shaking and tears. The taste of vomit was still strong in his mouth, but there was nothing to drink, so he just wiped it with his dirty sleeve and gulped in some air. They hadn't executed him yet, so maybe they weren't as sure as they'd been two weeks ago that he was Hugo Everly. Max knew that he was deceiving himself, but he was desperate for any shred of hope he could grasp at. Otherwise, he'd have to accept that he was living on borrowed time, and he wasn't ready to do that just yet.

Max had finally managed to reach some semblance of calm when he heard the scraping of the key in the lock. Dear God, were they going to question him again so soon? He'd barely had any time to recover from the last bout.

Max braced himself; holding on to the cot as if it could save him, but the guard barely looked at him as he admitted a short, slightly overweight man wearing a brown curly wig into the cell.

The man wrinkled his nose in disgust at the smell of vomit, sweat, and dried blood, but gave Max a stiff bow and asked if he might take a seat.

Max nodded, stunned that the man was being civil. He appeared to be around Max's age, his plump cheeks pale, and his muddy brown eyes devoid of any expression, save curiosity.

"My name is Gideon Warburton, Master Everly. I will call you that from now on, since it is your assertion that you are not Lord Everly. Is that correct?"

Max felt a moment of blinding hope as he faced the little man. "Yes, that's correct."

"I've been sent here by a benefactor who wishes to remain anonymous to help you prove your case, Master Everly. Is that acceptable to you?"

"I beg your pardon?" Max asked, confused. Who could

possibly be his benefactor, and why would they wish to remain anonymous? No one in this century knew him, or even of him, much less might feel the need to help him. As far as the world was concerned, he was Hugo Everly, pretending to have lost his mind in order to avoid the gallows.

"I need your consent to represent your interests," the man replied, not unkindly. "I know you've been through a lot," he said, taking in Max's injuries. "I've paid the guard to bring you some decent food, a candle, and some paper, should you wish to write a letter to someone. Is there anything else you might need, besides hot water for washing and a clean shirt?"

"You've paid the guard?" Max asked stupidly. "But I can't pay you back. I have nothing."

"I'm aware of that; that's why I paid him," Gideon Warburton explained patiently. "Now, shall we begin?" He pulled out a clean sheet of paper, a quill, and a pot of ink from his leather satchel and set them out carefully on the scarred wooden table, as if preparing to take copious notes.

"Begin what?"

"Planning your defense, sir. Now, is there anyone who can vouch for your identity, anyone at all?"

"Other than Hugo Everly himself? No."

"Surely there must be someone. Are you married, are your parents still living, do you have any children, a mistress, or even a faithful servant?"

"I've, eh... been out of the country for several years. My parents are deceased, and I'm not married, have no children or a mistress, and have done without servants for some time," Max answered, realizing that he was, for all intents and purposes, digging his grave even deeper.

"That's not very helpful, but we'll work with that. Your only hope lies in proving that you are indeed Maximilian Everly rather than Hugo Everly. Is there any way to do that?" Gideon

Warburton gazed at Max sternly, as if willing him to produce a battalion of credible witnesses.

"Master Warburton, I'm sorry to say that there's no one who can vouch for me. I'm quite alone," Max replied, fearful that the man would just give up on him and leave, but Gideon Warburton suddenly granted him a small, but warm smile.

"Not anymore, Master Everly, not anymore. You have friends, and those friends are willing to do everything possible to help. Bear up, man. Not all is lost." The man tried to look reassuring, but succeeded in looking more like a tired owl, but Max didn't care. He was the first person who'd been kind to him since coming to the past, and he wanted to prolong the interview for as long as possible just to have a friendly human being to talk to.

"Who are these friends?" Max asked, baffled. Who would be willing to help him, especially if it cost money? Perhaps whoever was paying the bill was one of Hugo's co-conspirators who thought that Hugo could be set free if his identity couldn't be proven.

Gideon Warburton scratched a few lines across the paper, closed the inkwell, put away his notes, and rose to his feet. He knocked on the door to summon the guard.

"I will see you very soon. We have much work to do." With that, he gave a wave of farewell and disappeared into the dim corridor. Max watched him leave with a mixture of hope and fear.

What if this is some kind of trick? Max thought as he stared at the gathering clouds outside the narrow window. It looked as if a storm was brewing.

Max was just about to lie back down on his lumpy cot when the door opened once again. The guard, who was a burly, bald thug whose nose must have been broken several times to look as misshapen as it did, came in. Max instinctively recoiled, fearing another interrogation, but the guard just set down a plate of something that smelled like roasted chicken, a jug of wine, fresh bread, and a hunk of strong-smelling cheese.

"Your paper and ink will come tomorrow," he spat out as he turned to leave.

Max fell on the food before the door was even closed. It hurt to chew, and his stomach contracted painfully after two weeks of nothing but thin gruel, but he finished every last bite, sighing with gratitude as the wine did its job and made him feel sleepy and relaxed. Whoever his benefactor was, he was a kind and generous man. Max lowered himself gingerly to his cot, feeling hopeful for the first time in weeks. His stomach growled with indigestion, but he didn't care. He was almost happy.

FIVE

SEPTEMBER 2013

Surrey, England

Purple shadows of autumn twilight crept shyly into the parlor, leaching the last of the daylight from the normally cheerful room. The trees whispered like conspirators, their conversation audible through the open window; the chill of the evening spreading its cold fingers over the hunched shoulders of the elderly woman who sat in front of the cold remnants of her untouched tea; the little cakes nearly dried up, and the sandwiches on the platter beginning to look wilted and unappetizing.

Lady Everly didn't bother to turn on the light or even to close the window even though she was chilled to the bone, continuing to sit in the gathering darkness which so aptly reflected her thoughts.

"Shall I turn the light on, my lady?" Mrs. Harding, the housekeeper, asked as she poked her head round the door and made for the tea tray, but Naomi Everly held up one hand, freezing her in her tracks.

"Just leave me please, Stella."

Mrs. Harding had worked for the Everlys too long to just accept the command, so she swiftly closed the window, pulled the curtains closed, and draped a cardigan over the old lady's shoulders before retreating into the corridor. She'd clear up the tea things later, but for now, her mistress clearly needed to be alone, and Stella knew exactly why. She sighed and made her way back to the kitchen to put away the items she'd taken out for dinner. Lady Everly wouldn't be eating tonight, and Stella was happy with a cup of tea and a sandwich in front of the TV.

Naomi Everly closed her eyes and leaned her head against the back of the sofa, allowing herself a moment of unguarded grief. Normally, her back was ramrod-straight, her hair perfectly coiffed, and her twinset and pearls clean and crisp, but tonight she wished she could curl up in a pair of flannel pajamas with the shaggy brown teddy bear she'd had as a child and allow the tears to flow.

Detective Inspector Knowles had telephoned earlier and asked if he might come by the house. Of course, Naomi knew that this couldn't possibly be good news. If it were, Max would have come home instead of the inspector.

She'd known Bobby Knowles since he was a little boy who incessantly annoyed his mother as she'd colored and set Lady Everly's hair in her beauty salon. *What a nuisance he was then*, Lady Everly thought, mentally deciding that it was that desire to annoy people that drew him to the police force. But she had to admit that D.I. Knowles was all tact and compassion when he'd come to see her. She'd offered him tea, of course, and he had shyly accepted a cup and a piece of cake as he broke the news. His words still swirled in her mind, forming a strange kind of colorful helix as they writhed and intertwined, at times making no sense at all, and at other times, clear as day.

"Lady Everly," the inspector had begun as he took a sip of his tea, mostly to hide his distress, "Max has been missing for several weeks now, and I'm sorry to say that the Super will not authorize any more funds on this case."

"But my son hasn't been found," Lady Everly had protested, knowing that it was futile.

"No, he hasn't been," the inspector had conceded. "Look, the truth is that there's absolutely no evidence of foul play. We've searched the woods inch by inch, dredged the stream, checked all of Max's credit card, bank, computer, and cellular activity, and went door to door questioning people. We have found nothing. There's no body, no sign of a struggle, no witnesses who saw anything out of the ordinary, and no cyberattacks on Max's accounts," D.I. Knowles had explained.

"Max hasn't accessed his bank account or logged on to his computer since September 4. He hasn't made any calls or charged anything on his credit cards." The inspector had grown silent, allowing Naomi Everly to draw her own conclusion. What he was essentially saying was that Max had either gone completely off the grid or was dead, in which case there was nothing more they could do than they had done already.

"Thank you, Inspector," Naomi had said, giving Knowles a weak smile. It wasn't his fault that he didn't have better news; he was only doing his job.

Detective Inspector Knowles had set down his teacup and quietly left the room, allowing Lady Everly the privacy she needed to deal with the news. Except, D.I. Knowles didn't know what she knew, so couldn't fully appreciate the complexity of Max's disappearance.

Naomi slid sideways on the sofa and hugged a fluffy cushion instead of a teddy bear. She'd refused to believe it when Neve Ashley had disappeared, had ridiculed Max for suggesting that such a thing could be possible, then told him to dispose of the evidence, not because she thought Neve had traveled through time, but because she didn't want anything sordid associated with the family name. Max was going to stand for

Parliament, and he didn't need anything, no matter how unrelated, to tarnish his campaign. The whole thing was preposterous anyway. Real people didn't time travel; they had breakdowns, went AWOL, and wound up getting years of therapy and being a drain on government resources, but they didn't time travel.

Naomi moaned softly as she recalled the conversation with Max in May when she'd returned from Cornwall. He had said Neve was back and had gone to London. She'd been in the seventeenth century. Max had been strangely tight-lipped about what had happened to Neve, but he had seemed very agitated and distracted. It wasn't until Max himself had disappeared that Naomi realized that he hadn't told her the whole truth. And now he was gone, and she had no way of getting him back. Not only did she have no idea of how to access the passage to the past, but she was too old and too frail to go searching for her son. It was clear that something terrible had befallen Max, or he would have returned by now, having satisfied his curiosity.

For one mad moment, Lady Everly thought of showing D.I. Knowles Henry's journal, and explaining to him where Max had gone. Perhaps he could interview that Ashley woman again and find out how she had managed to open the passage, but the idea was ludicrous. It was not as if a twenty-first-century detective was about to don period togs and go searching for her son in the past. It sounded like a plot of some misconceived television show, like *Doctor Who*. No, Max was lost to her, possibly forever.

"Oh, Max, where are you?" Naomi wailed into the pillow. "Please, please come back."

Until today, Naomi had refused to entertain the thought that Max might not return, but D.I. Knowles had brought it home to her that they had reached the end of the line. There was no way to find out where Max had gone, or what had happened to him once there. As a mother, Naomi felt an invisible tether to her child, and knew without a doubt that Max was in terrible danger. He was alone, penniless, and friendless. Endless scenarios raced through Naomi's mind until she felt as if her brain would explode, her heart hammering against her ribcage as she unwittingly imagined all the horrible ways a person could die in the past.

Was Max already dead? Was he lost to her forever? Was the Everly line now officially at an end? She was the last of the Everlys, the last of a noble and ancient family whose members had stood beside kings and made it into the history books.

A strange tingling originated in Naomi's right side. It started in the vicinity of her chest but seemed to spread higher and lower. It grew stronger until she felt as if electricity were being pumped through her flesh, but only on one side. She tried to call out, but her voice failed her, and she held on to the cushion tighter, hoping the feeling would just go away. Naomi felt as if a series of small explosions were taking place in her head, making her forehead feel tight, and her eyes bulge with unexplained pressure. The tingling seemed to subside, but numbness replaced it, making the right side of her body feel unbearably heavy. Naomi tried to move, but couldn't, the right side of her face frozen as she tried to scream.

It wasn't until two hours later that Stella Harding found her mistress on the sofa, half of her face paralyzed and her body immovable. She called Emergency Services, but it was too late. Naomi Everly had suffered a massive stroke and would require round-the-clock care, possibly till the end of her days.

"Oh, Max, where are you?" Stella Harding mouthed as she sat by Naomi's hospital bed. "We need you."

SIX

SEPTEMBER 1685

London, England

I was still in bed, luxuriating in the warmth of the blankets, when the sound of heavy footsteps brought me out of my reverie. Since our room was on the top floor, no one had any reason to be there unless they were coming to see us, and there was no one who knew where we were besides Bradford Nash.

Hugo was instantly by the door, dagger in hand, as he listened carefully. The footsteps stopped right outside, followed by a light knock that consisted of two taps, followed by one tap after a space of about thirty seconds, then three more.

Hugo's face split into a happy grin as he opened the door to reveal the fiery-headed Archie Hicks standing outside. The two men stared at each other; one in welcome, one in utter consternation, but Archie didn't question the transformation, merely entered the room, gave me a bow and an impish smile, due to my half-exposed breasts, and turned to face his master.

"I came as soon as I got your note. Harriet brought it. Seems Liza has been dismissed," he added meaningfully.

I noticed something in Archie's face but chose not to question it. Perhaps he'd had a relationship with the erstwhile Liza, or perhaps Jane had dismissed her for trying to warn the watch that we were in the area. It didn't matter. Archie was here now, and I felt better, knowing that a loyal, well-trained fighter was on our side. Hugo had two more men who'd traveled with him in the past, but I liked Archie the best. He was in his mid-twenties, with bright blue eyes, and a wicked grin that I was sure set many a heart aflutter wherever he went, but that wasn't why I was glad that Archie had come. Peter and Arnold were strong and loyal, but they were the type of men who followed orders without questioning them, obeying like drones. Archie was different; he was clever, resourceful, and charming, a quality that could be highly underrated, but could sometimes work wonders, particularly with women.

"Have you seen Jem?" Hugo asked, his face tense.

"No, can't say as I have. Haven't been to the house much, not since you left. Been at home, playing the farmer. My da is getting on in years, so he needs help around the place. Wasn't too happy to see me flying off to London at a moment's notice, especially just at the harvest. I asked Arnold and Peter to help him out while I'm gone."

"Did you tell them where you were going?" Hugo asked, somewhat alarmed.

"Nah. You didn't tell me to, so I kept my counsel. I have some questions though," Archie said, eyeing Hugo with undisguised curiosity.

"I'm sure you do, and I will answer them in due time. Now, why don't you go downstairs and allow Mistress Ashley to rise from her bed and put some clothes on, and I will meet you there presently."

Archie gave me an insolent wink and turned to Hugo with a wide smile. "It's good to have you back, Your Lordship, even if you do look like an overgrown angel with that golden hair and those wide blue eyes. Oh, and I believe your sister is awaiting you at Master Nash's house. She left for London yesterday, according to young Clarence. He was that glad to be rid of his mother for a few days, I can tell you. He was planning on going fishing today, and I think his tutor will not only be turning a blind eye but joining him on the riverbank."

"Jane is here?"

"Oh, aye." Archie let himself out, and I heard his boots thundering down the stairs.

"I'm glad Jane's here," Hugo mused as he finished dressing. "Brad will ask her if she's willing to testify on Max's behalf at the trial. I hope she doesn't refuse, although I can't imagine why she might have come if she doesn't wish to help."

"Perhaps she only wanted to see you. You know how reclusive Jane can be. She might not want the public scrutiny. I'm sure she's had to endure plenty since the day we vanished and left her to deal with the aftermath of your aborted arrest," I suggested as I pulled on my hose.

Jane never said anything, but I could only imagine the interrogation Captain Humphries put her through after Hugo and I had disappeared from the church. She knew nothing, but that didn't mean that anyone believed her. I knew that the house had been torn apart, because Max had told me so when he shared the story of Hugo's baffling disappearance. The soldiers had found nothing incriminating, nor any trace of Hugo Everly.

"Yes, I feel awful about that. Neve, I'm going to write Jane a quick note. Do you think you might be willing to take it to her? I can't go to Nash House, but no one will pay any attention to you. You can arrange a meeting with Jane. I don't think it would be wise to go back to Westminster again; we might become conspicuous. Perhaps we can meet at a tavern by St. Paul's. With all the construction and people coming and going, no one will notice us."

"Sounds like a good idea. I'll just have some breakfast and be on my way. I'm sure you and Archie have much to discuss."

I ate a few fresh buns, gulped down a cup of milk, and set off toward Brad's house, leaving Archie and Hugo deep in conversation over their own breakfast. Brad's house was located in a fashionable area, a few streets away from Whitehall Palace. The houses here were mostly built of stone and punctuated by large mullioned windows, the diamond-shaped mullions glowing in the morning sunshine and giving the residences a cheerful appearance. The streets weren't paved, but they were much cleaner than in Blackfriars and with less traffic rattling by.

This was the domain of the wealthy, and no place for the unwashed and boisterous masses which were found closer to the river. Brad's house was a three-story building, bordered on both sides by houses of similar architecture and size. It appeared almost as if the houses were holding each other up since they leaned into each other in a rather intimate way. The chimneys belched smoke into the bright fall sky, and several female servants came and went from nearby houses, baskets slung over their arms as they headed out to do their marketing.

An elderly servant opened the door and conducted me straight into the parlor, where Jane was sitting bent over her embroidery. Jane never just sat idly without having a work basket by her side. She set aside her work and came to greet me, apparently happy to see me.

"Neve, how wonderful it is to see you. Brad is not here, but I can offer you some refreshment on his behalf," Jane offered as she invited me to sit down.

"I just had breakfast, but you go right ahead," I replied, looking around the lovely room. It was paneled in blond wood, the upper half of the walls upholstered in a pastel fabric which gave the room an impression of airiness and light. Plump cushions padded the heavy wooden furniture, and a pastoral landscape hung on the wall, depicting what looked like Brad's estate in Surrey. The room was cozy and comfortable, something that couldn't be said of most parlors in this century which were not designed or decorated for comfort.

"I'm not very hungry, but perhaps a drink."

Jane called for some cider and I accepted a cup just to be polite.

"And how is my brother?" Jane asked, looking at me pointedly. "I thought you'd be in France by now. And to think that you had the passage booked and were hours away from leaving England."

"We would have been in France had it not been for this erroneous arrest. Hugo is looking for a way to help Maximilian," I replied carefully. Jane would know nothing of Max or her family's relationship to him, so I had to tread carefully and not let on that both Hugo and I knew exactly who Max was and where and when he'd come from.

"I just cannot begin to imagine where this man came from," Jane said irritably. "I've never heard of him before. My father had three sisters who had several sons between them, but none of them would go by the name of Everly. All marriages and births are recorded in the family Bible, and I have never seen anyone named Maximilian Everly. I would dismiss his claim out of hand if he didn't bear such an extraordinary resemblance to Hugo."

"You've seen him?"

"No, of course not, but several people in the village had, just before his arrest, and they could have sworn he was my brother. What is Hugo planning?" Jane asked, gazing somewhere just over my right shoulder. She seemed tense, but then again, I would never describe Jane as being relaxed or easygoing.

"Brad has a relative who is a man of law and will do his best to help Max through the trial. Other than that, there's not much to be done, I'm afraid."

"No, there isn't, is there?" Jane mused, suddenly brightening. She didn't seem overly concerned with Max's situation. He was nothing to her. "And how are you feeling, my dear? You look well."

"I'm all right. A little queasy at times still," I confessed. "And I have trouble sleeping."

"I know just the thing for sleeplessness," Jane said, perking up. "There's an excellent apothecary in Cheapside. I've often ordered potions from him while Ernest was ill. He'll have some dried chamomile, and perhaps some mint to settle your stomach. It's not at all far from here. Shouldn't take us more than a half-hour. I need some comfrey and willow bark. I keep it on hand in case Clarence gets a fever," Jane explained. "He's so often ill. An infusion of willow bark lowers fevers dramatically. Shall we go?"

"All right," I readily agreed. "Chamomile would be wonderful. I can brew it into some tea."

"Tea?" Jane asked, confused. "You mean a tisane? Yes, that's just the thing," Jane agreed, reaching for her hat. "I had trouble sleeping while I was pregnant too. I could hardly keep my eyes open in the afternoon and then at night I lay wide awake, my mind refusing to settle."

Jane opened a drawer and extracted a heavy purse of coin which she slid into a pocket inside her cloak.

"Is it that expensive to buy some herbs?" I asked, worrying that I didn't have enough money.

"That's all the money I brought with me. I don't like leaving it behind," Jane whispered, cutting her eyes at the door where the elderly servant had just passed.

I doubted that Brad would keep servants who stole from him, but didn't say anything and followed Jane out into the fall morning. I was surprised by her desire to take a walk. Jane wasn't one for outdoors and even avoided going into the village back in Surrey. Perhaps she'd missed London, since she hadn't been in a very long time. Jane was still in mourning for her husband, as her prim, black gown suggested. She looked like a raven with her dark hair, dark dress, and black cloak lined in dove gray, but there was a rosy blush on her cheeks, something I hadn't seen before.

The day outside was lovely, and I enjoyed walking arm in arm with Jane, breathing in the crisp September air. The tang of the river wasn't as strong here, making way for more pleasant smells, like those of baking bread emanating from the open window of someone's kitchen. I looked around with interest, trying to reconcile the London of my memory with the neighborhood I found myself in. I was sure I'd walked down this very street not so long ago, but in my time, it boasted several cafes, restaurants, and trendy shops lining the streets. There was no trace of the houses that we passed, save one or two historic buildings.

I smiled at Jane, thinking how nice it was to be surrounded by people who cared about Hugo and myself once more, despite the danger of being in London. She smiled back and squeezed my hand in a gesture of understanding and support.

We left the residential street behind and turned into Cheapside, which was a major commercial thoroughfare. The street was much wider, with countless shops displaying their wares inside and out. Wagons and carriages rattled past, and shoppers weaved between the vehicles to get from one side of the street to the other in search of a better price or a superior product.

Jane appeared to be overwhelmed by all the activity and steered me into a narrow lane, which was much quieter. Several shops were already open for business, but a few were still shuttered, their windows resembling closed eyes.

Jane glanced around nervously, as if expecting to be set upon by thieves at any moment, even though no one was within a few feet of us. I suppose it was daunting for her to be in a city of this size, after spending most of her time in the country and going no further than the garden and the church at the bottom

of the hill. Having been in mourning for nearly a year, Jane was
unused to being around people, especially of the lower classes
such as the ones who milled all around us now. I found it hard
to believe that she'd come here before in search of herbal remedies for Ernest. Jane wasn't the type of woman to go shopping
for anything; she'd just send a maid with written instructions,
but perhaps she'd had no choice, considering that Ernest had
suffered from syphilis, and she wanted to keep his condition a
secret from the staff.

"Where's the apothecary?" I asked, looking around. I didn't
see anything resembling that type of shop. The shops in this
street sold mostly leather and metal goods, their wares proudly
displayed as several women looked at pots and haggled over the
price of a pewter basin with the proprietor.

The people on the street were rough-looking and rude,
pushing past us unceremoniously as they went about their business. Jane seemed even more nervous than before, her eyes
darting up and down the street.

"Are we lost?" I asked, suddenly feeling nervous myself.
Jane's anxiety was contagious, and I regretted coming. Hugo
had told me to come straight back, and now he'd be worried.

"It's just up the street, I think," Jane replied. She looked
distracted; her head swiveling to the side as if searching for a
familiar landmark. She pulled me ahead, then suddenly
stopped as if she'd seen what she'd been looking for.

I bent down to take a pebble out of my shoe when I was
seized by rough hands; my arms pulled behind my back. Two
men shoved me up against a closed carriage.

"What are you doing? Let me go," I screamed. I assumed
they wanted to rob me and tried to free my hands to give them
whatever money I had.

One of the men slapped me hard across the face. I was
stunned into silence, my ear ringing where it had been hit. The
man in front of me didn't look much like a thief. He was simply

dressed, but his clothes were clean, as was the rest of him. He didn't have the grizzled look of someone who lived by stealing. He wore a sword, and I saw a hilt of a dagger protruding from his belt.

"I have money," I mumbled, but the man grabbed me by both shoulders and shook me, silencing me once more.

"I thought I told ye to shut up," he hissed as he held me pressed against the carriage. "Ye are under arrest for witchcraft, so say goodbye to yer friend."

I looked wildly for Jane, but her back was turned to me as she faced the second assailant, who was looking down at her as she fumbled with her cloak. I assumed that he was trying to steal her purse, but Jane was neither screaming nor struggling. She was relatively calm, especially for Jane.

The man bowed to her and seemed to thank her, just as I was roughly shoved into the carriage, which was dark as a coffin inside. The windows were covered up with squares of leather and the bench was unpadded, as were the walls of the carriage; it was nothing more than a wooden box.

I banged on the door, but no one paid any attention to me as the carriage lurched and began to move, picking up speed as it headed to an unknown destination. I put my head between my knees to combat the bile that rose in my throat. I was terrified. Who were these men? Where were they taking me? They hadn't been soldiers, nor did they have a warrant for my arrest. They had simply abducted me off the street. My only hope was that Jane would go straight to Hugo, but I suddenly realized that she had no idea where to go. I'd forgotten to give her Hugo's note asking her to meet by St. Paul's. I howled with fear as the carriage took a sharp turn and leaned precariously to the side, throwing me against the hard wood. I tried to hold on for dear life, praying all the while.

Eventually, the carriage stopped, and the men dragged me out. The sun momentarily blinded me after the total darkness of the carriage, but I saw a large, squat building with several doors and very few windows as they dragged me through the gate. It was a part of London I didn't immediately recognize.

The interior of the building was dim, several torches mounted on the walls throwing shadows into what appeared to be a dark, vaulted passage. The stench that hung about the place like a miasma felt like an attack on the senses; my eyes watering and my nose stinging as I tried not to breathe too deeply. It was like being taken into a septic tank.

I heard screams and cries of despair coming from darkened alcoves set into the walls which I recognized to be cells. Several faces peered through the bars, but they were so dirty that I couldn't even tell if they were male or female, the eyes of the inmates blank, showing neither interest nor any spark of life. They simply stared blindly, following the sound of my terrified screams.

"Please, I need to speak to someone in charge. This is a terrible mistake," I wailed, but the men completely ignored me as they dragged me along. My pleas echoed off the stone walls, bouncing right back to me and making me shake with desperation.

The men pushed me into a filthy cell and locked the door, leaving without a word. Their job was done.

I was left alone, standing in a tiny cell with no window or even a bucket to use as a toilet. The straw on the floor was crawling with vermin, and I could hear rats in the corner, even though I couldn't see them. They were just dark shapes that scurried from side to side, their eyes red pinpricks in the darkness.

I banged on the wooden door, calling out for what felt like hours, but no one came. Not then and not later. Eventually, I grew tired of standing and slid down the side of the wall to the sticky floor, beating the floor with my fists to scare away the rats. It didn't really work. I felt them drawing closer and closer with every passing minute. I was so scared, I could barely think; my body shaking with shock and cold, and my mind refusing to accept that this had really happened to me.

Where was Jane? They hadn't taken her. Had she returned to Bradford's house to get help? My mind was racing in circles, asking questions I had no answers to. The men had said I had been accused of witchcraft. By whom? No one knew that I was in London except for Bradford, Jane, and Archie, and how could the men have known that I would be in that particular street with Jane? Had they been watching Bradford's house and saw us leave? Did they know Hugo was back in London and had he been taken as well?

I wasn't sure how long I sat there until the cries of the other inmates subsided, and the prison grew quieter as people went to sleep. It must have been night, but I had no way of telling. It was dark inside the prison, and not a glimmer of natural light could be seen anywhere from my cell. I hugged my knees, rested my forehead against them and cried myself hoarse. I cried until there were no tears left. My head ached, and my eyes felt raw and swollen, but the storm had brought a modicum of release.

I must have fallen asleep but woke up with a start as a sharp pair of teeth sank into my ankle, and I cried out in pain and terror. I spent the rest of the night pacing the cell, afraid to sit down despite the exhaustion that weighed down my limbs like lead weights.

SEVEN

Hugo stared around the empty room. His gut burned as if someone had lit a roaring fire inside his belly, making him wince with pain. He had a splitting headache, and a tremor shook his left hand until he clapped his right hand over it angrily. They'd been over it a hundred times, but he still couldn't make sense of what had happened on this wretched day.

Archie poured Hugo a cup of ale and held it out to him. "Have a drink," he said.

"I can't," Hugo replied in clipped tones. His mouth was dry, but he couldn't bring himself to take a sip, feeling that his throat would just close up. Instead, he sat down on the bed, head in his hands.

What Archie had told him was beyond comprehension, beyond the realm of possibility, but he trusted Archie implicitly and knew that Archie would lay down his life if he asked it of him.

"Archie, tell me again," Hugo commanded.

"The whole thing?" Archie looked as if he wanted to die. It wasn't his fault, but he blamed himself, nonetheless, believing that there was something he could have done to prevent what had happened. He'd been too far away and unarmed, but he should have done something, should have tried to save his mistress.

"The whole thing," Hugo replied, looking up at Archie. "Perhaps we missed something."

Archie took a sip of ale and began again, guilt twisting in his belly like a sharp knife. "I followed Mistress Ashley to Nash House, as you instructed me to, and just waited around outside. I saw a man walk down the street. He seemed lost and was walking slowly, looking up at the houses as if searching for the right one. There were several other people in the street, but they were mostly servants going about their business. Mistress Ashley was inside for no more than a quarter of an hour, then she left with Mistress Hiddleston. The man I'd seen earlier had turned around and watched them leave, then walked briskly away. I paid him no mind and followed the ladies at a discreet distance, just to make sure they were safe." At this part, Archie nearly choked on the words, his hand reaching for the cup as he gulped down the remainder of the ale.

"Go on," Hugo insisted.

"They walked arm in arm and appeared to be in good spirits. Mistress Hiddleston seemed to be leading the way. They walked down Cheapside for a bit, then turned the corner. I grew concerned when Mistress Hiddleston turned off into a narrow alley just off Milk Street. She stopped and looked around, as if lost, so I thought of offering my assistance when I saw the carriage stop just next to them. The man I'd seen earlier, loitering outside Master Nash's house, jumped out of the carriage and went straight for your sister, and a second man who'd been driving the carriage grabbed Mistress Ashley and then hit her across the face when she began to scream. He then pushed her into the carriage and locked the door from the outside."

"How were they dressed? Were they armed?" Hugo asked.

"They wore leather doublets and stout boots. Both were wearing swords, and the one who confronted your sister had a pistol tucked into his belt. I couldn't see much more than that from where I was, but they were definitely not soldiers."

"Now, tell me the part about my sister," Hugo said quietly. He felt as if he were going to be sick, but he needed to hear it again.

"Mistress Hiddleston didn't appear to be startled or frightened. She seemed to know the man who approached her and handed him a purse of coin just as Mistress Ashley was bundled into the carriage. He opened the purse, took one of the coins out and bit on it, before thanking her. He bowed to her respectfully, then jumped onto the bench of the carriage," Archie recounted again. He'd been shocked to witness the transaction, but he'd had no time to question Jane. He had to follow the carriage to see where Mistress Ashley was being taken.

"What did Jane do after they left?" Hugo asked, his voice low and raspy with feeling.

"She smiled and gazed after the carriage until it turned the corner, then left," Archie recounted, inwardly cringing at the look on his master's face. "I don't believe she'd seen me."

Hugo just nodded, as if confirming something to himself. He'd raced over to Brad's house as soon as Archie had come running back with the news of Neve's abduction. Archie had run after the carriage but could barely keep up. He'd been too far away to do anything when the carriage had stopped in front of Newgate Prison and Neve was dragged inside by the men, who came out again a short time later.

Brad knew nothing of Neve's visit, having been out at the time, but he had confirmed that Jane had arrived the day before. The old servant, Billingsley, said that a lady had come by to see Mistress Jane and then they had both left. Mistress Jane had returned about forty minutes hence, took her belongings, and cleared off. He had no idea where she'd gone or why she had left in such a hurry.

It had grown dark outside as Hugo and Archie talked, but neither man made a move to light a candle. Sounds of talking and laughter could be heard from the taproom below, the appetizing smells of food drifting up the narrow stairs and filling the room. They hadn't eaten, and Archie's stomach growled in protest. He hadn't had anything since breakfast, when Hugo had asked him to keep an eye on Mistress Ashley just in case. Archie had sprinted out the door, never imagining what this day would bring.

"Is there anything I can do for you, Your Lordship?" Archie asked, but Hugo shook his head.

"Get some food and rest, Archie. There's nothing you can do at the present."

Archie gave a respectful bow and let himself out of the room, leaving Hugo sitting in the dark. It wasn't until Archie's footsteps receded that Hugo allowed himself to cry. He hadn't cried since the morning he'd held Jem's inert body in his arms, believing the child to be dead and himself responsible. He thought his heart would break, but that pain had been nothing compared to what he was feeling now.

Neve was completely beyond his reach. Even were he to reveal himself as Lord Everly, there was nothing he could do to get her out of Newgate. She'd been taken on a charge of witchcraft, a charge that no woman had ever beaten. The only question was whether she would be burned alive, drowned, or hanged. And, for some unfathomable reason, his own sister was complicit in the arrest. She'd had her suspicions about Neve, particularly after Hugo's miraculous disappearance and clever disguise, but he'd never for a moment imagined that Jane might be capable of such a betrayal. Why? Why would she do this thing? Why would she condemn Neve to die? And their child...

She knew that Neve was pregnant, carrying a possible heir who would ensure the continued survival of the Everly line.

Hugo couldn't begin to understand what drove Jane to do what she'd done, but he'd been noticing changes in her since she came to stay at Everly Manor shortly after Ernest's death, changes that he'd tried to ignore. She was irritable and quick to anger, suspicious of anyone who came to the house, and reluctant to so much as walk into the village. He'd simply assumed she was grieving and needed time alone, but perhaps there was more to it than that. Jane had complained of headaches and always sat close to the window or the candle, saying she needed extra light to see by, especially when sewing. Were these signs of illness? But even if she were ill, what had that to do with Neve and himself? Why would she go to such lengths to hurt them?

Dear God in Heaven, Hugo suddenly thought, *could she be doing this because of the child?* Was Jane's desire for Clarence to inherit the title and estate at the root of this madness? Hugo couldn't begin to guess at Jane's motives, but he knew that if he were to see her right now, he'd tear her limb from limb, and even that wouldn't do anything to tame the pain in his heart and the overwhelming fear tugging at his soul.

Hugo shook with terror and helplessness as silent sobs tore from his body. This was all his fault. Neve had begged him not to go back, but he'd had to do the honorable thing for Max, instead of putting the welfare of his family first. Now his beautiful Neve was in prison: alone, terrified, and without hope. She would die thinking that he had forsaken her and their baby; die a horrible, brutal death brought on by his own arrogance and Jane's malice. He'd turn himself over to the authorities in a heartbeat if that would save Neve, but right now he was her only hope, and there was absolutely nothing he could do to help her, nothing at all.

The only thing that could get Neve out of Newgate was a

pardon from the king, and Hugo was the last person, under the circumstances, who could petition James II for such a favor. He'd done everything he could to protect James's monarchy and make sure that a Catholic king remained on the throne, but no one, save a trusted few, knew of his motives, nor could prove that he was a loyal subject of the Crown. Hugo had been branded a traitor, his name synonymous with treason and betrayal. He could no more petition the king for a royal pardon than he could stop the events that would overtake James in just three years and turn him from a king into a fugitive—a sovereign without a country.

Hugo sank to his knees and keeled over onto the floor, lying in a fetal position in the darkness, unable to control the searing pain that was tearing through him every time he thought of what Neve must be going through. He remained that way all night, unable to close his eyes, staring at nothing, and feeling more than his mind or body could handle.

He winced with pain as the morning sun pierced the darkness of his soul. A new day had come, a day without Neve, a day without hope. A day in which he'd have to force himself to function when all he wanted to do was die.

EIGHT

"I wish I were a witch," Liza said with feeling as she blew out the candle and climbed onto her narrow cot. She laid her head on the lumpy pillow and pulled the blanket all the way up to her chin, since the room was in the cellar and the cold seeped through the stone walls and left her chilled to the bone. Liza couldn't even imagine how cold it'd get in the winter but hoped that she might find a better position by then.

She could hear sounds of laughter and the creaking of beds from the floor above, but her job was done for the day and she'd earned a few hours of rest. She'd been on her feet since early morning, clearing away the dirty cups and plates, scrubbing the floor of the salon where the girls entertained the gentlemen before taking them upstairs, and washing numerous shifts, stockings, and rags that the girls used to clean themselves after their clients finally departed. The rags were the worst, but Liza closed her mind to the unpleasantness and did her job, terrified that if she showed any disgust she'd be out on her ear.

She'd been working at the brothel for nearly two months now and there wasn't a day that she didn't seethe with anger, mostly at herself, for allowing herself to be taken in by pretty words and empty promises. Everly Manor might not have been the Promised Land, but it was a fine house, and she'd had a dignified and decently paid position. Finding new employment without a recommendation from her past employer had proved more difficult than she'd anticipated, and many a door had slammed in her face, leaving her to seek employment somewhere where the qualifications were less exacting.

Jane Hiddleston had been filled with glee as she'd dismissed Liza for lewd conduct and bid her to leave the house immediately. At that point, Liza had still harbored some hope that Captain Norrington would take care of her as he had so ardently promised when she had visited him in his room at the inn, but since following him to London, she'd learned what his promises were worth. He'd barely acknowledged her when she'd found him at the barracks where he was quartered—had turned his back on her and their child. He'd given her a few coins to send her on her way, without so much as a word of regret or apology, only the cruel announcement that he had a wife and children in Yorkshire.

She should have known better, but hope had gotten the best of her. Liza didn't much fancy being the wife of a soldier, but the thought of having a home of her own, a family, and a man who'd care for her more than made up for Norrington's unfortunate occupation. She'd fallen in love with him, truth be told, and allowed herself to trust the man since he'd proven himself to be gallant and kind.

Liza supposed it was easy to be kind when he saw her once a week and did nothing more than buy her a tankard of ale and a hot pie before taking her upstairs for an hour of pleasure. Now, she was all alone, pregnant, and destitute, and the only thing she had were her wishes. Well, if wishes were horses, beggars would ride, her mam used to say, and how right she had been.

"Ye'd best be careful, saying things like that," Liza's roommate, Mavis, said as she eyed her in the darkness. "Women have been burned for less. Why'd ye want to be a witch anyhow?" she asked, her eyes round with curiosity. "I've heard girls wishing they were fine ladies or wealthy gentlemen's mistresses, but I've never heard anyone wishing to be a witch afore."

"I wish I could be a witch so that I could get revenge on those who've wronged me," Liza explained patiently. Mavis was a good woman, the soul of kindness, but no one would ever accuse her of being overly bright. She used to be one of the girls who worked upstairs, but at nearly forty, she was too old, blowsy, and used up to even have for free, much less pay for by the type of men who frequented the establishment. Mavis didn't seem to mind, applying herself to cooking, cleaning, and looking after the girls.

"And who do ye wish to take revenge on, me girl?" Mavis asked as she shifted her considerable bulk on the cot. "That fine lord of yours? Did ye think he'd marry ye and make ye his lady?" Mavis chuckled. "Come now, Liza, even ye are not that dim. He was kind to ye; that's more than any woman of yer station could ask for."

"Oh yes, he was kind to me until he threw me over for some rootless whore who just showed up on his doorstep. She was no better than she should be, yet I could tell he wanted to marry her, wanted her to be the mother of his children. And that sister of his, that dried-up old stick. She'd not seen a stiff cock in a decade at least, I'll wager. She could have used one, and that's a fact. Would have made her a kinder person," Liza ranted as she warmed up to her tirade. "Had me thrown out without so much as paying me what was owed. Just tossed me out like the contents of a chamber pot."

Mavis chuckled in the darkness. "And how do ye know when was the last time she'd seen a stiff cock? I saw one just yesterday—too bad it weren't stiff for me. Would have made me a kinder person, I can tell ye." Mavis let out a bawdy laugh, which made Liza giggle. She really was a good sort.

"But most of all," Liza said as she stopped laughing, "I'd like to get back at that bastard captain who got me with child. Said he loved me. Said he'd take me to London and marry me. Too bad he forgot to mention that he was married already. If I were a witch, I'd cast a spell on him that'd make him so sick, he'd wish he were dead, and I'd get rid of this baby I'm carrying."

"Ye don't need to be a witch to do that, do ye now?" Mavis asked reasonably. "I haven't been a whore for more than half me life not to know how to get rid of an unwanted babe. I can help ye, if that's what ye wish."

"Goes against God, doesn't it?" replied Liza fearfully. She'd considered asking the girls for help but wasn't sure if she was ready to kill her unborn child. She was about three months gone; if she were going to do it, it had to be done soon, but she still harbored reservations. She knew that many women got rid of unwanted babies, but the notion of what was involved and the possibility of going to Hell had been enough to deter Liza thus far.

Perhaps, somewhere deep inside, she still hoped that Norrington would come to her and promise to take care of them, even if he couldn't marry her outright. She liked children, had always hoped to have some, and could almost imagine the baby she would have, warm and sweet in her arms, its eyes closed in sleep. Of course, it wasn't a fully formed child yet, but it was a life growing inside her, a life created in, what she believed was, love. What a fool she had been to be taken in so easily.

"Lying to a woman and making false promises goes against God too, but ye don't see the Almighty smiting down men in the street, for we'd have very few of them left, and where would we be then, I ask ye?"

"You've got a point there, Mavis," Liza said as she curled

into a fetal position and brought her knees against her belly for greater warmth. "Will it hurt very badly if I do it?"

"Of course, it'll hurt, ye stupid girl. Feels good going in, hurts something awful coming out, whether ye miscarry or give birth to it." Mavis looked serious now, her round face pale as the moon across the small room. "I'd done it a few times," she said quietly, her face crumpling with sadness. "Oh, the pain goes away soon enough, but the emptiness remains, like a great, big hole in yer heart. I didn't even know who sired me babes, 'twas too hard to tell with all the men I'd serviced, but it still felt like a loss. Mayhap, I'd been happier had I had a child, but I would've lost my place, me source of income, and I was scared."

"How did you do it? Did you seek out a wisewoman?" Liza asked. She might not make her decision today, but she wanted to know what to do just in case.

"No, I did it on me own. Ye stew some herbs of pennyroyal with a bit of blue cohosh and drink it. There's some as add some baker's yeast to it for greater effectiveness. I'd never done it and it still worked a treat. But never use the essence of the plant, just the herbs. Brings the pains on and forces the babe out of yer womb. I can make it for ye if ye like. Ye shouldn't be alone when ye do it."

"Because I might die?" Liza asked, her belly contracting with fear.

"Because it's good to have someone with ye at a time like that, someone who can offer ye a bit of comfort in yer hour of need."

"Thank you, Mavis. I really do appreciate your kindness," Liza said, meaning it. Mavis was one of the kindest, nicest women she'd ever met. She hadn't had an easy life, but she felt no bitterness, no anger. She just took things one day at a time, and never looked to the future, unlike Liza, who was always thinking ahead. "If I have this child, I'll never be able to get out of this place. I'll end up old and dried up, with no chance in life."

"Like me, ye mean?" Mavis asked without any heat. "Ye're right. Ye're a young woman still; ye deserve a chance at happiness. A child will only make yer life more difficult. Come now, my girl, let go of the past. It'll do ye no good at all to keep it. Just keep yer eyes open for an opportunity. The world is full of them if ye are clever enough to seize them. One might come along when ye least expect it."

"Like it did for you?" Liza asked spitefully, and instantly felt remorse. Mavis did not deserve her ire.

"Aye, like it did for me. I could have been out on the street, freezing and starving after me good years were over, but Madame offered me a place and I took it. I have a roof over me head, a bed, and enough to eat. And as long as those girls need looking after, I'll have a place."

"So, you're happy then, are you?" Liza asked, considering what Mavis had said.

"Aye, I am happy. I know me place, and so should ye."

"Perhaps you're right, Mavis, but my place is not here. I want to work in a fine house again, and if I do marry, I want a man who loves me and will cherish me and our children. I don't want a man who only wants a warm body to stick his cock into. I want a fair chance in life, and, by God, I shall have it. Let's do it next week when I have my half-day off."

"Ye just say the word and I'll help ye. Now, stop yammering and get to sleep. I'm tired."

NINE

I woke up with a start as a wooden bowl containing something gray was shoved through the door. A cup of warm, sour ale accompanied this meal, but I drank it greedily and forced myself to eat the gruel. I had to keep up my strength if I was to survive in this place. And I had to survive. Sooner or later, someone would come for me, take me to trial where I could prove my innocence. I had to. I refused to contemplate the notion that I might be condemned.

The only person who'd ever implied I was a witch had been Jane when she'd seen Hugo's physical transformation, but she was Hugo's sister, my future sister-in-law; surely, she'd never testify against me.

Who else could be called to bear witness against me? Lionel Finch? I'd insulted him, called him names, and helped abduct his wife, but I had done nothing that could be construed as witchcraft, nothing at all. But Finch wasn't a man of integrity; he could denounce me out of pure spite, to punish me for the part I'd played in rescuing Frances, and his testimony would carry plenty of weight.

And, of course, there was Captain Humphries, who could

attest to the fact that I had contrived for Hugo to bring me to the church, from where we had both vanished. Yes, I suppose that could be seen as magic, and, in a sense, it was. I still had no idea how the passage worked or if the wormhole in time opened only in that spot and was only between this year and the future. But Captain Humphries had not seen us enter the passage. For all he knew, we could have simply found some other way out of the church and ran for our lives, escaping into the woods and duping him and his men. Neither Captain Humphries nor his men had seen anything out of the ordinary with their own eyes, so how could they testify against me?

But someone had made an accusation of witchcraft, and someone had issued a warrant for my arrest. I was now known to the authorities, and I would be persecuted. The thought terrified me. This wasn't some hypothetical threat; I'd been arrested, snatched off the street in broad daylight, and incarcerated without so much as a chance to talk to anyone. I didn't know much about the prison system of the seventeenth century, but I knew that many prisons simply housed prisoners without keeping them locked up in individual cells. Prisoners could have their own belongings, buy food and wine, and have visitors. I wasn't sure if this only applied to debtors' prisons, but the fact that I was locked up in a cell and not offered a chance to buy anything meant that whatever my crime, it was very serious.

I wrapped my skirts around my ankles to keep the rats away from them and sat against the damp wall. The stench wasn't as strong anymore, since I'd become accustomed to it during the night. My eyes were swollen from crying, my throat raw from screaming, and my hands shook with fear, but I tried to come up with a way to calm myself. I'd thought of doing yoga, but I couldn't bring myself to stand up, so I came up with the next-best thing. I began singing softly to myself, first a lullaby, then a pop song I'd heard on the radio not so very long ago. I was able to keep this up for about an hour, but then I ran out of songs and needed to come up with something else.

I began to recite my favorite poem by Percy Bysshe Shelley.

> The fountains mingle with the river
> And the rivers with the ocean,
> The winds of Heaven mix for ever
> With a sweet emotion;
> Nothing in the world is single,
> All things by a law divine
> In one spirit meet and mingle—
> Why not I with thine?
>
> See the mountains kiss high Heaven
> And the waves clasp one another;
> No sister-flower would be forgiven
> If it disdained its brother;
> And the sunlight clasps the earth,
> And the moonbeams kiss the sea:
> What are all these kissings worth
> If thou kiss not me?

Hugo had loved that poem when I'd read it to him and had asked me to read it again and again. He said it reminded him of us. We were two people from different centuries who were never destined to meet or love, but we'd collided with each other, and produced something otherworldly. I was the moonbeam that kissed the impenetrable depths of his sea.

Thoughts of Hugo undid my hard-won calm, and I started crying again, whimpering this time like an injured puppy. He would be going mad with worry, tortured by his inability to do anything to help me. Perhaps Gideon Warburton could be called upon to do something for me, but that's only if Hugo and Brad knew where I was and why.

I suddenly realized that it was entirely possible that Hugo had no idea where I was. Jane had seen me get arrested, but she couldn't know where I'd been taken. Even if she got to Hugo and told him what had happened, Hugo might have no idea where to look for me, and he was in no position to search for me through any legal channels. I hoped he wouldn't do anything foolish and endanger himself further.

I wrapped my arms tightly around my legs and rested my head on my knees. I had never been so frightened in all my life, and I knew that my ordeal was just beginning.

Time crawled by. Another bowl of gruel was given to me hours later with the same cup of sour ale, and still no one came. I fell asleep with my head in my hands, and my ankles crossed and wrapped in my filthy skirts for protection. Had it really only been one day?

TEN

Hugo forced himself to get up off the floor and splash some water on his face. His shirt was filthy and smelled strongly of sweat and fear, so he pulled it over his head, threw it in the corner and rummaged for a clean shirt, donning it as he gazed around the room, his heart clenching at the sight of Neve's hairbrush and shift carelessly tossed over a chair. Doing common, everyday things felt absurd, but he needed to get a hold of himself and the best way to do that would be by walking.

Hugo let himself out of the room and walked toward the river. It was still early in the morning, the sun just rising over the rooftops and casting pink and gold ribbons of light onto the muddy waters of the Thames, making it look heartbreakingly beautiful as it sparkled and flowed through the heart of London, which was still lost in shadow, only the top floors painted light by the sunrise.

There were several ferrymen on the bank waiting for fares, and they waved to him, hoping he'd need to be taken across. Hugo just shook his head and walked on, eager for the exercise and fresh air. He felt stiff and achy after lying on the floor all night, but he welcomed the discomfort, knowing that it was

nothing compared to what Neve must be going through. The
thought of her and the baby nearly undid him again, but Hugo
gave himself a stern warning and walked on. He was practically
trotting, but he needed to release some of this tension in order to
focus his mind. Last night had been a moment of weakness and
self-pity, but today was a new day, and he'd be damned if he just
gave up.

Neve had said that the subconscious mind was a very
powerful thing, one that sometimes held the key to a puzzle or
the answer to a riddle. Hugo wasn't sure when the idea had
come, perhaps it had formed during the night when he'd
believed himself unable to even think, much less plan, but the
seeds had taken root, giving him a burst of energy and a seedling
of hope. He hadn't even realized that he remembered the story.
It'd made an impression on him at the time, and now he tried to
recall every detail of the Earl of Argyll's escape only a few years
before. The tale had been told at a dinner party, and everyone
had made much of the earl's daring, praising his ingenuity.

Archibald Campbell, the 9th Earl of Argyll, had been
imprisoned at Edinburgh Castle on a charge of perjury. A
sentence of death, as well as forfeiture, had been pronounced in
his absence after a letter had been received from Charles II
demanding that a sentence be passed without further delay.
The earl's estates were to be stripped from him, and his heredi-
tary jurisdictions reassigned, leaving his heirs disinherited and
disgraced. Argyll had expected to be executed within the
coming days but still held out hope, being a man who didn't give
up easily. He was surprised when a lady of his acquaintance
came to visit him in his chamber.

Hugo couldn't recall her name, but she must have been a
woman of great courage and cunning. The lady came accompanied by a page who wore a wig and a bandage over his head
since he'd recently been injured in a fight. She'd spent some
time with the Earl of Argyll, talking quietly, and was in tears

when she finally left, having bid goodbye to her dear friend for the last time. The page helped her into the carriage and got on the back of the conveyance as it drove through the gates of the castle and into Edinburgh. The page jumped off a few minutes later and melted into one of the darkened wynds, disappearing without a trace.

It was discovered a few hours later that the man who came and the man who left were not the same person. The earl had changed into the page's clothes, donned his wig and bandaged his head, enabling him to walk out of captivity without so much as a scratch. The page had been roughed up by the angry guards, but they could hardly keep him locked up since he was innocent of any crime other than duplicity. It had been a brilliant plan; one that Hugo had much to learn from. Hugo said a brief prayer for the soul of the Earl of Argyll, who had been executed only a few months ago in Edinburgh for his role in the Monmouth Rebellion. Argyll had been a brave and cunning man, and loyal to the last.

Hugo turned on his heel and began to walk back to the inn, suddenly impatient. He needed to wake Archie and discuss the plan with him. It was a good idea, but there would be many details to work out since they could hardly just walk into Newgate and walk out with Neve. But it was a starting point, a pinprick of light, and a beacon of hope.

Hugo burst into the inn and ran up the stairs, searching for Archie. He'd refused a room of his own and was sharing a bed with several other travelers who were still in various stages of undress and packed into the bed like herrings into a barrel. Hugo shook Archie by the shoulder until the young man finally awoke. His face was a mask of annoyance at being disturbed, but he instantly climbed over several men and began to hastily pull on his breeches.

"Get dressed and come to my room," Hugo said, leaving

Archie to finish getting dressed. He had no wish to speak in front of others, even if they were asleep.

"Did something happen?" Archie asked as he entered the room a few minutes later. "Is it Mistress Ashley?"

"No, nothing has happened, but I've been thinking," Hugo began, outlining his idea for Archie.

Archie stared at Hugo in utter disbelief. He didn't want to criticize the plan, especially since it was practically his fault that the mistress was in prison, but Hugo was waiting for him to speak, and he had to be truthful. Archie took a deep breath and plunged in.

"Your Lordship, I know you're angry and grieving, but that sounds a trifle far-fetched if you ask me. The lady in question found some poor sod who was willing to trade places with the earl, not knowing if they might throw him in prison or execute him instead out of sheer spite. Who would be willing to trade places with a woman accused of witchcraft I ask you? And how do you propose to get her in and your lady out?" Archie reasoned. "It's madness, pure and simple. Begging your pardon, my lord," Archie added apologetically. He took a step back just in case Hugo might fly into a frustrated rage, but Hugo just nodded, taking Archie's points into consideration.

"You are absolutely correct, Archie. No one in their right mind would agree to such a scheme, and even if they did, there'd be no way to get them in and Neve out, which is precisely why I wasn't planning the exact same thing as the earl. It is, however, a good idea, one worth exploring, and I have something in mind, but first we must make some inquiries, and that's where you come in. Here's what I need you to find out."

Hugo filled Archie in, itemizing a few things he'd thought of only a few moments ago on his way back to the inn.

Archie snorted with disbelief, his eyes growing round in his face. "You are really serious, aren't you?"

"Deadly serious," Hugo replied evenly, suddenly afraid that Archie was right, and his plan was insane.

"Well, it's a mad scheme. I don't see how we can pull this off, but I will do anything that's required."

"I know, Archie, and I appreciate it. You have the right to refuse, of course, seeing as how this might end up with you being in Newgate instead."

"You can't do this on your own," Archie protested, noting the look of desperation in his master's eyes. "I will do whatever it takes."

With that, Archie donned his hat, pulled it low over his eyes and left the room to pursue the first item on the list.

Hugo breathed a sigh of relief. Archie was right; there was no way he could execute this wild idea by himself. He needed at least one more man, a man who was willing to risk arrest, injury, and possible death. Not to mention eternal condemnation of his soul and an eternity in Hell.

Hugo put on his own hat and moved toward the door. He'd given Archie only part of the list. The rest he had to do himself.

ELEVEN

I woke up with a terrible cramp in my leg, and it took me some time to get to my feet and walk it off. I had no idea exactly how long I'd been in prison, but it was starting to feel like weeks. No one had come to talk to me, and any attempt I made at communication with the guard who brought my food ended in silence. The guard wouldn't answer any of my questions or even acknowledge that I was speaking. I'd seen several gaolers pass my cell from time to time, but none of them even looked in my direction or answered when I tried to call out. I could see the glow of a torch from my cell and hear fragments of conversation, crying, and moans, but for the most part, I'd been left completely alone.

I felt dizzy as I tried to walk, holding on to the damp walls and trying not to step into the piles of excrement in the corner or a pool of urine that hadn't dried yet. My gown was filthy, and my hair matted from lack of washing and brushing. I twitched as I imagined that something crawled over my skin and scratched my head frantically, fearing that I was infested with lice, although I wasn't sure if you could get them without contact with other prisoners. I supposed some lived in the straw that I was forced to sleep on.

I hadn't eaten anything but gruel since I got here, and I was dehydrated and starved. My body needed food for my baby, but I hadn't so much as had a piece of bread or any kind of protein in days. I was lightheaded and nauseous, and my legs buckled under me after only a few steps. I was starting to feel lethargic; my mind refusing to recite any more poems or sing any more songs. All I could do was sit hunched against the wall, desperate to remain upright in case I fell over in my sleep and the rats gnawed on my face.

My tongue felt like flannel in my mouth, and I would have sold my soul for a glass of cold water and a hot shower. At first, I had been concerned with the lack of hygiene, but now my main worry was malnutrition. I kept talking to the baby, begging it to hold on until help arrived, but after days of being locked up in this hellhole, I was beginning to doubt that it ever would. I'd truly believed that Hugo would get to me somehow. He was the most resourceful man I'd ever met, and, despite the hopelessness of the situation, I'd thought he might find a way to get me out, or at least to get a message to me. The horrible realization that he might have been arrested as well had come sometime in the night, draining away the last vestiges of hope and plunging me into a renewed panic.

Hugo wasn't coming, nor was anyone else. I'd be left here until I died of starvation or disease. It wouldn't take long if the bites on my ankles became infected. With no medical attention, I'd be dead within days, my body tossed into some unmarked grave by the guards. I'd seen them pass by from time to time with what looked like a dead body. They might have been grunting with the effort of carrying dead weight, but the prisoners were so malnourished that they were more like bags of bones rather than human beings, their appearance no longer resembling anything more than a scarecrow.

Memories of my last miscarriage snuck up on me from time to time, making me shake with apprehension. What if I miscarried in here, or, worse yet, what if I went into labor and gave birth to a live child? What would I do? How would I feed it? How would I care for it when I didn't have the strength to care for myself? I hadn't even been given any water, much less decent food or an opportunity to wash. They could leave me this way indefinitely since no one seemed in any rush to put me on trial. Not that that would be such a blessing.

There was only one outcome to a witch trial, and I knew exactly what it was. Suddenly, the idea of drowning didn't seem so bad. Slipping below the surface of cool, clean water, all my sins washed away as my lungs filled and I peacefully drowned. Well, there was probably nothing peaceful about it, but compared to the alternative, it seemed like a peaceful release. The idea of being burned alive left me convulsing with terror; my mouth going even drier than it already was, and my teeth chattering in my head until I bit my tongue. I couldn't imagine anything more horrific than being slowly roasted while blood-thirsty spectators watched my unbearable agony.

Hanging might be better than burning, but the idea of a rope tightening around my neck until my eyes bulged with lack of oxygen and my lungs burned as I strained to breathe was nearly as terrifying. I knew enough about public hangings to know that if the neck wasn't instantly broken, the victim took a very long time to die, sometimes as long as an hour. Contrary to the way that type of execution was portrayed in films, where, after kicking their legs for a few minutes in the aptly named "hangman's jig," and clawing at the rope, the victim was usually good and dead.

I found that the only way to make it through the day was to allow myself to float. I'd sit against the wall with my skirt tied around my ankles, close my eyes and relive various memories. Sometimes my mind went forward to the twenty-first century, replaying happy memories of outings with friends, walks in the park in the spring, and drives in the country as the leaves began to change, painting the world in glorious shades of burnished orange, blazing crimson, and golden yellow. I'd salivate as I remembered good meals and wine-soaked dinners in charming restaurants, and the feeling of contentment that came from knowing that my life was happy and well-organized.

But most of all I thought of Hugo. My mind frequently drifted back to the day we'd met in the lane when his huge horse had nearly run me down and he'd picked me up and carried me to the house, his eyes shaded by the brim of his hat, and his mouth set in a grim line as he'd contemplated me sullenly. I remembered feeling intimidated by him, believing him to be a callous, prideful man. How wrong I had been.

My mind produced snapshot after snapshot of Hugo laughing at something Jem had said, or dicing with Archie, Arnold, and Peter, and allowing them to win. I saw him watching me as I sang, his eyes full of quiet longing, and the feel of his skin against mine as he touched me and loved me, his lips paying homage to my body as if I were a goddess and he my most humble servant.

I would give anything to feel Hugo's strong arms around me and hear the beating of his heart, to know that he was still alive and searching for me, and that my hope wasn't in vain. I needed to believe in something while I was in here, or there was no point for me to go on.

As I imagined spending months in this filthy cell, my will to live seemed to waver; a desire for a quick death springing unbidden in my fevered mind as memories of happy times were replaced by more macabre images, ones I couldn't bear to dwell on without thrashing and screaming; my heart racing and my body shaking uncontrollably with terror. Was this really how my life was going to end? Was this some twisted way in which History righted itself and punished me for interfering with the timeline? Was Hugo meant to die this year, and getting me out of the way was the only way to accomplish that?

I squeezed my eyes shut and forced myself to breathe to calm my thudding heart. I was being ridiculous. There was no such entity as History; not one that could pull our strings as if we were puppets to attain a particular goal. History was just a series of events which had already happened, not which were about to happen. It couldn't retaliate against me.

Or could it?

TWELVE

"You must eat," Archie said forcefully as he placed a bowl of stew and a chunk of bread in front of Hugo.

Hugo was so consumed with their plan that he'd barely eaten over the past few days; his already lean frame shrinking noticeably. His hair had grown out over recent weeks, a line of black now visible close to the scalp, and his eyes were red—partly from lack of sleep and partly from those shards of blue glass he had inserted in them. Archie hoped he wouldn't be blinded by the friction. Nothing would induce him to put something in his eyes, much less something as hard and sharp as glass. As it were, Hugo's eyes burned with an unholy light as he feverishly made plans for Neve's escape.

"Eat," Archie said again, more insistently this time.

"Thank you, Archie, but I just can't seem to hold anything down," Hugo replied, pushing the bowl away. "You have it."

Archie pushed the bowl back toward Hugo, cocking an eyebrow. "How do you expect to get Mistress Ashley out when you barely have the strength to hold a spoon? You need brute physical strength for what we are planning, or have you changed your mind?" Archie berated him. "You do it for her, and you hold it down no matter what it takes."

Hugo couldn't help smiling at the determined young man. "Ever consider a career in the army? You would have been very good at leading men into battle. All right, give it here."

Hugo took a spoonful of the aromatic stew and chewed with determination before swallowing. Archie saw the throat muscles working as Hugo took a deep breath and closed his eyes as he turned green around the gills. He was clearly unwell, but he had to eat, had to keep his strength up. They would have one chance, and one chance only, and Hugo had to be in fighting form in order to carry it off. Hugo took another spoonful and forced it down, not chewing as much this time. He continued to shovel in the food without tasting it or smelling it, just to get it inside him. Archie could see that Hugo was fighting waves of nausea, but he finished the food and pushed the bowl away with an air of satisfaction at having completed the task.

"Good, I'll bring you more food in a couple of hours. Now lie down and get some sleep. You look like death." Archie stood firm until Hugo pulled off his boots and sat on the bed.

"I can't stop thinking, Archie. Neve's been in there for over a week now. I can't begin to imagine what she must be feeling. I have no way of getting word to her, so she must think I've forsaken her, or perhaps she imagines that I've been arrested as well, which would kill her. I don't know if she is all right, or if she's getting enough food. She's eating for two, and she must be starving," Hugo said quietly. "She's always hungry. Every time I put something in my mouth, I feel such guilt, knowing that her belly is likely gnawing with hunger. I would gladly go hungry if it would help her in some way."

"You have been going hungry," Archie reminded him, "and it's not helping anyone. Now, feet up, head down, and eyes closed. I will check on you in a bit and you better be sleeping. I have a wagon to purchase."

Hugo gave Archie a sad smile as he complied, wishing only to be left in peace so he could think about Neve. He dreamed of her every time he closed his eyes, and woke up bathed in cold sweat, terrified that his plan wouldn't work. There was so much at stake, and so much could go wrong. He'd gone over everything a hundred times, but there were aspects of the plan which were outside his control.

Eventually, Hugo began to drift off to sleep. Archie was right; he needed his strength, and he had to get hold of himself and do everything in his power to make sure that he wasn't the weakest link of this chain. They were planning to carry out their mission in two days' time, and he had to shut off his emotions and concentrate only on the task at hand. He owed Neve that much, and he would not fail her.

THIRTEEN

Bradford Nash gaped at Gideon Warburton in a way that made the other man uncomfortable. He'd told him what he'd learned the day before, but Nash seemed incapable of accepting the situation. It'd taken Gideon days to finally find someone who could answer his inquiry, but what he'd learned was so baffling, that he'd been reluctant to bring the information to Bradford, hating to disappoint him.

"Gideon, are you telling me that Neve Ashley, the woman held in Newgate, has never been formally charged with anything? There is no record of her arrest?" Brad asked again.

"None. She was brought in by some men who paid to have her incarcerated. No guard at Newgate will turn down a sizable sum, especially when they don't need to do anything for it but feed her some mush twice a day," Gideon replied calmly.

"And who were these men?" Bradford asked, gaping at Gideon.

"I can only assume they are mercenaries who'll work for anyone who's willing to pay. Someone clearly wanted to have Mistress Ashley out of the way," Gideon explained patiently.

"So, does that mean that she can be released?" Brad asked

with mounting excitement. "If there's no formal arrest, then there's no reason to keep her incarcerated. All we have to do is go see whoever is in charge of running the prison."

"No, my friend, it doesn't mean she can be released. Once someone is brought to Newgate, they leave either to be tried, executed, or buried. No one just leaves. They might not have needed paperwork to admit her, but they will need paperwork to release her. No one will take it upon themselves to just let a prisoner go for fear of being duped. With Mistress Ashley being there unofficially, it's even more difficult to get her released since she doesn't exist on any magistrate's docket."

"Oh, dear God," Bradford moaned, slumping into a chair. "So, what's to be done?"

Mr. Warburton shrugged. "Nothing. I'm afraid we have no legal options in this case."

"Are you suggesting that we simply leave her there to die?" Bradford asked, horrified. "That's unacceptable."

"There's nothing to be done. The only way for the lady to survive is to escape from the prison. It's difficult, but it can be done. Several prisoners have escaped over time."

"Gideon, how can she escape on her own? She is alone, pregnant, and without funds. She can't pay anyone off, nor does she have any knowledge of the prison or anyone on the inside who can help her," Bradford fumed, gazing at Gideon as if it were all his fault. Bradford was pacing the parlor like a caged animal; his hair standing up on end as he ran his hand through it repeatedly in his agitation. His eyes were blazing with anger, which wasn't really directed at Gideon, but still made him uneasy.

Gideon hated bringing the news to Bradford Nash, but he was a man of law, and it wasn't in him to repress information. He knew Brad would be very upset. This woman seemed to mean a lot to him, and it suddenly dawned on Gideon why. She was Bradford's mistress, pregnant with his child. Oh God, why hadn't he seen it before? Of course, Bradford would never admit to it, his wife being Gideon's cousin, but it was clear as day. Gideon didn't really disapprove of Bradford having a mistress; he simply hoped that Beth would never find out. It was better for everyone involved.

Bradford wouldn't be the first or the last man to keep a mistress and get her with child, but it wasn't often that a prominent man's mistress was accused of witchcraft, particularly in such an underhanded and malicious manner. She must have really crossed someone, or perhaps there'd been another lover before Brad, whom she'd thrown over without realizing the extent of his ire.

In either case, there was nothing to be done. Gideon didn't want to say out it loud, but the woman was as good as dead, as was her child. If it were born in Newgate, it would never survive, and given the fact that she wasn't due until next year, neither would she. There were some who received better treatment than others when money changed hands, but the people who couldn't pay for food were given just enough to be kept alive in order to face trial and execution. Few people were released.

Gideon supposed that someone could be bribed to look after the lady, but keeping her alive longer was not necessarily a good idea. With no chance of release, her suffering would only be prolonged, especially if she delivered her child while in prison. A quick death would be best for everyone involved, especially Bradford since it would spare him further suffering. If he wanted a mistress, there were plenty of women to be had by a man who was young, handsome, and generous. Mistress Ashley was lost to him now, and that was the end of that.

"Now, your other client seems to be doing better," Gideon said, hoping to steer Bradford's mind away from the problem with the woman. "Since I've taken on his case, he hasn't been beaten or tortured, has been receiving decent meals and candles, and is in somewhat better spirits. I believe a trial will be scheduled imminently. It will be presided over by a special committee since this is not only a matter of attempted murder and abduction, but of high treason."

"And do you know who the presiding members will be?" Brad asked. "Will it be the same as last time?"

"Not as of yet, but I have reason to believe they will be men who are difficult to sway and even more difficult to convince. However, I don't think George Jeffreys will be among them, which is excellent news."

Gideon rose to leave, having delivered his message. He was a man of few words, given to bouts of isolation from society. Unlike most men of his age, he didn't enjoy romps with whores, visits to Court, or outings to the theater or bear-baiting pits. He liked to be alone with his books, reading into the early hours until his eyes burned, but his mind felt sufficiently nourished. Gideon didn't have any friends, nor had he ever needed any. He was a solitary man, content to be in his own company.

The only person he'd ever enjoyed being with was Beth. She was a bright light among the darkness, a kind-hearted, sensitive soul who understood Gideon's taciturn nature. He'd thought he'd lose her when she married, but he had to admit that he genuinely liked Bradford Nash. He found him to be a man of great intellect, honor, and integrity, although this affair did tarnish his reputation in Gideon's eyes. Was this his first mistress or had he kept mistresses throughout his marriage to Beth?

Gideon himself had never had a mistress. He'd never been with a woman and felt no desire to alter his virginal state. What went on between men and women seemed obscene and disgusting. His father had taken him to a brothel when he was eighteen, and when Gideon had refused to go upstairs with a whore, had forced him to watch as he took his pleasure with a girl who was no older than Gideon. Gideon had been appalled, but fascinated at the same time, watching his normally reticent and stern father grunting and panting as he swived the girl, who had seemed to be enjoying the act. Perhaps she was paid to pretend, but the whole thing left Gideon with no desire to ever do anything like that himself. Women held no interest for him.

It wasn't until he'd met Bradford Nash that he began to experience the first pangs of sexual desire. He'd hated himself for what he felt, prayed for forgiveness, and mentally self-flagellated until his head hurt, but every time he saw Bradford, he felt like a moth flying too close to the flame. Bradford was so handsome, so polite, and so at ease in his own skin. He smiled easily, laughed without holding back, and appeared to Gideon to be like a gilded demi-god who'd come down to earth just to torment him. He'd had several sexual dreams about Bradford, waking with a wet stain on his nightshirt and a smile on his face, but that would never be, and his love had to be from afar.

When Bradford had asked Gideon for his help, he was overjoyed. Here was a service he could perform for the man he loved, and he would be happy to do it. Of course, bringing bad news and seeing Bradford so upset had not been part of the plan, but all Gideon wanted was for Brad to appreciate him and give him a smile of thanks. That was enough.

The two dilemmas that Bradford Nash had presented him with were interesting puzzles. Gideon Warburton felt absolutely nothing for either prisoner. They were just problems to be solved, riddles to be deciphered. What happened to the actual human beings was of no interest to him, but he would do anything he could to help Bradford, for to bask in the glory of his approval was more than Gideon could have hoped for.

"I will do my very best, Bradford. You have my word."

Bradford nodded his thanks and shook Gideon's hand before seeing him out. He returned to the parlor, poured himself a large drink and sat down in his favorite chair by the hearth. The fire was blazing merrily in the grate and the flames had a calming effect, as did the brandy.

Brad was drained by the events of the past few days and more than a little confused. Nothing made sense. This latest information from Gideon made things even more complicated, indicating that someone had wanted to intentionally hurt Neve and get her out of the way, but why? Someone, presumably Jane, had paid the men to abduct her and put her into prison on a trumped-up charge. The thought of imparting this bit of news to Hugo made him even more agitated, but it had to be done. Hugo needed to know, since it might have some bearing on his scheme. Brad had known Hugo since they were children and never had he felt as strong a kinship to him as he did now. The poor man was in Hell.

Brad walked out into the hall and called Billingsley. The older man shuffled into the foyer, having clearly been in the middle of his dinner. "I'm sorry, Billingsley. I didn't mean to interrupt your meal," Brad said apologetically. "I wanted to ask you to pack a small bag and travel to Surrey tomorrow morning. Take Matty with you."

"But who will see to you, Mr. Nash?" the old man asked, scandalized. He'd long suspected that the master was looking to put him out to pasture, so perhaps he was bringing in new servants. Matty was almost as old as Billingsley, having been cook and housekeeper to Master Nash's father. They'd been married for nearly thirty years and hoped to spend their twilight years in the Nash employ.

"Not to worry, my man, not to worry. I can see to myself for a few days," Bradford replied with what he hoped was a reassuring smile.

"As you wish, Master Bradford," Billingsley conceded, "as you wish. You do want us back, don't you?"

"Yes, of course. In a week or so, I should say. My wife will be most pleased to see you both. A spot of fresh air and rest might do you good," Bradford suggested, only aggravating his servant's fears.

Bradford fully realized what the old man was thinking, but there was no help for it. He needed the house to be empty, and there was nowhere else to send the elderly pair, save Surrey. They might be suspicious of the forced holiday, but he had to get them out of the house and then make sure that all the things Hugo asked for were on hand.

The clock struck 3 p.m. at a nearby church tower, and Brad hurried from the house. He had to meet Hugo to confer one last time before Hugo and Archie put their plan into action.

FOURTEEN

Max Everly wrapped himself in the thin blanket and huddled on his cot in the darkness of the cell. He'd run out of candles and would ask for some more when the guard came to bring him breakfast. He didn't really need the light anyway. He'd read the one book he had backwards and forwards and even memorized some of the passages, finding them to be a comfort. Gideon Warburton had chosen well when he'd brought the sonnets of John Dunne.

The days dragged on with a painful slowness, making Max wish for a speedy resolution, whatever it was going to be. He couldn't stand being cooped up this way any longer. His nerves were stretched to breaking point, and every time he heard a jangle of keys or a heavy footstep in the corridor, he wondered if someone was coming for him. Could they execute him without a trial? Was that legal in this time? He supposed they could do anything they wanted. It was not as if anyone would protest very loudly, especially when he was believed to be a traitor to king and country.

Damn Hugo Everly, Max thought for the thousandth time.

He realized that he had no real reason to be angry with

Hugo, but he needed someone to blame and Hugo was a ready target. Max couldn't help imagining Hugo, sitting at some local London pub with Neve, a frothy pint of beer in front of him as he watched football and cheered with the rest of the patrons. Hugo would have been in the future for four months now, so he'd have had time to acclimate and get his bearings. How convenient that he was living the high life while Max was under lock and key, awaiting a trial for Hugo's crimes.

Max shifted on the cot to get more comfortable and stared up at the dark ceiling. He had to admit—although he'd never say it out loud—that Hugo was a brave man. Seeing what Max had seen down on the green over the past few weeks would discourage anyone from plotting against the Crown, much less as openly as Hugo had been doing. This wasn't the twenty-first century where he'd get a jail sentence and then get out early for good behavior with a slap on the wrist; this was serious business. Max had seen several men executed since the young man, and he'd watched with admiration as they walked up to the scaffold, heads held high, shoulders back, and fully in control despite the gut-wrenching fear they must have been feeling. Some had even joked with the executioner before they laid their head on the block, knowing full well that in a few minutes it would be severed from their body in a barbaric and brutal way.

Had Hugo been prepared to die like these men? He was. Max knew that, just as he knew that Hugo wouldn't be afraid, wouldn't cower, or piss his trousers. Hugo would have been in control until the very last, not a trace of fear showing through the cracks. No wonder Neve had chosen Hugo over him. Hugo wasn't the class clown or the sugar daddy who could dazzle women with his wealth and power. Hugo was a man of conviction, a man of courage, a man whose cock was probably a foot long, Max mused bitterly. Damn, he hated the man!

FIFTEEN

I forced myself to sit up despite the dizziness that swept me along. A bite on my cheek was bleeding, and I wiped it with my hand, smearing blood and snot, no longer caring if it got infected. I wasn't hungry either. The hunger pains had disappeared days ago, leaving me lethargic and weak. I still forced myself to eat but couldn't get even half the gruel down my throat. I hadn't peed since yesterday; I was severely dehydrated. My lips were dry and flaky, and all my nails had broken off. My tattered dress hung off my frame; the fabric crusted with dirt, sweat and waste. There were bloodstains at the hem where the rats had bitten my ankles, and I felt as if I were constantly in some alternate state of being.

I had begun to hallucinate a few days ago and the hallucinations had grown worse, but I didn't mind. In them, I was always happy and healthy, laughing with Hugo and playing with the child who would never be born. I'd felt a flutter of movement in my belly. At first, I thought it was just hunger, but then realized it was the first time I'd felt my baby move. It would have been a joyous occasion had I been free. I'd closed my eyes and imagined Hugo's hand on my belly, smiling as he felt the butterfly wings brush against his palm as he made contact with his child for the very first time.

I might have cried, but I had no tears left, and no water left to spare in my withering body. I had no idea how long I'd been here, but my time was running out. I no longer knew if it was day or night, nor did I care. There was nothing to wait for, nothing to hope for except a quiet, peaceful death. Perhaps I would just float away, leave my body behind and simply disappear as if I had never been. At one time, that thought would have devastated me, but now it didn't seem like such a bad way to go, certainly a better alternative to being drowned or burned.

I leaned against the wall and closed my eyes as another wave of dizziness swept over me, making me nauseous. I barely registered the guard who stepped up to the door. He wasn't the usual thug who brought my gruel, but a younger man, possibly still in his twenties, with a thatch of dark hair and a broken tooth. His skin was severely pockmarked, and it reminded me of the craters of the moon as I crawled toward the door, hoping against hope that he might have some news for me.

"Come here, you," he hissed. "I brought you something to drink. You look thirsty," he said guiltily.

I took the cup with shaking hands, afraid to spill even a drop of liquid, and drank it all in one go. The ale tasted strange, a cross between bitter and sickly sweet, but I didn't care. It was hydration that I so desperately needed.

"Can I have some more?" I begged, but he just shook his head.

"Give the cup here," he hissed again, and I reached out and gave it to him as my knees gave way.

I had no energy to stand or to even sit. I lay down on the filthy floor and wrapped my arms around my belly, giving my baby one last ounce of maternal protection. My head felt like lead, and I was very cold as I began to drift. I tried to conjure up Hugo's face and focus on it, but I couldn't. It seemed to be swimming in front of my closed lids, the color of his eyes changing from black to blue and back again, his hair suddenly going platinum.

But it wasn't Hugo's hair; it was a warm, white light that beckoned me forward, and I longed for its embrace. I hadn't seen daylight since I'd been here, and it looked heavenly. The light seemed to grow brighter as I gravitated toward its warmth, eager to feel it on my face. My last conscious thought was of the baby as I finally succumbed and walked toward the light, feeling wonderfully at peace.

SIXTEEN

Hugo looked around the room one last time to make sure that nothing had been left behind, then closed the door and went to join Archie. Archie had taken all their possessions to Brad's house that morning, leaving only what they would need to facilitate Neve's escape. He'd purchased some secondhand clothes from the rag man, the only criteria being that they should be as plain as possible and dark-colored. Hugo and Archie needed to melt into the night and become one with the darkness, their grubby clothes marking them as men of poverty and low class.

The church clock had just struck 10 p.m. as they slipped out of the inn and made their way down the empty street. The evening was cool, but dry, a stiff breeze blowing off the Thames and carrying the smell of wet mud and a tang of fish. A distant splash of oars could be heard as someone made a late-night crossing to Southwark; the cheerful greeting of the ferryman clearly audible in the silence as he called out to an oncoming boat. Every sound carried on the wind, the night alive around the two men as they hurried along, their heads bowed, hands in their pockets. Hugo squeezed a leather pouch full of coin to keep it from jangling as he walked, moving stealthily behind Archie, close enough to the walls to become virtually invisible.

It took them nearly half an hour to reach their destination. Archie looked around, then fished a large iron key out of his pocket and unlocked the shed, speaking softly to the old mare that was munching on hay and gazing about without any interest. Archie took out an apple and fed it to the horse while Hugo checked the bed of the wagon to make sure they had everything they needed. Two shovels, a wooden ladder, and a length of rope were there, as was a lantern and an old blanket. A blunderbuss carefully wrapped in some old rags was hidden under the bench of the wagon in case of emergency.

Archie hitched the horse to the wagon and led it quietly out of the shed, locking it behind him. The two men climbed onto the bench and drove in silence down the empty streets. Most Londoners were already abed, so there was no light spilling from windows; the streets shrouded in nearly impenetrable darkness, making their progress slower than Hugo would have liked. A few taverns were still open, and there was an occasional burst of light and sound as a door opened and disgorged a few patrons, mostly drunk and ready for their beds, but otherwise all was quiet.

Archie held the reins, leaving Hugo to his own thoughts. Hugo muttered a heartfelt prayer. He'd lost count of how many prayers he'd sent up to the Lord, begging for Neve to be all right and for their plan to work, but the Lord was quiet, indifferent as usual.

They finally reached the church, and Archie hobbled the horse just around the corner, hoping it was sufficiently out of sight so as not to arouse anyone's suspicions. Hugo wasn't even sure which church this was, but it didn't matter. Archie had spent the last few days searching for what they needed and had found it here. Hugo didn't bother to ask, just jumped off the bench, reached into the back for the equipment and followed

Archie through the gate, casting one last look at the horse, who'd found some clumps of grass to chew on and seemed happy enough.

Thankfully, there was a full moon, but thick clouds floated lazily by, obscuring the shining orb for several minutes at a time and throwing the graveyard into almost complete darkness. Wind moved through the ancient trees, the leaves rustling ominously and blocking out the moonlight beneath them. Lighting a lantern was too dangerous, so they moved slowly, tripping over headstones which had nearly sunk into the ground, and cursing quietly as they made their way toward the southern wall where the grave was. It had no gravestone, having been dug only a week ago, but the mound of earth was fresh and still wet from last night's rain.

Archie squinted at the wooden cross driven into the ground at the head of the grave but couldn't make out the name until the clouds parted and the moon cast a beam of light onto the scene. "Mary Baxter," Archie read and nodded. "That's the one."

Hugo set the unlit lantern on the neighboring grave, threw down the rope and the ladder and drove his shovel into the earth. The ground had been soaked the night before, making the damp earth heavy and slippery. It would have been much easier to dig had it been dry, but they had no choice.

Archie removed his hat and hung it on the cross, then rolled up his sleeves. He'd tied a dark kerchief around his head, partly to cover up his bright hair, and partly to absorb the sweat that was freely running down his face after only a few minutes of digging.

Hugo took off his coat but kept the hat on to hide his blond hair. He should have gotten a kerchief too, but he hadn't thought of it. Sweat coursed down his face as he threw shovelful after shovelful of dirt on the mound growing by the side of the grave. His shirt was soaked with sweat, his arms burning with the effort, but they weren't even a foot in. Five more feet of earth to dig. Hugo had often helped out during the harvest and with the haymaking, but he wasn't used to this type of work. His arms were shaking with the effort; the muscles crying out in protest at the forced exercise. Hugo ignored the discomfort and continued to dig; his face set in grim lines as he tried to go faster.

Archie wiped his face with his sleeve, grunting with effort as he raised the shovel higher and higher to toss the earth out of the deepening grave. They were both filthy, sweaty, and covered with wet mud.

The handle of the shovel slid in Hugo's hands, so he put on a pair of coarse gloves and continued to dig. He tried not to think about what they were doing. Under normal circumstances, he'd never desecrate a grave. Someone's final resting place was sacred, and this was consecrated ground—a holy place. Hugo mentally asked the young woman for forgiveness, hoping that she would understand his need had she been able to hear him. This was an act of desperation, one he couldn't afford to get too philosophical about. It was the only way, so he forced thoughts of Mary Baxter from his exhausted brain and continued to dig mindlessly, intentionally clearing his brain.

Archie began to hum a song and Hugo joined in, finding that the rhythm helped with the digging. They were now about halfway down, so Archie jumped out and brought down the ladder to make getting in and out easier. The ladder sank right into the earth, but after they were finished, they could set it on the lid of the coffin to keep it from sinking further when they climbed out. It was also safe to light the lantern, since no one would see the feeble light coming from beneath the earth even if they passed by the cemetery at this late hour. The moon had disappeared behind the clouds about a half-hour since and failed to reappear, making the lantern necessary.

They continued to dig, painfully conscious of how much longer this was taking than originally anticipated. Hugo had allotted two hours, but they still had a way to go, not counting filling the grave back in once they were done.

Hugo breathed a sigh of relief as his shovel finally hit the wooden lid of the coffin. He was trembling with fatigue, his arms on fire from digging through six feet of packed earth.

Archie pried open the black-painted lid of the oak coffin with a crowbar and stood back. They stared in silence at the corpse wrapped in a linen shroud. Hugo crossed himself as Archie unwrapped the fabric around the face and held up the lantern to look at the girl. She was no older than twenty, her face pale and round, her lashes dark against her cheeks. Mary's hair had been carefully brushed and plaited, the end of the braid tied with a blue ribbon. She was wearing what must have been her best dress, but it was obvious that this girl had come from a poor family, the dress a prickly brown homespun.

Hugo briefly wondered what Mary had died of since her face showed no signs of illness, but Archie poked him in the ribs, and he set to work. Archie tested the ladder to make sure it was set securely in the ground and went up a few rungs before reaching for the girl. Hugo carefully lifted her out of the coffin and passed her to Archie, who climbed out and set her on top of the stone slab of the nearest grave. Hugo replaced the lid of the coffin, climbed out of the grave, and went to work hastily refilling the yawning hole. They had to hurry. The church clock showed 2:20 a.m., so they didn't have much time.

Filling in the grave was much easier than emptying it, so by 3 a.m. the site looked much as it had before it'd been desecrated. Hugo and Archie grabbed their tools and lifted the corpse. The clouds had dissipated somewhat, making it easier to see as they carried the girl through the graveyard toward the gate. Hugo hoped the horse and wagon were still there, and thankfully they were. The horse shied away as it smelled the corpse, which mercifully was in the very early stages of decomposition. The animal neighed in protest, but Archie gave it another apple and it quietened down and stood still, allowing them to lay Mary on the bed of the wagon.

Archie grabbed the reins, and Hugo jumped up onto the bench next to him. His hands were calloused and bleeding in some spots; the skin caked with dirt, as was pretty much the rest of him. His clothes were filthy, his hair damp with perspiration, and his face streaked with dirt. Archie looked no cleaner and smiled at Hugo as he noticed his gaze.

"We really look the part of grave-robbers, don't we?" he said as he maneuvered the horse around the corner. "I do feel sorry for what we've done. Feels wrong, but not much choice in the matter. I'm sure she would understand."

"I don't know about that," Hugo replied warily. "We disturbed her resting place and took her out of hallowed ground. Whoever loved her would not understand if they knew. I wish there had been another way."

"So do I. I'd seen her funeral. There were just her parents and brothers, but they were broken up with grief. I'd say Mary was much loved in life, and she will be missed in death." Both Hugo and Archie grew quiet, contemplating the young woman who bounced along in the bed of the wagon, going on a journey she'd never expected.

Grave robbing would not go unnoticed, and Hugo prayed they wouldn't have to do it again. It had taken Archie several days to find a grave of a young woman who'd been very recently buried. He'd been lucky to stumble onto the funeral of Mary and note the location of the grave. A lot of graves had no age marked on them, nor the date of death, so it was risky to just dig one up and find a woman who'd been seventy or been buried long enough to decompose. They'd needed a woman under thirty; one who was still fresh enough to pass for someone who'd just died.

The dark bulk of Newgate Prison finally came into view, making Hugo's heart beat faster. There were no lights in the few windows, only a torch burning at every exit. The building was low and squat, the walls made of solid stone, reminiscent of a tomb. For some, it was. Most people who entered the prison left either to be buried or to be executed. Few were pardoned or exonerated. It was a place of fear and death, a place of the worst kind of human misery, and Neve was inside. Hugo had never been inside Newgate, but he could imagine what it was like.

Archie counted the doors until he found the one he was looking for and walked the horse over with his hand on the bridle. He knocked softly.

A fat, youthful gaoler with very bad skin unlocked the door, his eyes round with apprehension.

"I thought ye wasn't comin'," he whispered urgently. "I'd been waitin' for hours; me shift's nearly over," he hissed. "Where's me money?"

Archie held the fat leather purse in his hand and let it dangle in front of the guard for a few moments as if he were trying to hypnotize him. The guard smiled, revealing a mouth that had only five teeth. He reached for the purse, but Archie snatched it away, giving the man a look of reproach. "Not till the deed is done," he said.

"Fine, but be quick about it. I don't want no trouble. 'Tis the last cell on yer left. The door's unlocked."

"Watch the horse and wagon," Archie ordered the guard, beckoning to Hugo, who'd remained silent. His educated accent would have given him away, so he had to remain mute. Archie took one look at Hugo and whispered urgently, "Stay here; I'll do the rest. You look done in. Believe me when I tell you that you don't need to see how things are on the inside. You have enough fodder for your nightmares."

"I'm coming with you," Hugo said quietly.

Archie didn't argue. "Help me get her off the wagon then."

They grabbed Mary under the arms and by the ankles.

Rigor mortis had set in, making her heavy, stiff, and difficult to maneuver through the narrow corridors.

Hugo gasped at the horrible stench inside the walls but didn't say a word. His boots stuck to the stone floor, making weird sucking and squelching noises as he moved his feet. The walls were weeping damp; the smell of mildew mixing with all the other odors swirling in the cavernous space.

The prison had absolutely no sanitation of any kind. The prisoners pissed, shat, ejaculated, and menstruated right where they sat, ate, and slept. No one ever cleaned the cells or allowed the prisoners to wash. The place was infested with fleas, lice, and rats, and was a cesspool of waste and infection. Most of the prisoners they passed seemed to be asleep, but a few just sat there, staring at nothing, mumbling to themselves, or moaning in their sleep.

Hugo could feel the desperation of the prison envelop him and wondered how God could permit such horrors to be inflicted on human beings, even if they were guilty of a crime. Not for the first time, he compared his own time to the future he'd visited and wished that there could have been a way for him and Neve to remain in the twenty-first century. She'd made a tremendous sacrifice by coming back with him, and this was her reward.

"That's the cell," Archie whispered as he pulled open the door and maneuvered the corpse inside.

Hugo lowered Mary's ankles and sank down next to the immobile woman on the floor. He pushed aside the filthy hair and stared at the face. His hands shook, and his vision blurred as he looked at Neve. She was barely recognizable, her cheeks sunken and her flesh so gray as to appear almost dead. Hugo lowered his head and listened to her chest. The heartbeat was faint and the breathing shallow, but thankfully she was still alive.

"The corpse is too clean," Archie whispered as he looked at

Neve. "Look at the state of her. They'll know right away something is amiss."

"What do you propose?" Hugo asked. He hated the idea of desecrating Mary's corpse, but they had no choice. She had to appear like someone who'd been in prison for some time: filthy, smelly, and barely human.

Archie unrolled the shroud and passed it to Hugo, who wrapped it carefully around Neve.

Hugo turned away as Archie unplaited the girl's hair and rubbed some excrement into it as well as onto her face. He unlaced his breeches and urinated onto the girl, soaking her clean homespun in a stream of urine. Hugo felt the bile rise in his throat but knew this was absolutely necessary. Archie rolled the corpse around the cell, getting her as filthy and ragged as possible before propping her up in the corner.

"I'm sorry, Mary," he said. Hugo could hear a hint of tears in Archie's voice, but this was no time for remorse; that would come later.

"Let's go."

Hugo lifted Neve into his arms as Archie held open the door for him to pass. She was so much lighter than before, her body weight depleted by the starvation rations of the prison. Compared to Mary's corpse, Neve was feather-light and terribly fragile.

The two men hurried through the dim corridors and out of the prison before someone noticed what they were about and tried to stop them. Hugo brought some extra coin in case they needed to bribe another guard to let them leave, but, thankfully, there was no one awake or sober enough to care.

Hugo and Archie gulped fresh air as they exited the prison. The autumn night had never smelled so good.

Hugo gently laid Neve on the bed of the wagon as Archie paid off the impatient guard.

"Did ye leave everything as ye found it?" he asked, already

closing the door.

"Aye, we did," Archie replied as he jumped up on the bench and took up the reins.

Hugo opened the shroud around Neve's face to give her some fresh air. Her lashes were stuck together as if from crying, and he could see tear tracks on her dirty face as the moon illuminated her sallow skin. Neve's lips were bloodless and cracked, her hair so dark with grime that it was a completely different color. Hugo wanted to howl with despair as he looked at her, but he couldn't afford to give vent to his emotions. They'd gotten her out, and just in time by the looks of it, and now it was imperative to get her back to Brad's house unnoticed, to be nursed back to health.

They drove away from Newgate at a stately pace so as not to draw attention to themselves. The clip-clop of the horse's hooves seemed unbearably loud to Hugo, the rattle of wheels deafening in the impenetrable silence of the night. In about an hour, the streets would start to fill up with produce and dairy wagons, farmers bringing goods to market and to the kitchens of the wealthy, but, for now, the streets were eerily empty.

Once they were sufficiently far away from the prison, Archie accelerated to a trot, taking them directly to Brad's house, which looked uninhabited from the outside. All the windows were shuttered, with not a chink of light showing through the cracks, and only a thin spiral of smoke curling from one of the chimneys into the inky sky.

Hugo lifted Neve out of the wagon and entered by the back way, leaving Archie to see to the horse and wagon. There could be no evidence of tonight's activities, so the wagon would have to be disposed of immediately. The horse would be sold off tomorrow, but, for tonight, it would stay in Brad's stable after pulling the wagon to some remote spot where it would be left for someone to find.

"Oh, thank God, Hugo," Brad breathed as he met Hugo

with a single candle. "Is she all right?"

"Far from it," Hugo replied, carrying Neve carefully up the stairs to a room at the back of the house, where a merry fire crackled, and buckets of water stood at the ready near a copper tub.

"The water has cooled. I was expecting you over an hour ago. Was it difficult?" he asked as he took a cauldron of boiling water off the flames and poured some into the tub to warm up the lukewarm water.

"It was," Hugo replied, not wishing to dwell on the details, particularly the disrespect they had showed to Mary's body. He felt terrible about that, but it couldn't be helped. The needs of the living came before those of the dead. "Did you bring what I asked for?" Hugo asked, looking around.

"There's a cake of soap, a jug of vinegar, honey, whiskey, towels, and a clean shift. Do you want my help?" Brad asked, but Hugo just shook his head and cut his eyes at the door.

Brad closed the door softly behind him just as Hugo pulled out his dagger and sliced off every stitch of Neve's clothing, throwing everything on the fire. His insides quivered as he took in her emaciated form. How was it possible for a person to change this much in ten days? Neve's face was gray, her mouth slack, and deep purple shadows formed half-moons beneath her eyes, but it was her body Hugo needed to examine. He forced himself to look down for signs of abuse. There were bites on her arms and ankles, but no other bruising. Hugo took a deep breath as he carefully pushed her legs apart, and nearly cried with relief when he saw no blood. She hadn't been raped or suffered a miscarriage, which was a blessing. Hugo's stomach unclenched a fraction as he went to work.

He placed Neve into the tub and scrubbed her until her skin glowed pink and her hair was clean. He had to do it with one hand since Neve would have just slipped under the water if he let go of her; she was as limp as a rag doll. The water in the tub was now murky, with bits of dirt floating on the surface, but he wasn't finished. Hugo soaked Neve's hair with vinegar and rubbed it in thoroughly, letting it do its work on the lice and fleas that took up residence in her thick tresses.

The smell made his eyes water, but he left the vinegar in for a few minutes, long enough for it to suffocate the vermin. Hugo rinsed off the vinegar and lifted Neve out of the tub, laying her on the towels spread on the floor. He dried her off, pulled on a clean shift, then used the whiskey to disinfect the bites, and treated them with honey, which would aid the healing. Hugo bandaged Neve's ankles and lifted her onto the bed. Her breathing was still shallow, but at least she was clean, which would make her happy when she finally awoke from the laudanum-induced sleep.

Hugo tucked the thick blanket around her, but not before he checked her pulse again. The apothecary had been very specific about the dosage of the laudanum, and Hugo nearly went mad imagining that the idiotic guard would give her too much. But they had no choice but to trust him. Money was a great motivator, and the man made enough money today to buy a farm somewhere and live comfortably for the rest of his life, if that's what he wished.

Hugo threw the dirty towels into the tub and moved a chair close to the bed so that he could watch over Neve. He was exhausted and crusted with dirt, but he couldn't even think of having a bath or going to sleep. He needed a little time to absorb the fact that Neve was there—with him. She looked worse than he expected, but she was free, safe, and alive. The rest would follow.

The fire burned down to embers by the time Hugo finally succumbed and allowed himself a brief rest. Archie tiptoed into the room and covered him with a blanket, then turned to leave, but not before he kissed the top of Hugo's head.

"Sleep well, Hugo," he whispered. "You've earned it."

SEVENTEEN

I pried open my eyes to find feeble light streaming through the opening in the bed hangings. It was no more than the pearlescent light of dawn, but it hurt my eyes after being in the darkness for so long, so I turned away from it, hiding my face in the bedding. It smelled of clean linen and a tang of vinegar, but I didn't mind. Where there was vinegar, there was usually fish and chips, and beer. I was so thirsty. I licked my lips to moisten them, but they felt dry and cracked and my teeth seemed to be made of flannel. On the bright side, the mattress was soft, and nothing was crawling, either in the bedding or in my hair. I could breathe freely, the air in the room a bit stale, but still amazingly fresh compared to what I'd been breathing in since my arrest.

Of course, I had to be dreaming—either that or I was already dead. I tried to remember where I was, but the last thing that came to mind was the fetid cell and the wonderful white light that had beckoned to me and made me feel safe and warm. If this was what death was like, then it wasn't bad at all. I supposed I might have expected more fanfare had I made it to heaven, but this wasn't half bad. Now, if someone would just bring the food and drink.

Were people still hungry after they died? I mused languidly. Did I still have a body? I tried to move my hands to check, but my arms felt awfully heavy, although I was fairly sure they were still there.

My mind seemed to be floating, disjointed thoughts tumbling over themselves as I tried to get my bearings but failed. My eyes kept closing of their own accord as if I were being pulled back into unconsciousness, but before I allowed my heavy eyelids to shut, I noticed a hulking shape sitting by the bed and forced myself to take a closer look, despite the dizziness that accosted me the moment I turned my head. The man looked like Hugo but wasn't quite him. He was dressed in filthy clothes, caked with mud and... honey?

No, that couldn't be right. His face, gray in the dim light, looked haggard and drawn, thick black stubble coating his lean cheeks and chin and a thin line of black visible just at the roots of his hair.

The man was asleep with his head hanging down and his arms crossed in front of his chest. His hands were cleaner than the rest of him, but I could see some calluses where the palms were visible, and there was dirt under his fingernails. He might have looked menacing, if he didn't appear to be so worn out.

So, definitely not heaven then, I concluded as I tumbled into darkness once more. My dreams were very vivid, and not altogether unpleasant. They were filled with color and light, things I thought I'd never see again. Fish and chips figured prominently. And bread. Fresh bread spread with butter and jam. I was still hungry. A part of my brain wanted to wake up, but I just couldn't. I felt as if I were under anesthesia, longing to wake but unable to until some of the drug had worn off.

I tossed and turned, thrashing as the dreams became more sinister and dark. I was running for my life; my hand pressed to my stomach as I darted barefoot from one dark alley to another, looking for a way out. Someone was chasing me, but I didn't know who; all I knew was that if they caught me, I was as good as dead. I was panting and stumbling, my legs turning to lead as I tried to move toward the ray of light I could see at the end of the twisty alley. I tripped over something, lost my balance and came crashing hard onto the ground. It woke me up.

I looked around again. The shutters had been thrown open, and golden light streamed through the bed hangings, illuminating the bed and the rest of the room. It didn't look familiar, and I was certain I'd never seen it before, but it was pretty and clean, a feminine room judging by the butter yellow and cream tones it was decorated in. Was I really in bed, or was this all part of the dream?

I took an experimental sniff. It still smelled of vinegar, but there was no foul smell of waste or sweat. I was gloriously clean and lying on a feather mattress beneath a canopy of embroidered flowers and vines on a background of sunny yellow. I was still hungry and thirsty, though.

Then my sluggish brain remembered the man from before, and I turned my head cautiously. I was still slightly dizzy, but less so, my vision clearer since my eyelids didn't insist on closing. He was still sitting there; only now he was Hugo. He was wearing clean clothes and must have recently shaved. His hair, which had been streaked with dirt before, appeared to be clean, and the dirt beneath his fingernails was gone, although his hands still looked raw and calloused.

Hugo seemed utterly exhausted, with the thin skin beneath his eyes smudged with purple shadows, and the hollows of his cheeks sunken deeper than I'd even seen before. He'd lost a considerable amount of weight, and a slight tremor went through his left hand now and again, something that always happened when he was overly tired or anxious. He appeared to be sleeping, but he sat up with a start, looking at me as if he'd seen a ghost. Was I really there, or was I still dreaming? If I were, I didn't want to wake up. Any dream where I was clean, safe, and with Hugo was my idea of heaven.

My head felt heavy, and my thoughts were still muddled, but I was sure I was awake. I tried to move my hand, but my limbs were like iron bars, stiff and immovable, as if I'd been welded to the bed. Only my stomach seemed to be back to normal, growling with hunger as it recognized the possibility of getting some food.

"Neve, you're awake," Hugo breathed. He was beside me now, sitting on the side of the bed, drinking me in with eyes that were clouded with worry. He pushed a lock of hair behind my ear and kissed my forehead so tenderly that I barely felt the brush of his lips. "You've come back to me," he whispered, gathering me up and holding me to him.

I could feel the wild racing of his heart and the hard outline of his ribs against my breasts. I wrapped my arms around him, finally allowing myself to accept that he was really there, and I wasn't just dreaming as I lay dying in my filthy cell. I clung to him for dear life, desperate to mold every inch of myself against him and feel his solid warmth as I slowly came back to life; back to hope that the nightmare was now behind me.

"I thought I'd died. I'd given up, Hugo," I mumbled into his chest. "I knew I was supposed to hold on, but I just couldn't go on in that place. How did you get me out? I don't remember anything at all."

Hugo finally released me, and I slumped against the pillows, so weak that I couldn't even sit up without being held.

"It doesn't matter. You're here now. I'll just go down to the kitchen and get you some food. You must be starved."

"Is there any fish and chips?" I asked hopefully, realizing that, of course, there wasn't. That particular delicacy would not be readily available in England for some time yet. "I'm thirsty," I added. "Hugo, where are we?" I called out after him.

"I'll explain everything later," he replied and disappeared.

* * *

I nearly cried with gratitude as Hugo spooned hot beef broth with chunks of mushy bread into my mouth. The warmth and richness of the broth seemed to spread through my starved body, awakening my senses with a rush. I couldn't eat more than a few spoonfuls without feeling sick, but I lay back down, closed my eyes, and commanded myself to hold down the food. I'd gulped down two mugs of apple cider and now felt as if liquid was sloshing around inside my belly, but it felt nice to be full.

While Hugo had been out of the room, I'd carefully allowed my hands to stray to my belly, holding my breath as I prayed for any sign of life. I wasn't sure exactly how long I'd been incarcerated, but I knew it was less than a month. Women had given birth to healthy babies in concentration camps and during times of famine and war. I had been starving, but the fetus would have taken what it needed from my body, draining me of vitamins and calcium to nourish itself. It had to have survived. *It had to*, I thought miserably. I couldn't bear to lose another baby, especially not Hugo's baby. A miscarriage would devastate us both, and I knew that Hugo would never forgive himself for putting me in danger, would never come to terms with the loss. I talked quietly to the baby, begging it to respond.

My heart nearly burst with joy as I felt a flutter beneath my palms. It was light, but unmistakable. It felt as if a tiny sea creature flipped over in its watery lair, causing ripples to spread out over the surface, subtle, but unmistakably alive. I'd breathed a sigh of relief and thanked God over and over for not taking my baby away.

The food seemed to have helped, and as the broth and bread became absorbed into my body, I felt a stronger response, the fluttering turning into more of an insistent pushing.

"Put the plate down," I whispered to Hugo as I felt it again. I was desperate to share the feeling with him, eager to reassure him that our baby was well.

"Do you feel ill?" Hugo asked, instantly concerned.

I grabbed Hugo's hand and placed it against my belly. "Do you feel it?"

I kept moving his hand around, trying to capture the light ripples, but Hugo couldn't seem to feel anything. Perhaps it was too soon to feel it from the outside. I was only... I let go of Hugo's hand and tried to concentrate. What date was it? What month? I wasn't even sure how pregnant I was.

"Hugo, what's today's date?" I asked urgently. "And do you have my vitamins? The baby needs them."

"Today is October second," he replied absentmindedly as he pressed his hand a little harder on my stomach, his face lighting up with an unspeakable joy. "I felt it. I think I felt it."

Hugo climbed into bed with me and pressed his hand to my stomach as he held me close. We remained that way for a while, cocooned within the tiny microcosm of the curtained bed, our little family, safe from the world.

My mind was teeming with questions, but I pushed them all aside, allowing myself to glory in feeling safe and loved. At some point, I would learn the truth of what had happened; would need to understand Jane's role in the events of that morning, and find out what Hugo had done to set me free, but I allowed myself a respite from all the pressing issues and gave myself up to the magic of the moment, realizing deep inside that the ordeal was far from over. There was more to come. I wasn't sure what shape events were going to take, but I was far from free.

Eventually, I fell asleep. I was so weak, I could barely move, much less attempt anything more strenuous. My body felt depleted and robbed of its vitality, so I gave myself up to sleep, knowing that it was the best medicine for getting back on my feet.

By the time I finally awoke, it was already getting dark; purple shadows gathering in the corners of the room and behind the furniture; the sharp angles of objects slowly dissolving into the twilight as the first stars began to twinkle in the sky—or would have, if not for the smoke belching from nearby chimneys. I saw the occasional pinprick of light just before it was obscured by billowing smoke. I must have slept through most of the day.

Hugo was no longer there, but he'd left a plate of buttered bread and a cup of milk for me, knowing that my stomach couldn't handle anything more elaborate, so I bit off a chunk and began to chew as I gulped down the milk. I was starving but had to take it slowly so as not to make myself sick. I ate half the bread, finished the milk, and leaned back against the pillows, exhausted by my efforts.

I was just drifting off again when I heard voices coming from the room next door.

"Neve is never to know what we did to get her out," Hugo said quietly, but with considerable force. "There's no need for her to be distressed. Nor does she need to know how she got there in the first place. Agreed?"

I heard the murmur of male voices but couldn't quite make out who they were. Likely Brad and Archie.

There was a silence, but I felt something was brewing, so lay still and listened attentively. What were they trying to hide from me and why? Exactly what had happened on the day I'd got arrested, and what could Hugo have done to get me out of prison that would distress me so? I'd assumed that money had changed hands or I wouldn't be here, but what else could he have done that he'd wish to keep from me?

"Archie," Hugo said, "someone who has no connection to me must claim the corpse of that poor girl. What we have done to her is appalling, and I want to make sure that she has a proper burial and is not just tossed into a pauper's grave in the state we'd left her in."

"There's no way we can rebury her in the same place," Archie whispered. "It's too dangerous."

"I know, but she can be buried someplace else. Now is not the time to reveal her identity, but maybe in the future, her proper name can appear on her stone."

I heard no answer from Archie, so assumed that he nodded in agreement.

"I've had word from Beth," Bradford said quietly. I could hear the acute tension in his voice, and it frightened me. Something was going on. "She'd ridden over to Everly Manor to see Jane, as I asked her to in the letter I sent on with Billingsley. The house is shut up and there's no sign of Jane or Clarence. Beth was able to locate Harriet in the village. She's working at the public house. The girl said that Jane had returned to Surrey on September twenty-fourth, approximately two days after Neve's arrest. She dismissed the servants, leaving only a caretaker and several grooms to see to the horses, and left with Clarence, presumably for her house in Kent, but Harriet wasn't sure. Cook is staying with a relative on the estate, and Liza was dismissed some time ago."

"And Jem?" Hugo asked, his voice breaking.

"Harriet said that she hadn't seen Jem since sometime in the summer. He just disappeared one day, and no one seems to know where he's gone."

"Did he leave on his own?" Hugo persisted.

"Harriet doesn't seem to know."

"And Liza. Where is she?"

"Jane dismissed Liza when she found out she was with child. Liza is not in the village, so she must have followed her captain back to London once Max was taken into custody and Captain Norrington was recalled. No one seems to know for sure." Brad's voice was soothing, but I could hear Hugo fuming through the walls. He wouldn't be too concerned with Liza, but he loved Jem like his own son, and the notion that no one knew what had happened to an eight-year-old boy would drive him mad with worry, especially when he was in no position to go searching for him.

"Brad, you have been my closest friend for decades. You have known me and my sister since we were children. Please explain to me what's happening, because I just don't understand. What am I missing? My sister lures the woman I love and who's carrying my child into a trap and pays some thugs to have her carted off to Newgate. There's no official warrant for her arrest, which is even more puzzling and sinister. Jane then runs off, presumably to Kent, to hide. A child I love has gone missing and no one knows or cares where he is, and a man I hardly know is in the Tower, awaiting trial and execution because the world believes him to be me. Did I leave anything out?"

"Yes, you did," Brad added grimly. "Liza betrayed you to Captain Norrington when you stopped by Everly Manor last month. She wanted to see you arrested and executed, and I can only guess why. You've made an enemy, Hugo, and you mustn't forget about her. The woman means you harm, and she's likely in London, her ties to Captain Norrington making her dangerous. She might think you're languishing in the Tower, but should Max be proven to be who he says he is, you will be in danger once again."

I stopped listening as my heart rate accelerated, and my head began to ache unbearably. Jane had lured me into that alley, had paid someone to arrest me and throw me into prison where she knew I wouldn't last long. Why? I suspected that she didn't wholly approve of me, but to go to such lengths to get rid of me? She didn't seem to mind me so much before. Was it because she thought I was merely Hugo's mistress and he would tire of me? Was it the child and Hugo's desire to marry me that had forced her hand? Was she so desperate to have Clarence inherit?

Of course, he was heir to the Hiddleston estate, which was very prosperous, by all accounts, but Ernest had not been titled, just wealthy. Perhaps Jane craved a title for her son, which would make him a much more desirable prospect once he was ready for marriage. At this point, the name of Everly was associated with treason, but by the time Clarence reached manhood, all this would have long blown over, especially once William of Orange took the throne three years from now as a result of the Glorious Revolution.

My head pounded unbearably as I tried to reason out what I'd heard. I could understand Liza's venom. She'd been in love with Hugo and he'd thwarted her affections, or perhaps he hadn't and had a liaison with her until he threw her over for me. Hugo never claimed to have been celibate, and Liza seemed an ambitious girl who would have done anything to better her situation. We had never spoken of it, but I knew there was more there than met the eye. She was a jealous girl, capable of great malice.

And Jem... Poor, sweet Jemmy. What had happened to him? Jane had said that he was well when we saw her only a month ago. Was she just lying to Hugo to spare him the worry, or had she done something to the poor boy? Where would he have gone? As far as I knew, Jem had no family to turn to and no income of any kind to fall back on. He was only eight, for God's sake, my mind screamed.

I suddenly felt very cold. Everything that had happened to Hugo over the past months had been either a direct or indirect result of my actions. I'd managed to save his life, but at what cost? Jane seemed to have become totally unhinged, Jem disappeared, Max wound up in the Tower, and Liza was nursing a grudge against Hugo that could conceivably cost him his life if he came across her by some unexpected twist of fate.

I sank deeper into the mattress and closed my eyes, the bread I'd eaten sitting in my stomach like a lead weight. When Hugo finally came into the room, I pretended to be asleep, unable to face him after what I'd heard. I knew he was devastated, and there was nothing I could do to help.

EIGHTEEN

As the sun finally set and the shadows of dusk began to pool in the corners of the tiny cell, Max cursed profusely as he fiddled with the contents of the tinderbox, desperate to light the candle. It still took him at least a half-hour to finally get the wick to catch once he produced a spark, leaving his forehead beaded with sweat and his hands shaking with the effort. What he wouldn't give for a lighter, or even a box of matches, he fumed as the tiny flame finally sprang to life, casting a pool of feeble golden light, just enough to dispel the gloom of the cell, but not actually light it.

Max sat down on the cot, resting his back against the rough stone of the wall. It felt hard and cold, but it was also the only back support he could get, since sitting on the low stool became uncomfortable after a time. He spent some time sitting on the narrow window ledge, watching the comings and goings on the Tower green below. He had no idea who all those people were, or what business brought them to the Tower of London, but it was a diversion, and as long as he didn't see any more executions, it gave him a way to spend some of the time that seemed to crawl at a glacial pace, especially during the early afternoon.

Max tried to impose a routine on his day, but it still seemed interminable with so many hours of idleness. Since his injuries had healed, he made sure to do at least an hour of exercise in the morning: walking around the cell, doing push-ups and jumping jacks, and at least two hundred sit-ups, to keep his muscles from becoming weak and lax from all the sitting he was doing.

At the rate I'm going, I'm going to be the healthiest corpse at the cemetery, he thought bitterly.

He tried to read when the light was brightest, but his mind kept wandering, his situation never far away, even when he was asleep. He'd been in the Tower for about a month now, a month during which he'd felt the kind of uncertainty and terror he'd never known in his twenty-first-century life. Max stared at the little flickering flame of the candle, thinking, not for the first time, that his life was much like that flame—burning steadily for a time, but vulnerable to any draft or breeze which could blow it out without warning, the flame extinguished forever.

Granted, Gideon Warburton gave him hope—more than hope. The man was a marvel, especially by seventeenth-century standards. He came once a week to check on his client and give him a brief update of his own activities on Max's behalf. Whoever Max's mysterious benefactor was, he wasn't sparing any expense in having his case proven to the best of Warburton's ability. Max wasn't sure that he liked the man himself, but he had to admit that he had a fine legal mind, one that liked the challenge of proving the impossible.

Warburton had been to see him only that afternoon. He'd thanked the guard graciously for allowing him in, took the proffered stool, and handed Max the latest care package, containing a new book, a jug of brandy, and several beeswax candles. Max could have used a clean shirt, since he hadn't bathed in a month, but couldn't bring himself to ask for one.

"How is it with you, Master Everly?" Gideon Warburton

had asked as he'd shifted his ample hips on the stool to get more comfortable.

"As well as can be expected," Max had replied, eager to hear what the lawyer had to say. "Is there any news?" Max was in equal parts eager and terrified to hear that a trial date had been set. The trial would either be an opportunity to prove his case and gain his freedom, or the final act before a public execution for treason.

"Yes, as it happens," Warburton had replied, giving up the stool and going to stand by the window. "I have obtained a sample of Lord Everly's writing and compared it with yours. Definitely not written by the same hand," he'd stated, nodding to himself in satisfaction. "Also, I have visited Lord Everly's tailor and bootmaker and requested a copy of his measurements." Max had thought it odd when, at their last meeting, the lawyer had insisted on measuring his height and shoe size, but now it all made sense. "You are two inches taller than Lord Everly, and your feet are considerably longer and wider. This in itself will not prove that you are not him, but it will certainly help our case. A man doesn't just grow in his middle years, nor does his shoe size change—unlike his girth," he'd added, patting his own round belly in an attempt at humor.

Max had smiled to make him happy, pleased that the man wasn't just sitting around twiddling his thumbs, but going out there and searching for evidence.

"Is that all we have?" Max had asked, trying not to sound desperate.

"We have several witnesses who will testify to your identity after being given a few minutes with you before the trial. I cannot get permission to bring them all here, but you will have ample time to prove that you are not Hugo Everly. Our best chance lies with Jane Hiddleston, Hugo Everly's sister. By all accounts, the two are very close, so she's sure to spot right away that you are not her brother," Warburton had explained. "Mrs.

Hiddleston seems to have left London for a time, but she will be induced to come back by royal subpoena once the date of the trial has been set. I have asked for several weeks to prepare my case and have been granted the extension. No one wants to execute the wrong man, Mr. Everly, of that you can be sure. The charges against Lord Everly are grievous ones, so it's in everyone's best interests that the right man be punished. I do hope that gives you some small degree of comfort."

"It does, Master Warburton, and I thank you for your work on my behalf."

The lawyer had peeled himself away from the windowsill and turned toward the door. He didn't smile or shake Max's hand, but Max had felt an aura of goodwill emanating from the man and could have kissed him had it been even remotely appropriate. "Please convey my regards to my benefactor and thank him for me," Max had called out as Gideon Warburton had disappeared into the corridor. He didn't hear an answer, but he was certain Warburton heard him.

Max turned over the book in his hands, wondering what had possessed the lawyer to choose this particular volume, but beggars couldn't be choosers and having something to read was better than nothing at all. He flipped through the pages, selected a poem at random and began to read.

> Death be not proud, though some have called thee
> Mighty and dreadfull, for, thou art not soe,
> For those whom thou think'st thou dost overthrow,
> Die not, poore death, nor yet canst thou kill mee.
> From rest and sleepe, which but thy pictures bee,
> Much pleasure, then from thee, much more must flow,
> And soonest our best men with thee doe goe,
> Rest of their bones, and soules deliverie.
> Thou art slave to Fate, Chance, kings, and desperate men,
> And dost with poyson, warre, and sicknesse dwell,

And poppie, or charmes can make us sleepe as well,
And better then thy stroake; why swell'st thou then?
One short sleepe past, wee wake eternally,
And death shall be no more; death, thou shalt die.

Max's soul felt lighter than it had in over a month. He felt undeniably hopeful, the taste of freedom intoxicating on his lips as if he'd already been released.

NINETEEN

Gideon Warburton breathed a sigh of relief as he came out onto the green. The thick walls of the Tower always made him feel as if all the air had been sucked out of the place, leaving just enough for the inmates to survive. The prisoners held at the Tower were much more comfortable and treated considerably better than the unwashed masses at the other prisons, but that didn't mean they wouldn't meet the same end. Gideon had tried to find as much evidence as he could to exonerate Maximillian Everly and hoped that his case was at least worth considering.

He'd petitioned to have the witnesses visit the prisoner to ascertain whether he was indeed Hugo Everly, but the request had been denied, which was ridiculous under the circumstances. How could a person testify in a case of identity when they'd had no opportunity to examine the accused? There was no doubt that whoever tried the case would be prejudiced against the prisoner, but there was little choice. At least legal representation had been permitted, which was a huge victory in itself.

Gideon allowed himself a moment of joy as he imagined Bradford Nash congratulating him on winning an impossible case and perhaps even giving him a hug—a bear hug, which would leave him breathless.

Bradford's approval means everything, Gideon thought as he passed through the gates and onto the crowded street beyond. Gideon realized that he was hungry, so he found an appealing tavern and went in, ordering himself a plate of roast beef. He was used to dining alone and entertained himself by examining the people around him.

A buxom girl brought the food and set a tankard of ale in front of him, bending over just low enough to stick her breasts in his face. She gave Gideon a winning smile and patted his hand. "Do let me know if you desire anything else, love. My name's Dulcie, and an extra coin can purchase delights you'll not likely soon forget," she whispered in his ear, making Gideon recoil. He couldn't think of anything more repulsive than touching Dulcie. She smelled strongly of woman—a scent that would drive most men wild, but left him mildly nauseated.

"Thank you, my dear," Gideon replied, "but I am very devoted to my wife."

"Well, lucky her," Dulcie said as she made an exaggerated face of disappointment. "If you change your mind..."

"I won't."

Dulcie shoved off, throwing a last sulky look over her shoulder, but Gideon had already forgotten all about her. Instead, his thoughts turned to Maximillian Everly. Gideon had visited him three times now and there was just something about the man that bothered him. Maximillian was attractive and clearly educated; he looked like a man who'd lived an active life, his body lithe and trim. He must have spent time outdoors, since there were traces of a most ungentlemanly tan on his face and hands. But his clothes were not those of a nobleman and his wording when he spoke was a trifle odd. He'd mentioned that he'd spent time abroad. Perhaps that accounted for his manner, but how was it possible that a man who'd been born and bred in England had no one who could vouch for his identity?

Gideon supposed that it was reasonable to assume that his parents were deceased, and he had no friends left in England if he'd been gone for a long time, but Max didn't strike him as someone who'd be alone for long. Did he not have lovers? Perhaps he didn't have a mistress but preferred the company of whores. Some men went in for that type of woman, one who had no shame and no inhibitions. A mistress would expect affection, some type of financial benefit, and promises of a future, even if they were utterly untrue. A whore asked for nothing, save her fee and a robust squiring, if that term was still applicable. Gideon wouldn't know.

He momentarily stopped chewing and tried on a fantasy of being with Maximillian for size. It didn't work. Gideon might not have ever had a lover, but if he had, he would be loyal till the grave, and Bradford Nash had his heart.

TWENTY

Over the next few days, I did nothing but eat and sleep. I now had a new appreciation for all the ordinary things I'd always taken so much for granted. A hot bath made me giddy with joy; a warm fire in the grate and light shining through the window appeared miraculous, and abundant food and drink were something to be grateful for every single day.

Since there were no servants in the house, the men didn't even attempt to cook, which was a blessing. Brad sent Archie to various taverns in the area to bring back our dinner and supper. This was the seventeenth-century equivalent of takeaway, and I was just fine with that. I was tired of broth-soaked bread and milk. My body craved protein, so Archie brought whatever meat dishes were available. I'd never been a huge fan of roast beef, but now, I could have eaten it three times a day given the opportunity.

I must be lacking iron, I thought as I inhaled the wonderful smell of beef wafting from downstairs. I was also craving apples, which Hugo bought at the market by the bushel. They'd been brought from the country by various farmers and were crisp, juicy, and full of the vitamins my body so desperately needed.

My little tenant seemed to be happy and rolled around inside my belly with greater frequency and vigor, which was the reassurance I needed that everything was well.

I was slowly regaining my physical strength, but not my peace of mind. The notion that I could be snatched off the street at any time haunted me; making me afraid to set foot outside, for fear that I was fair game. Did anyone know or care that I had escaped from prison? Was anyone likely to be looking for me? These questions swirled in my mind day and night, spawned by my desperate need to understand Jane's inexplicable behavior and my miraculous escape. Why didn't Hugo want me to know what happened? Who was the woman they'd referred to in their hushed conversation, and what had they done to her that was so appalling? I tried asking Hugo about that night, but he avoided my questions and told me not to worry and just rest.

I didn't want to upset Hugo or cause him any pain by insisting on talking about Jane's part in my arrest, but I couldn't carry this burden by myself any longer, nor could I stand his look of concern. I knew that he felt responsible for what had happened and had been through hell knowing what I'd gone through, but this had to stop.

Hugo insisted on sleeping on a truckle bed in my room, jumping to attention if I so much as sighed in my sleep.

"Hugo, come to bed," I whispered as he blew out the candle and settled on his cot, which whined in protest, being too flimsy for a fully grown man. It was usually used by young female servants or children, and not meant for someone of Hugo's weight and height. I couldn't imagine that he was very comfortable, but he insisted on giving me the use of the bed.

"I don't want to disturb you, sweetheart. You need your rest," he countered, sounding as stubborn as only a seventeenth-century man could when dealing with a hormonally charged pregnant woman.

Hugo hadn't touched me since I'd been brought back, limiting himself only to tender kisses and warm hugs. I could see perfectly well through his ruse; he wasn't afraid of disturbing me, but afraid of his own desire, which he felt was inappropriate under the circumstances. He thought it would be selfish of him to make love to me when I was still recovering from my ordeal. Little did he understand that I needed him more than ever; the feel of his body next to mine being the best protection he could give me, and his love and affection a shield against the terror I still felt deep inside.

I decided not to debate the issue, knowing full well that he would resist. His chest was being crushed by the magnitude of his guilt, and no words would make any difference. I slid out of bed, untied the ribbon of my chemise and allowed it to pool around my feet as I stood over Hugo, smiling in invitation. A few days ago, I wouldn't have liked for Hugo to see me naked, but tonight I felt more confident. I had regained some of the weight I'd lost, and the bites had begun to heal, leaving faint marks on my ankles and arms. My skin glowed in the golden haze from the fire, making me appear gilded and gloriously healthy. My breasts felt heavy, and my rounded belly rippled as the baby decided to participate in my grand plan of seduction and did a summersault.

"If you won't come to me, then I will come to you. The choice is yours," I said, getting on my knees next to his bed so that my breasts were practically in his face. "Don't you want me?" I asked petulantly.

"Neve, please," he whispered. "You are not ready. And the baby..."

"What about the baby?" I asked playfully. "It seems to be much more active than its father."

I pulled back Hugo's blanket and straddled him, grinding my hips against his, my eyes never leaving his face. I knew that'd be his undoing, and he reached up and gently cupped my breasts as I bent down to kiss him.

"I need you, Hugo," I breathed in his ear as I caught his earlobe between my teeth and nibbled it, making Hugo suck in his breath just as the cot collapsed beneath our combined weight. "It seems you no longer have a bed," I observed, giggling. "Will you come to mine or shall we sleep on the floor, because I'm not leaving?"

I fell onto the bed still laughing and pulled Hugo on top of me. He seemed to tense for a moment, unsure of whether he should be doing this, but nature won out, and he finally surrendered to his need for me, sliding into my body as carefully as if I were made of fine china.

"Let yourself go," I murmured as I moved more aggressively, urging him to stop holding back.

Hugo still seemed to be restraining himself, so I pushed him onto his back and impaled myself on him, moving my hips with deadly intent as I looked into his eyes.

"Please, Hugo."

He finally lost it and began to move inside me. His breathing was ragged as he raised his hips to meet mine and pushed harder, his desire obliterating his objections. I arched my back and moaned with pleasure as each thrust echoed in my womb, finally bringing me to a shuddering climax. As my body convulsed around Hugo, I felt happy for the first time in a fortnight.

Our bodies were still joined as Hugo pulled me against him and held me close as if he were afraid of losing me. I knew he felt torn between joy and guilt, so I took his face in my hands and kissed him gently.

"It wasn't your fault," I said, stressing every word as I stared into his eyes. "Do you hear me? None of it was your fault."

"You don't know the whole truth," he muttered, but I continued to hold his face, staring him down.

"I do. I know about Jane's part in my arrest; I heard you talking. Hugo, there is nothing— *nothing*—you could have done to make Jane behave as she had. Whatever she believes you, or me, to be guilty of doesn't begin to explain her actions. So, please stop blaming yourself; it's counterproductive," I added, for lack of a better word.

I felt Hugo let out his breath like a deflating balloon. He buried his face in my shoulder, unable to face me. "Neve, my own sister denounced you and paid to have you arrested. She wished for you to die, and die horribly—alone and abused. You keep telling me that it's not my fault, but I keep thinking that perhaps I'd done something to cause this, have hurt her in some way, or insulted her pride. What she did was not against you, it was against me. It was done to hurt me, to destroy me so completely that I would be reduced to nothing."

"Hugo, you haven't done anything, and even if you had, she's your sister. She's meant to love you and forgive you, or at least talk to you. What she'd done was monstrous. She condemned not only me, but our child to death. This wasn't about some minor slight to her pride, this was a vicious attack against both of us—an attack meant to divide and destroy. If you pull away from me, she would have succeeded, if only in part." I wrapped my arms around Hugo and held him close; needing to fill the hole in his heart that Jane's betrayal had carved so mercilessly.

I rolled off Hugo and pulled the coverlet over me. The fire was dying down and the room had grown colder; the wind howling outside like a desolate woman moaning with inconsolable grief.

Hugo slid in next to me and pulled me close, making me feel safe and loved. But I still needed answers, and the time had come for Hugo to come clean.

"Hugo, how did you get me out of prison, and is anyone looking for me? I need to know if I'm ever to have any peace.

You must tell me the truth," I added sternly, knowing that he'd try to protect me by withholding the worst of it.

"I don't think anyone is looking for you because they believe you to be dead," Hugo answered reluctantly. His face was illuminated by the dying embers, making him appear slightly demonic, his eyes dark holes in his pale face and his two-tone hair reminiscent of some punk rocker.

"What?!" I gasped, raising my head to gape at Hugo. "Why would anyone think I'm dead?"

I could hear Hugo's labored breathing as he worked up the courage to tell me the truth. It seemed that I hadn't been released legitimately, or even broken out of prison by paying someone off. There was more to it, something that Hugo had been keeping from me.

"Neve," he finally said, "Archie and I did something terrible to get you out. You see, there was no other way. Legally, we could do nothing at all, and to just help you escape would not only alert the authorities but bring attention to the fact that I must be in London, since you are known to them as my mistress, thanks to Lionel Finch and my sister. The risk was simply too great."

"Hugo, what on earth did you do?" I breathed.

"Archie found a gaoler who could be bribed to give you a drink laced with laudanum. Anyone who would pass by your cell would assume that you'd died. The guard would then turn a blind eye as we exchanged your inert body for the body of a woman who was already dead. To anyone in the prison, it would appear as if a corpse were being removed for burial in a pauper's grave, but, in actuality, we had removed a live woman and left a dead one in her place."

"Where on earth did you get a corpse of a woman?" I asked, horrified by the implications of Hugo's confession.

"We scoured several cemeteries, searching for a freshly dug grave of a woman who was no older than thirty. It was hard to find since many graves of the poor have nothing more than a name and no age or date of death. We had to make sure that the corpse was fresh."

"Dear God," I breathed. "You went grave robbing?"

"We did. I carried you out wrapped in the woman's shroud. So, to answer your question, as far as the authorities are concerned, you are deceased."

I felt a bubble of hysterical laughter well up inside my chest. I was now a non-entity, much as Hugo had been in the modern world. I supposed that I could no longer use my name as he couldn't use his since he was being hunted. We were a pair of ghosts, people who no longer truly existed, but were very much alive. There would come a time when we'd need to prove our identity, but for now, we were better off as we were —invisible.

"I'm sorry," Hugo whispered into my hair. "Please don't think badly of me, Neve. I would have happily killed a woman with my bare hands just to get you out; I was so desperate. With every day that passed, I knew that you were in greater danger. I was afraid that you might get assaulted or even killed once people discovered that you were the mistress of a suspected traitor."

I shook my head against Hugo's chest. "No one paid me any mind, except the rats. I was locked up in an individual cell, but I am so grateful that you did what you did. I couldn't have lasted much longer. I suppose the needs of the living come before the needs of the dead, don't they?"

"Yes, they do, but I will make sure the girl gets a proper burial and her own stone. We desecrated her body, Neve, to make it look as if she'd been imprisoned. I will never forgive myself for what we had to do to her. It was inexcusable, but we had no choice."

"Hugo, what do you plan to do now? Where do we go from here? We can't hide in Brad's house forever," I said, realizing for the first time that Hugo hadn't mentioned any plans for the future since I'd been back.

Hugo shrugged. I knew he was in turmoil, but it wasn't wise to rush into anything.

"I must confront Jane," he finally said.

"Hugo, if Jane is bent on revenge, she might betray you to the authorities. Right now, our only strength is in the fact that she doesn't know where you are, or that I'm still alive. Perhaps you need to let this go for now."

"I can't," Hugo replied stubbornly. "There must be retribution, but first I need to look her in the face and ask her why. I need to hear it from her lips; otherwise, I will never be at peace again. I need to understand what drove her to such lengths and know whether she feels any remorse," he explained.

"And will you be at peace if she tells you that she wanted me dead as well as our baby? Will that make you feel better?" I demanded, suddenly angry. I could understand his confusion and fury; I could understand his need for retribution, but we were in a precarious position, and this wasn't the time for the examination of fractured family relationships. I couldn't imagine that anything Jane said would make any difference, but Hugo obviously needed closure and would not be dissuaded from talking to Jane.

"I need to hear it from her. If that is indeed what she intended, then I will deal with the consequences, but I need to know for sure. And there's also the matter of Jem. No one has seen him since the summer. I'm worried about him, Neve. I must find out what happened to him."

"Are you proposing to leave London then?"

"I am. Max is in good hands with Gideon Warburton. He's working hard on Max's behalf, so there's nothing I can do at this moment. We must wait for the trial, so there's nothing to be gained by staying in London."

"Hugo, your disguise is no longer enough. Your own hair is

growing out rapidly, and you can't travel the countryside looking like yourself. It's too dangerous," I said, fearful for us both, for I had no intention of being left behind.

"Is there any other way of coloring my hair?" he asked.

Hugo could still hide his growing hair under a hat, but it was only a matter of time until that would no longer work and raise many a suspicious eyebrow.

"I've heard of using henna to turn hair auburn or black walnut husks for brown, but you need bleach to turn hair blond. I don't know if this will work, but I've heard of mixing vodka with lemon juice and sitting in the sun." I had a Brazilian coworker who swore by this method for getting lovely blond highlights, telling me that girls in Brazil did this all the time when they went to the beach. There wasn't much blazing sun in London in October, nor did we have any vodka, but perhaps something could be improvised.

"Well, I suppose whiskey might have a similar alcoholic content, and lemons could be obtained," Hugo mused. "As far as sunlight, do you think heat from the fire might do?"

"I don't know, but it's worth a try. If it doesn't work, you will have to shave your head."

"A prospect I don't relish."

TWENTY-ONE

Mellow rays of October sunshine pierced the gloom of the old-fashioned parlor, crowning the settle by the window in a halo of golden light. Dust motes lazily twirled in the shaft of sunlight slanting through the window to the rug covering the wooden floor and settled on the heavy wooden furniture and faded tapestries decorating the walls. Jane bent her head over her crewelwork, her hand shaking slightly as she stabbed the needle into the fabric and instantly pulled it out again. It went into the wrong spot, making Jane unbearably angry. She put aside the needle and began to rip up her work in such a frenzied fashion that the young maid who came in to call her to luncheon froze in the doorway, stunned by her normally calm mistress's behavior.

"Get out," Jane roared as she continued to destroy the embroidery she'd been working on for over a month. Pieces of colored thread littered her skirt and the cushion of the settle, but Jane couldn't stop until the whole pattern was torn out. She panted heavily as she hurled the piece of fabric across the room and covered her face with her trembling hands. Needlework had always been a source of solace to her, but over the past few months, it had become a source of incredible frustration instead. Jane's hands just wouldn't obey as they used to, refusing to comply as she strained to focus on the work. Not only had her vision become blurred around the edges, but her once deft fingers seemed to tremble too much to achieve the precision required.

Jane sighed and looked with irritation around the room. She hated this room; hated this house; hated the memories it all brought, but she couldn't go back to Everly Manor—not after what she'd done. Truth be told, she was scared. A messenger had arrived only a few days ago, informing her that Neve Ashley, accused of witchcraft and confined to Newgate Prison, had been found dead in her cell and subsequently buried in a pauper's grave. Jane's heart had lifted for just a moment until she'd realized what this would mean to Hugo. She didn't mean to hurt him, she really didn't, but given the choice between her only son and her brother, she had to act according to the dictates of her conscience.

Clarence was the best part of her; the only part she could steal from the man she had once loved, and the only thing that would be left behind once she was gone. He must never know, of course; he was only thirteen and as innocent as a babe in arms. He'd questioned Jane's absence when she went to London, and then argued incessantly about leaving Everly Manor. He liked it there and hoped that his uncle would come back soon. Clarence didn't want to return to Three Oaks—the house of his birth and childhood, a house where his mother had known only sorrow.

Jane finally forced herself to rise from the settle, brush the shreds of thread from her skirt, and glide regally toward the dining room. She ate with great ceremony every day, even though she dined alone. Clarence preferred to eat with his tutor, and that was just fine with her, but appearances needed to be maintained; Ernest had always said so. Of course, he'd also maintained an appearance of being a devoted husband and father, but nothing was further from the truth. Jane regretted telling Neve her secret, but, thankfully, Neve had taken it to her grave. Hugo must never know that the marriage he had so carefully arranged had never even been consummated. Her husband hadn't wanted any part of her. Instead, he'd chosen to spend his time with his devoted secretary, John Spencer, a man who had also shared her husband's bed for many years.

Of course, Jane didn't know this when she'd first arrived at Three Oaks, determined to make the most of her marriage. George had seduced and abandoned her, but Jane wasn't one for self-pity. She would build a new life, create a family and show George that he was nothing but a distant memory. But things didn't quite go as Jane had planned.

George was never far from her thoughts as she gazed upon Clarence, grateful that at least she had that much. Perhaps she would have married well had she not already been with child, but fate had other plans for her. Ernest had been kind and considerate, and acknowledged Clarence as his own, making him the heir to the Hiddleston estate, but he'd also used Jane to hide his proclivities from the world.

Jane glared at the portrait of Ernest hanging over the fireplace in the dining room. It had been painted in the same year as the portrait of Hugo, done by the hand of the same artist. The man liked making his subjects look stern and disdainful, but he couldn't hide the softness in Ernest's eyes or the twitch of a smile at the corners of his mouth. Ernest had been an attractive man; a man Jane could have come to love, had he ever seen her as anything more than a useful prop. Jane had tried her best to win her husband's affection, but Ernest had remained aloof and polite.

"Can you truly blame me?" Jane challenged the portrait, remembering the dark time in her life when she felt so lonely and unwanted that she'd turned to the only other man available to her at the remote estate. John Spencer had been younger than Ernest, and handsome in a chiseled, scholarly way. He'd always had a kind word and a smile for her, and later a secret touch or a seductive gaze. He'd often joined her for a walk in the garden when Ernest was out on the estate, and even took her on several picnics in a lovely meadow he'd shown her on one of their walks. He'd even played with Clarence, showering the little boy with praise and affection; unlike Ernest, who never did more than inquire after his health and occasionally pat him on the head absentmindedly, much as he did with his daughter Magdalen.

Had Ernest ever paid any attention to her, Jane might have resisted John's advances, might have acted with more propriety, but she was eighteen and she was lonely. She didn't protest when John kissed her softly under the green darkness of the willow tree, or slid his warm hand under her skirt, caressing her inner thigh until she was panting with desire. Only then had he slid his fingers inside her, exploring her expertly and bringing her to the first orgasm she'd had since George.

It didn't take long for Jane to start seeking him out under the pretense of needing to ask him a question or for advice. John was always happy to oblige, taking her swiftly in an empty room or behind a bush as she lay sprawled on the lush grass with her skirts about her waist. Jane's greatest fear in those days had been getting with child, since she wouldn't be able to pass it off as her husband's, but it seemed that life wasn't finished playing cruel tricks on her.

She supposed John Spencer got some perverse pleasure from bedding both the husband and the wife, but he seemed to truly enjoy both sexes. He wasn't picky about whom he lay with as long as he found pleasure in it. At first, Jane had protested when John took her in the rear, but he assured her that was the best way of keeping her from getting with child, so she'd agreed. She came to enjoy it in time, partly because John seemed to, but he pleasured her in other ways, especially when he disappeared under her skirts as she sat with her legs spread on a wrought-iron bench, and John feasted on her as if she were water and he a man in the desert. He'd finally come up and kiss her, the taste of herself still on his lips as he slid his tongue into her mouth, and whisper into her ear that it was her turn to return the favor. Jane didn't enjoy pleasuring him as much, but she did it with relish, eager to please her lover and prove to him that she loved him.

Loved him. The words stuck in Jane's throat, remembering the night when it all came to a head, her world crashing around her once again, but in a way she'd never expected. Seeing Ernest between John's legs, his tongue licking and teasing John's cock had been a terrible shock, but what had been even worse was John's face as their eyes had met. He had simply winked at her as if it was all one great, big joke. Jane had stood frozen as her husband had wiped John's seed from his mouth and flipped him over, taking him from the back like an animal, like John took her. Jane had watched in horror as her husband grunted and panted, his shaft slick in the candlelight as it slid in and out of John's body, John's eyes closed in ecstasy as he stroked himself. Jane had nearly fainted as Ernest had let out a gasp of pleasure and collapsed on top of John, who turned his face toward Jane and blew her a kiss, making her flee before her sobs could be heard by her husband.

Jane had never lain with John again and had spent hours on her knees, begging God for forgiveness and doing penance, but it seemed God wasn't satisfied with that. God, in his infinite wisdom, was just, and he had chosen to smite all three of them with his flaming sword. John had been the first to fall ill, followed by Ernest, and now Jane. Oh, she knew the signs, knew the symptoms as if they had been burned into her brain. She prayed for salvation, dared to hope that she might have been spared, but that was not to be.

It came on slowly, so slowly that Jane almost didn't notice the changes at first. She strained harder to see, had to focus intently to keep the tremor from her hands, and most of all had to try desperately to hide her disorientation and confusion. She'd tried to ignore the voices in her head, telling her that Hugo meant to dispossess her son and cheat him out of his inheritance, meant to produce another son. Yes, another son, she mused. He'd lied to her when he told her Jem wasn't his. Oh, she knew the truth. He'd fathered that boy as surely as he'd fathered Neve's bastard. Hugo said the boy had been a by-blow of an affair between Margaret the washerwoman and Ned the groom, but she knew better. She'd gotten rid of that meddlesome little pup as soon as she decently could, eliminating any threat to her son's inheritance. And now, Neve was dead, and so was her bastard. Perhaps Hugo had already married her, but it didn't matter. She was dead, and the child with her.

Clarence's inheritance is safe, Jane thought as she nearly spilled soup due to the shaking of her hands.

She picked up her cup and silently toasted Ernest. "May you rot in Hell, my dear," she said. "I shall be joining you shortly."

TWENTY-TWO

"That actually smells good," Hugo said as I doused his hair with a mixture of whiskey and lemon juice. I worked it into his hair and let him gulp down the rest, as I moved his head as close to the fire as he could stand in the hope that the concoction would do its work and lighten his hair. We would be leaving London tomorrow since Mr. Billingsley and his wife were returning from Surrey and mustn't find us in residence. Bradford was heading home to his wife and son, and Archie was coming with us to Kent to confront Jane. I was secretly glad that Archie would be accompanying us. He'd proven himself to be loyal and canny; two qualities that were in short supply just now.

I smiled as Hugo reached out and placed his hand on my belly, smiling gleefully as he felt a swift kick against his palm.

"Does that hurt?" he asked as I let out a startled yelp.

"Not really, but it does take me by surprise sometimes. It's amazing how much stronger the kicks have become in only a week. It kicks more after I've eaten and when I'm lying down," I said, marveling at the little person inside my body who seemed to have its own routine. "I often wonder what it will be like," I mused. "There are days when I think it's a boy, and there are other days, like today, when I think that surely it must be a girl."

"Well, if it's a girl, then I hope she looks just like you," Hugo said as he gazed up at me tenderly. "No one would want a girl who looks like me; she'd scare all her perspective suitors half to death."

"Do you think we can wait until she's born to start talking of marrying her off?" I replied, suddenly upset. It had never really dawned on me until that moment that our child would never see the future or have much as personal freedom as children had in my own time. He or she would be raised according to the strict rules of the seventeenth century, and I would forever be thinking of all the things they were missing. I was putting the cart before the horse, I knew that, but it saddened me to think of all the opportunities my child would never have.

I emerged out of my reverie to find Hugo watching me intently. He might have guessed at what I was thinking, but didn't say anything, simply took my hand and kissed my palm. I'd given up a lot to be with him, but I would never hold it over his head; the choice had been mine.

I gazed into the fire as I imagined myself in my flat in Notting Hill, surfing the internet as I prepared for my next work assignment, or dashing down a crowded London street to meet a friend at a bar in Soho for a quick drink. I think what I missed most was watching a movie as I sipped hot tea and indulged in that extra biscuit or browsed my favorite bookshop or art gallery. And music. I desperately missed music.

But none of the small pleasures I'd left behind could ever compete with what I felt when I was with Hugo. After four years with Evan, I was all right being on my own, but the thought of being without Hugo left me in a panic, my heart doing a mumbo of protest as I silently assured it that he wasn't going anywhere.

For the first time in my life, I felt a twinge of pity for my mother, who'd turned to drink after my father left, and eventually drank herself to death. I'd always felt a terrible resentment for the woman who'd chosen her need to numb her grief over the needs of her only child, but now, in hindsight—if looking at it from a seventeenth-century perspective could be called that—I realized she was so heartbroken by the loss of my father that she simply wasn't able to cope. I wanted to believe that I would be stronger than my mother, should anything ever happen to take Hugo away from me, and would love and care for my child properly, but the ache in my heart at the thought of being without Hugo mocked me and whispered in my ear that loss of love and hope could cripple anyone—even me.

My mother always said that home was where the heart was, and her home left the day my father walked out, leaving without a farewell or an explanation. He took her love and threw it back in her face, letting her know, in no uncertain terms that, in his eyes, it was a worthless commodity. My mother had never been able to make a home for herself with me. I simply wasn't enough.

Well, my home was right here; my heart carefully held in the hands of this man who reeked of whiskey and lemon and was studying me in a way that suggested that he wasn't oblivious to my thoughts.

"You smell like a brewery," I said to distract Hugo from whatever he was thinking.

"I've smelled of worse things in my life," he countered, his eyes still holding mine. "Neve, I would understand if you wanted to go back," he said, reading my mind with annoying accuracy. "Your world is much safer, especially for a woman carrying a child. I would go back with you, if that's what you wanted," he added, letting me know that he'd stand by my decision no matter what. "I'm yours to command, Neve, you know that."

"I don't want to go back, but I do wish things were a little less eh... volatile. I wish we were in some charming cottage in France, enjoying a peaceful existence and awaiting the birth of our child. I'm scared, Hugo," I confessed. "What is it?" I asked, sensing that Hugo wanted to tell me something, but had been waiting for the right moment.

"You are right to be scared, which is why you won't be coming with me to Kent," he said. There was a finality in his voice that I was only too familiar with. He'd brook no argument.

"Why?" I asked, my heart beating faster at the thought of being parted from him even for a few days.

"Because I won't endanger you, not if I can help it. Archie and I will take you to the Sacred Heart convent before making our way to Kent. The nuns will take good care of you, and I'm sure you'd like to see Frances again." Hugo thought that might soften the blow, but as much as I wanted to see how Frances was getting on, I was terrified of being away from Hugo and Archie.

"I won't be in the way; I promise," I pleaded, already knowing that Hugo would refuse.

"Neve, Jane meant you harm, and has likely been informed of your death in prison. I won't disabuse her of that notion. As long as you are dead, you are safe. I won't give her any ammunition against you or our child. I will keep you safe, even if that means forfeiting my own life. Now, please, say you understand and will willingly go to the convent."

"And if I don't?" I asked stubbornly.

"Then I will take you there anyway, but I would prefer that we parted on good terms and not in anger. Please, obey me in this; it's for your own safety."

Hugo was always reasonable and considerate of my needs, but there were times when once he'd made up his mind, there was no arguing with him. He was a man of his time, and a man protecting his woman was the natural order of things. He'd indulge me whenever he could, but this wasn't up for discussion. I felt a moment of annoyance, but instantly regretted it. Hugo had been to hell and back since my abduction, so I had no right to question his need to keep me safe. If he felt that this was best, I had to concede and respect his wishes; it wasn't until Hugo said it out loud that I suddenly realized exactly how dangerous Jane could be.

What if she wasn't satisfied with getting rid of me and the baby? What if Jane meant to do away with Hugo as well? I knew that I couldn't talk Hugo out of seeing her; he needed to have it out with her face-to-face, to understand, if at all possible, what had driven her to act so viciously against the person she claimed to love. I didn't expect that Hugo would find any answers, but perhaps he would find some closure. He needed to hear Jane admit what she had done for himself; otherwise, he would always try to imagine that there was some misunderstanding or coercion.

"All right, Hugo, I will obey you, but only because I know that your reasons are sound."

I reached out and ruffled Hugo's crusty hair to see if the mixture was working. The roots had turned a lighter color, if not exactly blond, so it was working. A few more minutes and I would wash Hugo's hair and see the result. The disguise would hopefully last for a few more weeks, but that wasn't my main concern. It was only a matter of weeks before the ships stopped sailing due to winter storms. If we didn't get out of England by the end of November, we'd be trapped here, in a place where Hugo was in constant danger, as was I.

TWENTY-THREE

I came downstairs the following morning to find Archie in the kitchen, slicing fresh bread. He looked up as I entered, smiling in greeting. The kitchen seemed strangely deserted, with no fire burning, nor a cook and maids going about preparing food for the day, no cauldrons simmering over the flames, nor the smell of baking bread filling the cavernous space. The table was bare, the pots gleaming, the hearth cold and clean.

Sunlight streamed through a small window set high in the wall of the basement kitchen, falling on Archie's hair and making it glow like flames around his lean face. His eyelashes were a darker shade of auburn, framing his deep-blue eyes and making them pop as our gaze met. Archie was tall and lean; his body exuding the grace and strength of a fencing master rather than a warrior. Not for the first time, I was taken aback by Archie's good looks. He wasn't vain in the slightest, wearing his beauty not as a badge of honor, but rather as one would wear a periwig at Court, a necessity that he would happily shrug off if possible.

"Where's Hugo?" I asked, suddenly worried. Bradford

didn't seem to be around either. The house was unusually silent.

"His lordship and Master Nash went to the livery to retrieve the horses," Archie replied soothingly, aware of my panic. "They should be back within the hour. Would you care for some breakfast, Mistress Ashley?"

"Will you join me?" I dreaded the thought of being left alone, even for a short while. Being with Archie made me feel safe, even if the two of us eating together in the kitchen wasn't exactly socially acceptable. But it's not as if anyone were watching.

Archie looked faintly horrified by this suggestion but was too polite to refuse. He treated me as if Hugo and I were already married, and I were a titled lady, not the pregnant mistress of his employer, who, by current standards, would be nothing more than a glorified courtesan.

I accepted a slice of bread and poured myself some milk from the jug. Archie silently pushed a dish of butter toward me and perched on the bench, feeling as awkward in my company as if I were the Queen of England. I thought that engaging him in conversation might help.

"Do you miss home, Archie?" I asked as I bit into the bread.

Archie considered the question for a moment and shrugged. "Can't say that I do," he replied. "I never did care for farming. Rising before the sun is up, toiling in the fields all day, then seeing to the animals before enjoying an hour or two of respite before going to bed and doing it all over again the next day never appealed to me. I suppose there's a certain pleasure in watching things grow and knowing that you are self-sufficient and can see to your family's needs, but farming's not an occupation for a man who longs for adventure or wants to see something beyond the next hill."

"So, what does appeal to you?" I asked, curious to know more about this reticent young man.

"I've always wanted to be a soldier, but my father begged me not to join the army. He'd witnessed the slaughter during the Civil War and feared I would die for naught. My da was a staunch supporter of the Republic, you know; idolized Oliver Cromwell until he grew disillusioned. I think he was actually relieved when Charles was invited back to take the throne but didn't want to appear foolish for changing his mind."

"Did he fight, your father?"

"Oh, aye, he did, and has the scars to prove it. The scars lasted a lot longer than the Republic."

"So, you stayed and farmed against your wishes?"

"My da and I came to a compromise, you might say. I stayed, but I didn't farm. I went into his lordship's employ and gave my earnings to my father to hire a farmhand. Worked for us both, for a time."

"You seem to be very devoted to his lordship. I can't believe it's only because he pays you," I observed. The relationship between Hugo and Archie mystified me. They were not exactly friends, but so much more than master and servant, and certainly loyal to each other in a way that belied their stations in life.

"He pays me rather well," Archie quipped as he finally smiled. "But you are right; it's not just the money. I owe Lord Everly my life."

"In what way?"

"Well," Archie said, suddenly looking sheepish, "I was a bit of a troublemaker as a small child, always trying to run away from my poor mother and getting into all kinds of scrapes. My mam was too busy to keep watching me all day long, so I was my sister's responsibility. Julia is five years older, so she considered herself to be quite the mature woman at the age of twelve. She ordered me about something fierce."

I could just imagine Sister Julia as a young girl, keeping a strict eye on her little brother. "She must have been formidable."

"Oh, she was. Never left me alone. One day, I managed to get away from her and snuck down to the river, where some of the older boys were swimming. I didn't know how to swim, but the water looked so inviting and cool. I felt grubby and hot and just wanted to cool off. The boys chased me away, but I hid behind a bush and watched them splashing around, hooting with laughter. I was so envious. I wished I had an older brother to tag along with, but I only had one annoying older sister."

"What happened?" I asked, already suspecting the answer.

"After the boys went home to have their dinner, I took my clothes off and waded into the river. It was bliss. The water was cool and fresh, the sun sparkling on the surface and making me feel as if I were in some enchanted place. I splashed around for a while and would have been just fine had I not decided to go in a little deeper." Archie gave me a rueful smile as he remembered that moment when everything changed. "It was a lot deeper than I'd bargained on. I lost my footing and went under. As the water covered my head, I felt a terror I haven't felt since. I was sure I was going to die. My heart was pounding, and my arms and legs were flailing like a windmill. I fought to keep my head above the water, screaming for my mother all the while. I remember thinking that if I ever got out alive, I would get my hide tanned like never before, so maybe drowning was preferable."

"Surely not," I said with a smile as I imagined a seven-year-old Archie, naked and terrified, fighting for his life.

"No matter the punishment, I wasn't ready to die just yet, but the current was strong in that part of the river and it carried me along, forcing me under. His lordship was fishing with his tutor and heard my screams. He waded in and fished me out before I drowned or was smashed against the rocks. The tutor, who was a dried-up old stick, tried to scold me and threatened to tell my parents, but Hugo just wrapped me in his coat and held me until I stopped shaking, then gave me some bread and jam that he'd had in his pack. He helped me find my clothes and then took me for a gallop on his horse until I dried off."

"Did you get in trouble once you got home?"

"My mother and sister were frantic. They'd looked everywhere for me, and Julia's face was all puffy from crying, which made me kind of glad, since she was always making me cry. My mam scolded her something fierce for letting me out of her sight. They both came running when they saw me astride a fine stallion with his lordship. Hugo told my mother that we'd been fishing together and lost track of time, so she couldn't very well punish me, could she?"

"And how old was your gallant rescuer at the time?" I asked, trying to imagine Hugo as he had been then.

"I reckon he was 'bout seventeen. He seemed very grown up to me, especially since he was old enough to shave. I felt stubble against my cheek when he held me and thought him quite the man. He came back the following week and took me fishing for real, and we had a sort of picnic afterwards," Archie reminisced happily. "I thought the sun rose and set on him that summer. Then he left for London come autumn. Went to Court with his father."

"And what of Jane? Did you see her much?"

"I'd seen her in church, but she never looked at anyone. She was a haughty little thing. I was glad to see the back of her when she married and left Everly Manor."

"And what about you, Archie? Have you never wanted to be married? Is there no fair maiden waiting for you back in Surrey?" I asked. Perhaps I was prying, but I was genuinely interested in getting to know Archie better. He rarely spoke of himself, and this was the first time we'd really talked.

"No, there isn't," Archie replied, reaching for another slice of bread. "I never stay long enough to make promises to a lass."

He seemed reluctant to speak of his private life, which made me even more curious. Unlike in my own time when people tended to overshare, and do so in the most public of ways, the men in this century were rarely willing to speak about their private lives. They kept their own counsel, which I found a lot more attractive than all the attention-mongering of modern men who often came off as crybabies and prima donnas.

"Do you not wish to settle down?" I asked, hoping I wasn't making him uncomfortable.

"No. Love and marriage kill," Archie replied with unexpected fire.

"Whatever do you mean, Archie?"

"I've never been in love, Mistress Ashley, but I know what real love looks like, and I know the power the loss of that love has to destroy the human spirit. I've seen what it did to my father after my ma passed, and I know what it'd done to my sister. Greater suffering, I never wish to behold."

"What happened to your sister, Archie?" I asked, carefully. Sister Julia was a lovely, warm woman. She'd been very kind to me and especially to Frances, who'd been brutalized and frightened when we brought her to the good sisters of the Sacred Heart. I'd assumed that something had driven Julia to renounce the world but had no idea what that might be.

"It's not for me to say, but I can tell you it nearly killed her, as it nearly killed his lordship when he thought he'd lost you. He was in a bad way." Archie stared down at the table, too polite to just get up and leave, but clearly not willing to continue the conversation.

"I'm sorry, Archie. I didn't mean to pry. I just wonder about you sometimes," I said, giving him a conciliatory smile.

"I'm not all that interesting, Mistress Ashley," he replied and rose from the table with a stiff bow. "Now, please excuse me; I have things to see to."

TWENTY-FOUR

The Convent of the Sacred Heart was hidden in a forest, reachable by a narrow path, more a deer track that forked off a deserted stretch of road, about a day's ride away from the city of Guilford. We'd been there once before, and now were on our way there again, once more in search of help. I had to admit that a part of me was relieved not to have to face Jane. I couldn't begin to imagine what my reaction to seeing her would be. I'd trusted her, considered her a friend, and had looked forward to becoming her sister-in-law, so the magnitude of her betrayal left me breathless with rage and hurt.

I suppose I never really knew her, but Hugo had, and he was just as bewildered and angry; a burning rage simmering inside him that would consume him if he didn't find a resolution. Hugo was one of those men who just retreated into themselves when hurt or angry, and he spent hours staring into space as we rode to Surrey, agonizing over the coming confrontation and probably playing out one scenario after another in his mind. I left him be, knowing that he needed to work this out for himself. There was nothing I wished to say in Jane's defense, nor did it seem right to tell Hugo how to deal with the situation.

Archie, who was always sensitive to Hugo's moods, was quieter than usual as well. He refrained from making jokes or singing, giving the master time to brood.

Normally, I would have been annoyed by Hugo's uncommunicative demeanor, but under the circumstances, he was entitled to a little silent reflection.

As we turned off the road and got deeper into the woods, the riotous colors of fall bloomed overhead—red, yellow, and gold offset by the occasional glimpses of the cloudless blue sky peeking through the branches overhead. Thankfully, it wasn't raining, the October day unspeakably glorious in its perfection. The forest smelled of decomposing leaves, damp wood, and that special scent of fall, which reminds one that winter is never far away. It was colder in the shadow of the trees, so I pulled my cloak closer around my body, suddenly remembering the last time we'd traveled this path.

It had been early spring, and the fresh green of new leaves had formed a canopy over our heads, shielding us from the weak April sunshine and teasing us with the promise of rebirth and redemption. We'd all been a little shell-shocked by the events that had taken place at the home of Lionel Finch, still recovering from the unexpected aftermath of Hugo's interference in defense of Frances. Jemmy had been severely concussed, after having his head smashed against the stone wall by Finch, and Frances nearly insensible with pain from the vicious beating at the hands of her husband.

Lionel Finch had assaulted me as well, and for the first time in my life I'd encountered someone who truly meant me harm. Strange, that I should be coming back to the convent after another such incident, but one even more frightening and real. In the twenty-first century, it was easy enough to cause someone irreparable damage simply by tapping a few keys or posting some damning information without ever meeting them face-to-face or sullying one's hands, but in the seventeenth century that wasn't an option.

Physical harm was the calling card of the day; harm that often led to death. I shuddered at the memory of Lionel Finch's eyes as they bore into mine, the cruel smile stretching his lips as he threatened to hurt me. Another few moments and he would have smashed in my face, as he had done to several others, whom he'd left blinded and permanently disfigured.

Hugo had saved me from the beating, but he'd paid a heavy price, having made a mortal enemy that day. It had been Lionel Finch who'd denounced Hugo and brought charges against him, and now Hugo was a fugitive, Max imprisoned in his stead, and Frances shut away in a convent in the woods just to keep her safe from Finch's vengeance. That one incident had changed the course of all our lives and had literally changed history. And now we were coming back after another such incident, seeking sanctuary.

I put Jane and Lionel Finch out of my mind as the sharpened spikes of the convent wall finally came into view, making my heart beat faster with the anxiety of the coming farewell. What I wouldn't give to be able to communicate with Hugo, but this wasn't the future, and he could hardly send me a text letting me know that he was all right and on his way back. I'd been happy enough to give up the relentless pull of the internet, with its alternate reality run on countless gigabytes of useless information, but the ability to communicate when necessary was one thing I sorely missed. Once Hugo left, I'd be completely in the dark, shut away from the outside world until he came back for me.

If anything happened to him, my only way of finding out would be to eventually leave the safety of the convent and go into the nearest village, where I might be lucky enough to overhear a little bit of gossip. With no telephones, television, or newspapers, there was no way for me to learn anything, and the total informational blackout was not something I was looking forward to, especially since Hugo was going blindly into a potentially dangerous situation.

Hugo dismounted and helped me down from my horse but didn't let me go. He held me close, inhaling the scent of my hair as he slid his hand between us to press his palm against my belly. The baby obliged him by giving a swift kick that startled us both. I didn't say anything; Hugo knew what I was feeling and understood my unease.

"I will be back in roughly a week," he said as he took my face between his hands and planted a kiss on the tip of my nose. "Two at most. During that time, you will not worry, understand? You will rest, enjoy the fresh air, and spend time with Frances."

"What if something happens to you? What if you get arrested?"

Being out in the open was vastly different than hiding in plain sight in London. There, Hugo was just one person among the multitudes, but riding with Archie down country roads where two wagons in one hour could be construed as heavy traffic was far more dangerous. This was Surrey, a place where Hugo was born and grew up. There were people who might recognize him, even if the possibility was remote.

"I will do nothing to put myself in danger; you know that. I will be back. But if anything changes, I will send Archie here for you. Agreed?"

"No, not agreed. I want Archie by your side at all times. I will wait patiently, I promise. Just stay safe."

Hugo kissed me soundly, turned me around, and gave me a pat on the bum. "Now go." He would stay behind with the horses, his altered appearance not something he wished to explain to the nuns, while Archie escorted me to the convent.

Archie banged on the thick door until the tiny window opened, and the anxious face of an elderly nun appeared behind the grille. She nodded in recognition and opened the door, ushering us inside.

"Good day to you," the nun said, smiling up at me. She was so tiny and withered that I had to almost bend down to hear her. Her face reminded me of a baked apple, all brown and wrinkly. I was sorry to say that I couldn't recall her name, although I must have met her the last time I was here. "I must admit, I never expected to see you two again," she added as she waited for us to explain our unexpected presence.

"We'd like to see Mother Superior, please," Archie asked politely as he gave my hand a reassuring squeeze. I could see his eyes darting around from building to building, searching for Sister Julia, but she was nowhere in sight.

The compound looked much as I remembered, with wooden buildings clustered around the yard, where the well held pride of place. Animals lowed in the barn, and the smell of something savory emanated from the kitchen behind the communal dining hall. I noticed several sisters emerging from the small shed where the laundry was done. They were red in the face from the steam; their habits damp down the front. It was laundry day.

A young nun I'd met on my previous visit gave us a huge smile of welcome as she hoisted a bucket of water out of the well and carried it carefully toward the kitchen. Otherwise, no one paid us any mind as the nun led us toward the tiny cell which served as the office of Mother Superior. We had come well before midday to make sure the nuns were not at prayer when we arrived. They would have been finished with Terce, the midmorning prayer, and at work until Sext, the midday prayer, after which they'd sit down to their dinner. It would have been disrespectful to disturb them during prayer or their meal, so Hugo had timed our arrival carefully.

"Master Hicks, Mistress Ashley, what a surprise to see you back with us. Have you come for Frances?" she asked, lines of concern appearing on her face. I noticed that she didn't say "Sister Frances," which was a surprise, but decided not to ask. Something must have happened since we'd left Frances here in April to make the Mother Superior appear so taken aback, but her face relaxed into a smile, and I decided that her reaction was probably just one of surprise, not worry.

"No, Mother," Archie replied as he kneaded his hat in his hands. "Lord Everly asks that you give his lady sanctuary while he goes on an errand that involves some danger. We shouldn't be gone more than a week or two, if that's all right," he added lamely.

Mother Superior noted my rounded belly and lack of wedding ring but didn't say anything. Hugo had made a generous donation to the convent's coffers, so to appear judgmental would not have been polite, although I couldn't tell if she was displeased or not to have me there. Her face was unreadable, which was probably a good thing for a woman in her position, but I suddenly felt a wave of apprehension.

"You are always welcome here, child. Please convey my regards to Lord Everly, Master Hicks, and tell him that we will look after Mistress Ashley as if she were one of our own. He needn't worry about her safety or that of his unborn child. Now, I expect you'd like to see Sister Julia before you leave."

"Yes, please. I would be most grateful."

"Master Hicks, follow me, and Mistress Ashley, why don't you go see Sister Angela. She'll be pleased to see you again."

I supposed that what Mother Superior was really saying was that Sister Angela would examine me to see if my pregnancy was progressing normally, but I didn't mind. I trusted Sister Angela after she'd taken such gentle care of Frances and Jem, and I was more than happy to have someone with medical knowledge reassure me that everything was going well after my ordeal.

"We will be back soon," Archie said as he took my hands in farewell. "I will take good care of him. You have my word."

"I know, Archie. And thank you again for everything you've done for me."

"There's no need for thanks. You are my mistress now, and you have my fealty." Archie gave me a deferential bow and followed Mother Superior outside. Somehow knowing that Archie was on my side made me feel better.

TWENTY-FIVE

The tailor positioned the cheval glass so that the light from the window fell just on the spot before the glass, illuminating the area like a stage. His hands shook slightly as he carefully unfolded the garment and laid it on the bed, hoping against hope that his client would like it, pay, and leave him in peace. Lionel Finch was a most difficult customer, his temper legendary among those who knew him. Normally, he had his clothes made in London, but he hadn't been to town since the spring and had summoned the tailor a few weeks ago most urgently.

There was much speculation in the surrounding area about the disappearance of Finch's wife. Rumors had reached far and wide about what had happened at the manor house in April, and there were those who quietly said that they were happy for the poor girl to have escaped the clutches of that monster.

Lionel Finch had quickly recovered from the physical assault, but his pride was not as easily mended. He'd been more difficult than ever, punishing the servants and tenants on his estate for the slightest transgression, and using his fists on anyone who so much as dared to look at him for a second too long or answer back.

Joseph Caxton had made several garments for Finch in the past, and hoped never to do so again, but couldn't refuse the summons. His shop was on Finch land, and everyone knew that Lionel Finch was a vengeful man.

The tailor brushed an invisible speck from the lapel of the coat and waited patiently for his client to arrive, growing more nervous by the moment. He was an elderly man and didn't have a young man's courage to stand up to such a tyrant. He squared his shoulders as Lionel Finch finally strode into the room, but forced himself to relax, his shoulders slumping in a gesture of submission and servitude.

"Ah, Master Caxton," Lionel Finch said, rubbing his hands with what appeared to be excitement. "Show me the garment."

The tailor lifted the coat off the bed and carefully held it out as Lionel Finch slid his arms into the sleeves. He adjusted the fit and preened in front of the looking glass, turning this way and that, but not saying a word. Joseph Caxton found that he was holding his breath as he watched Finch discreetly, so as not to offend, and praying that he was satisfied.

"You have outdone yourself, Master Caxton," Lionel Finch said, surprising the old man. "This is a splendid coat, just as I hoped it would be. I'll ask you to add some gold braid to the cuffs, but, otherwise, I will declare myself satisfied."

The tailor felt that there was enough trim on the already overly embellished coat, but he simply bowed and agreed. "I'm happy to see that you like the coat, sir," he said in his most agreeable tone.

"Oh, yes," Lionel Finch said, almost as if speaking to himself. He seemed to forget that Caxton was even in the room. "I will have a new coat for the trial, and a new wig. I might not have a title, but I will show those titled popinjays that I'm no worse than they are. Why, I have the money to buy them all twice over. And my testimony will send that villainous bastard straight to the execution block. He'll get what's coming to him, make no mistake," Finch said with great satisfaction. He practically glowed as he shrugged off the coat and passed it back to Joseph Caxton.

"Yes, Master Finch, he certainly shall," the tailor replied as he prepared to leave, but Finch wasn't finished.

"Well, off with you," Finch sneered, waving a hand in dismissal. "Have the coat back to me by tomorrow. I have no doubt that the summons will come any day now, and I must be ready."

"As you wish, sir," Caxton replied, bowing despite his aching back. He scampered from the room, eager to be gone. He was amazed by Finch's good mood and happy to have been dismissed, but then he remembered that he hadn't been paid. Joseph Caxton sighed, hoping Finch would pay him tomorrow. For someone as rich as he claimed to be, he was known for being overly tightfisted with his money.

* * *

Lionel Finch remained in front of the mirror, the smile now gone. Oh yes, he would have a fine new coat, a coat to rival that of the king himself. He spat on the floor at the thought of the king. The king was a useless, spineless puppet of Rome; a sniveling sycophant not worthy of the throne of England. Given the chance, he'd bring the Inquisition upon them all, with heretics burning in every square like Roman candles and suspects subjected to thumbscrews and the rack. Wasn't that what those heathens did to good, God-fearing Protestants like himself? Lionel had wholeheartedly supported Monmouth's claim and would have been happy to see him on the throne, instead of his brainless uncle.

He had to admit that Everly had done him a favor. Had he

not come barging into his bedchamber that night, Lionel might have contributed to Monmouth's cause. He'd have been accused of treason and gone to trial with the rest of those unfortunates who were now either dead or deported. Good men, all of them, especially the Duke of Monmouth. Now England had no hope, no future. If that Catholic poltroon had a son, that'd be the end for all of them; with a Catholic succession assured, England would be lost.

The thought of sons reminded Lionel Finch of his own childless state and Hugo Everly's part in the abduction of his wife. The memory made him seethe with anger, his guts burning with humiliation. Everyone knew that Frances had left him, and they were all sniggering behind his back, and calling him weak for not being able to control a slip of a girl, that stupid cow. He'd see Everly punished for what he'd done, punished to the highest degree the law would allow. Finch smiled at the pleasant fantasy he so often had of watching Hugo Everly hanged, drawn, and quartered. What a joy it would be to watch him suffer as he died inch by inch, his body mutilated before his very eyes, his severed cock tossed on the fire.

Finch knew that most likely he'd have to content himself with a beheading, but that was nearly as satisfying. He would stand right in front of the platform, his eyes on Everly's face, smiling as the executioner swung the ax. Lionel Finch would be the last thing Everly saw before his life was extinguished, and then he would see to his mistress. Oh, what a pleasure it would be to spend an evening with her. By the time he'd be done, she'd wish she were dead. No one would want her ever again, not after he was finished. She would beg and plead for him not to hurt her anymore and tell him where to find Frances. Of course, he could petition for divorce on the grounds of abandonment, but he wasn't quite ready to divorce the little strumpet. She was his property, his chattel, and he would deal with her as he saw fit before he got rid of her for good. Oh, how she would pay!

The thought of what he would do to Frances once he found her was enough to arouse him, so Finch unlaced his breeches and went to work, panting as he envisioned the scene in his mind. It was a fantasy he'd had many times, but it never failed to turn him on. He watched himself in the mirror as he pleasured himself, the image arousing him further.

TWENTY-SIX

The convent looked much as it had when we'd visited in April, and after the heaving, overly populated, noisy vastness of London, the enclosed compound made me feel rather claustrophobic. I steeled my nerves against the feeling of panic and reminded myself that it was only for a week or two. Not being part of the order, I wouldn't be expected to participate in the routine of the nuns or attend the prayers, but perhaps I could help with some chores to show my appreciation of their hospitality and to help pass the time.

I made my way past the barn and the well in the center of the yard, avoiding a muddy puddle that still hadn't dried since it had rained a few days ago, toward Sister Angela's sanctuary. A pleasant smell of dried herbs greeted me as I knocked on the open door and poked my head into the little hut. A merry fire burned in the grate, making the hut appear welcoming and cozy. Sister Angela's face broke into a grin of welcome as she ushered me in, putting aside the pungent mixture she'd been mixing in her mortar. I sniffed experimentally but couldn't quite place the smell, although it reminded me of something.

"Mistress Ashley, what a surprise," Sister Angela exclaimed

as she wiped her reddened hands on her apron and motioned me toward the bench by the wall. "What brings you to us this time?"

"I'm afraid Lord Everly had a rather dangerous errand to run and felt that I would be safer here, especially in my condition."

Sister Angela's gaze traveled over my generous bosom and rounded belly, straight toward my hand which bore no wedding ring. I could see momentary disapproval in her blue eyes, but she quickly rearranged her features into a bland expression and congratulated me. "Is the pregnancy progressing smoothly?" she asked as she studied my features. "This is your first, is it not?"

"This is my second pregnancy; I miscarried some time ago," I replied, not wanting to go into further detail.

Thankfully, Sister Angela didn't ask any prying questions regarding the first baby and its parentage.

"Well, you look very well, my dear, I'm happy to say. How far along are you?"

"Close to five months," I replied, my hand going involuntarily to my belly as I caressed the child within. "I'd like to make sure the child is all right." I tried to sound calm, but there was a slight note of hysteria in my voice. I was terribly scared that something was wrong despite the vigorous kicks of my little tenant.

"Well, let's have a look, shall we? Do you have any reason to believe that it isn't all right?" she asked carefully as she beckoned me to the other room and indicated that I should lie down on the cot. "If you are nearly five months along, you should feel the child moving by now," she added carefully.

"Yes, it's moving. Some kicks are rather painful actually, but I lost the first one..." I muttered, suddenly very nervous.

"Come now, my dear; just because you lost one child doesn't mean you'll lose the next," Sister Angela said in a soothing tone. "Sometimes God and nature have their own reasons for terminating a pregnancy. You mustn't fret; it's not good for the child. Why don't you just relax, and I'll take a look. I don't have much call for my midwifery skills these days, but some things one never forgets."

I reclined on the cot and tried to breathe evenly as Sister Angela palpated my stomach gently and let out a whoop of surprise when the baby kicked against her palm. She checked my pulse, nodding in satisfaction all the while, then reached for a long wooden tube and held it to my belly as she listened carefully, her eyes closed.

"The heartbeat sounds good and strong, and the child is active. I'd say that everything is progressing as it should. There's no reason for concern."

I just nodded in relief, happy to hear that everything was truly well.

"Your pulse is steady, but you are a trifle pale. Perhaps after the filth of London, you can benefit from some fresh country air, peace and quiet, and wholesome food. Lord Everly did right to bring you here." Sister Angela gave me a hand to help me up and smiled at me gently. "And there's someone who'll be very glad to see you again."

"How is Frances?" I inquired as I got to my feet and smoothed down my skirt. I hadn't seen her as I walked through the compound.

"Oh, well enough, under the circumstances," Sister Angela replied, rolling her eyes. I assumed that Sister Angela was referring to the fact that Frances came to the convent to escape an abusive husband and a miserable marriage, but she had a look about her I couldn't quite read. "Frances will be in the kitchen this time of day. She likes baking, so Mother Superior put her to work making fresh bread for our evening meal. Frances helps me here in the mornings. She likes learning about the various uses of the plants. I must say that she has a natural aptitude for herbology. Perhaps she can take over for me one day—if she stays."

I was somewhat surprised by that statement. Frances had expressed her desire to join the convent, so I just assumed that she would remain with the nuns. However, six months had passed, during which Frances might have changed her mind. She'd been injured and terribly frightened when we brought her here in the spring; the isolation and peace must have seemed like a godsend to her at the time. Being fourteen, however, she was too young to sign her life away, no matter what tragedies had befallen her in the past. Perhaps she'd had a change of heart and would, at some point, be ready to go out into the world again.

I hoped she might. I had nothing against religion, but being a person reared in modern times, I couldn't easily accept the notion of someone just giving up their life and hiding behind walls; particularly if their decision was influenced more by fear rather than true faith. Sister Angela looked very content with her lot, as did most of the other sisters, but I'd noticed something in Sister Julia that I had also seen in Frances—resignation and defeat, not peace and acceptance.

"I'll go find her," I said as Sister Angela returned to grinding her compound. "And thank you for reassuring me."

"You are most welcome," Sister Angela replied with her back to me.

I made my way back to the communal dining hall and toward the kitchens at the back. The long table in the hall was already set; wooden bowls, spoons, and pewter cups awaiting the nuns who would come to eat after prayer. An open Bible rested on the pulpit, ready for whoever was doing the reading today.

The midday meal was in about an hour and a half, and the sisters were busy cooking, the kitchen filled with a haze from the oven that dissipated as the fresh air blew in through the open door. An appetizing smell of fresh bread and cooked vegetables wafted toward me, reminding me that I was hungry, as usual.

Sister Gregoria was stirring a large cauldron that simmered over the hearth, and Frances kneaded dough at the table, her cheek covered with a smear of flour. She let out a squeal of joy as she saw me and came flying around the table, nearly knocking me off my feet as she threw herself into my arms.

I had only a few seconds to register several facts: Frances was not wearing the black habit of the order or a wimple, nor was she as thin as she'd been when we'd brought her to the convent. She wore a loose gray smock, which did nothing to drab down her angelic appearance, and a kerchief tied about her fair hair. I held her at arm's length, studying her round blue eyes and the bouncing blond ringlets that escaped the confinement of the kerchief.

"Go on, have a word with your friend," Sister Gregoria offered with a kind smile. "I'll finish the loaves."

Frances grabbed me by the arm and dragged me outside, straight to the herb and vegetable garden behind the kitchens. It smelled pleasantly of growing things and warm earth, the sound of a droning bee lazily circling a plant making the place appear even more peaceful than it already did. There was a wooden bench near the wall, and we took a seat, turning our faces to the weak October sunshine.

"Frances, you look well, but I thought you might have joined the order by now, as a postulate perhaps. Wasn't that your wish?" I was glad to see that Frances hadn't taken her vows. She still had time to change her mind.

"I wanted to," Frances replied, giving me a rueful smile. "Mother Superior was giving me instruction, but then things changed."

"In what way?"

Frances took my hand and laid it on her belly. I hadn't

noticed it under the loose garment, but now that she had pointed it out, I could feel the swell of advanced pregnancy under the smock. The child moved deep inside, turning and rolling against my palm like a large fish in a pond, causing ripples on the surface.

"Oh, Frances," I breathed. Would this poor girl never be free of her husband? In this day and age, leaving a marriage was difficult enough, but to have a child at fourteen without any means of support or family to rely on was practically suicide. I couldn't imagine that the nuns would turn Frances away, but with the change in situation, her options were now altered as well. I wasn't sure what to say, so I just took Frances's hand and held it silently.

"It seems Lionel got the last laugh after all," she stated calmly. "I couldn't stop crying when Sister Angela told me I was with child. I begged her to give me something so that I might be rid of it, but she wouldn't hear of it. Said it was going against God to kill a child, especially one that managed to survive the horrible beating he'd given me that last night. This baby is a fighter, to be sure."

"When is it due?" I asked carefully.

"About two months. Just after my fifteenth birthday. I'm not looking forward to that, I can tell you." I could understand the girl's fear. Her own mother had died in childbirth, and she had been much older and had already borne a child before Frances. Frances was hardly more than a child herself, her body still that of a prepubescent girl despite the noticeable weight gain.

Frances laid her head on my shoulder and closed her eyes. I wrapped my arm around her, and we sat in silence for some time, each lost in our own thoughts. I had some questions regarding the future of this child but didn't want to upset Frances. She looked so young and innocent as she leaned against me, her rounded cheeks reminiscent of a baby, not a woman who was about to become a mother.

"Sister Angela has taken good care of me," Frances suddenly said as she opened her eyes and smiled at me. "She says she'll help me through the birth, but that's not what I'm worried about, not really."

"No? What are you worried about?" I thought that statement was just bravado, but Frances seemed surprisingly serene as she reached for my hand.

"Whether I survive the birth or not is in God's hands, but what I choose to do after is in mine, and I just can't face the decision. I've discussed the choices with Mother Superior, and she has been very kind and supportive, but, ultimately, the final decision rests with me."

"What choices are there?" I asked, wondering what Frances was referring to.

"If the child is a girl, I can just keep her here with me, although I wouldn't be allowed to take my vows. I would be permitted to stay, for several years at least, until I decided what to do. Of course, I wouldn't be able to stay indefinitely, and no child should grow up shut away from the world. What kind of a life would that be?"

From what Frances had shared with me, I knew she'd had a lonely childhood. Her father had had no interest in her; her brother had used her as a butt of his cruel jokes, and the only person who had showed her any affection had been her nurse, who was eventually dismissed, being no longer useful in her father's eyes. Frances had been married off at thirteen, and kept a virtual prisoner by her husband, who forbade her to leave the grounds, probably out of fear that she might befriend other women or catch the eye of some young man. She was so lovely that it wasn't beyond the realm of possibility that she would find love outside her marriage, something Lionel Finch would never allow.

"But if the child is a boy," Frances continued, "I would be keeping him from his inheritance. A son of Lionel Finch would be entitled to a vast estate and great wealth, but only if I take the child back to its father."

Frances didn't need to elaborate. I knew what taking the child back to Lionel Finch would entail. Not only would Frances be putting her own life in danger, but that of the child as well. I couldn't imagine that Lionel would welcome Frances back with open arms. He'd abused her viciously on a regular basis. What would he do to punish her for the humiliation she'd caused him by leaving? He might want the child, but I doubted he'd want the mother. It was a known fact that Lionel Finch enjoyed very young girls, girls even younger than Frances. He'd lost interest in her once she'd reached puberty and took out his frustration by beating her savagely—an act that empowered him and made it possible for him to get an erection. What would prevent him from killing her or abusing the child as a means of punishing Frances?

"Are you actually considering it?" I gasped.

Frances shook her head in dismay. "I can't go back to that man. He'll kill me for what I've done, but do I dare deny my son what's rightfully his? I would be condemning him to a life of poverty and insignificance. Lord Everly has left some money for me with Mother Superior, but how long will that money last? A few years perhaps, and the only way I could give my son any kind of future is if I provide him with an education or an apprenticeship of some kind."

What Frances wasn't saying was that the most logical option to her dilemma wasn't open to her. Most seventeenth-century women who'd been left on their own remarried within a short time, unless they had independent means of support, which was rare. Women like Jane had the option of staying single since they were handsomely provided for, but average women needed the support and protection of a man. Of course, Frances couldn't remarry as long as her husband was still alive, and I didn't imagine that she would find that particular solution very appealing. She'd never known kind, caring men, so the idea of putting herself at the mercy of some man yet again would be terrifying. Even if she chose to return to her father's house, she would be promptly delivered back to her husband, so she was truly on her own, with no one to turn to.

"Frances, I can't tell you what to do, but you must put your safety and that of your child before any other consideration. No amount of money will compensate a child for being beaten and abused." I drew Frances close to me as she sighed dramatically.

"I know, Mistress Ashley, hence the conundrum."

"What does Mother Superior say on the subject?" I asked, hoping the older woman would talk some sense into the girl.

"She doesn't. She says that the decision is mine to make, and that I should make it wisely. Besides, a male child would not be welcome at the convent past infancy. I would have to give him up or leave the convent and brave the world outside. And who would want him? Most people can barely clothe and feed their own children. Why would they want to take in mine, unless I was able to pay them for his keep?"

I could understand France's anguish. Life had not dealt her a very fair hand, and although she was being admirably stoic, I could tell that she was barely holding it together. What a decision to make for a fourteen-year-old girl who had suffered more abuse in her short life than most people could even imagine.

Frances suddenly sat up straighter and turned to face me, her eyes full of hope. "Perhaps I can go with you," she whispered.

I opened my mouth to reply, but couldn't bring myself to squash her hopes, not when she was so desperate.

"Perhaps," I said, knowing that I wasn't being truthful.

TWENTY-SEVEN

A gentle wind moved through the trees, carrying with it the smell of hay, pine needles, and the tang of decomposing leaves. Fall had come to Kent, and the riotous colors of the season, which were so breathtaking during the day, were nothing more than dark shadows overhead as Hugo leaned against the trunk of a tree and watched Three Oaks from his vantage point. The house had been named after the ancient trees that grew along the drive, their massive branches intertwining overhead and forming a tunnel that was striped with shafts of sunlight on fine days and blocked out the rain on inclement ones.

The manor itself sat on a slight incline surrounded by acres of sloping lawns with a gravel path leading away from the house toward a lake stocked with fish. Ernest had been a keen fisherman, and often invited Hugo for an early-morning fishing expedition. Hugo preferred hunting to the endless hours of boredom that fishing demanded, but had indulged his brother-in-law, if only for Jane's sake.

As he waited patiently, his mind turned over various memories of his visits to Three Oaks, trying to pinpoint the beginning of Ernest's illness. He'd assumed that Ernest's deterioration had been the cause of Jane's bitterness and melancholy, but he now knew better. It had set in long before her husband got ill, long before John Spencer had died of syphilis.

If only she'd confided in me, Hugo thought for the hundredth time as he shook his head at his own folly. What would he have done? Would he have challenged Ernest to a duel? Ridiculous. What would have been the point? To punish him? To kill him? And then what? Jane would have been left widowed and disgraced, since the reason for the duel would not remain a secret for long. It was truly amazing that with no media outlets or telephones, the news traveled even faster at Court than in the twenty-first century, if such a thing were possible. The rumor mill never stopped, turning faster or slower, depending on the happenings at Court at any given time. Ernest might not have been a courtier, but the stain on his reputation would still be of interest to those who lived on spreading scandalous tidbits.

How could he have known that Ernest preferred men when he had arranged the marriage between him and Jane? Hugo asked himself yet again. There were no obvious signs or rampant gossip. Of course, there were men at Court who indulged their homosexual tendencies, but although they were discreet, rumors still abounded. Yet, there was never a whisper of doubt about Ernest. He rarely came to London, but he was believed to be a good, respectable man; a family man.

An image of Ernest with a man penetrated Hugo's defenses and seared itself on his brain. He still couldn't accept it, couldn't believe it to be true, although he knew the facts.

Poor Jane. What had the knowledge done to her? Did she believe Ernest's proclivities to be somehow her fault? Did she believe she didn't have the power to attract him? There were those men who went both ways, but Hugo wasn't sure if Ernest had been one of them. At this point in time, it was irrelevant, but he supposed that Jane would carry the scars of her marriage for the rest of her life. But were they enough to turn her mind, to drive her to kill? She might not have pulled a trigger or added poison to a cup, but what she'd attempted to do to Neve was no less attempted murder.

All these thoughts made Hugo's head ache, and he turned to Archie, who sat on the ground whittling away at a stout stick with his knife, while the horses munched on tufts of grass between the thick trunks of the hundred-year-old trees.

"Are you ready to go?" Archie asked as he looked away from his handiwork.

"Not just yet. A few more minutes," Hugo replied, wishing it was more like a year. The thought of confronting Jane made him anxious and physically ill, but he had no choice. It had to be done, even if it might be one of the hardest things he ever had to do.

The moon rose in the sky, the thin sliver hanging over the darkened outline of the house. Hugo watched patiently as the shutters were closed, and the tiny flickers of candlelight became extinguished as the servants made their way up to their attic bedrooms for much-deserved rest. Only one room on the ground floor remained occupied, a thin shaft of light just visible between the closed shutters. Both Jane and Ernest used to have their bedchambers on the first floor, but Jane had moved to the ground floor next to Ernest's room once he was no longer able to navigate the stairs. She seemed to have remained there. Clarence's room faced the back of the house, which was fortuitous since Hugo had no intention of involving his thirteen-year-old nephew in the confrontation with his mother.

Archie cut his eyes at the rising moon but didn't say a word. He could understand how Hugo felt. His own meeting with his sister in April had not been easy. He hadn't seen Julia in over five years; had not had a word from her since she had just left one day without so much as a goodbye to him or their parents. She hadn't tried to hurt anyone, but she'd hurt him by just leaving. They had been very close, despite their age difference, and Archie had felt as if he'd lost a limb once Julia simply wasn't there anymore. Of course, Julia had her reasons, valid reasons, but it was still painful for all of them. They'd tried to help her, tried to heal the wounds, not that such deep wounds could ever heal. The world was a cruel place, and despite the Church's insistence that God was all about love and forgiveness, Archie had his doubts. What kind of loving God put his children through such agony? And to what end?

His thoughts were interrupted by Hugo, who finally peeled himself away from the tree and nodded to him silently, his profile nothing more than a dark shape in the shadows.

"Shall I come with you?" Archie asked, knowing that Hugo would refuse.

"No, Archie, you stay here and mind the horses. I shan't be long. I can't imagine that what my sister and I have to say to each other will take more than a few minutes."

Hugo unbuckled his sword and tossed it to Archie as he began to silently move through the trees. The house was no more than a half-mile from the tree line, but he had no desire to be spotted by a random passerby or wakeful servant. Hugo skirted around the back and approached the door leading to the kitchen on silent feet. He'd been to this house many times since Jane's marriage, but never through the servants' entrance.

The door was locked for the night, so Hugo carefully inserted the blade of his dagger between door and jamb and drew it up until the blade lifted the latch. The kitchen was dark, moonlight painting the hanging pots a silvery hue, and casting squares of pearly light onto the flagstones of the floor.

Hugo sheathed his dagger and walked across the kitchen and up the stairs to the ground floor. The house was as dark as a tomb, the shutters effectively blocking all light, no matter how feeble. The corridor was lost in shadow, but a glow of light could be seen at the end, Jane's door slightly ajar. Hugo stopped just outside, suddenly unable to go in.

He could see Jane sitting at her dressing table, a brush in her hand as she pulled it through her dark hair. The candlelight softened her features, and the ripples of hair around her face made her look younger and less severe, the faded memory of the young girl suddenly apparent in her aging face. She'd been a pretty little thing, a bit pensive for one so young, but intelligent and inquisitive. There was barely a trace of that Jane in the woman she was today. The once-full lips were now thinner and stretched into a taut line, and the eyes were guarded and speculative, not trusting as they had been when she was a girl. Of course, Jane had a right to be bitter and angry, having endured her share of suffering and disappointment.

Jane's eyes stared at her reflection, a look of consternation on her face as she mouthed something to herself, maybe a prayer, or perhaps the words to a song. She used to hum to herself as she brushed her hair at night, Hugo remembered, enjoying the rhythmic strokes of the brush and the nightly ritual that she preferred to carry out on her own, sending her maid away.

Hugo stood still, watching Jane. He'd burned with anger and a desire for revenge all the way from London, but now that he was here, he felt lost and helpless; his heart reaching out to the sister he'd loved since she was a baby, his mind unable to accept that Jane had orchestrated this deadly charade against the woman he loved, the mother of his child.

"Well, don't just stand there," Jane called out. "Come in and say your piece, brother. I knew you'd come sooner or later." She carefully replaced the brush on the dressing table and turned to face Hugo, her face no longer passive but filled with scorn, her lip curling in a way that made Hugo want to slap her.

Hugo pushed open the door and came into the room but refused to sit. He needed to speak to Jane from a position of strength, but all he felt was a raging confusion as he took in her disdainful look.

"Cat got your tongue?" Jane asked playfully as she smiled at him in derision.

A hundred arguments had raced through Hugo's mind on the way from the convent to Three Oaks, but none of them seemed to fit now, his bravado gone in the face of Jane's hostility.

"Why, Jane?" was all he could manage.

"Do you really wish to know?" she asked conversationally.

"No, but I need to know. I need to understand," Hugo replied. His head ached, and his heart hammered against his ribs as he looked at Jane, who seemed to be enjoying herself. He'd hoped to see some remorse in her eyes, but there wasn't a shred of regret about what she'd done, only triumph.

Hugo hadn't even realized that he'd clenched his fists, but Jane noticed and let out a harsh laugh.

"Go ahead, Hugo, kill me. You'd be doing me a favor, you know, but you won't hurt me because you don't have it in you. You never did."

"I ask you again, Jane. Why? Have I not been a good brother to you? Have I not looked out for your welfare and bowed to your wishes when you needed me to, despite my better judgment?"

Hugo was growing angrier, but he forced himself to be calm, to uncurl his fists and lay them flat against his taut thighs. He needed to hear what she had to say, even if it tore his heart out. Neve called it "closure," but Hugo couldn't imagine that any outcome of this interview could possibly close anything. It would open an even deeper wound, one that would bleed for decades, if he lived that long, and never ever heal.

Jane watched Hugo; her head cocked to the side and a slight smile playing about her lips. She wanted to talk; he knew that. She needed to say her piece, and she would, in her own time.

Hugo realized that Jane had been waiting for this moment, waiting to explain, to torment him. She needed to; just as sometimes murderers needed to brag about their crimes and did so from the scaffold. What was the fun in planning something diabolical if you couldn't tell anyone about it? Jane had been clever, and she wanted that fact known. She wanted him to admire her cunning, to get angry enough to make her feel victorious.

Hugo remained silent, waiting for her to speak. He wouldn't beg for an explanation. She'd disclose everything sooner or later; he could see it in her.

Finally, Jane leaned against the hard back of the chair and folded her hands in her lap. She was ready. She looked calm, but her voice was tight with tension; her words rehearsed. Hugo was sure that she'd made this speech many times in her mind, preparing herself for the confrontation that was sure to come.

"I made one mistake, Hugo. I gambled and lost, and it ruined my entire life. You, being a man, can never understand what it is to have your virtue compromised or to bring a bastard into this world. Had you had a child out of wedlock, you'd simply throw some money at the problem and accept the pats on the back from your cronies, who'd make bawdy jokes about the woman whose life you'd ruined and make you feel virile and powerful. For such is the fate of women, that one mistake can send us straight to hell."

"I did what you asked of me, Jane. I found you a suitable husband and a willing father to your child. I saved you from disgrace and heartache. Clarence could have been taken away from you and raised in some peasant's cottage, but he sleeps upstairs, loved and assured of his place in the world," Hugo replied quietly, trying to contain his anger.

"Yes, you did, and I was grateful to you for that, until reality set in. You see, Hugo, I spent thirteen years married to a man who never so much as put his arm around me. He married me and forgot about me, treating me as one would a piece of furniture or a servant. Ernest not only didn't love me, but he didn't need me, not even for the conception of an heir. I was his façade of decency, his greatest sleight of hand. So, lonely and desperate, I turned to the only man who was available to me, his secretary John Spencer. You remember him, don't you, brother?" Jane asked with a sneer.

She looked old and ugly when she sneered like that.

"He was handsome, charming, and only too happy to service a lonely girl who was desperate for affection. I gave myself to him wholeheartedly, thinking that I could perhaps salvage some shred of a life for myself from the ashes of my marriage. But no, that was not to be. 'I am a vengeful God,' is that not what it says in the Bible? Oh, He is vengeful, indeed. I'd found out that my lover was also the lover of my husband; a man so depraved that he couldn't be contented with only one sex. He went from my bed to that of Ernest and allowed himself to be buggered and had buggered him in turn."

Hugo felt himself grow cold at the harsh sound of Jane's cackle. He'd known about Ernest, but not about John Spencer's part in Ernest's, or Jane's, life. He'd liked the man, had spent time talking and drinking with him. John had been cultured, attractive, and an amusing companion; a younger son of a noble family that had fallen on hard times, a situation which had forced John Spencer to accept the position of secretary. How smug John must have felt, knowing that Hugo was utterly ignorant of his role in the household, of his tastes.

"Oh yes, Hugo," Jane continued, her voice rising. "I saw them together, and it was a sight that still burns on my eyelids every time I close my eyes. Ernest was crouched between John's legs, sucking his cock with a look of such ecstasy that it nearly made me sick. John saw me, you know. He winked at me as he spilled his seed into my husband's mouth, just as he had into my womb. And then he turned around, and Ernest took him from the rear while John stroked himself, moaning with pleasure, his eyes locked with mine all the while. He was enjoying himself, and enjoying my humiliation," Jane recounted, her voice full of feeling as she remembered the moment that had changed her life once again.

"I ran back to my room, believing myself to be cursed and now sufficiently punished. However, that wasn't enough for our Lord God. He wasn't done with me yet. I spent months on my knees praying for forgiveness, doing penance, hoping that I might find some solace in devotion, but that was not to be. John began to display symptoms of syphilis shortly after. I didn't even know what it was. I overheard the physician telling Ernest what would happen. I was aghast. And even more so when I realized that this was an infectious disease. John had infected Ernest, or perhaps it was the other way around, and then myself. We were caught in a triumvirate of sin, punished most severely, for the only future I see in front of me is an eternity in a graveyard."

"Are you certain?" Hugo asked, dread flowing through his veins at Jane's implication. "Have you consulted a physician?"

"Yes, I am certain. I'm losing my sight, my coordination, and I'm plagued by evil thoughts brought on by impending madness. So, to answer your question, brother dear. Why? Because the only thing in my life that's worth anything is my son; my son who's innocent of all sin and deserves the best chance he can get—a chance that you threw away again and again. You could have made a suitable marriage, had a place at Court, perhaps even on the Privy Council. You could have expanded our wealth and influence, but instead you chose to marry that brainless twit and then spent a decade mourning her." Jane was panting now, her cheeks a mottled red in the candlelight.

"You turned your back on your sovereign and involved your-self in this sordid plot to back Monmouth, and when you should have been safely dead, you got some rootless trollop with child and decided to marry her, disgracing our family even further. You don't deserve any of the wealth and freedom that you've taken so for granted as a man. You deserve to spend the rest of your worthless life repenting and drowning in guilt for what your carelessness has caused. I heard your witch is dead and buried in a pauper's grave together with your unborn bastard. Well, serves you right, brother. Now you know what it feels like to have the ashes of your life scattered all around you," Jane spat out. Her face was contorted with rage and her eyes blazed with hatred, forcing Hugo to take a step back for fear of throttling her.

"And Jem? What have you done to Jem?" Hugo demanded.

"You mean your secret bastard?" Jane barked with disgust. "Oh, I took care of him. He'll never stand any chance of inheriting anything. He'll be lucky to live to see ten, much less adulthood. No one, you hear, *no one* will stand in the way of Clarence's inheritance."

Hugo lunged at Jane and pinned her against the wall, his hand around her throat. "What have you done with him? Tell me, or as God is my witness, I will kill you."

"And condemn your precious soul to the fires of hell?" She was mocking him now, and Hugo pressed harder, watching Jane's eyes bulge.

"I sold him," she croaked.

"To whom?" Hugo roared.

"To a brothel. Some men have a proclivity for young boys, did you know that? Perhaps Ernest was one of them. I know your sworn enemy Lionel Finch certainly does. Maybe he'll be Jem's first customer."

Hugo slapped Jane so hard that a trickle of blood ran from the side of her mouth, staining her teeth and giving her a demonic appearance as she smiled at him, her eyes dancing with crazed glee.

"Go ahead, do it again," she taunted him. "Save me from a lingering death, brother. It's the last service you can provide for me," she hissed.

Hugo let go of her as if she were suddenly too hot to handle, recoiling from her in disgust.

"I came here seeking retribution, but I see that I'm too late. You are condemned already, Jane, and nothing I can do is worse than what you've done to yourself. Yes, our God is a vengeful God, and He's not through with you yet. Rot in Hell, sister."

Hugo turned on his heel and stormed from the room, his blood boiling with rage and remorse. There was some part of him that had hoped to find the woman he knew and loved, but all ties were severed now. Jane would die a lonely, horrible death, befitting an adulteress, would-be murderess, and despicable shrew.

Hugo practically ran down the hill, needing the exertion to purge the anger he was feeling. Some small part of his brain pitied Jane, but there was no room in his heart for forgiveness. Yes, she was going mad, but not mad enough not to know what she was doing or saying. That was still to come. Right now, Jane was using her illness to justify the murder of Neve and his child and the assassination of Hugo's character, all to satisfy her need for revenge against a brother who'd loved and cherished her and did everything in his power to help her.

Hugo stopped, bent over with his hands on his thighs, and breathed deeply until his heart began to slow, and his mind stopped racing like rats in a maze. He'd wanted to know why, and now he did.

Closure, he thought and let out a bark of laughter at the ridiculousness of the term.

Hugo finally straightened and strode toward the woods, eager to put the episode at Three Oaks behind him, if such a thing were possible.

Archie was still sitting on the ground, his head resting

against the tree as he slept soundly, but he jerked awake as soon as he heard Hugo's stealthy approach. Archie didn't ask anything, just sprang to his feet and handed Hugo his sword.

Hugo hastily strapped on his sword and mounted his horse as Archie did the same. It was late, but he couldn't bear to stay here, so close to Jane. They'd stop off somewhere for the night as long as it was far from Three Oaks.

"What now, Your Lordship?" Archie asked as he followed Hugo through the darkened woods toward the road into the village.

"Now, we go back to fetch Neve and return to London. We need to find Jem."

TWENTY-EIGHT

Liza stared into the murky contents of the cup and sniffed experimentally. She expected the decoction to smell terrible, but it had a pleasant minty aroma that reminded her of the country. Mavis had prepared the mixture and left her alone while she went about her work, promising to check on her in a bit. It was just past noon, and Liza had the rest of the afternoon off. She got one afternoon off every fortnight, and it was a time she savored. Normally, she went for a walk by the river or looked at shop windows in Cheapside. She couldn't afford to buy anything, but it was nice to be able to look and pretend that she was just being choosy.

Once, she'd even gone to the Tower to see the lions. Liza didn't have the money to pay the entrance fee, but she'd managed to catch a skinny alley cat that had been too feeble with hunger to put up much of a fight and used the cat to pay for admission. The lions had been an awesome sight. They seemed oblivious to the crowd gathered on the viewing platform, one just walking around and the other lying on its side and licking its paws. *That one is probably a female*, Liza had thought as she'd edged closer to get a better view. She'd never seen a wild animal before, and she had been shaking with fright as the attendant had tossed a few cats into the dry moat.

The lions had fought over the spoils as the cats tried to run away from certain death. Liza had nearly bit her tongue as the male lion swiped a cat with its paw, knocking it senseless before tearing it to pieces with its teeth, the blood dripping down its chin as it fed. The other cats were still alive, their desperate screams turning Liza's insides to water with pity. She'd turned and ran, unable to get the memory of the carnage out of her head.

Liza had been responsible for the death of a cat, but if she drank the mixture, she'd be responsible for the death of a child; a child conceived in love—at least on her end—and very much wanted. It wasn't until this moment that Liza realized that what she felt for this baby was love. She'd felt angry, betrayed, and humiliated, but it wasn't the child's fault, was it? It was innocent of any wrongdoing on its father's part, and despite what Mavis said, Liza felt it was a grave sin just to snuff it out. She knew many women did away with unwanted babies, some even after they'd been born. It didn't take much to smother an infant, but the thought made her sick.

Liza's mam always said that God had a plan for all of us; it was just that sometimes it was hard to see it while events unfolded. Perhaps this baby was part of that plan. Liza had always longed for a family. Of course, that family always contained a husband, not just her and a child born out of wedlock, but families came in different shapes and sizes; she knew that. Her own mother had been wed four times; the house full of children sired by different fathers. Every husband had died after a few years, leaving her poor mother heartbroken and financially strapped. Most of the children had left home by now and were earning their own keep, but there were still three girls at home, helping their mother by taking in washing and sewing.

Swirling the liquid, Liza looked into its depths as if all the mysteries of the universe would be revealed. It was now or never. If she waited any longer, the babe would start to move, and she would never be able to do it, nor would the mixture be as effective. It might not work at all.

Liza raised the cup to her lips, intending to take the first sip, but her hand shook, and she spilled some liquid onto her skirt. She lowered her hand and closed her eyes as tears of frustration slid down her cheeks. She couldn't do it. She didn't want to do it. She wanted this child; wanted someone to love and care for, who would love her back in return and not just leave her. Perhaps it would be a son who would look after her in her old age.

Liza set the cup down on the three-legged stool by her bed and leaned back against the cold wall. The tears had stopped, but the feeling of overwhelming misery stayed with her. Liza didn't often give in to self-pity, but she felt she'd earned a few minutes of feeling sorry for herself. She knew that the decision had been made, but that didn't mean she knew how she would manage.

If only she could find a way to earn some extra money; just something to put by for when the baby was born. Then she would go back to the country and try to make do. Of course, she'd call herself Mistress Norrington, and tell everyone that she was a widow. No need to subject her child to the stigma of being born a bastard. Perhaps she'd even go back to her mother, but she needed coin, and she wouldn't earn it by scrubbing floors and washing soiled shifts.

Mavis had said that the world was full of opportunities. Perhaps she was right, Liza mused as she poured the contents of the cup into the chamber pot. She still had at least five months until the baby came; something might turn up.

TWENTY-NINE

I found going from the teeming streets of London to life in a religious community to be harder than I expected. The whole compound consisted of a few buildings clustered around the yard, with its well as the focal point. There were vegetable and herb gardens, but those weren't meant for walks, only work. The nuns kept to a grueling schedule that began with Matins before dawn and ended with Vespers before the nuns finally went to bed. The hours in between were filled with several daytime prayers, meals, and work. Each nun was assigned several tasks which she performed mostly in silence. The order was not a silent one, but excessive chatter was frowned upon and viewed as a sign of idleness. I could see why Frances was so lonely. Being only fourteen and not one of the order, she needed someone to talk to and spend time with, especially since her dilemma was always on her mind.

I'd been assigned to the kitchen, since I had no experience of livestock or the physical strength to do the weekly laundry. The work was easy enough, but monotonous and repetitive, as was the diet of the nuns. There was porridge with bread for breakfast, stew or pottage for the main meal at noon, and bread with cheese and boiled eggs in the evening. I spent hours chopping carrots, turnips, and wild garlic after breakfast, and then several hours washing up after the midday meal and helping Frances knead dough for fresh loaves of bread needed for supper and breakfast. My arms ached from the strain, and my mind chafed at the boredom. I asked Mother Superior if she might lend me something to read, but all she had were religious texts, and, frankly, I would have rather read the most boring of computer manuals than someone pontificating on various verses in the Bible and their possible interpretation.

Since candles needed to be conserved, we were expected to retire shortly after supper which was around 7 p.m., unless we were attending Vespers. Thankfully, I'd been allowed to share a room with Frances, so we huddled in our thin blankets against the cold and chatted for hours in the darkness; both desperate for the comfort of the other's voice. I didn't think I could bear to speak of it, but I told Frances of my experience at Newgate. It was easier to share in the dark somehow, the words melting into nothingness as the night settled all around us. Talking of it helped, especially since being in the dark monastic cell brought back the memories of that time. I had terrible nightmares, my ankles stinging when I awoke as if I'd been bitten by rats. I'd dream that I had awoken only to find that I was still in prison, and my escape had been nothing but a dream.

It took me some time to regain my composure when I woke, tears streaming down my face, my hands groping for the bedding and cot to make sure I was not on the floor of the cell. Frances would quietly talk to me to calm me down and reassure me that I was safe. The cell was so dark at night that it felt like a coffin, forcing me to throw on a shawl and grope my way outside for a breath of fresh air. Eventually, the feeling of being entombed would recede, leaving me freezing in my nightdress, my bare feet numb with cold. I desperately wished that Hugo would return for me, but days stretched into a week, and then nearly two with no sign of the men.

It was on one particularly dark night that I awoke, my forehead beaded with sweat as I dreamed once again that I was back at Newgate. My heart was hammering with terror, and my hands shook as I bunched up the coarse blanket and breathed deeply in order to calm myself. I thought that I'd screamed in my sleep, but the whimpering continued long after I awoke. I turned in the dark toward Frances. Her breathing was normally shallow as she slept, but still audible in the silence of our cell. Frances let out a low moan as her cot creaked in protest under her bulk.

"Frances, are you awake?" I whispered as I peered into the darkness.

"Yes. My belly hurts," she replied. Frances's breathing was labored. "I feel sick, and my back is quivering."

I got out of bed and felt my way toward Frances, settling on the side of her narrow cot, my face inches away from hers. I still couldn't see her, but I could feel the tension in her body as she convulsed and wrapped her arms around her stomach, desperate to contain the pain. I laid my hands on Frances's belly and felt the tightening of the skin as her womb contracted. These could be nothing more than Braxton Hicks contractions, since Frances was only about seven months along, but I couldn't be sure. In my time, we would just go to the hospital, but all we had at the Convent of the Sacred Heart was an elderly nun with some homeopathic knowledge.

"I'm going for Sister Angela," I said as I groped for my shoes.

"I'll be all right. Don't leave me," Frances wailed, but I was already halfway to the door.

"I'll be right back. Just keep taking deep breaths." *Much good it would do her*, I thought as I threw a shawl over my shoulders and pulled it tight to keep out the chill. But perhaps deep breathing would at least calm her. I found the door and opened it onto the misty night.

The moon was obscured by thick clouds, and a fine drizzle settled on my face and hair as soon as I stepped out into the open. The yard was slippery with wet mud, and I nearly lost my balance as I made my way to the other side, where Sister Angela's hut stood. Unlike the other sisters, she slept in her workshop, for fear of someone helping themselves to the medicines. A person unskilled in healing with plants might take the wrong dose or just use the wrong remedy altogether. Sister Angela kept the poisonous compounds on a separate shelf, but she still felt more comfortable in being on hand should anything happen. I briefly wondered if there had been a previous incident that had prompted this but put the thought out of my mind.

I knocked on the door and made my way inside, greeted as usual by the herbal smell of the hut. Dried plants hanging from the rafters caressed my face as I padded into the inner room, where Sister Angela's snores could be heard emanating from the blanket. The fire had gone out some time ago, and the acrid smell of ashes mixed with the pleasant smell of greenery inside the small chamber.

I gently touched her shoulder, but the sister didn't budge. It took several tries to finally wake her, during which time I could have poisoned myself and the whole compound had I really wanted to. Perhaps a lock on the door would be wise.

Sister Angela finally awoke and sat up looking confused, and more than a bit annoyed. Her gray hair was cropped short, and she looked older without her wimple. Being in her sixties, she was considered to be a woman of very advanced years, and she suddenly looked every one of them.

"Frances has a bellyache, sister. I think she might be in labor."

"Or she might have indigestion. It's common during pregnancy," Sister Angela grumbled as she got up laboriously from her cot and groped for her habit. "She's not due for two months yet."

The sister tied a kerchief about her head and followed me out into the night.

"I'm sure you're right, but she seems to be in terrible pain. Perhaps you can give her something."

"Hmm," Sister Angela huffed as she walked carefully through the mud. "Perhaps a decoction of mint might ease her. I need to make sure first. Light the candle," she ordered as she peered into the gaping black hole of the door to our cell.

I hadn't quite mastered the art of using tinder and flint, usually just lighting my candle on another flame or getting someone else to do it.

After several failed attempts, Sister Angela pushed me out of the way and lit the candle in one go before turning her attention to Frances, who was writhing in pain on her cot. Her face was a ghostly pale in the dim corner until Sister Angela moved the candle. Frances looked terrified; her pupils dilated just as they had been when I'd first met her and learned of her husband's wish that she use belladonna drops in her eyes. There was no belladonna now—just fear.

"There now, ducky," the nun said softly as she put her hands on Frances's belly. "It will all be all right. Let's have a look at you." She palpated the girl's stomach, then ordered her to lie on her back as she pushed a meaty hand between her legs. "Lie still for me now." Frances let out a pitiful squeak as Sister Angela pushed her fingers inside while probing the heaving belly with one hand. She looked thoughtful until her facial expression changed to one of concern. "Oh, Lord Jesus preserve us," she said as she extracted her hand and pulled down the shift.

"What is it?" Frances whispered.

I took her hand and sat next to her on the floor, there not

being enough room for both Sister Angela and myself on the cot.

"Your pains have started, my girl; you're dilating. Best if we get you back to my hut, away from the rest of the sisters. Get yourself dressed and help me, Mistress Ashley. I'll need you, if you are not squeamish."

"Don't leave me," Frances begged as I got up off the floor.

"I'll be with you till the bitter end," I promised as I kissed her clammy forehead. "Let me just get some clothes on. I'm freezing."

Together, we walked Frances to Sister Angela's hut, where we prepared for the hard work of bringing a new life into the world. Sister Angela got a roaring fire going while I went to the well for a bucket of water. I put the water to heat, while Sister Angela extracted some clean rags and a blanket from a wooden chest in the corner.

"Try to keep her calm," the nun said to me quietly. "She's too agitated and that might slow the labor down."

To say that Frances was agitated was the understatement of the century. She was in a panic—partly because the child was early, and partly because she was scared. Giving birth is frightening enough for grown women who are going into a hospital equipped with the latest equipment, experienced doctors, and handy drugs, but for a fourteen-year-old girl in labor in the middle of nowhere with only a nun to attend her —it's terrifying. The pain didn't seem to be too bad yet, but the terror had Frances in its grip, making her hyperventilate and shake like a leaf, which was making matters that much worse.

I left Frances for a moment and followed Sister Angela into the outer room for a quiet word. "Sister, have you ever delivered a child before?" I asked, wondering exactly what we were dealing with here. Giving out concoctions to relieve occasional constipation, diarrhea, or headache was not quite the same as delivering the child of a girl whose hips were no wider than those of a teenage boy.

"I have," Sister Angela answered a trifle defensively. "I've delivered more children than you might imagine, having been a midwife in my day, but I suppose you have every right to question me. I won't lie to you, Mistress Ashley; things don't look good for the girl. She's too young, too frightened, and too physically unsuited to the task at hand, not to mention the simple fact that the babe is two months early. I also don't have a birthing chair, which might have been helpful to her. It doesn't make the pushing easier, but it does offer some back support and something to hold on to, which helps when bearing down."

"Does the child have a chance?" I asked, already knowing the answer. A preemie might need an incubator to survive, not a drafty hut in the woods.

"I have seen premature children survive, but their chances are not good. It all depends on the child itself and how long it takes to bring it into the world. A long labor might rob it of its strength and make it more vulnerable than it already is. It's in God's hands now." The old nun rummaged along a shelf, searching for something. "Aha!" she exclaimed as she pulled down a bottle labeled "Valerian" and uncorked it. A strong medicinal smell filled the air as Sister Angela measured out several drops of the evil-smelling brown liquid into a cup of cider. "Here, have Frances drink this. Valerian root has calming properties and will help her overcome her panic. She'll accept it easier from you than from me."

I took the cup and held it to Frances's mouth as she drank and made a face.

"What is that?" she gasped in disgust.

"Just something to help you relax. Now lie back and count with me." I began to count very slowly until Frances stopped gulping air and began to calm down. She was still jittery, but the worst of it was gone now, leaving her exhausted and languid.

"Time her contractions, Mistress Ashley," the nun instructed as she threw another log on the fire and pulled the cauldron out of the flames to keep the water from boiling out.

"I don't have a watch," I replied, puzzled by the request.

"A watch!" Sister Angela exclaimed as if I said that I didn't have a spaceship. "Whoever's heard of such a thing? Just start counting as soon as one contraction ends and continue until the next one begins."

I began counting and got to three hundred by the time the next contraction took hold of Frances. "They seem to be about five minutes apart," I replied, wondering if that was good or bad.

Sister Angela nodded and sat down by Frances to examine her again.

"She hasn't dilated any further," she said softly, so as not to alarm the girl. "It's the same as before, about two centimeters. There's nothing to do but wait."

And, wait we did. By the time the milky light began to dispel the gloom of the night, and the first rays of sunshine burned through the mist, Frances was still laboring. I couldn't say how many hours it had been, but she'd dilated only about a centimeter more, and the contractions were four minutes apart. Frances was tired and cranky, her normally porcelain skin covered with a sheen of sweat and flushed from the heat of the fire.

"Is there anything you can do help her?" I asked the nun as we stepped outside for a breath of air.

"No. She's very frightened and that sometimes impedes labor. She needs to relax and allow nature to take its course, but she's holding on, striving for control."

"Perhaps another dose of valerian will help," I suggested. "Surely, it's worth a try."

"I don't want to give her too much," Sister Angela replied thoughtfully.

"Is it harmful?"

"No, but it might have the opposite effect and slow down the labor. We just have to wait. I've had cases where women were in labor for as long as a week," Sister Angela said with a frown of remembrance. "First-time mothers, most of them."

"Does that happen frequently?" Being in labor for so long was a terrifying thought. In my day, if a woman didn't deliver after a certain amount of time, the doctors suggested a C-section, which, by that point, the mother agreed to happily. The objective was to save the mother and child, but in this era, a cesarean was not an option unless the mother was willing to die to save the child. There was no way both would survive.

"No, but it does happen. Nature can't be rushed," Sister Angela said with a note of finality. "As a midwife, you learn that nature is in control, and your job is to assist rather than to take charge."

* * *

A few of the sisters, including Sister Julia, came by after Matins to see how Frances was getting on. Sister Julia sat with Frances for a while, talking to her softly, and telling her tales of Archie when he was a little boy and got into all kinds of scrapes. Sister Julia was normally so remote that I tended to forget she'd had a life before she joined the order and that the mischievous, red-haired Archie was her little brother.

I wondered if Sister Julia had red hair as well, but I'd never seen her without her wimple. She had a beautiful face, with wide blue eyes and a pert nose sprinkled with freckles, just like Archie. I couldn't help being curious about her. She had to be only a few years older than me. What had driven her to a life of seclusion? I suppose it was none of my business, but I didn't have much to occupy my mind, save fear for Frances, and by extension, myself.

I couldn't help but think about my own impending labor and where it might take place. Hugo had promised to find an experienced accoucheur in France, but we were a long way from France, and there was no guarantee that we would be able to leave England before the ships stopped sailing for the winter. It occurred to me that I might even have to give birth here at the convent, with the assistance of Sister Angela. Hugo would want me in a safe place, and this was the safest place we knew.

Thoughts of Hugo increased my anxiety. He'd been gone for nearly two weeks now. Of course, I had to take into account the time it would take to travel to Kent and back, but I was beginning to worry. I felt so listless without him, and so isolated. I had no way of knowing what was happening in London either. What if the trial date had been set for Max while we were away? I had to admit that Max was on my mind more than I cared to admit. After my own incarceration, I felt more of a kinship with him, although he wasn't forced to endure such vile and inhumane conditions as I had been. Gideon Warburton had made sure that Max had sufficient food, drink, and supplies, but I couldn't imagine that having wine and candles made imprisonment any easier.

Max, who was used to an easy, comfortable life, would be going mad with worry, especially knowing that he was all alone and that the odds were stacked against him. I'd never forgive him for his attempt on Hugo's life, but I did feel sorry for him—and for his mother. Lady Everly would never find out what had happened to her son if Max was unable to get back, and for her, that would be a fate worse than death. I'd seen the tenderness in her eyes when she looked at Max and couldn't begin to imagine the magnitude of her heartbreak. Had Max told her about the passage or what he was planning to do? Most likely not. Lady Everly was a no-nonsense type of woman, who'd probably just ridicule the idea. No, Max would slip away unnoticed, eager to explore the past on his own, and return when he was good and ready.

I sighed heavily as I considered the trial. Bradford had great faith in Gideon Warburton, but I had to admit that I did not. Hindsight is twenty/twenty, so I probably had a clearer perspective on the British justice system of the seventeenth century. Unless it could be proven without a doubt that Max was most definitely not Hugo, the outcome would be a foregone conclusion. Would Max really lose his life here?

If only there was some way to get him home, I thought as I turned to go back into the hut.

THIRTY

By midday, Frances fell into a fitful doze, waking up with a start with every contraction. They were still no closer together, which worried Sister Angela considerably.

I dashed over to the kitchen and brought some food for myself and the old nun, as well as some bread and cheese for Frances. She needed to eat something to keep up her strength, but a stew with rabbit meat and vegetables was probably not the best meal for a woman in labor. Frances took a few bites but couldn't eat any more.

"Perhaps she should walk around a bit," I suggested. My knowledge of birth was all theoretical, but just lying around for hours couldn't be helping.

Sister Angela seemed to consider this, and then allowed me to walk Frances around the well. Our progress was very slow, but the fresh air and the distractions of the outside seemed to help. The day outside was perfect. Blazing colors of fall burned just above the wall of the convent, and a fresh breeze moved silently through the trees, bringing with it the intoxicating smell of pine and wood fires from the closest village. The sky was cloudless, a vast expanse of blue that reminded me of a tranquil

Caribbean Sea. For all the rain in England, days like this were like precious jewels, there to be savored. Frances stopped every time a contraction gripped her but wanted to go on as soon as the pain passed, enjoying her escape from the stifling hut.

"Let's walk to the herb garden," she pleaded, pulling me along. "It smells so lovely in there."

I didn't see any harm in the suggestion, so followed Frances to the garden.

Frances sank down on the wooden bench, leaned against the wall and closed her eyes, turning her face up to the weak sunshine. She looked heartbreakingly young, and I felt suddenly angry that life should have been so cruel to her. She'd had her share of suffering, but I knew that no matter what happened in the future, it was far from over.

"I'm not scared anymore," she suddenly said. "Whatever is meant to happen will happen."

"What do you mean?"

"Don't you see, Neve; I have no say in anything that happens to me—never have. I didn't want to marry Lionel, but my father made me. Nor was I meant to come away with you and Lord Everly. I was meant to stay and face my fate. I managed to get away but found myself with child despite Lionel's beatings. I wanted to join the order but was prevented by my pregnancy. And now, whatever is meant to happen to my baby and me will just happen. I have no choice as I so foolishly believed I did. It's all been decided, hasn't it?"

"I don't believe that to be true. You can change your fate." I realized how patronizing I sounded the moment the words passed my lips. Perhaps in the twenty-first century, Frances might have been able to change her fate, but not now. She was a victim of circumstance, and her choices were practically non-existent.

"Can you?" Frances asked absentmindedly.

That was a very good question. I had tried to change Hugo's

fate and ended up creating a myriad of new problems that threatened to overwhelm us. Perhaps history was fighting back; trying to right the wrongs we'd done and steering us toward the conclusion that had been in place all along. Would Hugo end up dead while I was forced back into my own time without the child who was a bridge between the present and the future? The thought terrified me, but I resolved not to allow my doubts to overwhelm me.

"I'd like to think that we have free will," I said with more force than I intended.

Frances turned to me, her face scrunched in pain as a contraction seized her. "I've never known what it's like to have free will, and likely never will," she panted as she rose to her feet and began to walk slowly along the wall, holding on for support. "What happens today will change the course of my life, assuming I live through the birth," Frances said matter-of-factly. "Where's the free will in that? I'd like to leave here, but I'm in no position to support myself or my child. I want to go to France with you, but you're in no position to take me on, given your own set of circumstances, so I will probably remain here. So, you see, Neve, nothing I do is up to me."

My twenty-first century brain wanted to search for platitudes and assure Frances that all would be well, and everything would work out, but I knew that my words would be hollow. Frances was absolutely right, and by default, she was right about me as well. At this point, I had very little choice about what happened to me. I had no power to act, only to react, and the thought shocked me. I was as powerless as Frances, only I'd just realized it.

"I'd best get you back," I said as I steered Frances out of the garden. She didn't object, but there was a new look of determination on her face, which did nothing to reassure me.

THIRTY-ONE

Hugo stared pensively into the flames of the fire, watching as two rabbit carcasses sizzled over the flames, drops of fat dripping into the pyre and causing momentary explosions of burning fuel. The meat smelled good, and he was hungry, having had almost nothing all day, but his stomach felt as clenched as his fists. Hugo made a conscious effort to open his hands and lay them flat on his thighs in an attempt to let go of some of the anger. They might have stopped at an inn tonight, but he simply couldn't bear to be around people or hear the laughter and bawdy songs erupting in the taproom. He wanted to be alone, in the middle of nowhere, with only Archie for company. The young man always knew when to keep his own counsel and had left Hugo to stew ever since they'd left Three Oaks; understanding in an instinctual way that his master needed to work things out for himself.

Archie turned the spit and threw a few more twigs on the fire, before pouring Hugo a cup of ale from a stone bottle he brought from his saddle and taking one for himself. Hugo raised the cup in silent salute and drained it, enjoying the cool, sour ale as it slid down his dry throat. He'd spent the past twenty-four hours trying to reason out the events of the previous night, questioning his every act and decision since his father had died and left him guardian to his sister. Try as he might, Hugo couldn't think of anything he'd done to wrong Jane. He'd done his best for her, and although perhaps he might have made wiser choices in his own life, he'd always tried to take Jane's happiness into account.

Hugo momentarily considered the parentage of Ernest's daughter. If Ernest had never consummated his marriage with Jane, the same could likely be said of his first marriage. Or had he discovered his orientation after he'd married his first wife? Was it possible that Ernest had been in the dark until he married? Hugo doubted it. As a young man, Hugo had burned with desire. The swell of breasts above a bodice, a bare ankle, a sweet smile, were all it took to take his breath away. He'd been smitten with Margaret when he was fourteen, his mind tormenting him with images of her naked body until he could stand it no longer and would stroke himself until he found physical release from the torment. Surely Ernest had desires as a young man, but were they for men? Did Ernest get aroused by the sight of a groom with his shirt off or by a pair of strong thighs? He must have known, so Magdalen was most likely not his child. Thankfully, she was well married, so he need not concern himself with her.

Hugo shifted uncomfortably; suddenly aware of how much he missed Neve. He couldn't wait to hold her in his arms and bury his face in her hair, inhaling the scent that was so uniquely hers. He'd been worried about making love to a pregnant woman, but he liked the feel of her. Her breasts were bigger than before, filling his hands and spilling over in their abundance. And her body was like a ripe fruit, bursting with life. She was more sensitive to his touch, which made her like an explosive device with a lit fuse, ready to blow as soon as he entered her.

We will stay at an inn tomorrow, and I'll make love to her until she orders me to stop, he thought with an inward smile. Suddenly, he was ravenous.

Archie took the rabbits off the spit, tasted a piece to make sure it was well cooked and handed Hugo his share, along with a half a loaf of bread they'd purchased in the last village. Archie had barely said a word all day, and the silence was beginning to weigh heavily on Hugo.

"Thank you, Archie," Hugo said as he accepted the food and tore off a chunk of meat. He dispatched the little rabbit in record time.

Archie finished his meal and stared into the fire, his red hair a halo of copper in the glow from the flames.

"We should make the convent by tomorrow night," Hugo said, tossing the bones into the fire and holding out his cup for more ale.

"Aye," was all that Archie said.

"Archie, we need a plan. I've been turning the problem over in my mind, but I can't think of an efficient way to locate one eight-year-old boy in a city the size of London. What do you propose?"

Archie shrugged and set the empty bottle aside before answering. "I can't imagine that I have any better idea than you, Your Lordship. What have you been thinking?"

"The way I see it, we've got only the one choice. We visit every brothel in the city and ask for Jem. No one will be too eager to talk, but a purse full of coin has a miraculous way of loosening tongues. I suppose we should start with the finer establishments, since I can't see some rat-hole of a whorehouse paying much for the boy. Nor can I see my sister conducting a transaction in such a place," Hugo suggested.

"That's a sound plan, except for one minor detail. Going to the finer places might bring you face-to-face with gentlemen of your acquaintance. It's too dangerous by far."

"I have thought of that," Hugo replied with a frown, "however, I don't think many gentlemen visit brothels in the morning. Our best option is to pay them a visit just as they are waking up and are at a disadvantage. I can't bear to think of Jem in one of those places," Hugo sighed, his gut burning again. "He's so small and innocent. I can't begin to imagine the shock and pain..." His voice trailed off, but Archie took his meaning.

"He's a tough little blighter, and he's clever too. Let's hope for the best, shall we?"

Hugo just nodded, staring into the flames as if he saw the fires of hell.

Archie shifted uncomfortably in his seat across the fire, his eyes asking the question that had been on his mind for some time.

"No, Archie; he isn't," Hugo replied firmly.

"I'm sorry, Your Lordship, but you can see how people might assume..."

"Yes, I can, but Jem isn't my son. I made love to his mother when I was fourteen, or rather she made love to me, since I had no inkling of what I was about, but that association came to an end very quickly, once my father found out and threatened me with the strap."

"And never since?" Archie persisted.

"Never. There is absolutely no possible way that Jem can be my son. None. Can we move on now?"

"Ah, yes, as you wish," Archie stammered, chastened, but he wasn't convinced. Margaret had been a beautiful woman, with raven-black hair and eyes the color of the summer sky. She wasn't shy with her affections either. Archie had been only a child when Hugo was fourteen, but he'd known Margaret as a grown man—had known her better than he'd ever admit to Hugo. Archie had enjoyed his share of willing women, but few had been like Margaret. She didn't take men to her bed because she was lonely and needed a bit of affection; Margaret enjoyed her power to seduce. She was like a lioness that lived for the thrill of the chase and then played with her food before she devoured it. Archie imagined that a fourteen-year-old Hugo was probably enraptured with her, and Margaret would have played him like she played most men. She would have surrendered eventually and made him believe that he'd conquered her, when all the while she'd be the one doing the conquering.

There had been much speculation in the village once Margaret's pregnancy began to show, but everyone said that her brat was the son of a groom who'd taken off as soon as he'd found out that Margaret was carrying his child. He had a wife somewhere and wasn't interested in taking any responsibility for the child he'd so carelessly created. Archie had his doubts, though. Margaret had occasionally confided in him, mostly in bed when she was languid and sated, and she'd let it slip that Jem's father was a nobleman; a man of wealth and position. Of course, Archie assumed that she was referring to Hugo Everly, but perhaps she meant someone else, or simply wanted to adhere to the story that she was desired by men of power and influence. Margaret was too proud to admit that she had been ill-used by a mere groom.

Archie glanced at Hugo across the fire. He trusted Hugo Everly with his life and would give his own life in his service. If Lord Everly said that Jem wasn't his son, then it had to be the truth. Why would he lie? Hugo wouldn't be the first or the last man to sire a bastard. Everyone assumed that because Hugo took Jem in, he was acknowledging his responsibility, but Archie knew better. Hugo had been lonely for many years, despite having the occasional mistress. He longed for children of his own, and Jem filled a space in his heart that had been empty for a long time. Hugo might not have fathered Jem, but he loved him as a son and would turn London upside down to find the boy. Archie only hoped it was in time.

THIRTY-TWO

I woke up with a start as I nearly slid off the stool by Frances's cot. It had to be close to midnight, but there was still no sign of the baby. Frances was red in the face like a ripe tomato and panting like a locomotive. A low growl escaped from somewhere deep in her chest as another contraction rolled over her. She was too tired to scream, and she'd lost her voice hours ago.

"Please, make it stop," she pleaded as she looked at Sister Angela. "I can't anymore. I just can't." She sounded hoarse and desperate, but there was nothing either of us could do.

Sister Angela sighed and rubbed some oil on her hands before slipping her hand between Frances's legs again. She applied the oil to the perineum to make the birth easier once it was upon us and checked for dilation again, her face creasing in a smile.

"All right, my girl, I think it's time. I know you are worn out, but this is it. Mistress Ashley, get behind her and support her back. Frances, take a deep breath and push as hard as you can."

"I can't," Frances mewled as she shook her head.

"Yes, you can. On the count of three." Sister Angela took Frances's hands and locked eyes with her, counting slowly.

Frances gave it her best shot and fell back against me, panting.

"Again."

"No," she whispered, but Sister Angela was relentless.

"You're almost there. Just give it all you've got."

Frances took a deep breath and bore down, letting out a roar worthy of a lion. Her back pressed so hard against me that I could barely breathe, and I felt my own baby push back as it felt the pressure on my belly. Frances's legs were shaking with exertion, and her whole body was so tense that I thought her spine might crack.

"Again," Sister Angela commanded. "It's crowned. Now."

I was amazed to see the baby slither out on the third push. Frances slumped against me like a rag doll, her head drooping onto her chest as she tried to catch her breath. She was exhausted, but her legs were still bouncing on the cot, the tension still coursing through her body. I smoothed back her hair and held her as she threw her head back and rested it against my shoulder.

"Show me," she whispered as Sister Angela cut the cord and scooped up the baby.

It was no bigger than a loaf of bread, its little red face scrunched in displeasure. Sister Angela held the baby close to her chest, so I couldn't see if it was a boy or a girl, and quickly turned away toward the basin of warm water waiting on a stool by the fire. She cleaned the child with damp rags and wrapped it in a blanket to keep it warm. The baby didn't cry, but it whimpered and squirmed in its swaddling.

I carefully eased myself from behind Frances to allow her to lie down. Her eyes were closed, and her face flushed, but she was breathing evenly, probably already asleep.

"How is she?" the nun asked as she handed me the child and set about removing the afterbirth and cleaning Frances up.

"She's out," I replied.

I gazed at the little face. I'd never seen a newborn before, especially not a preemie, and I was amazed by how tiny it was. The baby opened its eyes just a fraction, and then closed them again as it yawned and settled into my arms as if it belonged there. I was glad that the ordeal was finally over for poor Frances. She was breathing deeply as she slept, her mouth slack and her damp hair stuck to her cheeks.

"Poor child," Sister Angela said as she pulled a blanket over her. "Her troubles are just beginning, aren't they?"

"Will it live?" I asked, gazing at the tiny bundle in my arms.

"I don't know. He's very small and weak, too weak to cry even. If he nurses well, he might have a chance, but the milk won't fully come in for another day or so. For now, we must hold him at all times and not put him down."

"Why?" I'd never heard of such a thing before, but the nun seemed confident in her methods.

"Babies are born with a survival instinct, but sometimes that's not enough. He needs our warmth and a sense of physical connection. He will draw the strength needed to fight to survive. I hope," Sister Angela added as she sank down on the second cot. "I'm done in."

"Why don't you rest, and I will take the first shift," I suggested, although I was bone-tired. I hadn't slept properly in over twenty-four hours, and I would have given anything for my bed, but the older woman looked near collapse.

She gave me a grateful smile, settled on her own cot, and promptly fell asleep without even removing her wimple or shoes, leaving me with the baby.

"So, you are a boy, are you?" I asked him conversationally. "Nice of you to finally show up. We were beginning to worry. I hope you like it here."

I studied the baby's face, curious to see whom it resembled. It was hard to tell, especially since both Frances and Lionel Finch were fair-haired and light-eyed. I imagined that Lionel had been a beautiful baby until his true nature began to emerge and hoped that this tiny child hadn't inherited his father's "finer" traits.

Actually, the baby's face resembled a Buddha with its round cheeks and slits for eyes. Sister Angela said that babies were usually puffy at birth and needed several days to recover. *I might not be here to see it,* I thought with a pang as I wondered once again when Hugo would come for me.

The baby yawned hugely, which made me laugh. "You think you're tired," I said to him as I sat on a bench in the corner and leaned against the wall for support. "Let's just take a little nap together, shall we?" I held the baby close as I allowed myself to nod off, desperate for rest.

THIRTY-THREE

It was fully light outside by the time I finally awoke. The baby slept in the crook of my arm, his tiny mouth forming an O and searching for a nipple in his sleep. He was a solid little weight in my arms, and I bent down and gave him a gentle kiss on his fuzzy head. In response, he opened his eyes and looked at me with an air of indignant accusation, assuming that I was the one denying him a breast. As I didn't comply, he let out a pitiful wail that woke the nun.

"Poor mite must be hungry," Sister Angela said as she adjusted her wimple and swung her legs off the cot. She looked better, if not well. The past twenty-four hours had taken their toll. She quickly splashed some water on her face and took a drink of cold cider from a jug on the windowsill, shaking her head to clear away the cobwebs.

Frances was still out, but Sister Angela gently nudged her awake.

"Time to feed your son, ducky," she said gently.

"My son," Frances murmured as she reached out for the baby. She stared down at it for a few minutes as if trying to fully comprehend that this thing was an actual human being. The baby stared back, still indignant, but curious. He must have recognized his mother's voice.

"Put him to your breast. You won't have much milk yet, but there's enough there to give him some nourishment. He needs to eat."

Frances obeyed and yelped in surprise as the baby latched on, sucking furiously. We watched in awe, happy to see him so active, but he suddenly stopped nursing and fell asleep, his mouth popping open to release the nipple.

"Must be enough for him for now," Sister Angela remarked as she reached for the child. "Now, let's get you cleaned up, changed, and fed," she said to Frances as if she were the baby. "You did well, my girl, well indeed, but you need to be ready to care for your baby."

"I'm tired," Frances whined as the nun helped her to her feet. Frances was shaky, but she allowed Sister Angela to help her wash, obediently put on a clean shift, and wolfed down some porridge brought from the kitchen by one of the sisters.

I was quite hungry myself, and still tired. I also felt emotionally raw. Witnessing the birth had been one of the most shocking yet miraculous events of my life, and I couldn't help thinking about my own impending delivery. Holding the baby had been indescribable. It was as if some fierce maternal instinct had been awoken in me, and I suddenly couldn't wait to hold my own baby.

Until now, I'd worried about the baby's well-being and development, but I hadn't given much thought to what it would be like to see it and hold it in my arms. I suppose I was too superstitious to think that far ahead and to allow myself to picture the child who was now growing inside me. I'd been so terrified of losing it that I blocked all thoughts of the future, refusing to think past the birth. Now, I felt a longing that was so intense, it almost hurt. I moved to pick up the baby, but Sister Angela stopped me.

"Go get some breakfast, and find your bed," she said. "I'll look after things here. You need your rest."

I nodded in compliance, gave Frances a quick kiss, and headed for the dining hall; exhausted and confused, but strangely euphoric after the night's work.

THIRTY-FOUR

I returned to Sister Angela's hut in the early afternoon, rested and well fed. Yesterday's weather had held, and I enjoyed the cool bite of October air as it caressed my face. Puffy clouds that resembled fat sheep floated overhead, allowing brief glimpses of the sun and casting shadows onto the ground. I felt an overwhelming need to go for a walk and stretch my limbs. I'd spent way too much time just sitting or lying, but there was nowhere to go, and I longed to see Frances and the baby. Perhaps, if she were up to it, I'd take Frances for a walk to the herb garden a little later.

Frances sat up on her cot, holding the baby as it slept peacefully. She still looked worn out, but her face was filled with joy.

"Have you picked a name for him?" I asked as I pulled up a stool and sat down next to her.

"I want to give him a strong name," she said, gazing at the baby. "Gabriel, I think, like the Archangel. What do you think, Neve?"

"I think that's a wonderful name. I'm sure he'll grow into it," I said, looking down at the tiny bundle in her arms. "Has he nursed?"

"Not much. My breasts are sore and hot, and the milk is starting to leak, but he seems too tired to suck for a long time. A minute or two and he's out."

"He's had a rough night," I said, hoping this was normal.

"Sister Angela has been pinching him," Frances confided in me as soon as the nun stepped into the next room.

"Why?"

"She says he needs to cry. It's good for his lungs."

"Does he?" I asked, curious at these methods.

"Only a little. He mewls like a kitten. Do you think he can see me?" Frances asked, frowning.

"Why wouldn't he?"

"His eyes are sort of unfocused."

"I'm sure he can see you, smell you, and hear you. Give him time. He's less than a day old," I reminded her. Frances was like any new mother, counting fingers and toes and checking that everything was as is should be. I supposed this was normal. I would be doing the same thing.

"He is, isn't he?" Frances conceded. "I keep forgetting. You know, I thought I'd hate him because he's Lionel's child, but I don't. It almost feels as if Lionel had nothing to do with him, and he's just mine. He's so small and helpless; all I want to do is take care of him," she confided.

"I believe they call that 'maternal instinct.' Shall I hold him while you rest?"

Frances handed over the baby and slid down onto the cot, her eyes fluttering closed.

I walked out to the bench and sat down, studying the little face. Gabriel had a pinched look to him that made him look like a worried old man. I ran my finger along the soft little cheek. It felt like a ripe peach, firm and a little fuzzy. Archangel, indeed, I thought as I smiled down at the baby.

Sister Angela came out of the hut and sat down next to me, her face creased with worry. She gazed at the sleeping infant in my arms and mumbled something that I didn't quite catch. She was clearly agitated.

"What is it?" I asked, suddenly worried myself. "Has something happened?

"I'd like to have him baptized as soon as possible," she said under her breath. "Just in case. I've spoken to Mother Superior, and she agrees. We should do it while Frances is asleep. I don't want to distress her by mentioning it, but I would just feel better if it were done."

I felt hot tears sting my eyes. There was only one reason why the nun would feel such urgency. I didn't ask any questions, just followed her meekly to the chapel, where Mother Superior was waiting. Normally, a priest or a vicar would perform the baptism, but under the circumstances, Mother Superior would have to do. The chapel didn't have a baptismal font, but I supposed any receptacle holding holy water would suffice. Three other nuns were in attendance, gathered by the altar. Everyone was subdued; their eyes downcast as I handed over Gabriel to Mother Superior. She took the baby, but her eyes remained on me since my agitation was palpable.

"This is just a precaution," she said softly. "The child might thrive, but should anything happen, it would distress Frances greatly if he couldn't be given a proper burial."

"I still think she should have been told," I replied, unsure of why I was arguing with Mother Superior. Her reasons were sound, but I felt as if something underhand were being done without Frances's consent.

Mother Superior acknowledged my statement with a nod and turned her attention to the baby. I felt as if I were being dismissed.

I suppose I had no right to interfere; I was an outsider in this community, and with my twentieth-century sensibilities couldn't grasp the importance of what they were doing. In my reality, everyone received a proper burial, whether they had been baptized or not. My modern-day brain simply couldn't grasp the injustice of denying burial in consecrated ground to an innocent child who had the misfortune to die before it had been baptized. It seemed cruel, not just to the hapless baby, but to its parents, who not only had to deal with the grief of losing a child, but also with the torment of knowing that their baby was denied heaven and would spend its days in Limbo.

I suddenly felt an overwhelming urge to leave and backed toward the door. No one paid me any mind, except Sister Angela, who gave me a scornful glance before turning back to the altar. I fled the chapel and made for the serene privacy of the herb garden, where I sank down on the bench and closed my eyes. I desperately wished that Hugo would come. The euphoria I had felt only a few hours before had been replaced by a feeling of dread, which seemed to leach all positive thoughts from my mind. I suddenly felt very tired, emotionally and physically, and wanted nothing more than to climb into bed with Hugo and have him hold me until I fell asleep.

The events of the past few months seemed to press down on me, making me realize just how dangerous a time I was really living in, and a wave of homesickness for the life I'd known washed over me. My hands instinctively reached for my belly, and I wrapped my arms around my middle in a futile gesture of protection. I couldn't protect my baby any more than I could protect myself.

A quarter of an hour later, I saw Sister Angela emerge from the chapel with baby Gabriel in her arms. A look of satisfaction had replaced the frown of worry on her face, and I felt admiration for her determination. She knew what she was doing, and I had to trust her. She had only good intentions toward Frances and her son.

I forced myself to get up off the bench and followed her.

Frances was still napping, but Sister Angela gently shook her awake and handed her the baby.

"Try feeding him again, ducky."

Frances's face lit up as she looked down at the baby. He seemed unaffected by having cool water poured on his head only a few minutes before and latched on to the nipple as soon as Frances pulled down her shift. We all watched as Gabriel's cheeks puffed out with sucking. He seemed to be working hard to get his nourishment. Frances sat perfectly still; holding her breath as the baby nursed. I knew she was praying that he would continue to suck despite the discomfort she was obviously feeling. Gabriel sucked for about a minute before his cheeks deflated and his mouth stopped moving. He seemed exhausted by the effort, and his breathing grew shallow as he fell asleep.

"Did he eat anything?" Frances asked Sister Angela, her expression one of concern.

"Enough to sustain him," the nun said as she turned away. I suspected she wasn't being wholly honest.

Frances just held the baby close as she pulled up her shift and leaned back against the pillow. She didn't seem up for taking a walk or even getting out of bed, so I left her to rest.

I was tired and felt a need to be alone for a while. For once, the austere cell didn't seem confining. I lay down on the cot and allowed my mind to drift, thinking back to the months when Hugo and I were in the twenty-first century. It was a difficult and uncertain time, but there were moments that stood out in my mind and made me smile. I concentrated on those, remembering Hugo's face when I took him to see a film, or his delight at seeing the twilit city of London spread out before him as we rode the London Eye.

I remembered the somber look on his face when we took a walking tour of the Tower of London and went down to the torture chambers containing the iron maiden and the rack. For most people, those items were just a gruesome piece of history, but for Hugo they had been real—the devices used in his time to break the spirit and the body.

I steered my mind away from those unsettling images and thought back to the night when he'd first told me he loved me. The memory made me feel happy, and I concentrated on that feeling as I drifted off to sleep, my mind and body needing a respite from the emotional roller-coaster of the past few days.

* * *

I woke up shortly before supper, my stomach growling with hunger and my limbs stiff with cold. I got up, splashed some water on my face, tucked my hair beneath the linen cap, and made my way outside. The temperature had plunged while I was asleep; the chill of the October evening reminding me that winter was just around the corner. I pulled my shawl closer about my shoulders and made my way to the dining hall.

Sister Julia was coming out just as I reached the door. She was carrying an earthenware plate covered with a linen cloth and a cup of ale for Frances.

"Would you like me to take those?" I asked. I assumed that Sister Julia would want to eat with the rest of the order and listen to that night's reading.

"You go eat," Sister Julia replied. "I'm not very hungry today, so I will stay with Frances and give Sister Angela a chance to eat in peace. She's more tired than she lets on."

"I will come and relieve you once I've eaten," I promised.

"Don't rush. We'll be just fine." She hurried past me, and I went into the hall.

I took longer than expected at the dining hall, since, after the nearly silent meal, all the sisters wanted a progress report on mother and child. It was strange to see them so animated, although a few hung back, obviously uncomfortable with the topic. I gave a brief report in lieu of Sister Angela, who never showed up, before making my way back to the hut. The elderly nun had probably been too tired to come. Her face had been crisscrossed by lines of fatigue, and she needed to rest. I suspected that she was eager to return to her normal routine of prayer, work, and doling out of the occasional headache or stomachache remedies. Hopefully, Frances would be up and about by tomorrow and return to our cell with the baby, but, of course, things would hardly be normal. Frances would stay at Sacred Heart at the very least until spring or summer, but then decisions would need to be made.

I was just nearing the well when Sister Julia erupted from the hut, tears streaming down her face. She was wailing like a banshee as she ran past me toward either the dining hall or the chapel. I couldn't imagine what might have caused such a reaction, but I was wary as I entered the hut. I was greeted by an ominous silence.

Sister Angela stood with her back to me, gazing out into the shadowy darkness through the small window of her stillroom. Frances sat on her cot, holding the baby just as she had before, her shift wet with milk stains and her face rosy in the glow of the fire. She didn't say anything, but the look in her eyes sent shivers down my spine.

I couldn't speak. I just stepped outside and wrapped my arms around myself, more for comfort than for warmth.

Sister Angela came out after me and motioned for me to sit down on the bench.

"What happened?" I muttered, although I already knew.

"Sister Julia was holding the baby while I was busy with Frances," the nun said. "She was singing to it softly, rocking it as it slept. All was peaceful," she added, as if not comprehending how life could change so quickly. "It must have been a quarter of an hour later when she stopped singing abruptly. I didn't pay her any mind, but Frances saw her face and started to cry."

Sister Angela wiped her eyes with her sleeve as she stared up at the star-strewn sky, which seemed so vast above this tiny island of humanity hidden in the woods. "He just slipped away quietly, without any fuss. I didn't think he would make it, but I was very hopeful."

"Why did you not think he'd survive?" I asked, needing to understand what it was that she had seen.

"I've brought many babies into this world, and after a time, you just know. He didn't cry, he was too weak to nurse, and there was a haze over his eyes, like a blind kitten. He just wasn't ready for this world. At least he went peacefully, knowing he was loved."

"Did he know that?" I asked through tears.

"Oh, I think so. That's why I said that we must hold him at all times. I didn't want him to die alone."

I choked back sobs as Sister Angela patted my hand. "It's probably for the best, but a shame that Sister Julia had to be the one who was with him when he passed."

"What does it matter?" I asked, feeling terribly angry with life, God, destiny, and whatever other celestial crap people usually blamed for tragedy.

"Sister Julia's had enough heartbreak to last several lifetimes. This was one that could have been avoided."

I didn't respond, so Sister Angela went on softly.

"Julia and I come from the same village, you now. I'd known her since she was born; delivered her, in fact. Her mother was my friend. They were a happy family, the Hickses, and Archie was such a rascal," she reminisced.

"What happened?" I couldn't help asking.

"Julia married very young. Couldn't wait. Her and Peter were so in love. She was a vision with her fiery hair and him so handsome with his dark good looks. I watched them exchange their vows and thought that there was hope for mankind as long as there was such love in the world." Sister Angela grew quiet, sniffling into her sleeve.

"Did he die?" I asked.

"They had six children in quick succession, five girls and a boy. Those girls doted on their brother. He had hair like a halo of sunshine while the girls all took after their father. They were poor but happy. It was five years ago now that some travelers passed through the village and stopped at the inn for supper. One had taken ill, so they asked for a room and stayed the night. The man was dead by morning, and the other two were fevered and had a sore throat. The pestilence spread like wildfire, and by the next day half the village was taken with the putrid throat. Julia's case was mild, but the children got it bad. She watched them die one by one. The little boy went first and then the girls. The oldest held on the longest, but in the end she succumbed."

I was crying hard now, unable to believe that such heart-wrenching misery was even possible. To lose six children in the space of a few days was more than any person could stand, much less a young mother.

"Peter was heartbroken; he hanged himself in the barn after the funeral. I think the only thing that prevented Julia from joining him was the fear that she wouldn't see her babies in heaven. She retreated from the world and just sat in her cottage, staring at the walls. Her parents came every day and forced her to eat and wash, but she barely acknowledged them. She was lost in her grief and unable to find a way back."

Sister Angela shook her head at the memory, as if trying to chase it away.

"I'd made up my mind by then to join the order. I was world-weary and ready to devote my life to Christ. It was a secret, but I thought that it might help Julia, so I went to see her. She just stared into the flames as I talked, but she must have heard me because she agreed to come. No one was to know where we'd gone since the location of the convent was to be preserved. I did tell her parents, however. They'd suffered enough heartbreak, losing six grandchildren and a son-in-law in one week; they couldn't lose their daughter as well without knowing what had happened to her. So, I brought her here with me in the hope that she might find some peace. It took her a long time, but she finally overcame the worst of the grief. To have that baby die in her arms is a terrible reminder," Sister Angela said with a sigh. "Well, I'd better see to Frances."

We found Frances in exactly the same position, holding the baby and rocking him as if he were asleep. She was humming softly, her finger stroking the little head. A faraway smile was on her lovely face, her eyes half-closed as she sang to her son.

"Let me have him, lamb," the nun said.

Frances obediently handed the baby over, but suddenly looked up, her eyes opening wide in alarm. "He's hungry. I must feed him," she said and began to pull down the shift, but I stayed her hand, my heart breaking at the look of incomprehension on her face.

"Frances, Gabriel has left us," Sister Angela said softly.

"Where has he gone?" Frances whimpered, her eyes wide with incomprehension. She seemed to be in denial.

"He's with God now, and with the angels."

"He's the archangel," Frances said, smiling through tears. "Why has he gone? Have I done something wrong?"

"No, ducky, you've done nothing wrong. The good Lord wants him by his side. He's somewhat short of angels just now."

The reality finally began to penetrate, making Frances shake uncontrollably as tears coursed down her cheeks. "Let me say goodbye to him properly," she wailed. "I need to say goodbye."

Sister Angela handed the baby back to her, and we watched with sorrow as Frances kissed the little face over and over and whispered words of love, before the sister finally held out her arms and Frances reluctantly surrendered her son for the last time.

I opened my mouth to offer some words of comfort, but none came out. A harsh sob tore from me, and I fled the suffocating hut, running for my life and taking refuge in the herb garden, where I wept until my throat was raw and my eyes so puffy, I could barely see.

THIRTY-FIVE

I sat in the herb garden long after most of the sisters had retired to their cells, and the chilly bite of the autumn evening began to seep through my gown and shawl. The garden was completely dark, but still I couldn't move, couldn't bring myself to go back to my cell. A gibbous moon hung in the sky, lighting up the thick clouds for brief moments in time as they passed over its bright face and moved on, disappearing into the inky darkness of the sky. Several candles burned in the chapel and cast a pool of light on the ground beneath the small window, but otherwise the compound was lost in shadow. The sisters either slept or prayed until it was time for Compline. News of Gabriel's death had spread through the small community, and I suspected that most of the sisters were praying tonight rather than just resting after a long day.

I barely looked up as a tall shadow materialized above me, gentle hands taking my own and drawing me into an embrace. He was so solid and warm that I just melted into him, allowing the tears to come again as Hugo held me and whispered words of comfort. I didn't even stop to question the fact that the nuns had allowed him inside the walls, but I supposed they all felt that on this day exceptions had to be made.

"How did it go with Jane?" I finally whispered. My voice was ragged and hoarse, and my question came out as barely more than a whisper, but Hugo heard me.

"Not well," was all he said, but I felt him stiffen against me as he pulled me even closer, nearly crushing my bones. My belly was between us, the baby kicking in protest at the imposition and Hugo released me, putting his hand gently on the bulge.

It was an innocent enough gesture, but I knew exactly what it meant when I gazed up at Hugo's face. Our time was limited, and my growing belly was just a reminder of that. Max was still in the Tower awaiting trial; Jem was missing, and we only had a few weeks left to find a ship bound for France, or we would be marooned in England throughout the winter—a dangerous proposition, to say the least, particularly if Jane was feeling as vengeful as Hugo's demeanor suggested.

"Get your things," Hugo said quietly. "We need to go."

"But what about Frances? I can't just leave her, especially not today." I gazed up at Hugo, whose face was silvery in the moonlight, his eyes hooded with fatigue. "Her baby died today," I added, suddenly realizing that Hugo hadn't even known Frances was pregnant, much less that she'd given birth or lost her child, but he didn't seem surprised. Someone must have told him already. "Hugo, she can't stay here," I cried vehemently. "There's no future for her here. She must have some say in her life, don't you see?"

"I do, but there's no future for her anywhere as long as she's still married to Lionel Finch. If he finds her, he'll kill her." Hugo looked deadly serious, and I felt a shiver down my spine. He was right, of course. Frances wasn't safe outside the gates.

"But we must do something," I persisted.

"Archie is with her now," Hugo replied cryptically.

"What does that mean?"

"It means that we need to go. I'll explain later." Hugo gently turned me around, slid his arm through mine and maneuvered me between the dark herb beds toward the dormitory. He couldn't go in but waited for me by the gate as I finally joined him, satchel in hand, but I couldn't leave. I couldn't just walk out on that poor girl who'd been through so much without an explanation or a farewell. I wished that I could stay for Gabriel's funeral, but Hugo's closed face told me that was not possible.

"I need to say goodbye to Frances," I blurted out as I shoved the satchel into Hugo's hands and ran toward the hut.

Frances was awake, her beautiful blue eyes unseeing as she stared at something above my head, her face puffy from crying. Sister Angela discreetly stepped outside to give us a moment of privacy.

"Frances, I have to go, but we will see each other again; I know we will. And when we do, it will be under happier circumstances." I pulled her close and enveloped her in a hug. After a time, her arms came around me and she buried her face in my neck, her tears wet on my skin.

"I know you must leave. I'm so grateful that you were here with me. We'll see each other soon," she murmured. "Archie promised to come for me. I will be waiting." I wasn't sure what she meant, but I just nodded and kissed her on both cheeks.

"Be strong, Frances. There will come a day when you will have choices."

"But that day is not today," she breathed, her eyes straying to the tiny bundle laid out on Sister Angela's worktable. "I would have loved him, you know, despite everything. God had no faith in me."

"I have faith in you," I said as I rose to leave. "Your story is only just beginning."

Frances gave me a weak smile as I walked out the door, wondering if I would ever see her again.

I was still enveloped in misery when Hugo escorted me up to our room at the top of the stairs in a tiny inn at the next village. There were only two rooms, and the other one was taken by a large family with several small children who squealed like a litter of pigs. Archie chose to bed down in the barn, despite Hugo's offer of our floor, realizing that after our separation, we needed some privacy. I wondered if he had seen his sister. Sister Julia had come undone after the death of baby Gabriel and shut herself in her cell, pleading for privacy. Archie hadn't said a word to either of us, but he would have understood what Julia was going through. He'd lost his nieces and nephew as well as a brother-in-law five years ago, and he'd lost his sister.

I ate my dinner without tasting what I was chewing, quickly undressed, and climbed into bed thankful that the children next door had finally settled down. Hugo blew out the candle and got in next to me. I didn't protest as he reached for me, nor did I actively participate. I was too numb after the events of the day. Hugo understood. He kissed me and caressed me until I finally began to reawaken, to welcome his touch. Only then did he push my legs apart and take me, rocking me gently and silently, like a ghost who wanted to possess me. I wrapped my legs around him, urging him to go deeper, to touch my soul. I cried out softly as I finally let go of my grief and restraint and allowed him to carry me along with him to a shattering physical release.

I didn't let him go as he rested his head on my shoulder, his breathing shallow as his heart slowed down in time to my own. We didn't speak, but eventually fell asleep in each other's arms.

THIRTY-SIX
OCTOBER 2013

Surrey, England

Stella Harding adjusted the blanket around the prone form of Lady Naomi Everly and stepped quietly from the ground-floor room she'd prepared in anticipation of her mistress's homecoming. The two orderlies who'd brought her from the hospital had already departed in the ambulance, leaving Stella alone. She walked slowly to the kitchen, put the kettle on to boil, and took out her favorite teacup and saucer. There were a few biscuits in the tin, and she arranged them on the plate, eager for a little bit of normalcy after the past week. She'd known as soon as she found Naomi on the sofa that things were dire but had still harbored some hope that she might rally. After a week in the hospital, the prognosis wasn't hopeful.

Stella poured herself a cup of tea, added a splash of milk, and dunked a biscuit in the cup, just as she had done every day for the past twenty-five years of working at Everly Manor. She liked her elevenses. It was a time to take a break and have a cuppa before starting on lunch. She wouldn't be preparing lunch today. Lady Everly couldn't take any solid food, so Stella would feed her some lukewarm broth through a straw. Naomi wasn't able to speak, but she occasionally moaned something that sounded like 'Max,' which nearly broke Stella's heart.

She was just finishing her tea when she heard the crunch of wheels on gravel as a silver Mercedes pulled up to the house. Dr. David Lomax emerged from the car, his medical bag in hand as he jogged up the steps to the front door. Stella put her cup in the sink, patted her hair into place, and went to let the doctor in.

"Hello, Stella," Dr. Lomax said as he kissed her on the cheek.

"Hello, David," Stella replied. She was suddenly very tired and glad to see a sympathetic face. Dr. Lomax was the type of doctor who never needed to work on his bedside manner. He was someone with whom patients felt instantly comfortable and put their trust in without question. Most modern doctors only saw patients at the hospital or in their private surgeries, but David still made house calls, and often simply stopped by if he felt his presence was needed. Stella had a sneaking suspicion that today's visit wasn't really meant for Lady Everly since she'd just been discharged from the hospital, but for herself.

"I'll just look in on Naomi," Dr. Lomax said as he walked past the housekeeper, "and then we'll talk."

"Would you like some tea?"

"No, thank you. How about a walk in the garden? It's a fine day, and you look as if you could do with some fresh air."

Stella just nodded. He was right; she'd barely had any time for herself between going to the hospital and trying to keep things functioning at the manor.

Stella watched as David disappeared into the room to check on his patient. She'd known David Lomax since she was a child. He had been something of a prankster at school and had sent her an unsigned valentine when she was twelve, gifting her with several

days of delicious anticipation until she'd found out that her mysterious valentine was none other than the class clown. Stella never
did figure out if the valentine had been in earnest, or just a joke
meant to humiliate her. She wouldn't have minded if David had
meant it. She'd had a secret crush on him since she was seven and
he'd generously offered to push her on the swing at the playground.

The clown had grown up and left for university, but not
before they had dated for a few months that summer. Stella still
remembered the warm kisses, sweet words, and the love they
made in the tall grass of the meadow, their bodies coming
together as if they were two halves of the same whole, a key
fitting perfectly into a lock.

Things might have been different had David not left, but by
the time he'd returned to Cranleigh, he had a medical degree, a
wife, and two children. They had remained friends, however,
and Stella had grown fond of David's wife. Clara Lomax was
too secure in David's love and her position to feel threatened by
an old flame, and Stella often came by the house for dinner or
tea and spent hours chatting with Clara. She had no resentment
or regrets. Life had its own plan, and nothing you did could get
in the way of that.

David finally emerged from the sickroom and motioned for
Stella to join him. The day was sunny but cold, so Stella
grabbed her coat, and tied a scarf around her neck for good
measure. She didn't need to get sick when she had Naomi to
take care of.

The garden was still in bloom, several rose bushes boasting
fragrant autumn blooms and flowers painting the beds in riotous
color. In a few weeks, the garden would be nothing but bare
sticks and shriveled up grass; but today, it was still a source of
pleasure.

David slid his arm through Stella's and steered her between
the flower beds toward an old wrought-iron bench beneath an

archway smothered with ivy. It was a pleasant spot, sheltered from the cool breeze of the October afternoon.

"How have you been, Stella? You look all done in," David said as he studied her pinched face.

"I am. I don't know what to do, David," she confided.

"Tell me."

Stella allowed her shoulders to slump as she stared at the ground. She needed to talk to someone, and David was the only person she trusted; he was the only one who knew the truth. It was time to share the burden.

"Max has been gone for almost two months now. No one knows where he is. The police have been to the house several times, but there's no new evidence. He simply vanished. Here one day, gone the next. At first, I thought that he might have just needed a few days away. Naomi had been grating on him, and he'd been generally agitated for months, ever since that woman left—Neve Ashley. I think he might have been in love with her, but the feeling wasn't mutual. You know how Max got when he couldn't have something he wanted. He became fixated on her."

"But you don't think he left of his own accord?" David asked, surprised.

"He had; that's what troubles me. You see, I was the last person to see Max before he vanished. He seemed very excited about something, hyper almost. He was mumbling to himself as he walked out the door, and his clothes were odd. I watched him from the window, and he practically ran toward the church."

"So, what do you think happened?"

"I haven't a clue. He simply never came back. At first, I thought it might have been suicide, but he just seemed so pleased with himself that afternoon. I can't imagine that he would take his own life. Something dreadful has happened to him, David."

"Yes, I'm afraid you're right. I'm sure Max's disappearance was the cause of Naomi's stroke," David said, taking Stella's hand into his own. "It would almost be easier if his body was found and she could have some closure. I can't begin to imagine the torment she's been going through since Max vanished."

Stella gazed over the flower beds, working up the courage to bring up what had really been on her mind for the past week. It seemed callous to speak of money at a time like this, but there was no choice; it had to be done.

"David, I can't look after Naomi and the estate without funds, but I have no access to the accounts. You said yourself that Naomi needs round-the-clock care. I can't hire a nurse if I can't pay her. The employees at the museum haven't been paid, and although I've been able to put household supplies on account, eventually the accounts will have to be settled."

Stella turned to David, relieved to see understanding in his face. His brown eyes looked sympathetic behind his glasses and Stella suddenly crumpled. She'd held it together since Max's disappearance, but now hot tears ran down her face as she leaned her head against David's shoulder. He put his arm around her and handed her his handkerchief, allowing her a moment to cry.

"Stella, you know what must be done," he said quietly.

"Oh, David, how can I? Do you know what that would mean?" Stella exclaimed.

"Yes, I do, but you have no choice. Your secret must come out; you've kept it long enough." David took Stella by the shoulders and turned her toward him, his face stern. "Stella, you have been silent for years, have even lied to your own son, but you can't do so any longer. Max has been gone for nearly two months, which means that he's most likely dead. He is the last of the Everlys, and the estate will go to some distant relation. Your son is Max's half-brother. It's his birthright to claim the Everly estate and the title. We no longer live in the Middle

Ages; illegitimacy can no longer prevent a person from inheriting what's rightfully theirs. Now is the time to act."

Stella shook her head, her eyes downcast. "I'm so ashamed, David. How do I tell Naomi after all these years that I had a relationship with her husband and that Simon is his son? She'd always believed that Simon was the product of a short-lived reconciliation with my husband. She's trusted me, relied on me, and confided in me. How do I tell her, when she's incapacitated and weak, that I've lied to her all this time?"

"Stella, Naomi Everly is many things, but stupid isn't one of them. She's known that her husband had been unfaithful to her practically from the start. She'd seen him with other women. Roland Everly was not a man who was ever content with only one woman. He'd slowed down in his later years, but, as you know, there was always someone. I wouldn't be surprised if another child materialized now that Max is missing. You must tell Simon the truth and have him fight for his inheritance. He deserves it. You deserve it. You'd been Roland's mistress for twenty years, and what had he ever done for you? He used you under his wife's nose, made promises, all the while treating you like a servant and making no move to acknowledge his son."

David Lomax had never liked Roland Everly. Roland had been an entitled, over-privileged prat, much like his son. As the family doctor, David couldn't allow his feelings to show, but Roland was dead, and Max was most likely as well, so he could permit himself an opinion. David could honestly say that he loved his wife and enjoyed a happy marriage, but there was just that little part of him which had always carried a torch for Stella and wanted to see her happy. Stella had married in her late twenties and divorced her husband soon after, possibly because of her feelings for Roland, who took her for granted and gave her a lot less than she ever gave him. It was time for Stella to fight for her rights, and those of her son.

"Roland paid for Simon's education and bought him his flat

in London. Simon always believed that the money had come from my ex-husband, who died when Simon was ten. I told him his father had left a trust fund for him. Now he'll know that I lied to him his whole life."

"You still have time to make amends to Simon, and Naomi doesn't have to know. Simon is an investment banker; he'll know what to do to access the accounts if he can prove that he's next of kin. You have his birth certificate, do you not?"

Stella nodded. She'd entered Roland Everly's name on the birth certificate just in case she ever needed to prove that Simon was his son. Now the time had come. Simon was nearly twenty-five; he had a right to know the truth.

"Stella, Naomi needs to go into a nursing home. You can't care for her yourself; it's too much. She need never find out that Simon is her husband's son. To be honest, I don't think she has long. She might not live to see Christmas."

"And what if Max comes back?" Stella asked, still looking for reasons to keep her secret. After all, the body had not been found, and according to Detective Inspector Knowles, there was absolutely no evidence of foul play. What would happen if Max returned to find the housekeeper's son playing the lord of the manor?

David gave her a searching look, his answer clear. "Call Simon, Stella. It's time."

THIRTY-SEVEN

OCTOBER 1685

London, England

We arrived back in London a few days later to find the city abuzz with the news that the date for the trial had been set. Judging from the snatches of conversation and comments in the taproom of the inn, public opinion was wholeheartedly against the accused. No one truly believed that the man held in the Tower was anyone other than Hugo Everly, the common folk having already cast themselves in the role of judge and jury.

"'Tis no use pretending to be mad, is there?" one particularly loud patron exclaimed, holding his audience rapt with attention. "Not like it will save you from the gallows. He was mad, if you ask me, to side with that traitorous cur Monmouth, but he got his just desserts, as will this overprivileged lordling. And they should go for the ultimate penalty, shouldn't they?" he demanded of his audience. "No beheading like they did for Monmouth, gruesome as it might have been. I'd felt a twinge of pity for him for a moment there, but he'd asked for it, hadn't he, that upstart bastard? No, I say, give him the highest punishment in all the land—drawing and quartering for the traitor Everly. And publicly, too. We, the people of London, deserve to see justice done."

The crowd roared in approval as Hugo calmly drained his tankard.

"We the people of London are bloodthirsty and short of entertainment," Hugo intoned, "and we won't be denied a nice, bloody execution, not if we can help it."

Hugo was going for humor, but I could hear the bitterness in his voice. No human being could remain aloof when total strangers were crying for his blood. After his encounter with Jane, Hugo was close to the breaking point, and although he put on a brave face for my sake, I knew that he was just barely holding it together.

"Shh, they'll hear you," Archie hissed at Hugo, suddenly afraid for him.

"No, they won't. They are so in thrall of their own sense of judicious righteousness that they wouldn't hear a volcanic eruption, much less one man mouthing off at the next table." Hugo was livid, his color high as he rose from his seat and pulled me to my feet. "Time to retire, I think. I've heard quite enough."

I meekly followed him to our room. I got undressed and climbed into bed, but Hugo made no move to take off his boots or coat. He just stood with his hands behind his back, staring out the window at the darkened silhouette of the Tower, where Max was awaiting his fate.

"Aren't you coming to bed?" I asked.

"Not just yet. I couldn't possibly sleep," he replied without turning around.

A soft knock on the door finally forced him to stir. Archie didn't bother to come in but handed Hugo a bottle of brandy and left to find his own bed.

I sighed and turned away, leaving Hugo to find oblivion in

the only way he knew how. He needed something to numb him
in order to allow him to get some rest. Ordinarily, I would have
objected, but tonight I could understand. Hugo wasn't just
upset for himself; he was thinking about Max. The more people
believed that he was truly Hugo, the more dire things looked.

I had to admit that I hadn't given Max all that much
thought this past week. Hugo and I had been back in the seventeenth century for only six weeks, but it felt more like six
months. So much had happened in such a short time that I was
on sensory overload, unable to process all the feelings that were
threatening to engulf me. I was still consumed with thoughts of
Frances. I knew I hadn't had much of a choice given our circumstances, but still felt awful for leaving her the way I had. She
needed me, and I'd left her, alone and bereft to cope with her
loss. I knew the sisters would be kind to her, but she didn't need
religious dogma; she needed a friend.

And, of course, there was Hugo. Hugo, being a man of his
time, was not someone who liked to burden me with his fears;
he believed it his duty to protect me and keep me from the
worst of it, but I knew that his meeting with Jane had virtually
destroyed him. He didn't speak of it, but he didn't need to. The
pain in his eyes was so raw that it broke my heart. Whatever
Jane had said to him had been bad enough, but selling Jemmy to
a brothel was monstrous.

Then again, compared to the fate she had in store for me, I
should probably think her generous of spirit, especially if she
believed Jem to be Hugo's son. I suppose Hugo could accept
Jane's ire against himself, but her vicious treatment of me and
Jemmy left him shattered. The search for Jem would commence
tomorrow, with Hugo and Archie visiting brothels and asking
for information. I hoped that they could at least pick up a trail.

I tried to sleep, but couldn't seem to settle down, even after
Hugo finally came to bed and drifted off, his arm protectively

around my middle, his breath saturated with alcohol. My whole body vibrated with terrible anxiety, and I lay awake until the small hours, trying in vain to convince myself that somehow this would all work out.

THIRTY-EIGHT

Max stared with dismay at the hunk of boiled beef and turnips on his plate, feeling his stomach clench in protest. He was grateful for the better fare, to be sure, but his guts were in an uproar from the harsh food and lack of exercise. He hadn't been outside in nearly six weeks, the only fresh air coming in through the leaky windows. It was getting cold at night. He probably wouldn't have noticed had he been able to sleep. The past week had brought news of the trial, which was to take place on October 30. At first, Max felt a twinge of relief at finally being able to state his case. He felt confident of the outcome. Gideon Warburton had worked hard on his behalf, rounding up reliable witnesses, procuring evidence, and researching cases which might have a bearing on Max's situation.

But, in the dead of night when the prison was quiet, and Max fancied he heard the cries of other inmates, he wasn't so sure. He tried to tell himself that since the trial hadn't been rushed, and the lawyer had been given ample time to find evidence, it was a good sign; a sign of the judge's willingness to entertain the notion that he really was who he said he was, but fear niggled at him in the dark. He had no home, no family, and no identity in this time, so no one could verify his claims. Whoever his mysterious benefactor was probably had his own agenda, an agenda that could only involve the apprehension of the real Hugo Everly. For what would be the point of proving Max's innocence if not to see the real traitor brought to justice?

Max had never been a particularly religious man. He'd attended services with his mother, whom he tried not to think of, for fear of completely breaking down and flubbing like a child, but he'd begun to pray during the last weeks. In a place like this, in a position of complete helplessness, there was nothing but God, nothing but faith—something that had eluded him all his life. He prayed every night as he lay awake, straining to hear some phantom response from the Lord, hoping that his fervent begging didn't go completely ignored. He'd been taught to believe that God was loving and forgiving, an omnipotent being who saw into men's hearts and offered no judgment to those willing to repent. And Max had repented. He'd prayed for forgiveness of his sins, his vanity, his ambition, but, most of all, his attempt on Hugo's life. It had been a moment of insanity, an isolated incident of a man driven to protect what was his. Perhaps he'd overreacted, but surely God would know that. He was so sorry—so very sorry—for the lapse in judgment.

But tonight, Max intoned a different prayer. Over the past week, he couldn't shake the feeling that something had happened to his mother. He had no way of knowing that what he was imagining was grounded in reality, but he'd learned not to ignore his instincts. His mother needed him, and he wasn't there.

Max sank to his knees and began to pray, as a brazen mouse scurried to his forgotten dinner plate and began to nibble on the meat, thankful for the bounty.

THIRTY-NINE

Liza made her way from room to room, emptying chamber pots into a large bucket. This was the absolute worst part of her job; worse even than washing the rags that the girls used during their monthly flow and to clean themselves between clients. She'd emptied plenty of chamber pots in her day, but not after twenty whores and their customers. The stink was unbearable as the bucket slowly filled up.

Most of the girls were still abed, but they were so exhausted by the night's work that they barely noticed Liza's presence. They were sprawled on their beds, their faces puffy from drink and smeared with traces of rouge. In the garish light of day, they looked blowsy and grubby, their faces appearing much older than their true age. Liza couldn't help but feel sorry for them. Most of them would be replaced by younger girls within a few years and forced to move on to seedier establishments where the clientele was of lower class and the fee they'd command would be halved, their earnings meager.

Liza held the bucket with both hands as she made her way down the stairs, terrified of spilling the contents, which she'd have to clean up. The steps were slippery since a steady drizzle fell outside, and several people with wet and muddy feet had already been up and down the stairs.

Jack, the thug who manned the door and kept the girls in line, had done his morning check, making sure that everyone was accounted for, and no stray customers were still in any of the rooms, having fallen asleep from too much drink. Mavis was in the kitchen, kneading dough and occasionally stirring the porridge to keep it from burning. The girls would start getting up soon and wandering into the kitchen in search of breakfast. Madame Nelly was in her office at the back of the house, no doubt counting money, as she always did, tallying the takings and recording them in her little calf-bound notebook. Nothing much changed from day to day.

Liza made her way to the privy behind the building and dumped the noxious contents of the bucket before rinsing it out with water from the barrel. It was full of rainwater, which came in useful for tasks like these. Liza had just turned to go back inside when she saw two men striding toward the front door. Their hats were pulled low over their eyes and glistening with moisture, but there was no mistaking the determination in their gait. They looked common in their homespun, so definitely not gentlemen. "Long on desire, but short on coin," as Madame Nelly always said about the numerous clients she was forced to turn away. Perhaps they thought they could pay less in the morning.

Liza was just about to turn away when something about the younger man caught her eye. She pressed herself against the wall and stared at the men. The older one had his face down, but the younger one looked up, confirming her suspicions. Archie Hicks. Liza would know him anywhere. Archie was a good lad who'd always been kind to her when she worked at Everly Manor.

She was just about to call out to him when the other man lifted his face. Liza's heart began to hammer wildly against her ribs, and she pressed deeper into the shadows, watching. The man had light hair and blue eyes, but there was no mistaking Hugo Everly. She'd know him anywhere, in any guise. She'd loved him once, had shared his bed. Liza had no idea what Hugo had done to alter his appearance; perhaps his woman had bewitched him. She'd heard Jane Hiddleston ranting and raving about her, calling her a witch, and asking God to smite her down. Perhaps she hadn't been as deranged as Liza had imagined her to be.

Mavis opened the door, her round face full of surprise at seeing customers at such an hour. "I'm sorry, gentlemen, but we are still closed," she said, not without sympathy. "Come back in the evening, if ye will."

"We are not here for the usual reason, mistress," the older man said.

Liza held her breath as his voice washed over her. It was him, definitely him.

"We are looking for a young boy who might have come here sometime in June. His name is Jeremiah. He's eight."

"I don't know of any Jeremiah," Mavis replied. "There are no boys here, only whores and several servants. If someone told ye he was here, they was mistaken." Mavis looked so earnest that the men didn't bother to question her further, just tipped their hats and turned to leave.

They were looking for Jem. Why? What had happened to him, and why would they think that he was in a brothel? Liza wondered as she watched the men walk away. Jem had still been at Everly Manor when Jane Hiddleston had dismissed her in June. Liza felt a pang of pity for the boy. He was a sweet lad; she couldn't deny that. He'd always given her a hand when she needed it and had delivered messages from her to Captain Norrington and back. Liza brushed away a tear with the back of her hand. She was very emotional these days.

The thought of something happening to Jem made her

think of her own baby, and what might happen to it if she didn't survive the birth. She couldn't allow herself to wallow in self-pity and fear, but the thought was always at the back of her mind. She had to leave enough money if she were to die for someone to at least deliver the child to her mother and not just leave it to die. She would leave a letter and some coin with Mavis and make her promise that she would see to the child should anything happen to her. Mavis would do it; she was very honest for an ex-whore.

Liza was just about to walk back into the brothel when she changed her mind. She draped her shawl over her head and trotted after the men, keeping a respectable distance. She'd get in terrible trouble with Madame Nelly, but she couldn't ignore this opportunity. If the man who'd come to the brothel was indeed Hugo Everly, then the man held in the Tower couldn't be, and that changed everything. This information could be worth a lot to the right person, and Liza knew exactly who the right person might be. She'd heard the talk. Lionel Finch had accused Hugo of kidnapping his wife and attempting to kill him. He'd be in London for the trial and might be willing to pay handsomely for learning the whereabouts of the real Hugo Everly. All she had to do was find out where Hugo was staying, and then she'd have something worth selling.

Liza kept to the shadows as she trailed the men from one establishment to another, until they finally gave up and walked to an inn in Blackfriars. Liza waited a few moments before poking her head into the taproom. Neither man was in sight, so they must have a room at the inn. She turned and fled, resolving to come back tomorrow to make sure that Hugo was still there.

FORTY

I stood on tippy-toes and tried to see out into the street. It was late afternoon, the city beginning to wind down as proprietors brought their wares into the shops and prepared to close for the day; the stalls wrapped up their awnings, and the servants disappeared off the streets to be at home in time to serve supper and then enjoy their own meal before cleaning up and retiring for the night. Darkness had already pooled between houses and in narrow alleys, but the sky above the rooftops was still ablaze with a glorious sunset; the violet heavens striped with blood-red ribbons of fading sunlight, the half-finished outline of St. Peter's black against the backdrop of vivid sky.

Yellow light from tallow candles began to illuminate windows before they were shuttered for the night, and the smell of bread and oyster stew wafted up the stairs from the taproom below. Thankfully, it was a weekday, so there weren't as many patrons baying for Hugo's blood, only a few strays who had nowhere to be at this hour; cradling their mugs of ale and gin and singing maudlin songs over the diminishing noise of the city.

Hugo had instructed me to stay inside, and I obeyed, terrified of venturing out on my own after my arrest. I felt safe inside the little room, although I had little to keep me busy. I had washed my undergarments and stockings, mended Hugo's shirt, and sewed up a slight tear in his coat, patched a hole in Archie's spare doublet and darned his hose, yet still time weighed heavily on my hands. It was now too dark to sew, not that I had any sewing left to do, so I just looked out the window, hoping to catch a glimpse of the men returning from another day of searching.

They'd been at it for days, coming back later and later every day since they went farther afield, but there was no news of Jem. The women at the brothels just shrugged, telling Hugo that few places had an interest in small boys, unless they were taken on for domestic tasks and the running of errands, but no one had any need to buy a child. There were plenty of orphans to be had for free, who would be only too happy of a place to sleep and scraps to eat in an establishment filled with women who were kind to the children despite their chosen profession.

Archie was usually angry and tired by the time they returned, but Hugo was withdrawn and silent, blaming himself relentlessly for Jem's fate and vowing to find him no matter what it took. I'd stopped asking after a few days, knowing that they had nothing to report. I could tell everything I needed to know from their tired faces and the sag of disappointment in their shoulders as they came in.

I finally left my post by the window and sat down on the bed. I was hungry but wouldn't go down to eat until the men returned. For one, I was scared, and for another, I felt guilty eating while they were out there hunting for a missing child.

One piece of good news was that Bradford Nash was back in London for the trial. He'd received a summons, as had several other people whose presence would be required.

I couldn't see the outline of the Tower from this room, but I was acutely aware of its forbidding façade, rising above the river; a silent reminder of the power of the Crown and all the innocent—and not so innocent—people who'd been incarcerated there and lost their lives. People still recounted with glee the execution of Monmouth, and I shuddered with the memory of that account, knowing that Monmouth's beheading was an example of brutality that still lived on in the memory of the British people.

I jumped up as I heard twin sets of footsteps on the stair, followed by a soft knock.

"It's us, love. Open up," Hugo's voice came from the corridor.

I unlocked the door and let the men inside.

"Why are you sitting in the dark?" Hugo asked as he went about the complicated task of lighting the candle. He seemed, for lack of a better word, lighter, as did Archie. Not cheerful exactly, but not nearly as defeated as they had been for the past few days.

As a perky little light flared into existence, Hugo sat down, pulled off his boots, and wiggled his toes. He was obviously worn out from walking all day, but he gave me a sweet smile and pulled me onto his lap.

"We had a small bit of luck today," he said as he kissed my neck and made me squirm away from his stubbled cheek. "One of the whores mentioned a place called 'The Orchid,' which caters to the needs of such gentlemen as are not interested in the charms of the opposite sex," he explained diplomatically.

"A den of iniquity, if I ever saw one," Archie chimed in with disgust, but Hugo just held up his hand, silencing him so that he might continue.

"It seemed a reasonable place to visit, so I sent Archie in, him being a pretty lad with those blue eyes and coppery hair. Any man would consider himself lucky to have such a fine-looking customer."

I was glad to see that Hugo was in a humorous mood.

"And???" I demanded. Whatever they had discovered was bigger than they made it sound. Hugo seemed determined to draw out the telling of the tale to torment me with curiosity.

"And the proprietor, who happens to be a young man not immune to our Archie's charms, did confide in him that he had purchased a little boy a few months since, but the wily devil had managed to squeeze himself through a tiny window and made off into the night before any money could change hands to offset the expenditure. The boy fitted Jem's description and was known only as Jeremiah. He was brought to the establishment by a lady of dark looks who seemed eager to be rid of him, selling him for a pittance."

I looked down into my lap to hide my dismay from Hugo. I supposed it was good news that Jem hadn't been abused or violated, but now that he was on the loose somewhere in London, or perhaps not, finding him would be like looking for a needle in several haystacks. I wasn't sure why Hugo was so optimistic but didn't want to ask and ruin his good mood.

Hugo lifted my chin with one finger and gazed into my eyes. "Yes, I know; finding him will be even harder now, but I take my victories where I find them. At least he wasn't hurt. Jem is a resourceful child. I've taught him a thing or two myself, and I know Archie had a hand in his education. Jem knows how to pick a lock, steal without being caught, and look after horses. He has the skills needed to survive, and that's a start."

"I suppose so, but how do you intend to find him?" I asked. The trial was only a few days away, and regardless of the outcome, we needed to see to our own future. Time was short, and our window of opportunity was shrinking with every passing day. Looking for an orphaned child in London could take weeks, possibly months, and there was no guarantee that Jem hadn't left the city to return to Surrey. He didn't have any family, but had I been him, I'd go to Bradford Nash for help.

"I haven't worked that out yet, but I will. For today, I will take what small joy I found and let it gladden my soul. Now, let's have some supper, shall we?"

"I'll go down and get it," Archie volunteered, but Hugo waved him toward a chair.

"Sit down, Archie. You've earned a rest. I'll get the food." Hugo didn't bother to put his boots back on, but went out in his stockinged feet, a couple of coins jiggling in his pocket as he skipped down the stairs.

Archie took a seat and stared into the candle, his face creased with concern. I'd gotten used to his silences, but something was on his mind, and although I didn't want to pry, I feared it might have something to do with Jem.

"Archie, are you all right?" I asked as I sat across from him and rested my chin in my hands. I could see the flame of the candle reflected in Archie's eyes, making it difficult to read his expression.

"Oh, aye. I just thought I saw someone," he replied, lifting his eyes to meet mine.

"Whom did you see?" I felt cold fingers of dread moving down my spine, terrified that someone had discovered our whereabouts, but Archie seemed more perplexed than worried.

"I've noticed the same woman several times over the past few days. I couldn't see her face clearly, but something about her seemed familiar. I suppose she works somewhere in this area and just happened to be passing, but I don't believe in coincidences," Archie explained.

"Do you think she was following you?"

"She might have, but to what purpose? If she wanted to speak to us, she'd had plenty of opportunity to do so." Archie shrugged, clearly confused.

"Have you mentioned this to Hugo?"

"No, I didn't want to ruin his good mood. Besides, I didn't see her again today. I will keep a lookout for her tomorrow, and if I see her, I will get to the bottom of this," Archie promised as the door opened and Hugo came in carrying a tray laden with a pot of stew, several loaves of bread, and a jug of ale. There was also a pewter cup of boiled water for me to brew some tea.

I ladled out stew for the men and took a bowl for myself. I was suddenly ravenous after hours of waiting.

Hugo and Archie talked of the coming trial, but I allowed my thoughts to drift to the woman Archie had seen as I tucked into my food. Perhaps we'd all become a bit paranoid over the past few weeks. What would this woman want with Hugo? She wasn't a noblewoman who might have recognized him from Court, so most likely she was just someone who lived or worked in the area. It didn't seem likely that she could cause him any harm, so I dismissed her as I took a sip of tea and joined in the conversation. Today was a good day, and I would not spoil it with fruitless speculation.

FORTY-ONE

Thanks to the tireless wheels of gossip that was seventeenth-century London, we barely had to leave the inn to learn the details of the upcoming trial, plus we had the invaluable input of Gideon Warburton, who was reporting to Bradford and keeping him abreast of the situation. It seemed that Max was in relatively good spirits, given that his fate hung in the balance, but Gideon was confident in his ability to prove his case. Bradford Nash and Jane Hiddleston were both highly respectable and trustworthy witnesses. It would have been helpful to call to the stand someone who could vouch for Maximilian Everly's identity, but Gideon was determined to work with what he had.

Despite my very vocal protests, Hugo insisted on having a meeting with Gideon Warburton the night before the trial. Having to sit and wait while Max's fate was determined would be torture, but Hugo needed to make sure that he did everything in his power to secure his freedom. We left the inn well after darkness fell, keeping to the shadows. Bradford had a closed carriage waiting for us a few streets over to take us to his house for this Council of War. I was worried about Hugo's safety, but Bradford assured us that Master Warburton was a man of discretion and utter moral conviction. He would never betray a client, or a friend.

Gideon had already arrived and was sipping a cup of claret, seated before a roaring fire in the parlor as if this was the most amiable of social occasions. He was still a young man, but his sallow skin, flapping jowls, and distended belly spoke of a man who wasn't in good health and likely suffered from gastric trouble. I could see the thinly disguised curiosity in his hooded eyes as he rose to his feet and extended his hand to Hugo.

"Lord Everly, a pleasure. I do hope you've found my service on your behalf to be satisfactory. I must confess, although much good it will do any of us now, that I, myself, was an ardent supporter of the young duke. England would do well to rid itself of the Catholic tyrant who sits on the throne, and replace him with a good, God-fearing Protestant who could lead this nation with dignity and unwavering faith."

"That is also my wish," Hugo replied smoothly as he withdrew his hand and accepted a cup of claret from Brad. Gideon Warburton had no reason to suspect that Hugo was actually Catholic, had wholeheartedly supported the "tyrant" currently on the throne and had done everything in his power to thwart the Monmouth Rebellion from within.

Gideon seemed to have exhausted his political agenda with that little speech and settled down to discuss Max's case, although I could see the confusion brought on by Hugo's appearance. Since Max was mistaken for Hugo, he'd expected to see a greater resemblance between the two men.

"I beg your pardon, your lordship, but Maximillian Everly doesn't favor you in looks or coloring. How is it that he was mistaken for your good self?" Gideon asked carefully.

"I was forced to alter my appearance to avoid arrest, Master Warburton," Hugo replied. "'Tis nothing but an illusion; a sleight of hand, if you will."

"I've heard of substances that might alter the color of a

person's hair, but your eyes are rather a startling blue," he exclaimed, leaning closer to gaze upon his client.

Hugo easily popped out a blue lens and allowed the lawyer a glimpse of his dark eye. "A bit of colored glass."

"My, how ingenious," Warburton exclaimed, getting up to see the lens for himself, but forestalled by Hugo's swift replacement of the modern-day object in his eye. Contact lenses would not come into existence for several hundred years, so they had to be kept a secret, even from Gideon.

"Shall we begin?" Hugo asked, leaning back in his chair and taking a sip of claret. He was clearly in charge of this gathering, so Brad retreated into a corner with his own drink and allowed Hugo to question the lawyer. "Do you feel yourself confident of proving your case, Master Warburton?" Hugo questioned, watching Gideon's reaction intently.

The lawyer, who'd been ingratiating and timid only a few moments before, seemed to draw himself up to his full height and meet Hugo's gaze with unflinching intensity. The law was his passion, and his knowledge gave him an upper hand. "I do. I have ample evidence and several credible witnesses who will swear to the fact that Maximillian Everly is not Hugo Everly. But there is a matter of some concern. I have only just found out that the judge appointed by the Crown has been replaced due to a bilious attack. George Jeffreys will now be presiding over the proceedings," he added meaningfully.

"Why do you find that concerning?" Hugo asked, suddenly tense. I could see that he was searching his memory for any mention of Jeffreys. Hugo had spent hours in the library while in the future, reading about the Monmouth Rebellion and the subsequent trials, but must have forgotten the name of George Jeffreys until he'd just heard it mentioned. There was a spark of recognition in his eyes as the piece of the puzzle fell into place.

"Were you not in London during the Bloody Assizes, your

lordship?" Gideon asked, surprised by Hugo's ignorance of the name.

"I'm afraid I was rather far away at the time," Hugo replied, referring to his sojourn to the twenty-first century. "I have heard about the trials, of course, but am not familiar with the details."

"George Jeffreys is rather—how can I best put it?—a bully. He doesn't have a reputation for mercy or compassion. He prefers to err on the side of extreme punishment," Gideon explained, clearly uncomfortable with enlightening Hugo.

So, Jeffreys was what we'd call a "Hanging Judge." I felt a shiver of apprehension as Gideon met Hugo's gaze.

"Jeffreys not only sentenced two hundred and fifty men to be executed, he condemned the rest to transportation to the West Indies to be sold as indentured laborers. Our case must be solid, which is where your sister comes in. People who have a slight knowledge of the accused might be mistaken, but a sister will be sure as to the identity of the man in the dock. I've had the pleasure of conversing with your sister, and she assured me that she knows the man in the Tower is an impostor, largely due to the fact that she likely realizes you are here in London. Eh, is she aware of your current whereabouts?"

"My sister knows I'm not the man in the Tower, Master Warburton," Hugo replied, avoiding the question. Given what had transpired, we couldn't afford for Jane to know where we were. "Will Maximilian be permitted to testify on his own behalf?"

"Prisoners are not allowed to speak in their own defense under the law, but I will be his mouthpiece," Gideon replied proudly.

I sat in the corner mulling over this information. I vaguely remembered that it wouldn't be until the end of the eighteenth century that William Garrow would begin to challenge the established British system and come up with the world-famous phrase "innocent until proven guilty." He advocated the adversarial court system while working at the Old Bailey, calling upon the cross-examination of the accused as well as the witnesses, who could be held in contempt of court or even arrested for perjury, as many witnesses were willing to testify to just about anything for payment.

Now, a century earlier, most individuals accused of a crime did not receive any legal help, nor were they entitled to a trial by jury. In most cases, it was the local magistrate who presided over a case, and his word was law. In a sensational case such as the trial of a traitor, a higher authority was called upon, such as George Jeffreys, who was held in high regard by King James, and would be elevated to the peerage and made Lord Chancellor, as we would discover in time.

"What do you suggest, Mr. Warburton?" Hugo asked. I could see the tension in his shoulders, but his voice was smooth and his hand steady as he cradled the empty cup, keeping his emotions under a tight rein.

"Rumor has it that Jeffreys has rather a taste for the finer things in life," Warburton suggested, eyeing Hugo to see if he took his meaning.

"You mean he's open to bribes?"

"Only very substantial ones, I'm afraid."

Hugo considered this information for a moment and turned back to the lawyer. "Master Warburton, I know that you will do everything in your power to defend your client, but should your defense fail, I authorize you to do whatever is necessary to ensure a desirable outcome."

"As you wish, my lord. Now, with your permission, I will leave you to your fine claret." Gideon Warburton rose a trifle unsteadily to his feet, bowed to Hugo and retreated toward the door.

Brad got to his feet, refilled Hugo's cup and patted him on the back. "I have the utmost confidence in Gideon's abilities," he said, which only signified to me that he was damn worried.

"Your friend's abilities might not be enough," Hugo countered, a look of consternation on his face. "If Jeffreys is as sadistic as his reputation suggests, we'd better have a substantial amount of money ready to buy him off. This is the last rebellion-related trial, and Jeffreys will not wish for history to remember him as being lenient or merciful, not at this late stage. He has a reputation to protect, especially if he hopes to elevate his position in the future. We must be prepared."

"I will make sure that Gideon has access to whatever he needs," Brad replied, nodding in agreement with Hugo. "I'm afraid you are right about Jeffreys. His last-minute appointment changes everything."

There didn't seem anything left to say, so Hugo draped the cloak over my shoulders and steered me toward the door. I was tired, and worried. Tomorrow would be a day I wouldn't soon forget.

FORTY-TWO

Liza waited patiently until most of the girls were occupied with clients, before quietly slipping out the back door. The night was dark, the moon obscured by thick clouds, which leached all the light from the sky. Here and there, a torch burned and cast a pool of light into the street, but there were long stretches of inky blackness.

Liza pulled her shawl over her head, partly for warmth, and partly to cover the large bruise blooming on her cheek. Madame Nelly had not been well pleased with Liza's unauthorized absences, and had made her feelings known very eloquently. She'd hit Liza until her teeth rattled in her face, but at least she hadn't been angry enough to turn her over to Jack. That would have been the end of her and her baby.

Keeping to the shadows, Liza hurried along the streets. It hadn't been too difficult to find out where Lionel Finch was staying the night before the trial. London was abuzz with news, and all one had to do was listen. There would be a heaving mass of people by the Tower tomorrow, waiting to learn the outcome of the proceedings, but Liza wouldn't be one of them, not if things went her way tonight.

She was relieved to finally see the sign for the White Hart Inn. It was a respectable establishment, within walking distance of Whitehall Palace; a testament to the fact that Lionel Finch considered himself to be an important man despite his lack of title or position on the Privy Council. According to the innkeeper, he'd taken several rooms, one for himself, and the rest for his men-at-arms, who were currently drinking and dicing in the taproom.

A burly man who looked as if he could squash Liza's head like a ripe melon came forward and eyed her belligerently. "What do you want?"

"I need to speak to Master Finch," Liza said, glaring at the man with all the authority she could muster. "It's urgent."

"He's not interested in the likes of you," the man replied, spitting a gob of saliva, which landed by Liza's feet.

"I have information about the trial that he'll be very interested in, unless, of course, you think you know best. Don't blame me if he guts you from chest to groin when he finds out you've turned me away," she hissed, hoping that the man was stupid enough to let her through. Lionel Finch had a reputation for violence, so perhaps her threat wasn't as empty as it sounded.

"Follow me."

The man rapped his knuckles on the door at the top of the stairs but didn't enter until he heard confirmation from Finch.

"This wench says she has information you desire," he said carefully, watching Lionel Finch for signs of rage.

"Let her through," Finch commanded.

Liza was surprised to see how insignificant the man looked. He wasn't very tall; his hair was thinning in the front, and he had a weak chin. Lionel Finch regarded her with his expressionless eyes as she stood before him. He must have been getting ready for bed since he wore just a shirt which was untucked from his breeches, and yellow stockings which made his skinny shins look like chicken legs.

"Well, what is it, girl?" Lionel Finch barked when Liza failed to speak.

"I have some information that could be valuable to you," she began, but stopped speaking as Finch let out a bark of laughter.

"What information could you possibly have, you stupid cow?"

"Information you'd be willing to pay for," Liza spat out. "Or do you not want to know where the real Hugo Everly is?"

"He's in the Tower, where he belongs," Finch replied, but he didn't sound certain. He was studying Liza, trying to figure out if she were having him on.

"No, he's not. But, if you're not interested in what I have to say, I suppose I'd better be going." Liza turned toward the door, praying that Finch would stop her. He did.

"Where is he? And how do you know?" he asked.

"I won't tell you where he is until you pay up. And as to how I know; I used to share his bed before that witch came along, so I'd recognize him anywhere. Seems he's here in London, searching for his little guttersnipe, Jem."

That seemed to pique Finch's attention, but he wasn't a man of business for nothing. Lionel Finch adjusted his expression to one of indifference and studied Liza in silence for a few moments before finally asking her to name her price.

"I want fifteen guineas," she announced, squaring her shoulders against Finch's gaze. Liza had thought long and hard about how much to ask for. She didn't want to reach too high, but she also didn't want to give up the information too cheaply. Fifteen guineas was a fortune to someone like her; a windfall that would allow her to live in comfort for the rest of her days. Of course, Finch would never just agree to the sum, but it was a starting point in their negotiation.

"I'll give you five, and only if your information is worth anything," he countered.

"Then I'm leaving," Liza said with disdain. Of course, five guineas was more money than she'd ever clapped her eyes on, but she was willing to walk away. This was her one chance, and she had to get as much as she could.

"All right, girl, I'll give you ten guineas, but if your information is worthless, I'll kill you with my bare hands. Is that understood?" Finch snarled as he reached for his purse. He slowly counted out ten guineas and laid them on the table in front of Liza. "Talk."

"Hugo Everly is staying at a small inn in Blackfriars called the Silver Cross Inn. He's been there for the past week at least. I've followed him several times to make sure. His whore and his man-at-arms are with him. What you do with this information is not important to me," she added, "but I want my money now that I've told you."

"And what's your stake in this?" Finch asked as he pushed the coins toward Liza.

"I was ill-used by Hugo Everly and dismissed by his sister, who threw me out without paying my wages or giving me a character reference, which would help me secure another position. I had to take a job in a brothel to survive. I won't spend the rest of my days cleaning up after whores; I have a child to think of," Liza replied. She had nothing to lose by telling him the truth.

"Carrying   a   bastard,   are   you?"   Finch   asked conversationally.

"I'm not the first, nor the last to be taken in by a lying cur of a man, but I will rise above my situation and make a life for myself," Liza retorted, color rising to her cheeks. She scooped up the coins and slipped them into the pocket of her skirt.

"I can have you thrown out of here without the money you

extracted from me, but I won't. You have spirit, girl, and I admire that," Finch said.

As long as it's not in your wife, Liza thought vengefully.

"Go back to your brothel, and don't be surprised when my man follows you. If your information proves to be false, you will pay dearly. Now go."

Liza turned and fled down the stairs. She heard Lionel Finch ordering his man to follow her, but she was already flying through the night, running for her life. Her pursuer might be strong, but he was clumsy and unused to running, especially down narrow, dark alleyways. She could hear him gasping for breath as he lumbered after her. She was getting winded herself, but she kept going, her feet landing lightly on the ground and making the minimum amount of noise. The distance between Liza and the man-at-arms was growing rapidly, so she began to look around for a place to hide. She'd be damned if she went back to the brothel now. If anyone found out, they'd take the money away, and she'd get a beating for leaving without permission. She just had to make it through the night, then she would be free. Her only regret was not saying goodbye to Mavis and thanking her for the friendship and help she'd given so freely.

Liza wandered the darkened streets until she came upon a church. The door was locked, but she hid in the church porch, pressing herself into a dark corner until she was invisible from outside. She'd wait until morning, then make her way to the city gates and hope that someone might offer her a ride in their wagon. She was going home, and she was rich.

Liza fingered the money in her pocket, amazed that she'd been able to get Lionel Finch to pay up. The coins were heavy, weighing down her skirt in a pleasant way. That's what it must feel like to have a full purse. Ten guineas was more money than she'd earn in a lifetime, enough to support her, her baby, and her mother for years to come. She might even be able to do something for her sisters, a modest dowry perhaps. All she had to do was make sure she didn't get robbed. If anyone heard the jingling in her pocket, they'd get suspicious, and she had no way of protecting herself.

Liza took out a coin and stared at it lovingly. It wasn't big, but still too big to swallow. She'd choke. She looked about her person frantically, searching for a place to hide her fortune. She thought of putting the coins in her shoes, but the soles were so thin, the coins might get pushed right through. Putting them inside her bodice was impractical as well. The coins might slide out. She needed a safe place, a place where no one would think to look should they have a mind to rob her. Liza swallowed hard as she thought of a solution. It was distasteful, but her fortune was sure to be safe. Liza lifted her skirts and pushed the coins one by one into her body. The metal was cold and hard, but she ignored the discomfort as she curled up in the corner and fell asleep, a small smile playing about her lips as she dreamed of the life to come.

FORTY-THREE

"You useless gob of dog shit," Lionel Finch bellowed. "I should make you pay me ten guineas in recompense for your unimaginable stupidity. How could you let that silly trollop get the better of you, Harvey?"

"She knows these streets, and it was dark," Harvey mumbled in his defense. "And we'd been drinking. I wasn't exactly steady on my feet, now was I?"

"You listen to me, you moronic lump of uselessness; you go to that inn, and you stay outside and watch until you see Hugo Everly, or you'll pay with more than a few coins. Am I making myself clear?" Lionel hissed, his eyes narrowed with fury. He was surrounded by morons; morons whom he paid handsomely for their services. He knew damn well that they felt no loyalty toward him; he wasn't the kind of man who inspired feelings of devotion, so he had to pay for them. But money couldn't buy good sense.

"I don't know what he looks like," Harvey protested, taking a step back.

"No, you don't, do you? But you know what Archie Hicks looks like. You diced with him half the night, if I recall. So, look for him. Everly can't be far behind. And DO NOT LET THEM OUT OF YOUR SIGHT!!!!"

"So, how will I keep you informed if I'm not to leave my post?" Harvey asked, perplexed.

"Not the sharpest knife in the box, are you?" Finch replied. "I will send Oliver there to find you. Now GET OUT!"

Harvey didn't need to be told twice. He shut the door behind him with a bang, leaving a furious Lionel Finch to pace the floor.

Lionel poured himself a cup of wine, drank it in one go, and slammed the cup back on the table. The trial was tomorrow, which meant that he had a decision to make. If the man on trial was not Hugo Everly, as he claimed, did it make sense to testify against him? What did it matter if he was released? However, if the accused were convicted in his stead, Hugo Everly would go free, which wasn't as straightforward as it sounded. Hugo would no longer be hunted, but he wouldn't be able to return to his estate or pick up the threads of his former life. Of course, Everly had enough money to leave the country and start a life some-place else, while someone managed his estate until he felt it was safe to return.

Lionel began pacing the small room, pivoting on his heel every time he reached the end. He would find Liza and kill her if she'd lied to him, but if she'd been telling the truth, then Lionel had been presented with a unique opportunity to get his revenge. If his theory was correct, then Hugo had no reason to remain in London after the trial.

No doubt he was waiting to hear the outcome and know how his own life would be affected. Of course, Lionel could just order Harvey to stick a knife between Everly's ribs and be done with it, but that approach lacked finesse. He needed Hugo Everly to know that he'd been hunted down and cornered, and he wanted to see the look on his face as he real-ized that death was inevitable, and he would go to his grave knowing that his woman would be left at the mercy of a vengeful enemy.

Lionel Finch stopped pacing and smiled. Yes, he liked that idea very much. There were a few details to be worked out, but the general plan was nearly fully formed in his mind. He suddenly lunged toward the door and ran down the stairs to fetch Oliver. Harvey was too stupid to handle this alone. He had brute strength and skill with a sword, but not nearly enough cunning to be trusted with something this important.

If this played out the way Finch hoped, not only would he get revenge on Hugo Everly and his whore, but he might get back Frances as well. Lionel Finch got a mighty cockstand when he considered what he would do to punish her for humiliating him.

FORTY-FOUR

The day of the trial dawned misty and gray; the city of London shrouded in a steel-wool blanket of thunderous clouds and chimney smoke, reducing visibility to roughly a few inches in any direction. The husk of St. Paul's looked as if it were wearing a periwig made of dirty cotton, and the usual morning sounds were muffled and distorted.

I pulled the blanket up to my chin, deciding to stay in bed a little longer. I watched Hugo pace the small room like a caged tiger but could offer him no words of comfort. The stage was set, and the players were due to start the performance at 9 a.m. Whatever the outcome, we had no power to interfere. Of course, Brad would fill us in once he got back, but even before then, we'd hear it through the grapevine.

There was a soft knock on the door before Archie materialized out of the dim corridor. "All right?" he asked, the question encompassing all manner of things, ranging from our general health to our frame of mind.

Hugo nodded absentmindedly, his mind miles away.

* * *

Max was somewhat taken aback by the manacles that were placed on his wrists and ankles for the short walk to the other side of the building. Even if completely unfettered, his chances of escape were nonexistent with soldiers stationed at every exit and various individuals milling on the green, their curiosity getting the best of them.

Max tried to eat some breakfast, but the dry bread and strong-smelling cheese stuck in his craw, making him feel queasy. He felt a small pang of relief when he spotted the tubby figure of Mr. Warburton hurrying along with a tidy sheaf of papers under his arm; a long, curly wig making him appear like a particularly well-fed poodle. Max smiled bitterly as he considered the fact that he could still make jokes when his life was in peril. It had always been his habit to deflect reality with humor, so at least that part of him was still intact—for now.

Pushed and prodded by two guards, Max walked slowly along the corridor. The chains between his ankles were heavy and clunky, making walking awkward and painful. The fetters chafed against his skin, so Max tried to pull his feet forward rather than lift them as he normally would.

"Will the fetters be removed for the trial?" he asked one of the guards, but the man barely even looked at him.

"No," he finally replied. "Not until you go back to your cell."

Max was admitted into a small, sparsely furnished side chamber, where a tall blond man and a dark-haired woman stood waiting anxiously. They both turned toward him when he entered, expressions of amazement and suspicion etched on their worried faces.

"You have five minutes," the guard announced as he took his place just outside the door.

The man hung back, but the woman came forward and laid her gloved hand gently on Max's cheek, smiling into his eyes. She was no more than thirty, with soulful dark eyes and a wide mouth, so like his own. He'd never seen a portrait of Hugo's sister, but that's who this angel had to be. The resemblance was too marked for her to be anyone else. Was she his mysterious benefactor? Max wondered as they studied each other in silence. The man was studying her as well, his expression difficult to interpret. He seemed almost repulsed by her, but instantly rearranged his face as he noticed Max looking at him.

"Who are you, my lady?" Max asked, hoping for a confirmation of his theory.

"I'm Jane Hiddleston, Hugo Everly's sister, and I'm not a lady. Plain Mistress Hiddleston will do," she replied, still gazing up into his eyes, her own round with wonder. "Yes, the resemblance is quite remarkable," she said at last, "but you are clearly not Hugo. I'd know my brother anywhere. You lack the arrogance and self-possession of the man."

"It's hard to be self-possessed and arrogant when you're chained like an animal and accused of a crime that can cost you your life," Max replied.

"So, you've never met my brother then?" she asked, as a charming giggle escaped from her mouth. She turned to beckon the blond man forward. "This gentleman is Bradford Nash, our closest neighbor and a devoted friend of my brother's. Brad, is there anything you wish to ask Master Everly to help you make up your mind?" She turned to the man, but he simply shook his head as he watched Max. It seemed his mind was already made up.

"Master Everly, I wish you the best of luck in these proceedings," Bradford Nash said as he gave Max a slight smile of acknowledgment. "I know that you are who you say you are. Jane, are you ready?" He took the woman by the elbow and steered her toward the door, but she turned back before leaving.

"You have nothing to worry about, nothing at all," she said with a smile of encouragement. "I will tell them the truth."

"Thank you, Mistress Hiddleston," Max replied, feeling overwhelming gratitude toward this kind woman.

"Oh, think nothing of it. I'm only doing my sisterly duty."

Max sucked in his breath as the guard returned to take him into the chamber where the trial would take place. It was a sizable room with a massive fireplace, and an iron light fixture hanging from the ceiling which held numerous candles, lit despite the early hour. Gray light crept through a narrow window set into the thick stone wall but did little to dispel the gloom. A wooden table stood facing the room, with three elaborately carved wooden chairs awaiting the judges. There were several benches for spectators which were already nearly full. There was no actual dock or a place for the accused to sit, so Max was made to stand to the left of the table and face the room. The chains rattled every time he so much as twitched, making him acutely aware of his position of helplessness.

Max found Jane Hiddleston, who was sitting behind a rather tall, bewigged man. He tried to make eye contact, but she looked through him, her gaze blank and her mouth pursed in displeasure as she stared at the wall. Bradford Nash was next to her, his expression still inscrutable, but not unfriendly as their eyes met.

Everyone rose to their feet as the examiners shuffled in.

It was immediately clear that the man who took the middle seat was the one to watch out for. He wore an elaborate wig of chestnut brown and an extravagantly embroidered coat in charcoal gray. Frothy lace showed beneath the wide cuffs, drawing attention to the pale skin of his bony hands. His deep-set gray eyes scanned the room from beneath heavy brows as he took his seat. The man was of average height, but rather too thin, which made him appear taller and grimmer. The other two were of middle age, paunchy, bewigged, and slightly nervous, their demeanor suggesting that they would be easily swayed by the head judge.

The representatives of the Crown were introduced as Lord Eastwick, George Jeffreys, and Lord Gray by a clerk who settled on a stool at the end of the table with a pot of ink, quill, and paper to record details of the trial and draw up a document proclaiming the verdict.

The man called Jeffreys, who was clearly the head judge, spoke first.

"Ladies and Gentlemen, the individual on trial is accused of attempted murder, kidnapping, and most importantly, high treason. Since he insists on denying his true identity, the first order of this court will be to ascertain whether he is truly Maximillian Everly, as he claims, or Lord Hugo Everly, playing at being mad in the hopes of making a fool of the Crown. He has solicited legal representation, which is unusual, but, due to mitigating circumstances, has been permitted by our sovereign, who is just and merciful. You may proceed, Master Warburton, and be quick about it."

Gideon Warburton rose to his feet and stood before the table, half turned toward the judges, half toward the assembled spectators. "Ladies and Gentlemen, I won't waste your time with a lengthy opening statement. I will only say that the cornerstone of any legal action is to ensure that the right man is being tried. As I will prove today, with the help of physical evidence, as well as statements from several credible witnesses, the man before you is not Hugo Everly, despite the physical resemblance. The man on trial is Maximilian Everly, a distant relation of the lord who happened to be in Cranley and was arrested in error."

Gideon Warburton grew momentarily silent to allow everyone to digest what he'd just said before turning to the table of judges with an affable expression.

"First and foremost, I would like to present to the court a sample of Lord Everly's writing, as well as a sample of my client's. They differ radically." Gideon Warburton triumphantly laid two sheets of paper in front of the judges, but George Jeffreys didn't even glance at the evidence before dismissing it.

"Master Warburton, I hate to think you naïve, but it's not a great feat to disguise one's writing, particularly when plainly aware that the two will be compared. I do not accept this evidence. Move on," Jeffreys ordered, waving away the two writing samples.

"Yes, Your Honor," Warburton replied, clearly taken aback. He took a deep breath and instantly rallied, moving on to his next piece of evidence. "Here, I have a list of measurements of Lord Everly obtained from his tailor and bootmaker. As you can see, Lord Everly is somewhat shorter than the accused and his foot measures nearly two inches less."

The lawyer made to hand the document to the judges, but Jeffreys once again waved it away, his face a mask of annoyance.

"Unacceptable. Lord Everly could have easily paid these men to falsify the measurements. There is no proof whatsoever that these are accurate. Proceed."

"I call Bradford Nash," Gideon Warburton intoned.

Max couldn't help noticing that Gideon Warburton seemed less sure of himself than before.

The blond man rose to his feet and took his place in front of the judges.

He never looked at Max, but Max felt a certain sympathy emanating from him, and rightly assumed that this witness was in his corner.

"Master Nash, how well do you know Lord Everly?" Gideon Warburton asked.

"Hugo and I have known each other since childhood. We grew up together and are still the closest of companions." Bradford Nash had a deep, soothing voice which resonated through the stone-walled room, and his demeanor was one of calm assurance as he faced the examiners.

"In other words, you are here to prove your loyalty to your friend by supporting his fraudulent claim," Jeffreys roared, rising to his feet and slamming his hand on the surface of the table. He was much shorter and thinner than Nash; a shortcoming he instantly recognized before he sat back down to avoid looking ridiculous.

"I'm a loyal subject of the Crown and a man of honor. I do not lie under oath," Nash countered, his color rising as his eyes locked with those of Jeffreys, daring him to impugn his honor.

Jeffreys did not reply but motioned for the lawyer to continue.

"Master Nash, is the person here today the man you know as Hugo Everly?" Gideon Warburton asked, cutting through the tension with his reedy voice.

"He is not. This man does bear some resemblance to Hugo, but he is most certainly not the man I've known all my life," Bradford Nash stated calmly. His eyes never left Jeffreys' face, his expression challenging him to question his honor again. Jeffreys was the first to look away, clearly unsettled.

"Take a seat, Master Nash," Jeffreys ordered. "I'd like to call a witness for the prosecution before allowing you to proceed, Master Warburton. I call Lionel Finch."

Max shrank back as he watched the man rise and take his place. He knew who Finch was, of course, from the charge of attempted murder and kidnapping, but he'd never seen the man. He wasn't very tall and wore a curly blond wig that accentuated his pale skin and colorless eyes. There was nothing overtly threatening in the man, but something about his demeanor made Max's flesh crawl. *If Hugo had tried to kill this man, he probably had very good reason*, Max thought as he tried to adjust his expression to one of neutrality. Showing any animosity would only prove the prosecution's case, so Max tried to appear as bland as possible.

"Master Finch," Gideon Warburton began, "do you know the man on trial today?"

Finch turned slowly about and studied Max at length, his eyes meeting Max's for a long moment before finally turning to face the judges.

"I do. This is the man who came to my home in April with the purpose of soliciting my support for the rebellion of the traitor the Duke of Monmouth. While there, he took it upon himself to interfere in my marriage, assaulted me most viciously, and stole my lawfully wedded wife, whom I still have not found."

"Where's his wife?" Jeffreys demanded, looking directly at Max for the first time.

"I don't know. I've never met him or his wife."

"Your insolence will not be tolerated, sir. I repeat: where is his wife?"

"As God is my witness, I don't know," Max replied. He tried to appear calm, but his innards were turning to jelly as he looked into the pitiless eyes of the judge.

"Step down, Master Finch. Master Warburton, I'm allowing you one more witness before I make my decision on the identity of the accused."

"I call Jane Hiddleston, sister to Lord Hugo Everly," Gideon Warburton announced triumphantly. Jane was his trump card, his unassailable witness.

Max smiled at the woman as she rose slowly and took her place. She appeared small and vulnerable as she stood in the middle of the room before the table, and the judges noticeably relaxed and even nodded to her in encouragement.

"Mistress Hiddleston, you are very fond of your brother, are you not?" Gideon Warburton asked softly.

"Indeed, I am, sir, which is why it makes it so difficult for me to speak the truth in front of this court. That man *is* my brother," she said, pointing at Max as her eyes bored into his mercilessly.

Max felt his heart drop to the floor and shatter at his feet as he stared at the woman who'd been so kind to him only a few minutes ago. She'd promised her support and told him not to worry, but now she was swearing that he was Hugo Everly, when she knew damn well he wasn't.

"Mistress Hiddleston, please look again. Are you sure?" Warburton squeaked, panic written all over his face. His star witness had gone over to the other side without any warning, and he had no idea why.

"I am absolutely certain," she said and buried her face in her handkerchief, plainly distressed. "I'm sorry, Hugo," she sobbed as she was led back to her seat by the clerk, who'd jumped to his feet and took it upon himself to assist the lady.

Jeffreys smiled at the assembly like a shark who'd just smelled blood. "I think it's painfully clear that the accused tried to deceive this court and failed. Therefore, we will now turn our attention to the charges."

Jeffreys was clearly enjoying his position of power. His shoulders were drawn back; his chest puffed out with self-importance, and his lips twitching with suppressed mirth. He turned to the other two judges, who nodded in agreement, eager to be done with the trial and scamper to the nearest tavern for a tankard of ale. They were visibly uncomfortable with the tactics Jeffreys had employed but didn't care to draw attention to themselves by disagreeing.

Jeffreys turned his gaze back upon the audience as he took a moment to gather his thoughts and allow tension to build. He was nothing if not a good showman, and this was a performance he relished. When he finally spoke, his voice was smooth and controlled; his hands steepled in front of him, almost as if in supplication.

"Master Finch, since you are very much alive, the charge of attempted murder is hereby dismissed. The accused is presumably guilty of abducting your wife, but I have no proof that she didn't leave with him of her own accord. Much luck in finding her, sir, and if you do, I suggest greater vigilance and stricter supervision. A woman requires her husband's guidance and moral instruction since she's too feebleminded to think for herself. I suggest you look to your own lack of husbandly discipline for an explanation."

Lionel Finch turned puce at this little speech but remained silent and bowed to Jeffreys stiffly in acknowledgment of his judgment and advice. Max had no idea what his marriage had been like, but he could only assume that the wife wasn't so feebleminded if she had decided to turn her back on her husband and leave with Hugo. It wouldn't have been an easy decision for a woman to make in this day and age, so, presumably, she'd been justified. Had she been Hugo's lover before he took up with Neve Ashley? Max wondered.

Of course, the charge of abduction never really posed much threat. The worst he could get for that one was a slap on the wrist, according to Gideon Warburton. It was the charge of treason that would decide if he were to live or die.

Jeffreys once again grew silent, waiting for everyone to focus their attention on him before speaking. He clearly enjoyed theatrics, a trait which would have been valuable in a TV judge on a reality show, but not nearly as appreciated in a seventeenth-century courtroom. The audience was growing restless, eager to hear the outcome of this much-awaited spectacle.

Finally, he spoke. "Now, the only charge that truly matters in these proceedings is the charge of treason, which we have ample physical evidence in support of. We have letters of correspondence between the conspirators, as well as a letter from the Duke of Monmouth himself." Jeffreys pointed to a stack of papers in front of him, which could have been pages from a

Shakespeare play for all anyone knew. "It is, therefore, clear to me that Lord Hugo Everly is guilty of high treason."

A hush fell over the room as Jeffreys glared at the audience, daring anyone to contradict him. The other two judges nodded once again, and Gideon Warburton momentarily sank deeper into his seat, but forced himself into action in a last attempt to save his client.

"Master Jeffreys, if I might have a word in private, sir, before you pronounce the verdict," Gideon Warburton muttered, giving Jeffreys an imploring look.

Jeffreys sneered at the little man but appeared to consider the request and motioned Warburton to join him in the side chamber.

"A five-minute recess," he called out as he disappeared through the door.

Max stared around the room uncomprehendingly. How was it possible that their well-prepared defense had fallen apart in a matter of minutes? Why had that woman lied when she clearly knew he wasn't her brother? Did everyone in this damn century have an agenda? Max felt his knees give way as he realized the magnitude of what had just occurred. He was helpless and at the mercy of the Crown; a Crown that had executed nearly everyone associated with the rebellion. He'd truly believed that he had a chance of proving his innocence, but Jeffreys' mind had been made up long before he took his seat at the table. Max had been doomed from the start, and no amount of evidence could have made any difference to the outcome of the trial.

Max tried to force himself upright, but his knees felt like water, and his stomach was seized with cramp. He could barely see through the haze of tears, which threatened to overwhelm him as his legs buckled.

The guards came forth and held Max up as Jeffreys and Warburton returned to the room and took their places. Neither face betrayed anything, but there seemed to be a slight shift in

Jeffreys' belligerence, a satisfied gleam in his narrowed eyes as he took his seat and gazed around the room. The murmuring and shuffling of a few moments before now turned to dead silence, everyone waiting to hear the fate of the accused.

Jeffreys didn't bother to consult with the other two judges; they appeared to be purely ornamental since the final verdict clearly rested with him. He took a deep breath before splaying his hands on the table, as if wrestling with a difficult decision, then finally spoke.

"I have considered the verdict most carefully, and although my initial instinct had been to sentence the accused to death by beheading, I have decided to be merciful. Hugo Everly did not physically participate in the rebellion, but merely incited it, which is still treason, but not on the same scale as taking up arms against the king. Therefore, I sentence Lord Hugo Everly to transportation to the West Indies, to be sold into indenture for a period of seven years. It will be considered unlawful for anyone to try to purchase Lord Everly's freedom before such a time and an affront to the Crown. Arrangements will be made for transport. Good day to you all."

Jeffreys rose to his feet, followed by the other two judges, who hadn't so much as uttered a word. Everyone shuffled from the room, a buzz of conversation flowing over Max as he was hauled from the room and back to his cell. His mind was numb, but the words "beheading" and "indenture" were spinning in strange concentric circles, making him feel nauseous and lightheaded.

He collapsed onto his cot as soon as the fetters removed, but immediately rolled to the side and threw up into the chamber pot, emptying his already empty stomach as dry heaves wracked his body. He couldn't even begin to understand what had just happened, but the reality of his situation was beginning to dawn on him, making him shake violently as he continued to retch, his insides turning themselves inside out until his stomach muscles began to spasm, leaving him gasping for air.

* * *

Bradford Nash walked through the gate of the outer wall, his mind in a whirl. Jane had disappeared as soon as the proceedings were over, for fear that Brad would confront her about her testimony, but he couldn't honestly say he was surprised. After what she'd planned for Neve, it stood to reason that she had an agenda of her own. He supposed the fact that Max wouldn't be executed should be considered a triumph, but he felt hollow inside, knowing full well that the man was innocent.

Seven years of indentured labor in the West Indies. What were the chances he'd survive? His death would be a fitting punishment in the eyes of the law, and would pave the way for Clarence Hiddleston to inherit, which is precisely what Jane wanted. Brad suddenly felt an overwhelming hatred toward the woman he'd known nearly his whole life. He hoped that Jane would get what was coming to her, and if God were truly just, she would.

Brad pushed his way through the crowd outside, hardly conscious of the mob demanding to know the outcome of the trial and cursing with disappointment when they heard that there was to be no public execution. Brad barely noticed as a dirty ragamuffin catapulted from between the legs of two burly men and threw himself at him, wrapping his scrawny arms around his legs. Brad looked down in annoyance, his hand already reaching for a coin to toss to the urchin but was suddenly distracted.

FORTY-FIVE

"Transport to the West Indies," Archie announced as he burst into the room. "Commuted from beheading after a closeted meeting with Master Warburton."

"What's the mood like downstairs?" Hugo asked, his head bent as he processed the news that Archie had just delivered.

"Vehement outrage," Archie replied. "The masses feel that he—*you*... got off lightly. They were hoping for a nice, public execution to fuel their bloodlust." Archie looked utterly indignant as he imparted the news but was disappointed when Hugo didn't seem to share his anger.

"As expected then," Hugo quipped as he sank into a chair and crossed his feet at the ankles, completely unperturbed, which I found to be surprising, given his devotion to providing Max with the best defense and campaigning for his release.

"You don't seem particularly upset," I remarked, watching him from across the room, my expression probably mirroring Archie's grimace of confusion.

"I'm not. I've done everything in my power to save Max from being executed. I can only assume that the reduction in sentence came after a very generous offer from Master Warburton, one I can't really afford under the circumstances but felt obligated to make, nonetheless. I consider my duty to Max Everly to be fulfilled," Hugo replied, looking from me to Archie in a way that suggested he needed our understanding.

"What do you think will happen to him?" I asked. "Is there any chance of helping him escape?"

"Max will be heavily guarded on the way to the port, and on board the ship as well. Any rescue effort would be foolhardy and bound to fail. I hope that he will serve his sentence and find his way back to England, where he can hopefully return to his rightful place," Hugo added meaningfully. "We must leave as soon as possible to find a ship bound for France. Time is of the essence."

"What about Jem?" Archie and I asked in unison.

"Brad will continue to look for Jem. He will offer a reward for information about his whereabouts. Money always helps people remember what they'd have otherwise conveniently forgotten. Brad will look after him should he be found. Right now, my priority is getting to France, marrying the very pregnant mother of my child, and making contact with friends abroad who can help pave our way into the court of Louis XIV. Do you feel this to be the wrong course of action?" Hugo asked, watching me with narrowed eyes.

"Not at all. I just wasn't expecting this particular outcome, I suppose. I hoped Max would be set free." My hopes had been naïve, given the gravity of the charge, but somewhere in the back of my mind, I believed that Max would be able to return home.

"That was never really an option," Hugo replied as he rose to his feet and folded me into his embrace. "This is the best outcome we could have hoped for. Now, why don't we get some good brandy to celebrate and begin to make plans for our departure?"

I abstained from the brandy but did have a cup of cider to

celebrate this "win," if that's what it was. I could completely understand Hugo's point of view, but I did feel sorry for Max. He was a spoiled, pampered scion of a wealthy, titled family. He'd never survive on some sugar plantation, working fourteen-hour days in extreme heat and poor conditions. I admit that I'd initially felt very angry and wanted to leave him to his fate, but the more gullible part of me wished that we could help him somehow.

"Let it be," Hugo said to me, putting his warm hand over mine. "There's nothing more we can do for him."

"I know," I sighed.

Hugo stiffened when there was a loud knock on the door. He reached for his dagger while Archie opened the door a crack to see who'd come calling.

"Message for Master Tully, sir," a young girl announced, handing over a square of paper sealed with a blob of wax.

"From Bradford Nash," Archie said, examining the seal and handing the note to Hugo.

Hugo broke the seal and unfolded the note, quickly scanning the few sentences scribbled on the sheet, his expression changing from curiosity to surprise.

"Well, what does it say?" I asked, trying to see over his shoulder.

"It says to come at once to the Black Dog Tavern in Cheapside. And to come alone."

"Could this be a trap?" Archie asked as he took the note from Hugo and looked closely at the imprint of the seal.

"No, that's Brad's stamp on the seal. It's from him; I'm sure of it. Neve, stay here. Archie, follow me at a safe distance just in case. I don't like the sound of this," Hugo said as he finished his brandy and slammed the cup down on the table with more force than he intended.

Hugo strapped on his sword, pulled his hat low over his eyes and gave me a quick kiss before disappearing through the door, followed by Archie. I was left to wait and fret once again, an occupation I was getting used to.

I locked the door behind them and settled near the window with my sewing. I could mend things, sew on buttons and darn socks, but actual sewing was a bit of a challenge. I thought I might try sewing a gown for the baby. How difficult could it be to make a sack-like garment with an opening for the head, the legs and something resembling sleeves? Clearly more difficult than I imagined since I'd probably have to twist the baby's arms to get them into the too-narrow sleeves that appeared to be at the wrong angle. I ripped out the seams and tried to figure out how to make the openings for the arms bigger without ruining the rest of the gown.

As I battled with the tiny garment, my mind whirred like a crazed bumblebee, imagining all kinds of scenarios which would induce Brad to send such an urgent message. Clearly, going to his house wasn't safe, so what was so important that they had to meet in some flea-infested tavern in Cheapside? Part of me was very worried, but part of me reasoned that Brad would never do anything to put Hugo in danger. Whatever it was had something to do with the trial, or perhaps Jane's arrival in town.

I finally gave up on the gown and stretched out on the bed, suddenly exhausted. My last thought as my eyes fluttered closed was of a tropical beach in the Caribbean where indentured servants were sold at auction to burly, sweating plantation owners, who eyed the merchandise and poked them with riding crops.

FORTY-SIX

Lionel Finch tore off his new coat and threw it across the bed as he poured himself a generous measure of wine. He wanted to smash something, but there was nothing worth breaking that would give him any satisfaction. Instead, he drove his fist into the wall. He yelped with pain as the plaster gave way and his fist sank into the hole, making him lose his balance and smack his head against the wall. He righted himself, pulled his arm out of the hole, and sank onto the bed, suddenly tired.

The whole morning had been a disaster from beginning to end. He'd stepped into a pile of horse shit on his way to the trial, got a tear in his breeches when they snagged on a protruding nail, and then got a lecture from that high-handed imbecile of a judge about his lack of husbandly guidance and discipline. Jeffreys had thoroughly humiliated him in front of the entire assembly, not only turning him into a laughingstock, but utterly dismissing the charges against Everly. He could have ordered some recompense, but instead, he'd made him look like a complete fool and a possible cuckold, by implying that his wife had left with another man of her own free will. Lionel Finch had been the injured party in all this, but now he was made to appear a buffoon in the eyes of London society. The popinjays at Court would have a good laugh at his expense, of that he was certain.

The verdict had been a surprise as well. Lionel had decided to testify against the impostor on trial, and an impostor he was, to serve his own ends. The man physically resembled Hugo Everly, but the likeness ended there. Hugo wouldn't have permitted himself to nearly faint; he was strong and proud, not a sniveling weakling like the one in the dock. The two men were very different; anyone who cared to look would see that at once, which made Jane Hiddleston's testimony that much more puzzling. Seemed the comely Mistress Hiddleston had an agenda of her own. Perhaps her brother had wronged her some-how, but enough to want to see him dead? It was hard to fathom. Lionel would gladly pay a coin or two to find out that story, if only for his personal entertainment. This morning's performance had been better than the theater, particularly for those who had nothing to lose either way.

Yes, beheading would have suited Lionel's needs very well. It would ensure that Hugo Everly could never go back to his former life. He'd be Lord Everly no more, for how could he prove his identity after supposedly being executed for treason? It would all have worked out very nicely had that pig-faced poltroon, Gideon Warburton, not intervened. Must have offered a hefty bribe to get the sentence commuted. Lionel couldn't help wondering who'd financed that maneuver.

Still, the plan was in place, and everything was at the ready. All he needed was the word from Harvey that Hugo was on the move. Lionel put aside his injured pride and smiled to himself as he pictured the coming encounter. Hugo Everly was a dead man.

FORTY-SEVEN

It was well past 3 p.m. by the time Hugo reached Cheapside. Ordinarily, it would still be light outside, but the dreary weather and miserable drizzle left the narrow streets and alleys dark and slick with moisture. Thick clouds blanketed the autumn sky and seemed to float right above the rooftops, giving the impression that the sky was falling. Candlelight spilled from most windows despite the early hour, the shutters firmly closed on others to keep out the wind and rain.

There were a few people about, but most tended to stay indoors if they could afford to; it was too raw and wet to be out. Hugo had no trouble finding the tavern; a peeling sign of a ferocious-looking black dog swung in the wind with a creak that could raise the dead. The taproom was nearly empty; a few old-timers nursing their tankards of ale rather than heading out into the cold. The dinner crowd had departed; the news of the trial already grown stale as people's attention shifted to other things.

Hugo looked around the pub, not noticing Brad sitting in a dark corner at first but going to join him when he heard himself addressed as "Master Tully." Brad was leaning against the dark paneling of the wall, an empty mug in front of him, his face a study in pensiveness.

"What is it?" Hugo asked as he took in Brad's mystifying appearance.

Brad gestured toward a chair across from him and signaled for the barmaid to bring a tankard of ale for Hugo.

"Hugo, I have good news and bad," he began once the wench had slammed the tankard in front of Hugo and another in front of Brad, giving them both a sour look.

"I'll take the bad first."

"Jane's testimony was most damaging. She knew perfectly well that Max wasn't you. She said as much to him when she met him, but she went on to swear under oath that Max Everly was indeed her brother, knowing that he would most likely be executed. It's bad enough what she tried to do to Neve, but this is an innocent man she'd never met. She seemed to have no qualms about sending him to his death."

"I can only assume that she was hoping for the death penalty, which would open the way for Clarence to inherit the title and the estate. Having me deported to the West Indies was not in the cards, but seven years is a long time, during which much can happen. I'm sure Jane is very pleased with the day's work. Now, tell me the good news. I'm more than ready for some." Hugo smiled at Brad, who suddenly looked aglow now that his duty of telling Hugo about Jane was done.

"Finish your ale and come with me," Brad said.

"Won't you just tell me?"

"No, you need to see this for yourself," Brad replied as he drained his tankard and set it down with a bang of satisfaction.

He asked for a candle and led Hugo up the narrow stairs to a corridor, which was nearly pitch-black. Brad fumbled for a key and opened the door to a room at the end of the passage, preceding Hugo into the dim interior. An empty plate sat on the scarred table, and water swirled in a basin, the liquid nearly black with dirt and grime. A tiny figure lay huddled on the bed, but Hugo's heart gave a lurch as he recognized the mop of dark curls.

"Oh, Brad, is that...?" He nearly choked on the words as Brad nodded happily. "He nearly knocked me off my feet outside the Tower when I left the trial. He'd been waiting for me."

Hugo sat on the side of the bed and bent over the sleeping form of Jem, who instantly came awake, sat up, bumped his head on Hugo's chin, and threw himself into his arms, sobbing pitifully.

"I knew it wasn't true," he mumbled into Hugo's chest as his thin arms held on for dear life. "I knew it wasn't true."

"What wasn't true?" Hugo asked gently.

"Mistress Hiddleston said you bid her to sell me to a brothel since I was a useless burden, and the money would go to pay for what you'd spent on me already. She kept saying it, but I knew it couldn't be true."

"Of course, it's not true. Oh, Jem, I'm so happy to see you, my little lad. Are you all right?" Hugo held Jem away from himself and examined him by the feeble light of the guttering candle. Jem looked much thinner than he'd been, his hair greasy, and his clothes nearly in shreds, but his face and hands were clean, and his eyes shone with such happiness that Hugo was nearly brought to tears.

"I ran away from the brothel," Jem announced proudly. "There was a small window in the cellar. I climbed up on a barrel, smashed the glass, and managed to squeeze through. I got a few cuts, but I was able to get away. I was so scared of what they would do to me. I heard some of the other boys talking. They didn't seem to mind it so much, but I couldn't..." Jem's voice trailed off as he recalled what he had heard.

Hugo felt a blinding rage as he imagined what Jem must have endured. For a child, who believed that adults were to be trusted and respected, to hear that grown men would want to use him that way must have been terrifying and utterly beyond comprehension. Hugo could understand two willing participants finding pleasure in each other, but to force a small child was monstrous. Of course, it wasn't all that different from the regular brothels where girls as young as eleven were on offer; some of them highly valued and sold to the highest bidder since they were still intact.

"Did anyone hurt you?" Hugo asked, his voice tight with fury.

"The man in charge wasn't unkind," Jem replied, "he ordered me to bathe, and I was measured for new clothes. He wanted me to wear velvets and silks. I knew it was just a matter of time before he'd force me to do things. There were no women in that place," Jem confided, "not even servants." He wiped his nose with his filthy sleeve as he fought tears that weren't far away. "I found work in a livery, but they didn't pay me. Just gave me one meal a day, and a sorry one at that, and allowed me to sleep in the hayloft. Once I'd heard about the trial, I knew that Master Bradford would be there, so I resolved to see him and find out the truth for myself. I can come back, can't I?" he suddenly asked, his face growing pale with concern as his eyes swam with unshed tears.

"Jem, I'm not going back. I am a wanted man, and there are those who won't rest until I'm dead. I'm going to France, but I will take you with me, if that's what you wish. If not, you can go back with Master Bradford, and he will look after you until such a time as I'm able to return to England."

"I want to go with you," Jem wailed, alarmed. "Not that Master Bradford hasn't been most kind," he added with a glance at Brad. "Please, take me with you, Your Lordship. I won't be any trouble; I promise."

"Of course, you won't. Mistress Ashley will be overjoyed to see you. We must get you some clean clothes, though.

These reek," Hugo said, wrinkling his nose and making Jem laugh.

* * *

I nearly went out of my mind with anxiety as I watched the gloomy afternoon turn into a wet, dark evening. The pitter-patter of gentle rain turned into the drumming of a downpour, but Hugo still had not come back. I tried to light the candle, but my hands shook so badly that I finally ventured downstairs and lit my candle against one of the candles in the taproom, returning upstairs with my hand around the flame to keep it from blowing out, thanks to the numerous drafts coming in from beneath doors and through window frames despite the shutters.

If there was one thing I truly missed about the modern world, besides electricity and plumbing, it was the welcome distraction of television, books, and phones. With nothing to do but worry, the time dragged interminably, my imaginary scenarios growing more harrowing with every passing hour. I nearly jumped out of my skin by the time I heard a gentle rap on the door and Hugo's voice.

"Where in God's name have you been?" I tore into him but grew silent as I realized that someone was hovering behind him in the dark corridor. A little shape materialized from behind Hugo's back, the wide smile making me forget all my worries as my heart leaped with joy. "Oh, Jem," I cried as I drew him into my arms, kissing the top of his head, which smelled as if it'd been freshly washed. Jem was wearing clothes that were way too big for him, but he seemed so happy that my heart nearly burst. "Where did you find him?" I asked Hugo, who looked pretty happy himself.

"Jem found Brad after the trial. I always said he was a clever little lad."

"And where's Archie?"

"Organizing supper and bullying the innkeeper's wife into making Jem a gooseberry tart." Hugo looked around the room, which was still in disarray. "You haven't packed. We're leaving tomorrow morning."

"I couldn't settle down to anything. I was too worried," I replied. "It won't take long; not like we have much."

We had a merry feast that night with a gooseberry tart for dessert. No one mentioned Max, but his sentence felt like a two-thousand-pound elephant perched on the narrow bed in our tiny room. But we'd done all we could, and now it was time to go. Hugo invited Jem to sleep on a pallet in our room, but Archie tactfully maneuvered Jem out of the door. Archie slept in a communal bed shared by several travelers, despite Hugo's offer of his own room. Archie was a simple man who felt more comfortable in haylofts and barns, and I suspect didn't want to put Hugo to any extra expense. Jem would be safe with him, and probably warmer and more comfortable than he would be on the floor.

Jem pushed Archie out of the way and threw himself at Hugo one more time before leaving. He wrapped his arms about Hugo's waist and pressed his cheek to Hugo's chest; his mouth curved in a sweet smile. "I love you," he whispered as Hugo held him close, his own blissed-out expression a testament to his feelings for the child.

FORTY-EIGHT

The morning of All Hallows' Eve found Max huddled in the corner of his cell; his head pounding and his eyes burning from lack of sleep. He'd tried to rest, but every time he so much as nodded off, he came awake with a jolt, remembering the trial and the sentence that awaited him. Knowing that he'd avoided the death penalty was a cold comfort when he thought of what awaited him. He'd always been in good shape, taken care of himself, and watched his diet, but a healthy twenty-first-century man who could walk for miles or run on the treadmill was no candidate for seven years of indentured labor on some plantation.

Max had no illusions about what to expect. He'd seen the films and knew that reality would be that much worse. Even without cruelty, poor diet, and fourteen-hour days, he wouldn't be likely to last more than a year. He was a spoiled, pampered, thirty-eight-year-old man who'd never done a day of hard physical labor in his life.

And, even if he somehow managed to survive this trial by fire, what then? How would he ever find his way back to England with no money, no friends, and no connections? Max had begged Gideon Warburton to give him the name of his benefactor, but the lawyer had refused, saying that the person in question wished to remain anonymous. Whatever compelled this man to help him seemed to be at an end. He'd been spared beheading, at great cost to his patron, but now he was on his own—left to fight for his life with whatever life skills he possessed.

Thoughts of his mother had tormented Max all night. He'd never see her again; never have a chance to tell her that despite all the tongue-lashings, the criticism, and the pressure to get married, he loved her. He was the last of the line, so once he was pronounced legally dead by the authorities, the title and estate would go to his next of kin, and that would kill Naomi Everly, if she weren't already dead. God, he wasn't even sure who that would be. There were a few cousins on his father's side, but Max had never had much time for them, had never gotten his affairs in order or made out a will.

Max realized that he was shaking—whether from fear or cold he couldn't say, but his teeth were chattering, and salty, hot tears ran down his cheeks as he heard the scrape of the key in the lock. Two guards hauled him to his feet, fettered him, and pushed him out the door, jeering at him the whole time. They weren't the usual guards who'd been handsomely paid by Gideon Warburton; they were men he'd never seen before, but they obviously knew all about him.

"Oh, but we will miss ye, Yer Lordship, won't we, Dick? Such a model prisoner, and so well-mannered. I reckon that'll serve ye well where ye're going." The guard laughed at his own wit, showing brown, crooked teeth.

"Oh, aye," the other one chimed in. "He'll be the most admired slave in the West Indies, till the other 'guests' find out what he's been sent down for. No one likes a traitor, not even murderers and thieves. Oh, ye'll have a fine time of it down there, to be sure."

Max didn't bother to reply, just allowed himself to be manhandled until he was standing outside in the cool, misty grayness of Halloween morning. He filled his lungs with what passed for fresh air in seventeenth-century London and stepped into the open wagon that was to transport him to his destination.

"Where are you taking me?" he asked, knowing he'd get no answer.

The one named Dick shoved him, making him fall to his knees on the wagon bed. Max tried to get up, but the wagon lurched into motion, pitching Max forward onto his face, his fettered hands caught in front of his stomach, the iron slamming against his ribs as he fell hard.

Max finally managed to sit up and lean against the rough wood of the wagon, but eventually the motion lulled him into drowsiness, and he sank to the bottom of the wagon, lying in a fetal position on the smelly straw and staring at the ominous-looking sky until he fell asleep, welcoming the temporary oblivion.

FORTY-NINE

I huddled deeper into my cloak and pulled on my hood to keep out the bitter wind off the river. The air was fresher today, most of the muck having been washed away by the hard rain of the night before and carried down to the riverbank and into the Thames itself. The water was mud-brown, with various bits of rubbish floating on the current and bumping against the sides of the packet boats which were already out in full force, their lanterns glowing as they swayed from side to side with the rolling of the boats. The ferrymen called out to each other, their voices muffled by the fog, which was as yellow as pea soup and nearly as thick.

London was stirring to life; the shutters flung open to the gray day outside and the empty streets beginning to grow congested with passing wagons and pedestrians. The dark outline of the Tower loomed to my left; the screeching of the ravens loud in my ears as we cantered past. The streets were nearly dark despite the hour, the angry clouds obscuring the sky like a filthy blanket.

Hugo and I rode in front, with Archie and Jem, who was

seated in front of him, bringing up the rear—our little party leaving London for what could be years. I wanted to feel hopeful, but we still had to get to Portsmouth and find a ship. At this point, we'd take a ship bound for just about anywhere as long as it took us from the shores of England, where Hugo was still in constant danger. We'd left at dawn, hoping to reach Portsmouth by late afternoon tomorrow. Archie would leave us in Surrey to go fetch Frances from the convent before meeting us in Portsmouth.

I had to admit that I was glad Frances would be coming with us. I thought of her all the time; the tiny face of baby Gabriel often in my dreams. I smiled and cooed to him as I held him close, watching the pink eyelids flutter as he fell asleep in my arms. I'd remembered the desolation I'd felt after my miscarriage, so I could only imagine what poor Frances must be feeling after having given birth and holding her live baby, believing that they had a future together. A new place would mean a new lease on life, a new beginning, and she deserved that much. Frances would be fifteen in December; she still had her whole life ahead of her, and I wanted to believe that Hugo and I could help make it a happy one.

Once we left London behind, the road to Portsmouth, which had been so congested only a month ago, was now nearly empty. An occasional coach passed us in the opposite direction, or a lone traveler on horseback, but for the most part we were alone, especially at such an early hour. Had it been market day, countless wagons would be streaming into the city, laden with grain, produce, and dairy products.

I was glad that it was easy-going, despite the gathering clouds which threatened an epic downpour sometime soon. I'd seen a flash of lightning split the sky off to the south, and a distant rumble of thunder rolled through the deserted countryside. I dreaded the idea of being out in the storm and getting soaked through, but we had little choice. Stopping at an inn and waiting out the storm would put us back by several hours, which we couldn't afford.

Hugo was unusually quiet this morning, a stark contrast to the joy he had felt last night when his eyes hardly ever left Jem, and his lips stretched into a happy smile as Jem devoured the last of the tart and licked his sticky fingers.

I glanced behind us. Archie was staring off into the distance, his hand relaxed on the reins, and Jem looked the picture of contentment as he leaned against Archie and gazed around with interest, his troubles already forgotten. I maneuvered my horse closer to Hugo and reached out to touch his hand. "Are you all right?"

Hugo turned to face me. He looked tired and stern. His hair, most of which was thankfully hidden by his hat, had faded to a shade of bronze, and his eyes were red-rimmed from the prolonged wearing of contacts. We didn't have any contact solution, and although Hugo took them out at night, and I washed them out with water before he replaced them in the morning, his eyes were irritated. I was beginning to wonder if they impaired his vision, but he never complained.

"I keep trying to come to terms with the fact that my sister knowingly condemned an innocent man to death, for that's what she thought would happen to Max, but I simply can't. My mind keeps searching for some explanation or an excuse for her behavior, when I know full well that there isn't one."

"The syphilis..." I murmured.

"No, Neve. This is not the act of a person whose mind is teetering on the brink of insanity. This is pure malice, carefully planned and flawlessly executed. She wanted me dead, and if she couldn't have that, she wanted me dead in the eyes of the law."

"I'm sorry, Hugo. I can only imagine how much that must

hurt you," I replied, remembering my mother passed out on the kitchen table in a pool of her own vomit. That had hurt. Knowing that my mother got drunk every night without any thought for my well-being had been a terrible betrayal, but my mother had been weak and broken-hearted, not driven by a desire for a title and financial gain. "It's always the people closest to us who hurt us the most," I said, and Hugo nodded, realizing what I was referring to. He didn't say anything but reached for my hand and held it in his warm one, silently promising not to be one of the people who caused me pain. I squeezed his hand, sealing the pact between us.

We rode in silence for a while. Jem had fallen asleep against Archie's chest after devouring a buttered roll I'd brought for him from the inn. The child was so hungry and tired from his ordeal that it would take weeks for him to fully recover. I'd made sure to bring enough food to give him something to eat every two hours or so. It wasn't much, just some bread, cheese, a few slices of cold pork and several apples, but it would tide him over until we stopped somewhere for a hot meal once it began to grow dark.

I was actually feeling peckish myself, so I pulled out an apple and bit into it, enjoying the juicy firmness and the sweet-tart flavor of the freshly picked fruit. I still had a few prenatal vitamins left, but I tried to eat as many fresh fruits and vegetables as I could find to augment our diet, which consisted mostly of bread and meat. British cuisine had never been in the same vein as French, Italian, or even Spanish, but in the seventeenth century, the fare was so unvaried and devoid of nutritional value that it made me long for the lovely food we might eat once in France.

I had to admit that I was nervous about the future. With my rudimentary knowledge of French and my limited exposure to the ways of the nobility, the thought of being presented at the

Court of Louis XIV was frightening. I'd heard how cruel and unforgiving French courtiers could be, and dreaded being the subject of scrutiny and ridicule, but I didn't want to burden Hugo with my worries; he had enough to concern himself with, not the least of which being the birth of our child.

Despite nearing the third trimester, I tried not to dwell on the coming birth, repeating to myself like a mantra that everything would be all right. I knew no such thing, but I had to believe it, or I would come undone and take Hugo with me.

I finished my apple, threw away the core, and rubbed my hand over my belly, which suddenly shifted sideways. The baby had woken up from the nap it had been lulled into by the motion and was reacting to the sugar in the fruit. "Hello, there," I whispered as either a foot or an elbow pushed against my hand.

We had to be about two hours south of London by the time I heard, or rather felt, the thundering of hooves coming from the direction of London. Hugo motioned for us to shift to the side of the road to allow the riders to pass. There appeared to be four of them, riding hell for leather. The day was bleak, but the gray light still reflected off the breastplates and scabbards the men wore. Their hats were pulled low over their bearded faces, their features difficult to make out. I hoped they would just pass us quickly and be on their way, but something about their breakneck speed on the sleepy road made me anxious, especially since Hugo took my horse by the bridle and pulled it closer to the side of the road. I assumed that he did it to keep me out of the way of the mud that flew from beneath the hooves as they churned the damp dirt of the road.

I turned to Hugo just in time to witness the dramatic transformation in his face, which he quickly rearranged into his normal expression. My head whipped back, and I stared at the oncoming riders, alarmed by what Hugo had seen.

The men were riding two abreast. The first two appeared to be men-at-arms, rather than soldiers. They were dressed as civilians, except for the breastplates and swords, but wore no helmets, nor bore any sigil identifying them as soldiers of the king. They were big men, broad across the chest and wide of shoulder, with blunt features that were so common in peasants and yeomen.

A third, similarly attired man rode next to someone of smaller stature who wasn't wearing any armor but was decked out in a flowing velvet cape which streamed behind him like a full sail. His hat displayed colorful plumage, and his face was clean-shaven, but framed by his blond wig, its curls hanging halfway down his chest.

I would have recognized the man anywhere. Lionel Finch. My heart began to hammer against my ribs as my extremities grew cold with fear. What was he doing here, and could this be a coincidence? He might not recognize Hugo with his lighter hair and blue eyes, but he knew me, and he'd seen Archie as well as Jem. There was no way he could just gallop past us without noticing.

My head swung back to Hugo. I wasn't sure what I expected, but it wasn't the passive calm with which Hugo watched the men approach. I expected that there was a storm brewing inside him, neurons firing at an alarming speed as Hugo appraised the situation and weighed our options, but, outwardly, he was the picture of self-control. There was no chance of escape; he knew that much—not with a pregnant woman and a child. Our horses were good, dependable beasts, but could never outrun our pursuers. They were solid and reliable, but certainly nothing like Hugo's Arabian, Aamir, which Jane had probably sold at the first opportunity.

Jem was wide awake now, his eyes huge with alarm as he perceived that something unexpected was happening. He twisted and turned, trying to get a better look, but Archie put a steadying hand on his shoulder and said something to him quietly, which seemed to have a calming effect on the child. I wish I knew what it was because I was shaking like a leaf; my hands were icy, and I suddenly felt a shortage of oxygen despite being out in the open country.

I gulped in the ozone-scented air to calm myself, but only succeeded in becoming lightheaded. Hugo didn't say much but held my hand and my eyes in a manner he thought was reassuring. Nothing he could have done at that moment would have curbed my panic, but seeing him calm and collected did help.

"Maybe they'll pass by," I breathed as they drew closer, knowing that was wishful thinking.

"They won't," Hugo replied. "They're here for us. I knew we were being watched."

I opened my mouth to respond, but there was no point. Whatever Hugo had known was irrelevant now since it wouldn't change a thing. He'd chosen to take no action, which made no sense to me, but I knew Hugo to be a keen strategist. He would never knowingly put us in danger or allow himself to be taken unawares. All I could do was trust in him.

We waited by the side of the road until the riders were almost upon us. I still prayed that they would just pass us, but, of course, that was not to be. The three men-at-arms stopped just behind us, allowing Lionel Finch to canter to the front to face Hugo. He tried to look nonchalant but couldn't keep the glee from his colorless eyes. He was practically glowing as he looked at us one by one, his eyes stopping on me and sliding down to my belly as his mouth twisted in a mirthless grin.

"Lord Everly, what a pleasure to see you again," Lionel Finch exclaimed as he tipped his hat to Hugo in a gesture of mockery. "And how very different you look." He turned to me, pinning me with his snakelike stare. "Mistress Ashley, a delight, to be sure. And how's your head, young man?" he called out to Jem. "All healed?"

I didn't dare turn around, but I could hear Jem crying softly behind me. He was terrified, and he had every right to be.

"What do you want, Finch?" Hugo asked warily, although I was sure he already knew.

"I want you," Finch replied softly. It sounded almost intimate, which made it all the more frightening.

"How did you know where to find me?" I knew it cost Hugo a lot of pride to ask that question, but he needed to know. We'd obviously been betrayed by someone.

"Funny story, that," Finch replied with obvious relish. "Liza —I'm sure you remember her well—saw you at the establishment where she works, searching for your urchin. Seems your dear sister dismissed her without pay or reference when she found herself with child, and she now scrubs floors at a brothel where she'd hoped to advance her career after the child was born and promptly smothered. Being a clever girl, Liza deduced that the information would be worth more to me than the authorities, so she followed you to your lodgings and came to find me. As you might imagine, I was very interested in what she had to say, and we came to a mutually beneficial arrangement. Liza got to leave the brothel and will perhaps even keep her bastard, and I get you. Now that's money well spent, if you ask me," Lionel Finch gloated.

"I'd say it was," Hugo agreed. "Now what?"

"Now, you and your man dismount, lay down your swords, and follow us into the woods. If you do that, your lady and brat might not be harmed."

"Might?" Hugo demanded.

"I might change my mind after you're dead," Finch replied, "but you'll never know, will you? I see she's with child; that will make things more interesting for all involved."

I began to shake more violently, my whole body convulsing with overwhelming fear as the meaning of Finch's words sank in. He had no intention of sparing me if he got past Hugo; he'd make me pay for what had happened with Frances, and this time there would be no one to protect me from his rage. My hands automatically went to my belly, which seemed to amuse Lionel Finch greatly. *As if you could protect it,* his eyes seemed to say.

Hugo squeezed my hand, but he wasn't looking at me, his attention fixed on Finch, who clearly meant business. We were outnumbered, outarmed, and completely surrounded. I snuck a peek at the other three men. They seemed to be enjoying the performance, their eyes traveling between Finch, Hugo, and myself. One of the men caught me looking at him and gave me a leering smile, which made my flesh crawl. He moved his meaty hand to his groin suggestively, letting me know in no uncertain terms that whatever awaited me would involve rape. These men felt no personal sense of vengeance against us, but the promise of coin and spoils was enough to motivate them.

"I want a guarantee that Neve and Jem will be allowed to leave," Hugo demanded.

"You are in no position to ask for anything, nor will you know if I kept my word, but if it will make this go quicker, you may leave once the men have dismounted," Finch said to me magnanimously.

"Neve, you are to go as soon as I get off my horse," Hugo whispered. "Get as far as you can while they deal with us, then turn off the road and hide in the woods. Take care of Jem."

"I'm not leaving you."

"Yes, you are." Hugo gave me a look that spoke volumes as he reached over and squeezed my hand, reminding me of our pact. He did not want to be responsible for Jem and I being hurt, although the chances of us getting away were practically nonexistent. "Please. Promise me."

"I promise," I stammered as I looked at him. "I love you."

"I've felt more alive with you these past few months than I have for most of my life," Hugo said as he leaned over and kissed me tenderly. "Please get out of the way," he whispered so no one could hear.

"Well, this is all very touching, but we really must get on with the business at hand," Finch said. His patience was running short, and he wanted what he came for—Hugo. All this had been foreplay, and now he was ready.

I nodded as I swallowed bitter tears, but Hugo was still watching me, his eyes telling me something I didn't understand. He slapped my horse's rump, and it began to walk past Finch. Archie jumped off his horse and did the same, Jem ending up next to me, his tear-stained face contorted with grief and fear. I couldn't just leave, so I turned around to catch a last glimpse of Hugo, desperate to remember his beloved features.

Was this how it was going to end? Finch wouldn't give Hugo a clean death. He would torture him and probably disfigure him before he finally had his fill. He might even leave Hugo to die, rather than finishing him off, just to prolong his own enjoyment. I could see by the malicious look on Finch's face that he meant to draw this out for as long as possible and humiliate Hugo as much as he could.

Hugo looked undaunted as he gracefully dismounted, unbuckled his sword, and bent down in front of Finch's horse to lay it down in the dirt. A terrible sob tore from me as I reached out and grabbed Jemmy's hand. The three men were still where they'd been before, a few feet away, watching the proceedings with interest. It seemed Lionel Finch wanted to do the deed and needed the men more as backup. He would never take his chances with Hugo alone, but he felt invincible with three heavily armed men at his side.

Hugo appeared to lay the sword on the ground. His shoulders slumped with defeat, and his eyes rose to meet Lionel Finch's in mute appeal. Lionel Finch's chest swelled with confidence as his eyes drank in his enemy, now all but on his knees. Archie was not far behind, watching Hugo as he lowered his own sword to the ground. Did Hugo really think that Lionel might show him mercy?

I couldn't bear to see Hugo brought down so low, but I couldn't look away, couldn't forsake him in his final moments. The men couldn't see Hugo's face; only Lionel Finch and I could. They appeared relaxed and almost bored as this ceremony took place; ready to do what they'd come for.

Hugo's eyes never left Finch's, but the expression in them seemed to change. It went from supplication to murderous intent in the space of a moment, giving Lionel Finch about a second to comprehend that Hugo wasn't surrendering at all. I gripped the pommel with both hands. It seemed to be the only thing tethering me to this moment, this life. Whatever Hugo was about to do was his only chance, which is why he needed me out of the way.

Hugo suddenly unsheathed his sword, grabbed it with both hands, and brought it down with all his might behind the knees of Finch's horse. The horse screamed in terror and pain as its severed legs buckled, and it pitched forward hard, tossing a shocked Lionel Finch over its head. He landed hard on his back, the wind knocked out of him, his face a mask of rage and disbelief. But he didn't have long to be angry. Hugo was above him, his sword gripped in both hands as he brought it down on Lionel's chest, driving the steel into his heart. There was a sickening crunch as the blade crushed the ribs to get to its mark, and then a crimson stain bloomed around it, unfurling like a red rose. It all happened so quickly that the men barely had time to react. Their faces were slack with shock, their hands going for their swords as the reality sank in.

Archie had already grabbed his sword and placed himself between Hugo and the men-at-arms. It was two against three now, but the men were mounted, which gave them an advantage. They could cleave Archie from shoulder to groin without much effort and then turn their attention to Hugo, who now stood facing them, sword in hand.

"Wait," Hugo called out as the men drew their weapons. "Finch is dead, and you have your payment for this day's work. There's nothing to be gained by coldblooded murder other than a noose around your necks."

The men considered the wisdom of this and turned to the one who appeared to be their leader, eyes narrowed in speculation.

"What say you, Oliver?" one of them asked.

The man looked down at Hugo, his gruff face thoughtful as he considered this unexpected turn of events.

Hugo deftly cut Lionel's purse strings and tossed the heavy pouch to the man. "You have now been doubly paid for the day's work," he said. "Be on your way then. We have no quarrel with you."

"Nor we with you, Lord Everly. Godspeed," the man said, and the riders turned back toward London, eager to get away. Their master was dead, and tomorrow they would be in need of employment, but today they had freedom and coin, which usually implied a few hours in a tavern, getting thoroughly drunk, having a good meal, and maybe moving the celebration to a nearby brothel if the spirit moved them.

I was shaking hard as Hugo pulled me off the horse and held me close. He kissed my face and whispered endearments as I buried my face in his chest and inhaled his familiar scent. His heartbeat was strong and steady, and I listened to it until I began to calm down and finally allowed myself to believe that he was unharmed.

"They can still turn you over to the authorities," I whispered, terrified.

"They can, but I doubt they will. There's nothing to be gained by it. The authorities have their Hugo Everly, so reports of some man on the road to Portsmouth might not get as much of a reaction as they might hope for, and judging by their demeanor, they might want to keep a low profile for a time."

Hugo kissed me again and gently set me aside, turning to Archie, who still had his sword out. Archie cut his eyes at the horse, asking permission to put it out of its misery, but Hugo waved him aside. He knelt by the dying animal and laid his hand on its head. It was snorting, its eyes rolling wildly with pain and fear, its teeth bared. Blood pooled beneath its legs but was already congealing in the cold autumn air.

"I'm so sorry," Hugo said to the horse. "There was no other way."

The horse seemed to quiet down, as if it understood what Hugo was saying. I think it instinctively knew what was about to happen. Hugo pulled a dagger out of his boot and drove it into the animal's chest. The horse convulsed for several moments before finally growing still, its mouth growing slack. I briefly thought that Lionel Finch would not have appreciated his blood mingling with that of the horse, but he was no longer in any position to object. His eyes stared at the lowering sky, a scowl on his face, even in death.

I normally found it tragic when anyone died, especially a person who was still young, but Lionel Finch's death left me unmoved. He was a parasite and a sadist; a man who derived joy from the pain of others. I felt no pity for him. All I wanted was to get away from this awful spot. I was dimly aware that I was in shock, and eventually the dam that held my feelings at bay would give way and allow the floodwaters to drown me.

Hugo and Archie stood for a moment over Finch's corpse, their faces expressionless. Archie shrugged with indifference and turned away, but Hugo crossed himself and offered up a prayer. "Hail Mary, full of grace. The Lord is with thee. Blessed art thou amongst women, and blessed is the fruit of thy womb, Jesus. Holy Mary, Mother of God, pray for us sinners, now and at the hour of our death. Amen."

I turned away as Hugo and Archie carried Finch's body off into the woods, leaving the horse on the road. No one would be too astonished to see a dead animal, but a corpse would raise questions. They returned a few moments later, ready to move on. I was secretly glad that they didn't bother to bury Finch. He didn't deserve the honor, or the delay it would cause us. *Let the animals have him,* I thought savagely as I mounted my horse with Hugo's help and took up the reins. Archie vaulted up onto his horse and held Jem close as the little boy pressed his body against him.

"I promised you all would be well, didn't I?" Archie asked him as Jem dug his fingers into Archie's hand. His face was deathly pale. He nodded but couldn't speak. I wasn't surprised to see him passed out a few moments later. He'd been overcome with fear, and this was his body's way of relieving the stress. Jem snored softly as he began to relax, molding himself to Archie's chest. "Poor little mite," Archie said as he drew up alongside me. "Are you all right?" he asked.

I found that question to be ridiculously inadequate after the events of the past half-hour, but what else could he say? I forced a smile, "Yes, I believe I am."

I barely spoke as we rode south, not that I would have been heard. Loud crashes of thunder were followed by flashes of lightning as the heavens finally opened up, and a downpour soaked us in minutes. The water was frigid, and I was shivering with cold, especially once the water began to drip into my shoes, but we couldn't afford to stop, not yet. Visibility was poor, and the road quickly turned into a sea of mud, which slowed down our progress even more.

I hardly noticed Archie leave us. He galloped off with a quick wave after handing off Jem and conferring with Hugo regarding our rendezvous in Portsmouth. Jem huddled against Hugo's chest, his hair plastered to his face, and his oversized coat clinging to his narrow chest as we continued on. Water from the brim of Hugo's hat dripped onto his head, but he didn't complain, just burrowed deeper into the coat. Hugo's face was set in grim lines, his hands tense on the reins, but he turned to me and smiled. He was soaked, but he was all right, and so was I, and that was all that mattered for the moment.

FIFTY

It wasn't until the dreary day began to turn into dusk that we finally stopped at an inn in some nondescript village situated about a mile off the road. The inn was full to the gills, but thankfully there was one room left. It was just beneath the roof and about the size of a cupboard. A steady drumming announced that the roof had a leak.

Hugo's head brushed the rafters of the ceiling as he shed his cloak and pulled a chair close to the fire. I was so numb with cold and the dramatic events of the day that I was unusually unresponsive as he tried to talk to me. Hugo gave up on making conversation, removed my cloak, and sat me down in front of the fire. He rolled down my stockings and began to methodically rub my feet until some feeling began to come back into the frozen flesh. Steam rose from our wet garments, but I was still shivering violently, my teeth chattering.

"Jem, go get a pitcher of hot water," Hugo ordered as he pulled me to my feet and began to unlace my bodice and skirt. He had me down to my shift, which was damp but not soaked, and unpinned my hair to allow it to dry from the heat of the fire.

When I closed my eyes, images of Lionel Finch danced

before them until I was shaking and crying again. Lionel's dead eyes seemed to be staring at me in accusation as Hugo and Archie dragged him off into the woods. I felt no pity for him, but I was overcome by the danger we'd been in. Had things gone differently, Hugo might have been dead now, and I could have been at the mercy of those crude men, who would have hurt me very badly given the chance. The idea of losing Hugo had me bawling once more, and I pressed my head against his belly and wrapped my arms around him, holding him close.

"I almost lost you," I wailed, finally allowing my feelings to vent. My nose was running, and I was getting snot all over Hugo's shirt, but he didn't seem to care. He was cradling my head as he spoke softly to me, his voice strangely distant over the roar in my ears.

"I'm right here with you, love," Hugo reassured me. "Don't you know that I'm indestructible?"

"No, you're not. He would have killed you; he would have tortured you, he would have broken you," I sobbed. "Why didn't you tell me we were being watched?" I demanded, suddenly remembering what Hugo had said earlier.

"I didn't want to frighten you."

"And having armed men surround us threatening to kill you wasn't frightening?" I retorted, my grief turning to anger. "You knew that would happen?"

"No, I didn't. I wasn't sure who was watching us or why. I thought it might have been Jane. I had to bide my time and see what they had planned. I assumed that once we left London something would happen, but I wasn't sure what. It was a waiting game; that's why I had Archie guarding you at all times."

"Game?" I stammered. "*Game?*"

"Shh, calm down, my sweet. It's all over now. You need to warm up, eat, and get some sleep. It was all just a bad dream."

"Dream," I repeated stupidly. Yes, I liked thinking of it as a dream, a nightmare. It was over. "I've woken up, just like Alice," I said. "Where am I?" I suddenly began to feel very hot. My cheeks were flaming, and my chest felt constricted. I was very thirsty, and my stomach heaved in protest as the baby reacted to whatever was happening. My teeth were still chattering even though I was no longer cold, and I couldn't get any words out for fear of biting my tongue.

"You're burning up," Hugo said. His voice was full of alarm, but I was already slipping away.

I tried to pry my eyes open but couldn't. Fatigue settled into my bones, making me feel as if my limbs were weighed down with iron dumbbells. I'd been hungry before, but now my stomach was twisting and roiling; bile rising in my throat as I fought the urge to throw up. I pushed Hugo away just in time as I vomited into the basin again and again. I was heaving, sweating, and falling all at once.

Hugo caught me before I hit the floor and tucked me into bed. His face swam before my eyes, which were open to mere slits.

"I feel sick," I mumbled.

"I know, love." Hugo was sitting on the side of the bed, his face anguished. At least I wasn't convulsing anymore. "Here, drink this."

"Hmm, that's what the bottle said in Wonderland," I giggled.

"What is she talking about?" Jem asked. He sounded very frightened. "Where is Wonderland?"

"She's delirious, Jem."

I gulped down whatever Hugo was giving me. It was brandy. My muddled brain recognized that brandy was probably the only medicinal thing available to him in this godforsaken place. There was some reason why I couldn't drink alcohol, but I couldn't remember it. I seemed to be sinking into oblivion, my body floating as I succumbed to sleep.

I felt Hugo's body next to mine during the night, heard him talking to me softly, but couldn't respond. He held me and tried to get me to drink more brandy, but I just turned my head away, disgusted by the taste. Jem's worried voice seemed to be coming from somewhere, asking if I would be all right, but I couldn't really tell where he was. Perhaps he was on the floor by the fire where it was warmest. I was warm enough as it was; burning in fact. I was sure that if I tried, I could breathe fire like some fairy-tale dragon.

I was no longer sure if I was asleep or awake, hovering somewhere between the two worlds, on the brink of falling into oblivion. I felt strangely happy. I was floating on a cloud of peace, my body weightless and my mind serene for the first time in months. No one could harm me now. I was safe.

FIFTY-ONE

Sun was streaming through the leaded window when I finally opened my eyes. A patch of blue sky was just visible, and the annoying drumming of the leak had stopped sometime during the night. I was warm, but not burning, and the raw, damp cold of the previous day had left my bones. I was ravenously hungry, and slightly hung over. Hugo must have given me a lot of brandy last night.

I closed my eyes against the bright sun and put my arm over my face, suddenly realizing that I was alone in the room. I sat up alarmed, only to see Jem asleep on the floor. His face was relaxed in sleep; his lips curled in a beatific smile.

The door creaked open, and Hugo came in bearing a tray.

"You're awake. How are you?" he asked as he studied my face for the telltale flush of fever. "You need to eat something."

"I feel better," I said, as I sat up and accepted a warm buttered roll.

Hugo handed me a cup of milk and watched happily as I ate.

"Another?" He handed me a roll without waiting for my answer. "You were very ill last night," he said. I could see the worry in his eyes as he reached out and touched my forehead to check my temperature. "I think it was a combination of shock and chill. How do you feel now?"

"Weak, tired, queasy, but much better. I can travel," I added.

"Are you sure?"

"Yes," I replied. "Are those cakes for Jem?" Two oatcakes sat on a plate next to the remaining rolls.

"Those are souling cakes," Hugo explained. "It's November 2, All Souls Day. I was going to leave them out for my parents."

I'd never celebrated All Souls Day, so wasn't familiar with the custom. All I knew was that it was a day to commemorate the dead. Hugo would have gone to church, had there been a Catholic church to go to, but he had to make do with what he had. I was surprised that the tiny inn offered the cakes, but I supposed it was just another way to make a profit.

"Do you think Archie has reached the convent yet?" I asked, as I returned my empty cup to the tray and made a move to get up. "Will they let Frances go without a fuss?"

"I don't see why not. They might keep the money I left," Hugo replied, "but they took good care of her, so it's their right, I suppose. I only hope she won't be too spooked to go with Archie."

"Why would she be?" I asked, surprised by Hugo's comment. I didn't for a moment think that Frances would have any reservations about leaving. She wanted to come with us; she trusted us.

"Archie is a young, strong, virile man whose body will be in close proximity to hers as they ride to Portsmouth," Hugo explained. "After what Frances has been through at the hands of her husband, she might find that threatening. She has every reason to fear men, and being alone with Archie is not the same as being with all of us."

I was sure that Archie wouldn't do anything to make

Frances feel uncomfortable, but I hadn't considered this aspect. Would he sense her fear and act accordingly, or would he just wrap his arms around her and pull her against his chest as they rode at speed, her buttocks grinding against his crotch for hours? I wasn't sure how much Archie might be in tune with what Frances could be feeling. He was a clever lad, but few seventeenth-century men were keenly aware of the feelings and fears of women. Frances had trusted Hugo, but Hugo was old enough to be her father, and she saw him as being mine. Archie was a single man, one who exuded sex appeal even when dirty and disheveled, which could be threatening to a girl who'd been assaulted repeatedly.

"Oh, dear," I sighed. "Perhaps you should have gone to get her."

"I wouldn't leave you, not in the state you were in. Frances will just have to grin and bear it," Hugo said as he shook Jem awake. "It's nearly noon; we must get going if we mean to arrive in Portsmouth before the closing of the gates for the night," Hugo said.

"Noon? How long have I been asleep?" I asked, aghast.

"Since about seven last night. I didn't want to wake you. Your body needed time to rest, and your mind needed time to cope," Hugo replied.

"Sometimes you sound very modern, Hugo Everly," I said with a smile. "The twenty-first century was good for you."

Hugo just grinned in return as he lifted Jem off the floor. The child was still dead to the world, so Hugo tried to tickle him to wake him up.

"Noooo," Jem moaned. "I'm tired."

"I have fresh buttered rolls and milk," Hugo offered, knowing that Jem couldn't resist food.

The boy rubbed his eyes and finally forced them open.

"All right," he mumbled.

"Do you think I can persuade you to eat your breakfast

downstairs?" I asked, suddenly aware of urgent physical needs. "I need a few moments to freshen up. And wash your hands and face, Jem."

Hugo scooped up Jem, who grabbed his rolls and then left me alone, and just in time too. I'd never been so happy to see a chamber pot; my bladder was about to burst.

It was just past 1 p.m. when we finally left the inn and returned to the road. It was still slow-going due to the mud from yesterday's downpour, but at least the day was sunny and bright, and I did my best not to dwell on the events of the day before.

Hugo seemed in better spirits as well, but he looked over at me from time to time to make sure I was all right. Last night had scared him; I knew that. If there was anyone with medical knowledge, they would most likely be in Portsmouth, not in a tiny hamlet which probably didn't even have a name. My hand went protectively to my belly. We needed to get to France, and soon, before the baby was born.

FIFTY-TWO

The ride to Portsmouth was uneventful, but I couldn't help looking back every so often, expecting to be pursued by soldiers of the Crown. I couldn't ignore the tension in Hugo's shoulders and the rigid set of his back. Despite his reassurances, he wasn't as sure that we were free as he claimed. I didn't question him, but every time I heard hoofbeats on the road, I nearly shrieked with terror. By the time the walls of Portsmouth came into view, I was exhausted from worrying and relieved to have finally arrived. It was easier to hide in a town full of people than on the open road where we were constantly in full view.

Hugo took us to an inn where we had previously stayed, awakening a bizarre feeling of déjà vu. Was it only two months ago that we were here, ready to sail for France on the *Mathilde*? It seemed more like two years.

I tried to eat some supper, but ended up just moving food around my plate, my stomach too knotted with anxiety to eat, and my hands shaking with fatigue. I finally gave up and pushed the plate away despite Hugo's concerned gaze. Normally, I was always hungry, so he knew I wasn't as well as I claimed to be. Jem seized my plate and finished my meal, completely ignoring the silent exchange between the adults.

"I think I'll retire," I said as I began to undress. All I wanted was to go to sleep and find oblivion in my dreams, but the laces proved to be a challenge. My fingers refused to obey since I was achy and tired, my mind worn out by constant worry and fear. I yanked on the strings in frustration, close to tears, but they wouldn't give.

Hugo came up behind me and pulled me against his chest. "I know what will help," he whispered, his breath in my ear making me shiver.

"Are you mad? Jem is here," I whispered back, appalled by the suggestion.

"So? This is not the twenty-first century. Most children sleep in the same bed while their parents copulate. Jem will not be shocked by anything he sees or hears," Hugo added matter-of-factly.

"Absolutely not," I replied, shaking my head, but my body was saying something different, entirely betraying me. I was melting into Hugo, leaning my head back to allow him to kiss my neck as he cupped my breasts and massaged them gently, moving his thumbs over my sensitive nipples.

"Jemmy, find your bed," Hugo instructed.

Jem gave him a wicked grin, but obeyed, and spread his bedroll by the fire, turning his face away from the bed as Hugo deftly untied my laces and lifted me off my feet.

"Close the bed-curtains," I hissed. That was perhaps the last coherent thought I had that night.

Hugo did as I asked and proceeded to spend the next hour turning me into a quivering mass of desire. At first, I was still tense, but little by little, I began to let go and succumb to the release he was offering. Hugo took his time, kissing and caressing me until I could no longer think, much less resist. My hips arched toward his in silent demand, but he held off, making sure that I was good and ready. This was the only therapy he could think of to help me deal with everything that had happened. He couldn't offer me analysis or prescription drugs to numb my pain; all he could offer me was his love and the promise of the future.

By the time he finally took me, I went off like a firework after a few thrusts, convulsing around him with an intensity I hadn't expected after the last twenty-four hours. My body seemed to let go of the fear and tension and just did what came naturally. He needed me too, and I gave myself up to him completely as he rocked me gently, seeking his own release, which was quick and powerful.

"Better now?" Hugo asked as he rested his forehead against mine. He could see the answer in my drooping eyelids. "Good-night, my sweet," he said as I fell asleep in his arms.

FIFTY-THREE

Frances looked in dismay at the firmly shut gates built into the city wall around Portsmouth. Several torches burned bright in their sconces, casting pools of light onto the stretch of road approaching the city. Archie had warned her that the gates would be closed by now, but she didn't believe him and needed to see for herself to be sure that he was telling her the truth.

Frances drew the cloak tighter around her body and gave Archie a stubborn nod, acquiescing to spending the night in a barn they'd passed on the way.

The farmhouse had been burnt out, but the barn was still intact, offering shelter against the cold November night. The day had been sunny, but now thick clouds obscured the rising moon, and the wind had picked up, effortlessly penetrating the thick folds of Frances's cloak and making her shiver with cold. They'd ridden hard the whole day, and Frances was tired, hungry, and afraid. She longed to see Neve and Lord Everly and feel safe at last.

Archie had come to collect her just as the sun was rising above the tree line beyond the convent wall, and furious bird-song had erupted all around, creatures large and small waking to another day. The rain of the night before had finally stopped, and shy golden rays had filtered through the riotous colors of the fall, the leaves burning like tongues of orange and red flame in stark contrast to the cloudless blue sky. The nuns were still at prayer, so Archie had had to wait outside until they finished, and someone could open the door. Frances had been overjoyed to see him until she realized that he was quite alone.

Archie was escorted directly to Mother Superior and emerged a few minutes later having completed his business. Frances had hovered nearby, eager to hear the news. Was her life about to change, or was Archie here for a different reason?

"Get your things, Frances," Archie had announced gruffly, "you're coming with me. We are to meet Lord Everly and Mistress Ashley in Portsmouth, hopefully tonight."

Frances had been torn between excitement and fear as she'd dashed to her cell to collect her few belongings. She had only one gown and the cloak in which she had arrived. When at the convent, she wore a gray sack-like garment which covered her from head to foot. Under the circumstances, it seemed best to leave it on. Frances had folded her clothes into a small sack and threw a last look at the cell that had been her home since April. She wouldn't miss it, but it had offered safety, for which she'd be eternally grateful.

Archie was already by the gate, waiting for her. He was chewing on a hunk of bread liberally spread with butter and topped with a slice of cold pork. Sister Julia was by his side, talking quietly. They wouldn't be seeing each other again anytime soon, not if Archie left for France. The thought of seeing France had buoyed Frances's spirits, but there was one last thing she had to do before saying goodbye to the sisters. She'd imagined this moment several times before, and it broke her heart, but this time it was for real and needed to be done.

"Master Hicks, I need to visit Gabriel's grave," she had said as she handed him her sack. "I won't be long." Frances had turned to walk away, but was surprised to find Archie walking alongside her, his breakfast finished. "Where are you going?" she'd asked, glaring at him.

"I'd like to pay my respects, if you have no objection," Archie had replied as he continued to walk by her side.

Frances didn't say anything, but she was touched by the gesture.

Archie had removed his hat, and they had stood side by side over the mound of dirt where her son slept. A plain cross stuck out of the ground bearing his name. Archie had bent his head and said a prayer for Gabriel's soul, then had turned to leave, giving Frances a few moments of privacy. She had promised herself she wouldn't cry, but hot tears slid down her cheeks as she gazed upon the tiny grave.

"I will never forget you, Gabriel. Never. You will always be in my heart, as long as I live," she'd whispered, hoping that Gabriel knew she wasn't deserting him. "You'll be safe here. The nuns will look after your resting place, my angel, and I will come back some day. I promise." Frances had kissed her fingers and pressed them against the wood of the cross before she turned on her heel and ran toward the gate, unable to stand the guilt she felt for leaving her son alone.

The nuns were gathered by Sister Angela's hut, ready to say goodbye. They had been kind to her, and Frances gave each one a kiss on the cheek, despite their aversion to physical affection. It was the only way she could show them how much they'd meant to her, especially Sister Angela and Sister Julia, who'd taken her under their wing and tried to help her cope, especially after Gabriel's death.

Mother Superior had come forward and kissed Frances on the forehead. "Take care, my child, and never forget that God loves you and is looking out for you. Bless you."

"Yes, Mother," Frances had replied. She wasn't so sure that God loved her at all or had been looking out for her when

Lionel beat her half to death or when her baby died, but she chose to remain silent and accept the blessing. What harm could it do?

The nuns had begun to disperse as Frances walked toward the open gate, followed by Sister Angela and Sister Julia.

"Be well, ducky," Sister Angela had said as she drew Frances into a hug. "I know you think God has forsaken you, but the best is yet to come; you'll see. Just don't close your heart to love."

Sister Julia had squeezed Frances's hand, smiling sadly. They shared a bond that women who'd never lost a child could ever understand. "It gets easier," Sister Julia had said, "but it never goes away. He'll stay with you forever, but I'm not sure that you'd want it otherwise."

"No, he'll always be with me, as will the two of you. Thank you," Frances had said as she smiled at the two women. "I will never forget you."

"Go with God, Frances, and give our regards to Mistress Ashley."

Archie was already outside, stuffing her sack into the saddlebag. There was only one horse. Frances had tried to bite back her panic, but her only option was to remain at the convent, and she'd be damned if she chose to stay in this sad, desolate place. Frances had taken a deep, calming breath and approached Archie carefully.

"I'd like to ride sidesaddle, please," she'd said, praying that Archie wouldn't ask for an explanation. She was still bleeding after the birth, and to sit astride would make it difficult to keep the thick rag between her legs in place. She would feel more comfortable if she could keep her legs pressed together.

Archie had looked momentarily surprised but gave her a quick bow. "As you wish." He'd grabbed her by the waist and raised her onto the horse before mounting himself. It was very awkward for them both. "Are you certain you wouldn't rather ride astride?" Archie had asked as he shifted in the saddle to give Frances more room.

"Yes."

He didn't say anything else, just took hold of the reins as the horse picked its way carefully along the narrow woodland path.

Frances had turned to wave to the nuns, but they had already shut the gate, leaving her to her fate. She was no longer a part of their orderly life. She strongly suspected that Mother Superior had been glad to see the back of her. She'd brought nothing but problems to the convent, and her pregnancy and Gabriel's birth had brought back certain memories and longings in the nuns, causing a ripple of discontent which would take some time to quell. They were better off without her.

Frances had sat stiffly, her back straight until they finally reached the road, where the horse picked up speed. Her back had burned with tension, and her legs had felt as if they were sliding off the horse. She had held on to the pommel for dear life, praying that she wouldn't fall off like a sack of grain.

Archie was aware of her discomfort but didn't say a word. He had gazed ahead, his arms loose around Frances. She'd wished she could lean against him, but she was too afraid of physical contact. Lord Everly and Mistress Ashley trusted Archie, so she had to as well, but her fear was so deeply rooted that she couldn't find the strength to overcome it. Any male touch sent her into a panic, and she shrank away from Archie, acutely conscious of him next to her. He'd been traveling since yesterday morning and smelled of sweat, horse, leather, and something of his own. It wasn't a repulsive smell, but it was overwhelmingly male, which made her wary.

After an hour, Frances had thought she would die. Her whole body was on fire from sitting in such an awkward position, and they had hours to travel yet. She'd shifted in the saddle, dimly aware of Archie's eyes on her.

"Is there something you wish to tell me?" Archie had asked conversationally.

"No," Frances had replied stubbornly.

"So, are you insisting on sitting this way to be ladylike?"

"No," she had said again, unsure of what to tell him. She couldn't last this way till Portsmouth; she knew that much.

"Frances, you have nothing to fear from me," Archie had said firmly. "I would never do anything to hurt you. You would be more comfortable if you would just lean into me."

"I can't," Frances had mumbled, her cheeks turning crimson with embarrassment. "I'm still bleeding after the birth. I can't sit astride, but my back aches something dreadful."

"I see," Archie had replied as he'd turned off the road onto a narrow track in the woods. The trees had whispered above them, the forest filled with sounds of animals and birds and the breaking of twigs beneath the horse's hooves.

"Where are you going?" Frances had screeched, alarmed.

"Just off the road where you can get a bit of privacy," Archie had replied. "Don't worry."

They had stopped just as soon as the road could no longer be seen through the trees, and Archie had dismounted and helped her down. He'd rummaged in his saddlebag until he pulled out a large linen handkerchief and handed it to Frances.

"Have you ever seen a baby's nappy?" he'd asked. "Tie it just like that. It will keep everything in place."

Frances had thought she would die of shame, but she went behind a bush and did as Archie told her before returning to the horse.

Archie had lifted her up, and she'd sat astride, feeling her legs relax around the smooth flanks of the animal. Archie had sat behind her and gently pulled her to him until she was resting against his chest. Frances had resisted at first, but finally allowed herself to get comfortable as they left the woods and got on their way once again.

Archie didn't say much, but his presence was comforting and solid behind her. Frances finally began to relax; she'd even managed to sleep for a while after they stopped at midday to eat at a small tavern. *Archie's idea of the handkerchief had been ingenious*, she'd thought, *but she could hardly tell him that*. The rag was held firmly in place, giving her freedom of movement. And, thankfully, she wasn't leaking milk anymore. Sister Angela had bound her breasts right after Gabriel had died, and the milk had dried up within a few days. Seeing it seep out had been a heartbreaking reminder of the child who wouldn't need it. It would take a few more weeks for her body to return to normal, according to the old nun, and Frances looked forward to that time. It would make Gabriel's death a little easier to cope with. As long as her body was still recovering from the birth, she felt the loss very keenly.

The rest of the ride to Portsmouth had been smooth until it began to grow dark. "The gates will be closed by now," Archie had said. "We should find a place to hole up for the night."

"No, we must get to Portsmouth," Frances had whined, panicked. She couldn't spend a night with Archie—she just couldn't. She had been acutely aware of his hard prick against her lower back for the past few hours. Archie had shifted uncomfortably from time to time as her buttocks ground against him but continued as if nothing were amiss. Frances had been terrified at first, but he seemed to be ignoring his arousal, so she had as well. But, once they were dismounted and lying side by side, there would be nothing to stop him. She didn't know much about the appetites of men, but she knew that they rarely denied themselves, especially when there was a woman nearby. She wasn't willing, but that might not be deterrent enough. She just wanted to be with Neve. Neve was only twelve years older than Frances, but she'd been the closest thing she'd had to a mother since her nursemaid. Neve made her feel cared for and safe.

"Frances," Archie had said patiently, "the gate is closed, and we cannot get into the city until morning. We must find a place to sleep since I have no intention of just sitting here all night. We passed a barn about a half hour ago. That will do. Now, shall we go?"

Frances had no choice but to agree. She fretted all the way to the barn, trying to think of a way to sleep on the other side.

The barn was relatively large, but cold. Wind blew between the wooden slats, making the inside just as frigid as the outside. Archie saw to the horse, while Frances looked around the barn. The dirt floor was covered by bits of straw, but it was moldy and smelly, left over from when the place was still inhabited. There was a hayloft, however, which seemed cozier.

Archie carefully stepped on the rungs of the ladder to make sure they weren't rotten until he made it to the top.

"Frances, come up here," he called. "It's much warmer and there's clean straw."

Frances considered sleeping downstairs alone but moved toward the ladder. She'd rather take her chances with Archie than with someone who might enter the barn during the night.

Archie was right; the loft was warmer since there wasn't as much of a draft.

Archie unfolded an old blanket he'd brought up and spread it on the straw. He sat down and held out an apple to Frances. "Here, you must be hungry."

"I'm all right; you have it."

"I have one for me too," he said and tossed the apple to her.

Frances caught it and bit into it but remained standing. Archie moved over and cut his eyes at the blanket, inviting her to sit down. Frances reluctantly complied but kept as much distance between them as she could. She was surprised to see Archie grinning at her in the darkness.

"What's funny?"

"Frances, I will not lie to you and tell you that I'm as pure as driven snow, but I do not routinely force myself on unwilling young maidens. You are quite safe," he said, still smiling at her.

"But I felt your... eh, you know," she said, blushing hotly.

"That happens to men, but that doesn't mean I have to act on it. Just lie down and rest, woman. I will deliver you safely to Lord Everly in the morning."

Archie threw away his apple core, stretched out on the blanket and rested his arm over his face. He was asleep in minutes, but it took Frances considerably longer. She wrapped herself in her cloak and tried to sleep, but was too nervous to relax. The horse was snorting below them, and an owl hooted somewhere, but still Frances lay awake. It must have been close to midnight when she finally fell asleep, curled into a fetal position.

Frances awoke to find herself rather warm and comfortable. She was lying on her side with Archie behind her, his body molded to her, and his arm protectively wrapped around her middle. Her cloak was spread out over the two of them, keeping them warm and snug. Frances grew as rigid as a wooden plank and drove her elbow into Archie's stomach. He sat up with a surprised yelp of pain, rubbed his face, and smiled at her guiltily when he realized how intimately they'd been lying. There were bits of straw in his hair, copper stubble on his cheeks, and an expression of such sheepishness that Frances had to turn away to keep from smiling.

"I'm hungry," he said, dispelling the tension, "but my belly hurts for some reason." Archie rubbed at the spot where Frances had hit him, his eyebrow raised in mock confusion.

Frances suddenly let out a peal of laughter. She'd been such a ninny for fearing Archie. Any other man would have throttled her by now, but Archie was attempting to make jokes to make her feel more at ease rather than giving vent to his temper. Aside from Lord Everly, Archie was the noblest, kindest man she'd ever met, and she had insulted him by doubting his honor.

"I'm sorry, Archie," she said as she took hold of his hand in a conciliatory manner and smiled into his eyes.

"For what? For me being hungry or for my bellyache?" he asked, but he knew what she meant. "Don't worry yourself about it, little dove. You have every right to be scared, and as long as I'm with you, you have my protection. Now, let's go find some breakfast and then ride into Portsmouth. We must wait an hour or so till the soil wagons pass out of the city anyhow. The stench is unbearable when they do."

Archie shook out the cloak to get rid of some bits of straw sticking to it and draped it over Frances's shoulders. He gently tucked a stray curl beneath her cap, then lifted her onto the horse before swinging into the saddle behind her. Frances leaned against him with a sigh of contentment as his arms went around her to take hold of the reins. The sun was just rising, the golden haze blurring the harsh lines of the burnt-out cottage and making the dew glitter on grass. The whole world seemed to be new and sparkling, and suddenly Frances felt much lighter than she had in years.

FIFTY-FOUR

When I awoke in the morning, I was quite alone. I pulled aside the bed hanging and squinted at the window. Judging by the position of the sun, it had to be well past eight in the morning. Normally, the sounds of the town would have woken me long before, but our room faced the back of the house, and it wasn't as noisy as it would have been on the other side, with wagons rolling down the street, townspeople going about their business, and cargo being loaded or unloaded at the port. I had seen the dark outline of several masts against the evening sky as we'd ridden into town and prayed that one of those ships might carry us to France.

Hugo and Jem had gone downstairs to find their breakfast, so I took my time getting ready. I washed, brushed out my hair and pinned it up neatly beneath my cap, then cleaned my teeth before getting dressed. My stomach growled with hunger as I finally left the room and went downstairs. I felt much better, and more at peace. Hugo had known what he was about last night. I blushed at the memory of Jemmy being in the room with us, but then dismissed my concerns. Hugo was right; in this day and age, no one enjoyed the kind of privacy they did in the future, and thanks to the bed hangings, Jem wouldn't have seen a thing; maybe just heard a moan or a sigh. I was sure we hadn't damaged him for life.

I heard familiar voices even before I descended the last steps. Archie's deep baritone intermingled with Hugo's gravelly voice and Jem's high-pitched chatter. I couldn't hear Frances, but I saw her as soon as I entered the room, and the joy in her eyes when she saw me told me everything I needed to know. She didn't say anything, but rose to her feet and came toward me, wrapping her arms around me. We stood like that for a few moments, happy to see each other again, and silently acknowledging everything that had happened. She was a widow now, but she'd also lost a child only a few weeks ago.

I held Frances away from me and studied her face. "How was the ride to Portsmouth?" I asked carefully.

"Oh, it was all right," she replied, shrugging. "We got here just after they closed the gates. We had to find a barn to bed down in for the night," she said as a charming blush stained her cheeks. "It was drafty and uncomfortable, but we survived." Her eyes strayed to Archie, who nodded in agreement. There was nothing in her manner to suggest that she had been put off by Archie's company. He turned to look at her, and I saw a softness in his eyes that I hadn't noticed before. He had taken on the role of protector, and Frances had been happy to accept.

"Has Hugo told you about Lionel?" I asked as I sat down and accepted a piece of bread and some bacon. It smelled heavenly, but I couldn't eat until I knew that Frances was all right, emotionally as well as physically.

"Yes, he has," she said quietly. "I'm not quite sure how I feel about his death, but I am happy to be free of him. I would like to use my maiden name again, if that's all right," she said, glancing at Hugo. "I'd like to sever any connection to him and that part of my life."

"By all means, Frances," Hugo replied as he meaningfully

pushed the plate closer to me. "Eat," he said, "you barely ate anything last night."

I took an obedient bite and turned back to Frances.

"From this moment on, I am no longer Frances Finch. I am Frances Morley, an unmarried woman traveling under the protection of my benefactor," she stated, smiling at Hugo.

"Indeed, you are."

I noticed a fat purse of coin attached to Hugo's belt. Mother Superior must have returned the money Hugo had left in safe-keeping for Frances. I had to admit that I was glad. We'd need all the funds we could get in the coming years to keep us afloat. We were a bedraggled group with hardly a change of clothes between us and would need to start our lives from scratch once we left England.

Hugo and Archie finished their meal and pushed away their plates, their faces full of determination. "We're off to the quay to inquire about ships bound for France. Neve, please stay here with Frances and Jem, and *do not* leave," Hugo added.

He didn't have to tell me twice. After everything that had happened, I had no desire to be out on my own; I didn't feel safe, and judging by Frances's frightened eyes, neither did she. Her gaze flew to Archie, who gave her a reassuring smile before leaving.

"Can we play a game?" Jem asked as he followed me back upstairs. "I borrowed some dice from the innkeeper's son. I'll teach you how to play," he added when he saw my look of ignorance.

"I know how to play," Frances said, "and I will win every time."

"Oh, no, you won't," Jem replied and stuck out his tongue at the girl, who swatted him upside the head and ran up the stairs giggling before he could retaliate. I suddenly imagined what it might feel like to be a mother to two nearly grown children.

FIFTY-FIVE

Max shivered with cold as he was pushed out of the wagon and herded toward a waiting ship, which was bobbing gently on the swells of the iron-gray water. He had nothing besides the clothes he stood up in, and the wind off the water was bitterly cold. Max had only a few moments to catch his last glimpse of England before boarding the vessel. He thought he might be in Southampton, but he couldn't be sure. The three-masted wooden ship looked like a toy compared to the vessels of the twenty-first century, and Max's stomach clenched with fear at the thought of crossing the ocean in November in something hardly bigger than a yacht.

Sailors purposefully crisscrossed the deck as someone shouted orders over the din. They were rough-looking men with weather-beaten skin and shaggy beards, dressed in loose trousers and shirts made of homespun. One stocky fellow passed directly in front of him, and Max took him to be in his sixties until he saw the man's face. He was no older than Max. Several barrels were rolled up the gangway and taken down to the hold, and a reluctant goat meehed as it was pulled aboard by a boy who appeared to be no older than ten. The deck rolled beneath Max's feet, but he tried to keep his balance, knowing that his guards would likely kick him if he fell.

No one paid Max much attention as the soldiers walked him across the deck. An imposing man, presumably the captain or the first mate, directed the soldiers to the wooden ladder leading below deck. Several men were already in the hold, their faces stern and their clothes filthy and smelly. They were chained to iron rings set into the wall. An iron grille was built into the ceiling—it was the only source of light and air. The cabin was bare of any furniture. There wasn't so much as a bench to sit on. The men would make the voyage locked in this cage, sleeping and eating in their designated spot. Their exercise would consist of walking to the bucket in the corner which would serve as a toilet.

The other men eyed Max as he was pushed inside, but no one said a word while the soldiers chained him to a vacant ring and departed in silence.

Max looked around in dismay. He'd expected terrible conditions, but this was even worse than he had anticipated. The stench was overwhelming, and they hadn't even set sail yet. The men glared at him through matted hair, their faces feral and primitive.

"They'll take the fetters off once we're out to sea," a man close to Max said. Max couldn't be sure, but he appeared to be in his thirties, with bright blue eyes and a face that must have been handsome at some point. "Should take a few weeks to get to where we're going," he continued.

"And where is that?" Max asked.

"Oh, I don't know. I suppose we'll find out once we get there. I'm Dick, by the way. And you are?"

"Max."

"Pleased to meet you, Max. That there is John, next to him is Cecil, and the other three aren't talking yet. Too scared, I reckon."

Max nodded to the men, who reluctantly nodded back. Max was curious what their crimes were, but it seemed too soon to ask such personal questions. Not like they didn't have time to get acquainted.

Max sank to the floor and leaned against the rough wall, closing his eyes. All he wanted was to open them up again and find that everything that had happened to him had been a bad dream, and he was at home in his own bed. Max smiled bitterly at the fantasy. If only... He was starting out on a new chapter of his life; a chapter that was bound to be somewhere at the very end of the book since he wasn't likely to survive for long. He tried to remain calm, but a tear slid down his cheek. He wiped it away angrily, but not before the men saw this sign of weakness. He'd just made a terrible mistake, and he knew it.

Max wasn't sure how much time had passed since he was brought aboard the ship. No one had come, and no food had been given. The grille above their heads grew dark as day turned into evening. Max must have fallen asleep, but woke up with a start when he heard the unmistakable sound of a heavy chain clanking against the hull as the anchor was raised. The rolling increased as the ship began to move out of the harbor toward the open sea. One man muttered a prayer, while the others remained silent, their faces hardly more than pale ovals with hollow eyes in the darkness of the cell. Max was about to pray when he realized the futility of it. God had forsaken him. He was alone.

FIFTY-SIX

I leaned on the railing as the massive vessel heaved into life, the deck vibrating beneath my feet as the anchor was lifted out of the water. Several men went up the rigging, climbing like monkeys despite the bitter wind and the rolling of the ship. The deck was a beehive of activity, and it wasn't long until I heard the sails unfurling and snapping loudly overhead as they filled with wind. Eventually, the activity subsided somewhat, and the crew dispersed, everyone now at their post. The sailors went about their duties cheerfully, occasionally exchanging a brief comment or joke in French.

Frances stood next to me, her face rosy from the cold, but her eyes alight as she watched the coast of England slowly recede. I suppose to her this was a wonderful adventure, but I felt a terrible melancholy steal over me. We were now officially in exile, and it would be years until we could safely return.

I turned, my eyes searching for Hugo, but he was nowhere in sight, and neither were Archie or Jem. If I knew Jem, he was probably down in the galley, begging for food and learning his first words in French, which were probably, "go away, boy." I wrapped my arm around Frances, and we stood like that for nearly an hour, just watching the churning gray water and listening to the screaming of the seagulls overhead, both of us lost in our own thoughts.

I leaned back as Hugo came up behind me and wrapped his arms around my ever-expanding waist, instantly making me feel warmer. I was nearing my third trimester, and the baby was moving around and doing summersaults as if it were training for a career in the circus.

"Come with me, I have a surprise for you," Hugo whispered in my ear.

"I've had enough surprises," I replied churlishly, hesitant to leave my safe little spot. I was still feeling unexplainably sad; my insides hollow with the uncertainty of things to come.

"It's a nice one; I promise," Hugo said. "You too, Frances."

We took one last look at the distant shoreline and turned to follow Hugo. He led us to the captain's cabin, situated in the stern of the ship. The windows along the back wall allowed in feeble November light, which was supplemented by numerous candles, giving the cabin a pleasant warm glow. Archie was already there, as was the first mate, who seemed impatient to get on with whatever we were there for. Jem was practically dancing with excitement, his dark eyes watching me as I entered.

Captain Lafitte was casually leaning against his desk, hands resting on the smooth surface. He was Hugo's age, with lively dark eyes fringed by lashes that most girls would kill for. His arched brows nearly disappeared beneath his wig as Frances and I entered, his gaze clearly fixated on the lovely, young girl at my side. Frances had been through hell, but none of her suffering showed in her beautiful China doll face. Her blond ringlets framed her porcelain skin, and her blue eyes opened wider as she took in the splendor of the captain's cabin.

"Mademoiselles," Lafitte intoned, giving us an elaborate

bow of greeting and welcome. "Are you ready, *ma chère?*" he asked, looking directly at me for the first time.

"Ready for what?" I asked, suddenly suspicious.

Everyone present seemed to be vibrating with suppressed excitement, even Archie. I couldn't help noticing that Frances moved closer to his side, her hand reaching for his. Archie seemed taken aback by the gesture, but allowed his hand to be held, assuming it was just excitement on Frances's part.

"Why, for your wedding, of course," he replied in his accented English. It sounded charming.

"You could have warned me," I mumbled to Hugo as we took our places in front of the captain.

He leafed through the Bible until he found the passage he was looking for, gazed upon us with grave seriousness, and began to recite the wedding ceremony, his face glowing with such fervor as if he were God himself.

Hugo slipped a silver filigreed band onto my ring finger after making his vows, but then added a line from the Protestant service for my benefit. "With this ring I thee wed, with my body I thee worship, and with all my worldly goods I thee endow: in the name of the Father, and of the Son, and of the Holy Ghost. Amen."

"I now pronounce you man and wife," Captain Lafitte said in his lovely accent. "You may kiss your bride, Lord Everly," he instructed, clapping his hands like a child as Hugo gave me a long, tender kiss and pulled me close enough to feel our child kicking between us.

Everyone stilled as we stood together, lost in each other's eyes. I no longer felt melancholy, just wonderfully content and loved. I suddenly recalled seeing Hugo's likeness for the first time at Everly Manor, his scowl making me want to rush past his portrait. The man who looked at me was nothing like that haughty nobleman. He looked vulnerable, happy, and a little nervous, like any bridegroom who was not only embarking on marriage but was about to become a first-time father. I felt a wave of tenderness wash over me as I leaned over and whispered into his ear. "I love you, husband."

"I thought of you as mine from the moment we met, and now you are mine at last in the eyes of God and man," Hugo replied. "I never truly understood what it meant to love someone until I found you."

Our audience began to grow restless, and the captain stowed away his Bible and turned to us before returning to his place on the bridge. "It would be my great honor to invite you all to dinner in my cabin tonight to celebrate your nuptials.

"Thank you, you are most gracious, Captain Lafitte," Hugo said, returning the captain's generous bow. "We'll be happy to join you. And now I think Lady Everly and I need a moment alone."

I giggled as Hugo shut the door to our cabin behind us and lifted me off my feet, nearly smacking my head on the low ceiling. The berth was too narrow and the cabin too tiny for much of a honeymoon, but Hugo sat down and lowered me onto his lap, kissing me tenderly. I undid his laces and lifted my skirts around my waist, sighing with pleasure as he slid easily into me and began to move carefully, his hands on my hips to keep me from falling. We instinctively fell into the rhythm of the moving ship, our joining a fluid motion of two bodies.

"Mine," Hugo whispered, tipping me over the edge of reason as my body joined his in a climax.

We fell back into the berth, snuggling together as I pushed down my skirts and laid my head on Hugo's shoulder. "Why now? Why not once we got to France?" I had a vision of getting married in some quaint French church, our union witnessed by fat cherubs diapered in frothy clouds as they cavorted overhead.

"No French priest would marry us unless you agreed to convert and go through a rigorous course of the Catechism. I promised that I would never ask that of you, so this was the most logical solution. The captain is a Catholic, which is good enough for me, and he will provide us with a marriage certificate—in duplicate. One for me, and one for you, should you ever need to prove that you are Lady Everly and that our child was born in wedlock."

"You always think of everything, don't you?" I asked, astonished as usual by Hugo's practicality. His mind was always three steps ahead.

"I have to, don't I?" He slid his hand under my skirt and laid his palm on the warm skin of my belly as he kissed me.

I didn't need to ask what he was thinking. I knew.

EPILOGUE

The rain came down hard as a lone woman walked through the All Hallows by the Tower Church cemetery. She wore a dark hooded cape, but tendrils of dark hair escaped and were soaking wet and plastered against her pale cheeks. She moved slowly despite the driving rain, undaunted by the thunder and lightning that illuminated the cemetery and bathed it in an eerie light for just a moment before allowing it to be swallowed by the darkness once more.

A welcoming light glowed through the stained-glass windows of the church, offering shelter from the rain and solace for the tormented, but the woman resolutely ignored it. She raised her gloved hand and tore something off a tree as she passed, before putting her hand back into the pocket of her cape. She continued to walk, looking left and right until she found what she was searching for.

It was the only plot in the cemetery marked with a statue. It was the grave of a duchess who was much beloved by her husband, or so the inscription read. The marble angel stood pensively over her final resting place; its wings folded demurely, its arms outstretched. It seemed to be welcoming the dead, or merely opening its arms in a shrug of acceptance. Everybody dies, it seemed to say.

The woman slid down onto the ground and leaned heavily against the legs of the angel. She closed her eyes for a moment as she muttered a prayer, crossed herself, then brought out the berries she'd picked from the yew tree and tossed them into her mouth, chewing slowly.

Jane stared up at the leaden sky, rivulets of water coursing down her face as the poison began to spread through her bloodstream, making her face contort with agony as she convulsed in the last throes of death.

"I'm sorry, Hugo," was the last thing she whispered as the light went out of her eyes, and she slumped at the feet of the indifferent angel.

A LETTER FROM THE AUTHOR

Huge thanks for reading *Wonderland*, I hope you were hooked on Neve and Hugo's epic journey. It continues in book three, *Sins of Omission*. If you want to join other readers in hearing all about my new releases and bonus content, you can sign up for my newsletter!

www.stormpublishing.co/irina-shapiro

If you enjoyed this book and could spare a few moments to leave a review that would be hugely appreciated. Even a short review can make all the difference in encouraging a reader to discover my books for the first time. Thank you so much!

Although I write several different genres, time travel was my first love. As a student of history, I often wonder if I have what it takes to survive in the past in the dangerous, life-altering situations my characters have to deal with. Neve and Hugo are two of my favorite characters, not only because they're intelligent and brave but because they're fallible, sensitive, and ultimately human. I hope you enjoy their adventures, both in the past and the present, and come to see them as real people rather than characters on a page.

Thanks again for being part of this amazing journey with me and I hope you'll stay in touch – I have so many more stories and ideas to entertain you with!

Irina

Printed in Great Britain
by Amazon

39528757R00199